The Challenge of Entail

by

Jann Rowland

One Good Sonnet Publishing
Publishers of Fine Romance
and Fantasy Fiction

By Jann Rowland
Published by One Good Sonnet Publishing:

PRIDE AND PREJUDICE VARIATIONS

Acting on Faith
A Life from the Ashes (Sequel to *Acting on Faith*)
Open Your Eyes
Implacable Resentment
An Unlikely Friendship
Bound by Love
Cassandra
Obsession
Shadows Over Longbourn
The Mistress of Longbourn
My Brother's Keeper
Coincidence
The Angel of Longbourn
Chaos Comes to Kent
In the Wilds of Derbyshire
The Companion
Out of Obscurity
What Comes Between Cousins
A Tale of Two Courtships
Murder at Netherfield
Whispers of the Heart
A Gift for Elizabeth
Mr. Bennet Takes Charge
The Impulse of the Moment
The Challenge of Entail

COURAGE ALWAYS RISES: THE BENNET SAGA

The Heir's Disgrace

Co-Authored with Lelia Eye

WAITING FOR AN ECHO

Waiting for an Echo Volume One: Words in the Darkness
Waiting for an Echo Volume Two: Echoes at Dawn

A Summer in Brighton
A Bevy of Suitors
Love and Laughter: A Pride and Prejudice Short Stories Anthology

THE CHALLENGE OF ENTAIL

Copyright © 2019 Jann Rowland

Cover Design by Jann Rowland

Published by One Good Sonnet Publishing

ISBN: 1989212069
ISBN-13: 9781989212066

To my family who have, as always, shown
their unconditional love and encouragement.

PROLOGUE

August 1804

Never had Mr. Bennet of Longbourn in Hertfordshire thought his life would go so wrong. The scion of a long line of gentlemen, respectable, though not prominent, he had always intended to marry a good woman, a woman who would provide him an heir, companionship throughout the days of his life, and contentment, if not happiness. But now, after almost seventeen years of marriage, he found it difficult to abide his wife, and the situation was wearing on him.

Marrying Maggie Gardiner had been a mistake, Bennet was forced to own to himself, if to no one else. After a short acquaintance in which her sunny character and warm openness had recommended her to Bennet as a desirable marriage partner, he had proposed to her immersed in the throes of infatuation. It was only after they were married when he had learned the truth of his companion in life—she was a silly woman, one with a paucity of intelligence and interests which did not at all align with his own.

Still, Bennet was a philosophical man and had looked at the situation with the self-deprecating humor for which he was known.

She may not be Aristotle, but Maggie was possessed of a sunny disposition and her share of beauty. As he was joined with her, Bennet thought to make the best of the situation. As patiently as he was able, Bennet began to teach her, to instruct her in the ways of proper behavior and, at least in part, to open her mind to the world.

For many years, it seemed to have worked. As Maggie had improved, Bennet had found her companionship to become more pleasant and engaging. While he could not say that his infatuation for her had deepened into an abiding devotion, he was at least happy with her. And equally important, Bennet thought Maggie was happy too. Was this not what any man wished for the woman he had taken into his care?

But then things had changed — so slowly that Bennet had not even realized it until it had become impossible to ignore. The woman Bennet had married had given way to a creature even sillier, one who was ruled by her imagined "nerves," one fretful and frightened. It could all be traced back to the unfortunate fact of the entail on Longbourn and, even more unfortunately, the Bennets' lack of a son.

Maggie had loved Jane from the moment she was born, and who could not? Jane had always been a beautiful child, quiet, calm, patient, and happy. Doting on the girl was something that had come easy to his wife, and Bennet was no less pleased with his eldest daughter. When she had been with child a second time, Maggie had convinced herself the child would be a son, only to be disappointed with the emergence of another daughter. And Lizzy's character, so different from Jane's, which delighted in knowledge, her open ways more similar to Maggie's than she wished to confess, made her more difficult for Maggie to understand and guide.

Then, with each subsequent girl born to them, Maggie's nerves had become more prevalent, the unattractive parts of her character more obvious. When Lydia, their youngest, was born, his wife had taken to her bed, wailing against the injustice of it all. Then when no other children were to come to them, her behavior had worsened, her thoughts consumed with her certainty their unknown cousin — his heir — would throw her from the house as soon as Bennet was cold in his grave, never mind the fact that Bennet was only a few years older than his wife.

These past years had been difficult. Gone was the sunny and happy woman he married, replaced with the nervous creature whose company Bennet found difficult to tolerate. Bennet had had no illusions about his own character. He was not an industrious man, preferring the comforts of his library to work done on the estate. With the possibility of an heir scorched, leaving nothing more than dim embers, seeing to an estate from which his children would not profit became less appealing. It was short-sighted, he knew, but there it was. Maggie, convinced her salvation lay in marrying her daughters off to whomever would have them, began to spend more of their income, determined they should present themselves to greater advantage, though not one of them was yet out. And Bennet found he had not the firmness of purpose to curb her. It all seemed like so much work, akin to struggling against the tide.

Though he had managed to put some money away for his family's eventual support, his determination became a casualty in the face of his wife's ever more strident worries. Bennet even found himself beginning to treat the woman with disdain and ridicule. This was a disgusting way for a gentleman, one charged with the care of his family, to behave, but though he attempted to curb it, Bennet often responded without thinking. Soon, he wondered if it might have become habit.

Not long after Jane turned fifteen years of age, prompting Maggie's insistence she debut in society, Bennet received a note from his brother, Mr. Phillips. Phillips was married to Maggie's sister, a woman sillier than even Bennet's own wife. But while he was a stuffy man, fonder of port wine than Bennet's own prodigious taste for it, he was a good man who served as the town's solicitor. He had also been absent from Meryton for the past week, attending some gathering or another. Phillips served as Bennet's own attorney in most matters, so his summons was not unusual. The man's demeanor when Bennet joined him in his office *was*, however.

"My apologies, Bennet," said Mr. Phillips when Bennet entered the room. Gesturing to a cane propped against the side of his desk, Phillips continued: "I would have attended you at Longbourn, but I turned my ankle my last day in London and have had a difficult time getting around."

"It is no trouble, Brother," replied Bennet. "You said you had an urgent need to see me?"

"Not so urgent, as it seems," said Phillips. "But I have discovered something extraordinary, which will be of great interest to you." Phillips leaned forward in his chair. "I believe I have stumbled upon a solution to your problem."

Bennet frowned, uncertain to what Phillips referred. "I do not believe I have informed you of any problems of late."

"The entail," clarified Phillips.

"What of it?"

"It is not so iron-clad as I might have thought. In fact, I have learned that a simple entailment is rarely used any longer—or at least not by itself."

A rush of hope surged in Bennet's breast. "Then, by all means, let me know what you have learned. Are you telling me I have the means to do away with the entail in favor of my own children?"

Phillips nodded once, his mien betraying his excitement. "You can end it and leave Longbourn to whichever of your daughters you wish, and the process is not at all onerous.

"You see, I happened to mention your situation to a colleague of mine I have not seen nor heard from in many years." Sitting back in his chair, Phillips's look became one of introspection. "It was not that I expected to learn anything new, you understand. I do not even recall the genesis of our conversation, to own the truth. But when I mentioned the entail on your estate and your fears for the future of your family, he asked why I did not bar the entail and end it.

"I was shocked, of course. To the best of my knowledge, entails were near impossible to break in a legal sense. It appears they still are in Scotland. But in England, a process referred to as common recovery has been in place for many years, which allows a man to bar the heir from ever receiving the estate."

"And this common recovery is available for our use?" asked Bennet.

"It is available for anyone who possesses an entailed estate," confirmed Phillips. "My colleague informed me he had not seen an entail used in some time, though they might still be preferred in some small neighborhoods which may, I suppose, be called backwards." Phillips paused and chuckled. "As you know, I spend less of my time in London than even you do. I have practiced the law for many years, and those matters in which I have experience I understand well. But Longbourn is the only estate hereabouts which has an entail, and I have never had to contend with it on any other property. It is clear your ancestor who instituted it had no knowledge of the matter either, else he would have used the newer method of ensuring the solvency of the estate—strict settlement."

"So, to be clear," said Bennet, steering the conversation back to the matter at hand, "you can file for this common recovery? Then what happens?"

"Then the estate is yours to do as you wish." Phillips leaned forward. "Your legal will would then take precedence, allowing you to leave the estate to any of your daughters, or even divide it up between them."

Bennet frowned. "That is one reason for an entail in the first place — to prevent an estate from being broken up, along with protecting it from profligate heirs."

"That is true," said Phillips. "Then you could leave it to Jane, or to Lizzy." Phillips smiled. "Your second daughter might be the better inheritor, given her quickness."

Gripped in his thoughts as he was, Bennet nodded without thinking. "Perhaps, though she is still full young. Maggie might object, for Jane *is* the eldest. Jane might feel passed over, should I leave it to Lizzy. Furthermore, it is the girl's future husband who would own the estate and must be my concern."

Phillips shrugged. "Then when your daughter marries, you utilize a strict settlement agreement with him — that way the estate cannot be broken up or sold for the next generation. Thus, you would have protected it as much as you are able. Either way, with one of your daughters as your heir, you protect your wife and any remaining daughters, as you can write any conditions you wish into the contract. And if the man who marries your heir does not agree, you can disinherit her in favor of one of her sisters."

"Then it is settled," said Bennet. He laughed as a sudden thought came into his head. "My cousin may well suffer apoplexy when he hears of this if he does not beat down my door in his rage."

"Given what you have told me of the man," replied Phillips, "saving the estate from him is as much of a relief as providing for your family."

"That is true," said Mr. Bennet, shaking his head in disgust. "Collins is a brute of a man, one I hope I never have the misfortune to meet again."

"Good riddance, then," said Phillips. "I shall draw up the papers and bring them around to Longbourn when they are complete." Phillips paused and grimaced. "Or I shall if this ankle will allow it."

"If you are the means of my family's salvation," replied Bennet, "I shall ride to Cumbria to retrieve the papers. Let me know when they are complete, and I shall return."

"Excellent!"

Bennet shook his brother's hand, thanking him once again, and then rose to depart. During the ride back to Longbourn, Bennet considered the changes about to take place in his life. If he was to leave

Longbourn to Jane—for Bennet was uncomfortable with passing her over—she would be provided for. Given what Phillips had told him, Bennet knew his other daughters would be similarly cared for. But perhaps with the change in their fortunes, he might convince Maggie to put some extra money aside for their other daughters' dowries to make them more marriageable or provide for their support if they were not inclined to marry. If Longbourn *was* to benefit his family, perhaps Bennet himself would take more interest in it. The feeling of being in control of his destiny was intoxicating—Bennet felt freer than he had in years.

The return to Longbourn was accomplished quickly—it was doubtful Maggie had even known of his absence, so ensconced had he been in his library of late. As he entered the house, Bennet could hear her raised voice, and he grimaced because of it. As he was still uncertain about Phillips's information and wary of exciting Maggie's hopes, only to dash them later, he would say nothing for now. Once it was an established fact, Maggie would be the first to know.

"Papa?" a girlish voice interrupted his thoughts, and Bennet, who was handing his hat and gloves to Mr. Hill, noted the approach of his most intelligent daughter. "Where did you go?"

"Just to Meryton to visit your uncle," said Bennet, smiling at Elizabeth with pleasure. "I hope nothing has happened in my absence to upset your mother."

A smile crept over his face as Elizabeth looked skyward. "Lydia was running in the sitting-room after Kitty and tore Jane's new gown."

Bennet shook his head, another thought working its way through his consciousness. Kitty and Lydia, though only ten and eight years of age respectively, were already showing high spirits which bordered on impropriety. Should the matter of the entail be overcome, perhaps it would be best to ensure the girls were taught decorum. It would be best if they were instructed whether Longbourn was his to do with as he pleased or not.

"No suitors have beat down my door for your sister's hand?"

"I am certain Jane does not wish for a suitor," said Elizabeth, frowning at his jest.

"Nor should she," said Bennet, forcing his humor away in favor of earnestness. "Do not fear, Lizzy—I shall speak with your mother. This business of pushing Jane into society when she is not ready must cease."

Though he surprised the girl by the firmness of his tone, it was clear from her approving smile she agreed. And Bennet realized he had become far too distant from his family if this simple statement was a surprise to his closest daughter. Maggie was not the only one who needed to alter her behavior.

"Do not concern yourself, Lizzy," said Bennet. "There will be changes made at Longbourn, for I have just learned a most surprising thing from your uncle." Bennet held up his hand with a laugh at Elizabeth's blatant curiosity. "Please allow me my secrets for now, my love. You shall learn of them before long."

"Very well, Papa," said Elizabeth.

And she turned and departed for the sitting-room. The open door allowed the sound of his wife berating her youngest to reach his ears more clearly, and he shook his head. The return of the Maggie he had married would be a boon, indeed. The changes he was contemplating would benefit them all. Hopefully, Phillips's information, was correct, for it may become the salvation of his family.

CHAPTER I

October 1811

*L*aughter punctuated a typical meal at Longbourn, home of the Bennet family near Meryton in Hertfordshire, coupled with conversation, a healthy measure of teasing, and a smattering of gossip common to families of the area. But while the reader might be excused for assuming the family was one improper and difficult to tolerate, nothing could be further from the truth. For while their spirits were high, they were not improper, and though laughter and teasing prevailed, affection prevailed among them all. The passage of seven years had done them all much good, their worries for the future now far in the past.

The presence of Mrs. Garret at the table ensured good behavior, particularly of the youngest members of the party. She was a widow, stern but fair, knowledgeable yet compassionate. Mr. Bennet had retained her after he had put the entail aside, and for a time she had served as both companion for the elder girls and governess for the younger. Now she was companion to all, but her focus was on Kitty and Lydia, the only two not yet out in society.

The sound of laughter rang out over the table and Elizabeth, the second eldest of the Bennet girls, noted that a sharp look from the elder woman moderated Lydia's response to whatever jest her mother had made. By her side, Mary was listening to something her father was saying, interest unfeigned. Jane, as was her wont, was quiet, while Mrs. Bennet was speaking with Kitty and Lydia, her voice as always voluble.

It was a balm to Elizabeth's soul to see such a sight as her family in harmony, all behaving as the gentlefolk they were. Even as a young girl of thirteen summers, Elizabeth had recognized the alarming behavior of her mother and had seen the way her youngest sisters were beginning to emulate it. Many times she had sat at that table, listening to her mother lament some ill — real or imagined — and wondered what would become of them all. Now she pondered what might have happened to her family had their course remained unchecked.

But checked it had been, and whether one considered the circumstance which had led to the change to be blind luck or the natural order of the world, the entire family had benefited from it. Elizabeth could not be more grateful. At thirteen, she thought her future fraught with uncertainty. Now, at twenty, she knew she would be cared for, would always have a home, regardless of what happened. She even had a small dowry to allow her some modicum of freedom in the future.

This was not a universal opinion. Elizabeth turned and looked at her father, noting the affectionate way he was sporting with Jane over some matter or another. From a few comments he had made over the years, it seemed his former heir's condemnation had been swift and unrelenting. Mr. Collins, the cousin, had passed some two or three years after the entail had ended, and from what she understood, he had not been a good man, his loss unlamented. The son was as implacable in his own denunciation, though her father had told her several times, his words on the subject were much more plentiful, the language almost absurd.

As Elizabeth did not expect to ever make Mr. Collins's acquaintance, given his offense over being passed over, his opinions did not concern her overmuch. But the comical way in which her father portrayed his cousin's reproachful letters was a source of amusement for them all. Mrs. Bennet, to whom the Collinses had been evil incarnate, tolerated mentions of her former tormentor with an indulgent exasperation. That night, however, the conversation concerned another matter altogether.

"I wonder what you will all do now," commented Mr. Bennet as he carved the roast beef which was their supper. "When our new neighbors did not appear at the last assembly, I thought the young ladies of the neighborhood might expire of disappointed."

It was a mark of the changed relationship between husband and wife that the comment was not meant to provoke his wife, nor was the response offered in a flurry of nerves. In fact, Mrs. Bennet sat calmly, regarding her husband with a slight smile.

"I dare say we shall all survive our neighbors' absence until they see fit to grace us with their presence."

"But is it not strange?" asked Mary. "Mr. Bingley came to Netherfield, professed to our uncle how much he liked the place, signed the lease, and then disappeared again, greeting no one in the neighborhood."

"It seems a matter of urgent business arose which necessitated his absence," said Mr. Bennet, handing the tray of now cut beef to his eldest daughter. "Or so your uncle informed me."

"Then he will come when he will come, Papa," said Elizabeth. "Though we might all relish the opportunity to make new acquaintances, Mr. Bingley must see to his own affairs."

"That is wise of you, Lizzy," said Mr. Bennet with a smile. Then he directed a sly look which seemed to encompass both Elizabeth and Jane. "I might have thought you both would repine their loss as much as Miss Goulding or the Long sisters do., Mr. Bingley was said to have a friend who intended to visit also. Had they come, you might already be caught in the throes of infatuation!"

While Jane protested any such notion, Elizabeth only smiled at her father. "For my part, I shall not pine after the attentions of gentlemen with whom I am not acquainted."

"Then you are more sensible than Chloe Goulding," said Mary with a sniff of disdain. "At the assembly, I heard her boasting of how she would have caught Mr. Bingley if he had only attended."

"Chloe Goulding has a high opinion of herself," said Mrs. Bennet. "Everyone knows Jane is the most beautiful girl in the neighborhood. Had anyone caught Mr. Bingley, it would have been Jane!"

The words proved that Mrs. Bennet was not quite reformed. But knowing her mother's character, her words did not surprise Elizabeth. Rather than pushing her girls forward at every opportunity, Mrs. Bennet had learned to become more circumspect, to take their opinions into consideration. But she was a fierce defender against any slights, and a critical observer might claim she was less proper than might be expected of the wife of a gentleman.

Elizabeth loved her mother, but she did not lack understanding of her. Many of the things that interested Elizabeth were a mystery to Mrs. Bennet. But she was a good wife and mother, kept house with as much flair as anyone in the neighborhood, and no one could complain about the table she set.

"If Jane should be inclined toward the gentleman, I would have no objections." Mr. Bennet smiled at his eldest who had colored in embarrassment. "But let us leave that sort of conversation until after we have made the gentlemen's acquaintance, as our Lizzy says.

"Besides," said Mr. Bennet with a sly look that suggested a coming tease, "it seems to me my daughters will be well occupied, regardless. For I have heard there will be a company of militia quartered in Meryton for the winter."

There was a variety of reactions around the table to Mr. Bennet's news. While Jane looked on with interest, the same as Elizabeth herself, Mary was indifferent, her huff speaking volumes if the rolling of her eyes did not. Mrs. Bennet appeared somewhat interested, understandable given her occasional stories of the regiment of militia who had stayed in the area when she had been a girl. The most demonstrative reactions were reserved, yet again, for the youngest members of their company.

"It is unfair!" exclaimed Lydia, though she did not do so in a screech which had characterized her outbursts years before. "The militia is rarely quartered nearby, but as we are not out, Kitty and I will have little to do with them! Even Maria Lucas shall have more fun with the militia than we!"

"I do not care to socialize with officers," ventured Kitty in that tentative voice she always used when contradicting her younger sister. "It should be much too dull, I would think."

Lydia directed a glare at her sister, though it had little effect, as Mrs. Bennet spoke up. "And it is well you are *not* yet out, Lydia, if this is how you would behave."

With a harrumph, Lydia sat back, annoyed with her mother for not taking her part. Mrs. Bennet noticed and looked down the table at her husband, who joined her in indulging in a shaken head at their youngest daughter's attitude.

"Militia officers are not some mythical standard of masculine perfection, Lydia," said Mr. Bennet. "I suspect you would agree they are nothing special, should you meet them. And you *will* have occasion to meet the officers in the appropriate settings. But you must remember —" Mr. Bennet's tone became firm " — to adhere to decorum, for should you not, I will deny you their company the next time the opportunity arises."

The pout with which Lydia regarded her father almost set him to laughing. As it was, he maintained his firm demeanor, prompting Lydia to sigh and give up her objections.

"It is hard being the youngest, Lydia," said Mrs. Bennet, grasping her daughter's hand and giving it a consoling squeeze. "But you must remember all your sisters endured the same restrictions when they were your age, and they all passed through the experience, I hope, a little wiser."

The three eldest Bennet daughters chorused their agreement. It did not quite placate their younger sister, but at least she ceased her objections.

"Listen to Mrs. Garret," said Mrs. Bennet, nodding at the girls' companion, who nodded back. "If you wish to join your sisters at society events, you must learn how to act properly. Only then will your restrictions be lifted."

It was a sullen Lydia who nodded, ending the discussion. They turned to other matters, and for a time she was silent. Elizabeth watched her youngest sister, noting her returning spirits, wondering, not for the first time, what character she might have possessed had her father not had the foresight to curb her. Elizabeth shuddered to think of it.

The days passed as most days do, and the absence of the promised new residents at Netherfield meant there was little excitement in the sleepy little neighborhood. The local ladies' imaginations were soon full of red-coated militia officers, and more than one young lady would sigh in dreamy anticipation of the delights they were certain would soon attend them. Until the company arrived, there was little other than imagination to satisfy those longing for their presence, but when other forms of amusement are absent, such internal musings must suffice.

At length, however, the company marched into Meryton, one afternoon with many of the neighborhood watching and cheering. It should not be a surprise the Bennet sisters did not take part, though they received accounts of the event from more than one source. Soon scarlet-clad officers attended every gathering of the area, and the younger Bennets, eager for any news, badgered their siblings without mercy.

Aside from her annoyance with her younger sisters' determined questioning, Elizabeth found she did not think of the officers much when they were not before her. They were, she had decided early, a creditable and gentlemanly lot, though many seemed a little lacking in experience and too young to be out in the world. There were pleasant men among them, and some who were not. But Elizabeth, who was not looking for a husband — or even a man with whom to flirt — did not consider them much.

That changed, however, only two weeks after their arrival. On the night in question, the Bennets' friends of Lucas Lodge had invited the neighborhood for an evening party. Sir William, the patriarch of the family, was a bluff, kindly soul, one impressed with a knighthood he had received many years earlier and deemed it his duty to act as the spokesmen for the gentlemen of the area, leading in civility and banality in equal measure.

The Lucases were the Bennets' particular friends. Their eldest daughter, Charlotte, was Elizabeth and Jane's closest friend and the second daughter, Maria, was close to Kitty and Lydia, though the latter two were not to be in attendance that evening. There had been some talk of Elizabeth making a match with Sir William's eldest son, though it had died down in recent years — this was agreeable to Elizabeth as she did not much care for him.

"I am glad you have come," said Charlotte when she saw Elizabeth enter the room.

"When do we shun your home?" asked Elizabeth with a laugh. "You know we are happy to attend. How else would I obtain intelligence of our finest officers if we did not attend?"

Charlotte laughed. "Maria is not best pleased with your parents. When Father discovered your father did not intend to allow your sisters to attend, he decreed that Maria should not attend either. She was quite vexed when my parents sent her to bed before our guests began to arrive."

"Then I am sorry for her," replied Elizabeth, joining her friend in her mirth. "But I do not disagree. I hope she will take solace in hearing our accounts. Perhaps Mrs. Garret can help her understand why she could not attend."

"I am grateful to your parents for their forbearance," said Charlotte. "Many would not appreciate another girl of the neighborhood joining in lessons with their daughters."

"They are happy to do it," replied Elizabeth. "It helps Maria, true, but it also helps Lydia if she knows there is some company in her misery."

As the night progressed, Elizabeth met more members of the militia than she had before. Whether it was speaking with Captain Carter, one of the most well-regarded officers, or listening to poor Mr. Littleton who stuttered and stammered his way through conversations, Elizabeth found herself well entertained. But there was one among the officers' number to whom Elizabeth had not yet been introduced, to whom the eyes of almost every young maiden seemed to be inexorably drawn.

Mr. Wickham was a fine figure of a man—even Elizabeth, who thought herself less affected than most by a handsome mien, could confess it. He was tall, wavy brown hair framing a face with a strong jaw and high cheekbones, his blue eyes capturing the attention of even the most aged matron. Furthermore, his address was gentlemanly, his voice soft and melodious, and his observations engaging. Elizabeth was witness to more than one young lady sighing in dreamy worship of the young man.

Though it might be supposed Mr. Wickham was a man who was well aware of his looks and manners, he never drew attention to himself, though Elizabeth thought she detected a hint of basking in it when it came to him regardless. Still, it was understandable that any person blessed with such attributes would be conscious of them, and perhaps even a little vain. There seemed to be no such pretension in Mr. Wickham—or at least no more than normal for any man.

It was to the Bennet sisters that seemed to draw Mr. Wickham after a time in their company, to the chagrin of several other young ladies. Elizabeth supposed it was their disinclination to dominate his attention that saved them from becoming unpopular, and Mr. Wickham seemed content to speak with any young lady who wished to exchange words. In that way, everyone seemed happy.

"I understand you live nearby?" asked Mr. Wickham at one point when both Elizabeth and Jane were standing with him.

"At Longbourn," supplied Elizabeth. "It is less than a mile distant. The Lucas family have been our particular friends for many years now."

"They seem like excellent people," was Mr. Wickham's easy reply. "The regiment has been fortunate in being assigned to billet in this neighborhood. Though I have not been with the regiment long, I have heard Colonel Forster say a regiment of soldiers does not receive a ready welcome in every neighborhood they visit."

"I hope we are as welcoming as the next town," replied Elizabeth. "There are some among our number who are eager to welcome you."

Mr. Wickham laughed, as at that moment one of the Long sisters was smiling at him, her coquettish simper seeming to invite him to abandon the Bennets and join her instead. Though sorely tempted, Elizabeth avoided laughing when Mr. Wickham did nothing more than smile and turn his attention back to them.

"There are many pleasant people here. You are blessed, indeed. In the past, I, too, have been welcome in many situations and have had the good fortune to be the protégé of one of the best men I have ever known. I am no stranger to society."

"Such a thought never would have crossed my mind," said Elizabeth, Jane agreeing. "But I am interested—you have not been a member of the regiment for long?"

"Only a few months," said Mr. Wickham. "I purchased my commission two months before we came to Meryton. It was my intention to enter a seminary and become a man of God, but it seems to have worked out for the best that my journey in life brought me here."

"That is good news, Mr. Wickham," said Elizabeth. For a moment she thought she had disappointed him by not asking further of his previous intention to become a parson. Elizabeth ignored the matter, instead saying: "One's journey through life is enhanced with happiness if the circumstances match one's character."

"That is true!" cried Mr. Wickham. "Though I cannot say being a parson would not have suited me, the life of a military man is satisfying too."

Elizabeth thought it an odd statement. A parson's life was so different from that of an officer, she might have thought it unlikely a man would find either equally suitable. But Mr. Wickham changed the subject back to extolling the welcome he and the men of his regiment had experienced since their arrival. It seemed he had much to say on the subject, for he spoke at some length.

As often happened at gatherings of this nature, some of the younger members of the company began to express their desire to dance not long after. Mary, who possessed little fondness for the activity was drafted to play the pianoforte, and soon several of the officers were leading young ladies of the neighborhood to the improvised dance floor. It appeared Wickham was not about to be left out, for he turned at once to Elizabeth.

"Might I have this dance, Miss Elizabeth?" asked he with a gallant bow.

Though she thought he appeared a little ridiculous, Elizabeth assented and allowed the gentleman to take her hand. But before they joined the other dancers, Mr. Wickham turned to Jane, who had been watching with some amusement.

"And Miss Bennet, if I might petition your hand for the next dance, I would be very pleased, indeed. It is rare one is in the position to secure the hands of the two brightest jewels in succession."

"Of course, Mr. Wickham," said Jane, not responding to the man's obvious flattery. "I shall be pleased to dance with you."

A beaming smile lit up Mr. Wickham's face, and he bowed and led Elizabeth to the other dancers. There was little doubt the man had spread his flattery a little thick in his praise of the Bennets, but Elizabeth, who had seen many men make fools of themselves over Jane's imagined approval, could only look skyward as Jane once again proved her power over members of the other sex. That Mr. Wickham had asked Elizabeth to dance first was a surprise, for it was usually the opposite. To be compared to Jane was a compliment of the highest order.

It seemed Mr. Wickham was, in addition to all his other perfections, a consummate dancer, for he was light on his feet, performed the steps with precision, and did not come near to treading on her toes. Elizabeth received many looks of envy as she partnered with the handsomest man in the room. But Elizabeth would have given up his company without hesitation. Though his conversation was interesting, and his handsome countenance was beyond dispute, he did not interest Elizabeth as anything other than a casual acquaintance.

Soon after it became Jane's turn to dance with the gentleman, and she did so with her usual poise. If there seemed to be some further conversation between him and Jane than he had with her, Elizabeth did not concern herself over the matter. She was not in love with the man, and neither was Jane. Let him attempt to charm the Bennets. Elizabeth thought she and her sisters were more than capable of withstanding his manners and comely features.

CHAPTER II

Between the Bennet and Lucas families, it was a custom to gather the day after an event of significance to speak concerning it. It was not gossip, though those of a particularly rigid moral bent might consider it as such. But their conversation was more of their observations, items of humor or interest, or nothing more than a discussion of unrelated topics. It was so innocuous that even Mary, the most pious of the Bennet girls, felt comfortable in attending them.

That day there were few subjects to be canvassed which did not involve the militia regiment. More particularly, the Bennet sisters were curious concerning Mr. Wickham, for he was not the sort of man one forgot quickly. While they were familiar with all the principal officers of the regiment, none of them had made Mr. Wickham's acquaintance before that evening.

"It is my understanding Mr. Wickham was late joining the regiment here," said Charlotte when Elizabeth asked. "My father does not know the details, but Mr. Wickham had been given a commission by Colonel Forster which delayed his arrival."

"I wonder what it might have been," mused Elizabeth. "While the colonel might send men in advance to prepare a new camp, being left behind seems odd."

"It seems he must be highly trusted," added Jane. "No one who did not have the complete faith of the commander would be sent on a task which would delay him for two weeks."

Elizabeth directed a long look at her sister, wondering what her comment presaged. Jane had not seemed enamored of Mr. Wickham the previous evening—had Elizabeth been mistaken? The opportunity provided by her elder sister was too much for Charlotte to resist, and she took advantage to the fullest extent.

"Is that admiration I hear in your voice, Jane? If it is, I should not blame you—Mr. Wickham was deemed handsome by every woman in attendance last night."

"On the contrary," replied Jane, her color suspiciously heightened, "I have no admiration for Mr. Wickham."

"But you must confess he is far more appealing than any other man in the regiment."

"Based on nothing more than a handsome countenance, I must agree with you," said Jane, drawing her self-possession about her like a cloak. "I will own he seemed like a good man. But I hope I am no more turned by a handsome countenance than any other young lady."

"Good for you, Jane!" exclaimed Elizabeth. "There are other qualities in a man a woman must take into consideration."

"Such as?" prompted Charlotte with good-humored mirth.

"The ability to support a wife," said Elizabeth. "Being a member of the militia, Mr. Wickham must not be a wealthy man. While he might receive some support from his father, these militiamen all seemed to be second sons or less." Turning to Charlotte, Elizabeth fixed her friend with a curious look, asking: "Do you know anything of Mr. Wickham?"

"Nothing at all," replied Charlotte. "Before last night I had never made his acquaintance, and even my father, whom you must confess knows most of the local gossip, could say nothing more than that Mr. Wickham was a friend of Mr. Denny. It was on Mr. Denny's recommendation that Mr. Wickham joined the local regiment."

"Then perhaps Mr. Denny has more information concerning Mr. Wickham. Thus, you need only apply to him, Jane, if you wish to know more of your future beau."

Once again Jane colored, though it did not affect her glare at Elizabeth. "I have already said I have no admiration for Mr. Wickham."

"Methinks the lady doth protest too much," said Charlotte, *sotto voce*.

The friends laughed together and her sister, who almost never looked on anyone with censure, was peering at them with an expression resembling annoyance. This did not halt their amusement — quite the contrary.

"Even if I did," said Jane, "I do not believe Mr. Wickham possesses any admiration for me."

"Though I believe you when you say you have no admiration for Mr. Wickham," said Elizabeth, gazing at her sister with affection, "the reverse is not true, Jane."

"Mr. Wickham asked for your hand first," challenged Jane.

"Perhaps he did," replied Elizabeth. "But when my dance ended, he then danced with you, and for the rest of the evening, he could not be moved from your side."

"The fact of the matter, Jane," said Mary, who had heretofore remained silent, "is *you* never think *any* man has singled you out. *We*, however, always know when a man is singling you out, which is almost always!"

The three ladies laughed at the shamefaced Jane, who soon joined them, though with not nearly as much mirth. Their conversation brought Mrs. Bennet's attention, as she entered the room, looking on them with some interest. Elizabeth smiled in greeting to her mother, beckoning her to join them.

"You are speaking of last night?" asked Mrs. Bennet, aware of the ladies' habits.

"Yes, Mama," said Elizabeth. "More particularly, we were speaking of Jane's future courtship with Mr. Wickham.

Once again, the friends collapsed in laughter while Jane stammered her mortification. Mrs. Bennet appeared amused at the scene, entered and laid a commiserating hand on her eldest daughter's shoulder.

"I see your sister is at it again, Jane." Then she sat next to her daughter and added: "Mr. Wickham is, indeed, a handsome young man. I dare say he is even more handsome than Lieutenant Balderee, who was the talk of the regiment that camped here when I was a girl. Many a young lady liked him very well, indeed."

A dreamy look stole over her mother's countenance such as to make her appear many years younger. Elizabeth stifled her chuckles, sharing expressive glances with her sisters and friend. Their mother was so uncommonly improved in her comportment since the threat of the entail was removed and Mrs. Garret arrived that when she displayed an echo of her former behavior, it provoked a measure of mirth in them all. As a woman of more than forty years, to see her wistful sighs over the memory of some officer from many years ago struck Elizabeth as hilarious.

"I know you girls find my introspections amusing," said Mrs. Bennet, turning a pointed look on Elizabeth. "But I hold such remembrances dear. As Mr. Wickham focused more on you girls, I did not speak much with him. He seemed to be a very pleasant man. The question is, whether Jane likes him."

Jane smiled at her mother, her usual serenity returned. "While I agree with you, Mama, I found Mr. Wickham to be a pleasant man and no more. I was not enamored with him."

"That is not the issue we were discussing, Jane," said Elizabeth. When her sister glared at her, Elizabeth leaned forward and, grasping her hand, squeezed it. "I do not tease, Jane. It was obvious to us all that Mr. Wickham admires you, even on such a short acquaintance."

"That much was clear," said Mrs. Bennet, prompting Jane's frown. "But there is more to consider than whether a young man is amiable or possesses a handsome countenance."

That was not a statement Elizabeth might have expected to hear from her mother. Then again, Mr. Bennet was not what most women would refer to as exceptionally handsome, though Elizabeth did not think her father was in any way ill-favored.

"That is true," said Mary. "A man must have something with which he may support a family."

"Which Mr. Wickham would obtain should he marry Jane," observed Charlotte. "Jane *is* your father's heir now."

"Is showing such a quick interest in Jane not a sign of a fortune hunter?" asked Mary. "Since Papa dissolved the entail, Jane has become the most eligible young lady in the neighborhood."

"I think it is yet early to ascribe such self-interested motives to Mr. Wickham," said Jane, as always, determined to think the best of everyone.

"That is true," said Elizabeth. "There is no indication that Mr. Wickham even knows of Jane's good fortune. He *has* only been here for a few days."

"Actually, he does," said Charlotte, her manner faintly apologetic. "When he was speaking with my father last night, the subject arose, and my father was not hesitant to share his knowledge."

"It would have become known regardless," said Mrs. Bennet. "It is no secret in the neighborhood."

Charlotte smiled in thanks, but Mrs. Bennet was already considering the matter further. "It would be my preference," said Mrs.

Bennet, "that Jane did not marry a penniless man. It would be beneficial for her to connect herself with a man who already has some means. But if Jane truly liked him, I should not stand in her way."

"Which is exactly as it should be," said Elizabeth. "Look for a man of more means, but if Mr. Wickham is the man you wish to wed and he is a man of good character, there should be nothing to prevent you from following your heart."

"Thank you, Lizzy, Mama," replied Jane. "But to repeat myself, I am unmoved by Mr. Wickham. A handsome man he is, and he seems to be a good man. But one meeting does not leave me in love with him. While that may change, I suspect it shall not."

"Then the matter is settled," said Mrs. Bennet, rising from her chair. As she stood she smiled at her eldest, caressing her cheek with one finger. "I hope, my dear, that the disposition of Longbourn means I shall have your company after your marriage, but I would not have you married to a man for whom you do not possess any esteem." Mrs. Bennet turned to Elizabeth and Mary. "While I understand your wishes, your situation will not allow you to be as fastidious. Let us find good men for you, but your dowries will mean you must take the best available."

"My sisters are welcome to stay with me as long as they wish, Mama," said Jane.

"Of course, my dear," said Mrs. Bennet. "But the best a woman can hope in our society is protection in marriage. I wish that for all of your sisters."

Then Mrs. Bennet nodded toward Charlotte and excused herself and left the room. It did not take long for the sisters to exchange looks and descend into chuckles, though they took care to remain quiet.

"It seems there are some things about Mother which shall never change," said Mary with a shaken head.

"At least she does not throw us at gentlemen." Elizabeth turned an arched brow on her elder sister. "Do you not remember Mama's comments as she prepared you for your grand coming out when you were fifteen?"

"Without a doubt," said Charlotte, her eyes dancing with mirth. "I remember thinking many times that dealing with *my* mother was hard — being required to withstand your mother would be more than I can bear."

"I remember it too," said Jane, sighing and shaking her head with regret. "But she is uncommonly improved."

"Aye, that she is," agreed Elizabeth. "Believe me, Jane, I can endure these lectures concerning the superiority of the married state far better than I could being propelled toward any man with more than a penny to his name."

"She was not *that* bad," protested Jane.

"Yes, she was, dearest sister." Elizabeth rose, approached her beloved sister, and kissed the top of her head. "Though I do not say it to criticize, I must disagree with you. Mama was much worse than I said.

"Come, Charlotte," said Elizabeth, turning to her friend. "Do you fancy a walk on the back lawn?"

Charlotte smiled and agreed, and the two women excused themselves.

A little later, Elizabeth found occasion to visit her father's study. It was a handsome, bright and airy chamber, one Elizabeth had always found comforting, especially in the years of her mother's increasing manic lamentations about the evil of the entail. Whereas then she had been the only one her father would allow into the room on a regular basis, now all the girls were welcome to come and select a book or to speak of what they read with their father. Mary and Elizabeth were the ones who most often availed themselves of the privilege, though the other girls did so occasionally. It was a wonderful change, and the entire family had had some engaging discussions in that room.

That day nothing in particular brought Elizabeth to her father. There was nothing of which she wished to speak to him of a literary bent, nor did she have a problem she wished to discuss or an anecdote to relate. Being in there calmed her, allowed her to set her worries aside and lose herself in the written word. But she did none of those things on that day. Instead, she walked along the bookshelves so lovingly attended to by her father, ran her fingers along the spines of the books, relishing the feeling of the leather on her skin. It was an action borne of nothing more than love for the written word, though her mind was not on it. She felt at peace.

"It seems, my dear, something weighty is on your mind. Would you care to talk about it?"

Turning, Elizabeth smiled at her father and shook her head. "There is nothing troubling me, Papa. All is well."

"Yet you have been deep in contemplation since you entered, and I have not seen you walk around my room in such a manner for some time. When you do, it is almost always a result of you either contemplating something or worrying a problem over in your mind.

Since you have declared you have no concerns . . . ."

Elizabeth easily understood the inference, smiled, and sat in the chair in front of his desk. Mr. Bennet put the book in his hand down and turned his full attention on her. It was attention which might have been foreign to him only a few years ago, even when confronted by his favorite daughter. More than just Mrs. Bennet had changed in recent years.

"When Charlotte visited this afternoon, we spoke about several matters, one in which Mama took part."

"Your mother," said Mr. Bennet, a chuckle betraying his amusement. "I had thought she was past worrying you girls, but she backslides from time to time."

"It is not that, Papa," said Elizabeth. "The subject *was* marriage — or at least it was to some degree. But Mama did not discompose us."

Then Elizabeth proceeded to explain the subject they had discussed, while her father listened intently. He made no comment while Elizabeth was speaking, then after she fell silent he leaned back in his chair and considered the matter for some moments. Then he sighed and leaned forward.

"Though I am certain you already apprehend this, your mother is not incorrect. Provided a woman can find a good man for a husband, the protection of marriage is the best way to live your life. On the other hand, I know your wishes and I cannot say you are incorrect."

"I am aware of that," said Elizabeth.

"Of course, you are," replied Mr. Bennet. "When Jane marries, I can include articles in the contract which guarantee the support of you, your mother, and any remaining unmarried sisters. If her future husband does not agree to your support, I can change my will to make *you* my heir, or one of your sisters. And you will all have some money — not much, perhaps, but enough to support yourselves. But yes, I would like to see you all in fulfilling marriages when the time comes."

"As would I, Papa," replied Elizabeth. "But I do not wish to settle for a man for the sole purpose of attaching the title 'Mrs.' to my name."

"That is understandable. I do not wish any of you to be miserable in marriage." Mr. Bennet bestowed a singular smile on Elizabeth, one which had always made her feel treasured and special. "Especially you, Lizzy. It has always been my thought your disposition is such that you would never be happy in a marriage with a man you could not respect."

"That is true," said Elizabeth. "And I do not wish for it. I wish to love and respect my partner, to find fulfillment in the state of marriage. Perhaps I wish for too much—I know many would abuse me for having such fanciful notions. But I want it all the same."

The smile fell away from Mr. Bennet's face and he leaned forward again, bracing his arms on his desk and fixing Elizabeth with his expressionless eyes. "I know it is what you want, Lizzy. But let me also caution you, for the pangs of infatuation can sometimes mislead us into thinking our hearts are engaged, when, in fact, they are not."

Elizabeth knew her father was speaking of his own experience. While it had all turned out well, she knew her father might have made a different choice if he had been a little wiser, understood her mother a little more. He was not unhappy now, but those years in which her mother had betrayed the worst parts of her character had been a trial on his temper.

"Furthermore," said her father, "I must ask you to be careful in choosing a man, to look through to his heart and see him for what he is, rather than what you might wish him to be."

"Surely you do not think I will choose rashly!" exclaimed Elizabeth.

"I know your character, Lizzy," said Mr. Bennet. "That you will intend to be a rational creature is in no doubt whatsoever. But the heart is no rational organ. You never truly know a person until you are married to them, and I would not have my little Lizzy married to a man whose character you did not discover until after you had taken an irreversible step."

"I understand, Papa. While I cannot say for certain if I will choose with wisdom, I will assure you I intend to make every effort to do so."

"That is all I can ask for, Lizzy," said her father, sitting back in his chair once again. "There was no doubt in my mind you would do as I suggest. A little reminder every so often does not go amiss, now does it?"

Laughing, Elizabeth agreed with her father. "It does not. I will do as you say. But in the end, I believe I will attain happiness with any man I love, regardless of his station in life. I do not require a wealthy man. There are more things in life than great wealth."

"That is true. Wealth does much to smooth the path, though it may create other problems. It is right you should consider such matters as less important, though I would not advise you to forget about them altogether."

With those words, her father once again retrieved his book. Elizabeth, as she was now situated comfortably in the chair, allowed her mind to wander along paths of thought, considering what the future might hold for her. Though she had rarely considered what kind of man she might wish to marry, an image sprang to mind, of a tall handsome man. She could not see his face or anything of his features or person, or even the clothes he wore. But he was a good man, one devoted to her and their children, a good provider, intelligent and well-read, yet considerate and eager to hear her opinion on a variety of subjects.

The thought heartened her. Elizabeth Bennet did not have much to tempt a man other than her person. Despite that, she had always thought her lack of a substantial dowry would help her discern whether a man wished for her as a wife, or wished to obtain her money, had she possessed a great fortune. There were blessings, even in trials.

CHAPTER III

*O*ften, Elizabeth found younger sisters—especially younger sisters of high-spirited natures—to be more than a little bothersome.

Mary was quiet and thoughtful, and no trouble to tolerate. Kitty and Lydia were a different matter altogether when they got it into their heads they were being unfairly treated.

Unfortunately for the two youngest Bennets, the events of the neighborhood with the officers' attendance continued as autumn progressed. And every time there was mention of a party, dinner, or other amusement which would inevitably include the attendance of their elder siblings, the two younger Bennets would complain their exclusion was unjust. Elizabeth did not think their whining was nearly so bad as it could have been, but it was irritating, nonetheless.

The day of a gathering not long after the function at Lucas Lodge was evidence of this. It occurred in the morning at the breakfast table as the family discussed the evening's activity together. While Elizabeth suspected the two girls would prefer to remain abed in the mornings, Mrs. Garret was of the opinion that young girls needed to rise early to obtain the greatest benefit from the day. Thus, they were present for the discussion, which, to them, seemed more of a punishment than being required to rise early.

"Mama?" asked Lydia in a wheedling tone when Mrs. Bennet had made some comment of the evening. "Shall we not attend tonight's party? I promise we would be ever so well behaved."

"Perhaps it would be best to demur," said Mrs. Garret, eying Lydia in a manner which dared her to contradict. "Though I will defer to *Mr.* Bennet in this matter, I think neither Miss Catherine nor Miss Lydia is ready."

"And you would have my agreement," said Mr. Bennet. The stern manner in which he spoke left no option of changing his mind, and Mrs. Bennet's nod to support her husband closed that avenue as well. "The officers, my dear Lydia, would not provide you the excitement you think they might. In truth, they are a rather dull lot."

"Maria Lucas says they are far more interesting than any gentlemen who reside here," muttered Lydia, petulance coloring her voice.

"Oh? And how would Maria know? By my account, I do not think she has spent time in their company at all. The time is not yet right for you to attend.

"And remember, Lydia," continued Mr. a stern Bennet, "you are yet fifteen and will not be allowed out for some time yet."

What remained unsaid was that Kitty would be allowed before, which prompted a hesitant smile from the girl, but no comment. As she had been known to trumpet her status as the next to enter society in the past, her forbearance was an improvement, and Mr. Bennet noticed. His approving smile heartened her, allowing her to return to her meal.

"But, Papa—"

"That is enough, Lydia," said Mrs. Garret. "Your father has made his decision, not that I would have expected him to yield. If you had considered the matter yourself instead of complaining, you would have known it too."

"Thank you, Mrs. Garret." Mr. Bennet turned back to his youngest daughter. "Should we host a party at Longbourn, I *may* allow you to attend for a short time, and there are visits to consider, though your lessons must come first. Patience, child, for all you desire will come to you in due time."

It was clear Lydia had little notion of practicing patience, but she nodded and returned to her breakfast. If her mouth was pulled down in a sullen frown as she pushed her potatoes around her plate, no one saw fit to mention it, preferring to speak of other matters.

For Elizabeth's part, she considered the girls for a few more moments. High-spirited and petulant though they may be at times they were good girls. They were on the way to becoming estimable young ladies, she thought, if they could only move past this trying time of young girls on the cusp of adulthood.

At the gathering that evening, Mr. Wickham's admiration for Jane became obvious. There had been other gatherings at which he had paid her attention, but that evening it seemed he could hardly be moved from her side. It started as soon as the regiment arrived.

The Bennets, as was their custom, were among the earliest of the company to arrive. Their hosts, the Robinsons, greeted them as old friends, and they stood speaking as other families began to trickle in. Sarah Robinson, the only Robinson child left at home, was a year younger than Elizabeth, and as she was a friend of Elizabeth's, they stood for a time, speaking about recent events in the neighborhood.

"Did you hear of the butcher's son and the tanner's daughter?" asked an eager Sarah. "It is quite the scandal in Meryton."

Elizabeth laughed, for Sarah was one of the most determined gossips in the neighborhood. "I have not, Sarah, but I assume you are bursting to share every salacious morsel with me."

"Of course, I am!"

Then she made good on her statement, occupying Elizabeth's attention for the next quarter of an hour. Elizabeth was not a gossip herself, though news of their neighbors interested her. But she was willing to listen to a friend speak, though she did not take part herself. Then, after Sarah had canvassed that, and several other subjects besides, she moved away, ready to find another willing ear for her tales.

"Is Sarah finished?" asked Mary when she approached a moment later. In contrast to Sarah, Mary quite disapproved of gossip, and while she liked Sarah, she would absent herself whenever she spoke of such matters.

"With me, I suppose," said Elizabeth with a laugh. "Others will certainly be treated to the same stories."

"It would be best if you did not encourage her to such behavior," said Mary, the note of judgment in her voice unmistakable. "Gossiping is unseemly."

"Though I agree it is not the best behavior," replied Elizabeth, "Sarah relates nothing with malicious intent. I do not carry tales myself, but I willing to listen to her."

Mary sniffed with what sounded suspiciously like disdain and moved away, Elizabeth watching her as she went. A good girl though Mary was, she possessed a moralizing streak which could be maddening. Elizabeth did not think Mary thought herself better than others, but there were times when she gave that impression. It did not always make her popular in the neighborhood.

A little later, Elizabeth was standing with Jane when the officers entered. While Denny, Sanderson, Carter, and most of the rest entered and began making themselves agreeable, Mr. Wickham stopped in the doorway and surveyed the room. Then, when his eyes fell upon Jane, he brightened and made his way over to them, bowing when he arrived.

"Miss Bennet, Miss Elizabeth," said he. "It is wonderful to see you both this evening. How do you do?"

"Very well, Mr. Wickham," said Elizabeth, speaking as she usually did when someone addressed them together. "You are a little late this evening."

"Yes, there was a matter of which Colonel Forster wished to speak to us before we departed. It, unfortunately, deprived us of a few precious moments in your company."

"Nothing serious, I hope," said Elizabeth.

"Not at all," replied Mr. Wickham. "There have been a few times when some of the junior officers have not behaved with perfect decorum in recent days. Colonel Forster wishes to preserve the good reputation of the regiment."

"A worthy goal, to be sure," replied Elizabeth.

"And you, Miss Bennet?" asked Mr. Wickham, turning to Jane. "Have you been here long?"

It seemed Jane was near to being startled by Mr. Wickham's sudden question, for she stammered for a moment before responding. "Yes, we arrived perhaps thirty minutes ago."

"I wish we had come earlier," replied Mr. Wickham. "I have longed to speak with you since our last meeting, for you mentioned several matters which intrigued me."

Jane did not know what to say, and Elizabeth frowned and looked at the gentleman. While Jane had spoken to him, Elizabeth had been nearby, and she could remember nothing of any substance being canvassed between them.

"Your connections, for example," said Mr. Wickham. "I assume you must have many relations as worthy as your immediate family. Are you related to anyone present?"

"No one closely," said Jane.

Elizabeth, sensing Jane was not inclined to say anything more, spoke in her stead. "If you trace our lines back far enough, I suspect we have some connection with most everyone in town whose family has a similar history in the neighborhood. But we have no near relatives living nearby."

"But you have them." Mr. Wickham's words were once again directed at Jane.

This time, Jane put forth the effort to respond. "A few. The Bennets have been a small family for some generations."

"We have no living relations who bear the same name," said Elizabeth. "My father has a sister in Dorset, but we do not see her much. Our nearest relation aside from our aunt is a cousin three or four generations removed."

"Ah, that resembles my family," said Mr. Wickham. "For I, too, lack any near relations."

"Oh?" asked Elizabeth. "Then you have some?"

"Yes, I do," replied Mr. Wickham. Then he turned back to Jane. "And your mother's family? Is she from one of the other families in the neighborhood?"

"She is," replied Jane. "But not a gentle family. My mother's father was the local solicitor, a position now held by my aunt's husband. My mother's brother lives in London and is quite successful there."

"That is interesting," replied Mr. Wickham. "Then might I assume he is a man of business?"

"You may," replied Elizabeth, drawing his attention back to her. The way his eyes gleamed at her, Elizabeth began to wonder if Mr. Wickham was becoming annoyed with her responses. "Mr. Gardiner is successful too, as he owns his own business and many investments and interests in other companies."

"A remarkable man then," said Mr. Wickham. Then he turned back to Jane yet again. "And this is the extent of your relations? No other uncles or cousins lying in wait for the unwary?"

While Mr. Wickham laughed at his own jest, Jane responded with nothing more than slightly upturned lips. Elizabeth smiled along with her sister, but Mr. Wickham was so intent upon Jane that she might as well have been a thousand miles away.

"I shall look forward to making *all* your family's relations. If they are anything like you, I cannot imagine they will be anything other than the finest people."

"I believe we would all agree," said Elizabeth, this time speaking without waiting to see if Jane would muster a response. "I am curious about your family, for you said it was small?"

"Yes," was Mr. Wickham's only reply.

If he thought Elizabeth would be content with his answer, such as it was, he was destined to be disappointed. "Then you have few aunts and uncles or cousins? And your parents?"

"I have no siblings," replied Mr. Wickham shortly. "My mother passed on many years ago, and my father almost five years gone."

"Ah, then you have my condolences, Mr. Wickham." By Elizabeth's side, Jane murmured her own sympathies. "It must be hard to lose those precious to you."

"It is," replied Mr. Wickham. Then he turned again to Jane. "You are very fortunate to still have your mother and father, Miss Bennet,"

"Yes, we are," replied Elizabeth. "Pardon me, but where did you say you are from?"

By now the annoyance was clear to Elizabeth, who was looking for it, though she thought it would be hidden from a casual observer. Mr. Wickham regarded her for several moments before he made a short reply.

"I do not believe I did say—I am from Derbyshire."

"Ah, Derbyshire," said Elizabeth. She looked at Jane. "Aunt Gardiner is from Derbyshire, from a little town called Lambton, I believe it was."

That seemed to catch Mr. Wickham by surprise, and unless she missed her guess, she thought him a little worried. "I am familiar with Lambton. Did your aunt live there long?"

"Many years as a girl," replied Elizabeth. "I understand her father was the parson there."

"Then she likely left some time ago," replied Mr. Wickham. "Mr. Thorpe has been the parson since I was a boy."

Then Mr. Wickham turned back to Jane and addressed her again. Though Jane did not seem inclined to speak much, Mr. Wickham more than made up for her lack, ensuring there was rarely silence between them. Elizabeth exerted herself to interrupt a time or two, and every time she did, she noted his increasing annoyance. It seemed to Elizabeth that Mr. Wickham wished her gone, though he said nothing to suggest such a desire. Their conversation with Mr. Wickham lasted for some time until Elizabeth gathered her sister and excused them to speak to someone else.

Mr. Wickham let them go with a broad smile and a stated wish to see them again. Then he allowed them to depart, turning his charming smile onto another young lady of the neighborhood. But that did not last long either, for he soon made his way toward Jane again, seeming disappointed when Elizabeth joined them a few moments later.

It was a game of cat and mouse. Elizabeth watched Mr. Wickham's movements throughout the night, and whenever he accosted Jane, Elizabeth was there soon after. And while Jane was her usual reticent self, not making much response to his overtures, it did not seem to matter much to Mr. Wickham. Then when they were together, the interesting three-way conversation would play out, Mr. Wickham speaking to Jane, Elizabeth responding, and Jane saying nothing more than a monosyllable. And the longer the evening went on, the more pointed Mr. Wickham's looks became.

Finally, Elizabeth decided she wished to know more about the man, and since he would not talk of himself, she knew she would need to ask another. Since it was well-known that Mr. Wickham had been Mr. Denny's friend before joining the regiment, Elizabeth knew no one else could provide the information she required. Thus, during a lull in Mr. Wickham's attentions to Jane, Elizabeth beckoned Mary to her and gave her a few quiet instructions.

"Please stand with Jane for a time, and should Mr. Wickham come, do not allow him to intimidate you into leaving."

While Mary looked at Elizabeth askance, she did not protest, instead nodding and making her way to Jane's side. Elizabeth, thus freed from protecting her sister from a man of whom she was growing suspicious, made her way to the other side of the room where Mr. Denny stood speaking with a pair of his fellow officers.

"Miss Elizabeth," said Mr. Denny with a wide grin. "How do you do?"

"I am well, Mr. Denny," said Elizabeth, noting the man's eagerness to speak with her. Absently she wondered if he thought her approach was evidence of her preference for him. If he did, he would be disappointed.

"Should I feel privileged to receive your attention, Miss Elizabeth?" asked Mr. Denny before Elizabeth spoke again. "I have noticed you Bennet sisters do not seem to care much for our poor band of soldiers."

"I would not put it in such terms," replied Elizabeth. "There is nothing wanting with the officers of the regiment. But I have known those of the neighborhood for many more years. Is it, therefore, any wonder I speak more to them?"

"Perhaps not," replied Mr. Denny. "It is possible I misunderstood your character."

"How so?"

"Nothing shocking, I assure you," said he with a laugh Elizabeth detected as contrived. "It is only that I would have thought you eager to expand your circle of acquaintances by meeting new and interesting people."

"Oh, I am always happy to make new acquaintances, and no objection to interesting characters."

The way Denny regarded her, Elizabeth thought he was trying to divine whether she considered the officers—or perhaps himself in particular—at all interesting. Just as Elizabeth had intended, for though she did not think there was any harm in him, he was eager to come to know her more personally. He would do nothing improper without encouragement, but she had little doubt he would if she gave him any perceived encouragement. How fortunate her intended questions would do much in dissuading him from any such hopes!

"Speaking of interesting characters, I *am* wondering about something. I understand you knew Mr. Wickham before he joined the regiment."

The slow smile which began to spread over his face was wiped away by her reference to Mr. Wickham. It was all Elizabeth could do to refrain from laughing at him. As it was, she waited with guileless patience while Mr. Denny shot a glance at Mr. Wickham, who was, Elizabeth noted, once again with Jane, Mary looking on with some disapproval.

"Ah yes," said Mr. Denny, his pique not as well concealed as he might have liked. "Wickham is always popular with the ladies. I have seen him paying considerable attention to your elder sister of late."

Turning back to Elizabeth, he added: "I can see the appeal. Miss Bennet is a fine woman."

"I cannot agree more," said Elizabeth, clenching her teeth to avoid slapping him. "But I do not think Jane favors him. Mr. Wickham is charming, to be sure, but his prospects are poor, I think. A man such as he is unlikely to touch Jane's heart.

"Of more interest is that Mr. Wickham does not speak of himself. As his friend, I am certain you must know something of him?"

"I could not bear tales, Miss Elizabeth," said Mr. Denny.

"Nor do I ask you to," was Elizabeth's easy reply. "The purpose of my query is not to learn some gossip or anything of an improper nature. I wish to understand more of him—his family, connections, history. The usual information only."

Mr. Denny smiled, a quality inherent in it that Elizabeth could not like. "I understand and know why you would wish to have this information. Your application is in vain, however, as I know little of Wickham before I made his acquaintance. It seems he has been as circumspect in speaking of himself with me as he has been with you."

Then Mr. Denny bowed and moved away, indicating the end of their conversation. Elizabeth watched him go, wondering how to interpret his words. While she was thus engaged thinking of the matter, Charlotte approached her, fixing her with a questioning look.

"What was that about, Lizzy?" asked she.

"Merely attempting to learn more of Mr. Wickham," said Elizabeth with an absence of mind.

"I *have* noticed his attentions toward Jane. Do you suspect him?"

"There is something smooth about him, something which suggests his interest in Jane is more about Longbourn than Jane herself."

"You suspect him of being mercenary."

"Do you not?" asked Elizabeth, turning her attention to her friend.

Charlotte sighed. "He does seem to be inordinately interested in her."

"Yes, he is. He displays no care for her feelings, for Jane does not respond to him. In fact, I have been speaking for her all evening, and yet he continues to address her regardless of what I say. Furthermore, I have thought he has become more impatient with me throughout the evening as if I have interrupted his conquest. No, Charlotte, I do not trust the man in the slightest."

"Will you inform your father?"

Upon considering it for a moment, Elizabeth nodded slowly. "It seems likely to me that Papa has already noted Mr. Wickham's interest. But perhaps it would be best if I did. First, however, I wish to know Jane's feelings. While she does not respond to his overtures, she is as withdrawn as always, and I do not know if she feels threatened or does not wish to encourage him."

"If I know Jane at all," said Charlotte with a laugh, "it is the latter. When does Jane ever attribute anything other than the best motives in anyone she meets?

Elizabeth could not help but join her, regardless of the strain of the evening. "I cannot say you are incorrect."

"For what it is worth, I will assist you in keeping him from Jane's sole company. We do not wish her to be taken in by a man of poor character."

"Thank you, Charlotte," said Elizabeth. "You are a good friend."

When Elizabeth returned to Mary's side, she noted that Mr. Wickham had moved on, and Jane was now sitting by her mother, speaking with some of the other ladies. What Mr. Wickham thought of her present circumstance Elizabeth could not say, for he appeared to have focused on his new companions. But the frequent glances he cast in Jane's direction spoke to his interest.

"Did Mr. Wickham behave?" asked Elizabeth of Mary.

Mary turned to Elizabeth, her gaze curious. "Did you expect him to be the opposite?"

"I do not know what to expect of Mr. Wickham. The man is charming, winsome, and strikes me as utterly false. You must have noted his displeasure as I stayed close to Jane this evening."

"It seemed curious to me you would not leave Jane's side," said Mary, her eyes finding Mr. Wickham. As Elizabeth was also watching the man, she noted when his eyes flicked to Jane once, then back on his companions, and then once again only a few moments later. The frown it prompted in Mary informed Elizabeth her sister had seen it too.

"Is he a fortune hunter?"

"He shows every indication of it. Given Charlotte's testimony, he knows of Jane's position as our father's heir. As she is the one he is determined to entice, it seems suspicious, does it not?"

"It does," said Mary. "Though it could mean nothing more than inclination."

"It would if he did not keep watching her, or if his interest was not so blatant. The man is too polished by half, his manners seem calculated to please. I have little trust in him, and Jane is incapable of warning him away herself."

Mary nodded. "If I may be of any assistance, I will do it. We can keep him away from her together."

"Thank you, Mary. Tomorrow I will speak with Jane."

With a nod, Mary moved away, leaving Elizabeth to her thoughts, which were filled with no cordial feelings toward Mr. Wickham. Though Elizabeth knew she might be mistaken concerning the gentleman, she had learned to trust her instincts. And they were screaming at her to be wary of this man who portrayed himself as being without flaw.

Chapter IV

*J*ane Bennet was a woman eager to ascribe the best of every virtue to everyone. Elizabeth had always known this about her sister. It was a mark of Jane's angelic nature that she was mild and trusting, forgiving and thoughtful. Everyone who knew her considered Jane to be as good a woman as had ever breathed.

Such a trusting nature, however, opened her up to being deceived, to an unscrupulous character taking advantage of her and using her for their own purposes. Though there were few in Meryton to whom Elizabeth might have attributed such tendencies, those who were not as well-known were a concern. That was not to say Jane was incapable of reason or discernment — Elizabeth possessed the highest confidence in her sister's intelligence. However, when a woman's first instinct was to trust, the possibility existed for harm, for she might not realize the truth until it was too late.

In herself, Elizabeth knew the opposite problem existed — or perhaps it was not correct to suggest she had the opposite problem, for Elizabeth was not possessed of a suspicious character. Even so, Elizabeth was capable of taking care in a person's company and not trusting them until they had proven themselves. She was something of a cynic, more prone to expecting the worst of those she met, and in that respect, Elizabeth was the diametric opposite of her sister.

Thus, when Elizabeth determined to approach Jane, she hoped she could persuade her sister to her point of view. Jane had been quiet enough in Mr. Wickham's presence that it did not seem improbable she would listen. Then again, Elizabeth had seen her sister in the company of men who professed an interest in her when she did not return the sentiment, and in those times, Jane's usual means of informing them of her disinterest was avoidance. It was likely Jane already thought she was doing enough to dissuade the gentleman.

But Jane had never faced a suitor as determined as Mr. Wickham seemed to be. Even Mr. Harrington, the son of their neighbor to the southwest, who obviously had his eye on uniting the two estates under his future ownership, had not persisted when it became clear Jane had no interest in him. Mr. Wickham showed all the signs of a willful misunderstanding of Jane's indifference.

That morning, Elizabeth awoke early as was her habit and departed for her constitutional, returning before most of the rest of the house arose from their beds. Though Jane was not an early riser, neither was she usually abed late. It was, therefore, at breakfast when they met for the first time that day, and after that Elizabeth arranged tête-à-tête with her sister.

"I wished to speak to you about Mr. Wickham, Jane," said Elizabeth without preamble. She had learned through experience it was often best to be direct with her concerns.

"Mr. Wickham?" asked Jane with some surprise. "What of him? Surely you do not suspect me of being partial to Mr. Wickham."

"No, I do not. I have seen enough of your reticence with him in company to know you are in no danger of that."

Jane frowned with confusion. "Then what is your concern? Once Mr. Wickham understands my disinclination for his company, he will leave me be."

"Do you truly believe that? After his performance last night, I cannot imagine that Mr. Wickham will be content with rejection."

"I do not understand."

Suppressing a huff of annoyance at Jane's blindness, Elizabeth essayed to speak rationally, but with the firmness of her conviction. "Did you not witness the same as I, Jane? Mr. Wickham spent the evening continually returning to your company, and he was not at all deterred by your refusal to respond to his overtures. Did you not also see him becoming more frustrated with my interference as the night wore on?"

"It did not seem to me like you were interfering, Lizzy. We often stand together at society events."

"Of course, we do," said Elizabeth. "But Mr. Wickham has not been here long enough to know our habits. And for your information, I *was* interfering with Mr. Wickham's efforts, for his motives were clear."

"How could you suspect him so quickly?"

"By observing him, Jane." Elizabeth grasped her sister's hand and squeezed it with affection. "Mr. Wickham is a man with wooing on his mind, and none of the other ladies of the neighborhood are good enough for him, for he is after Longbourn. For me, he had no more than a few glib words, even though I was the one who continued to respond to him in your stead. Furthermore, he began to become more annoyed with me as the night wore on. When I left you late in the evening and Mary stood beside you, she reported that his wish for her absence was beyond dispute."

"Really, Lizzy," said Jane, a hint of exasperation creeping into her voice, "there is no need to concern yourself for Mr. Wickham or for me. I have no interest in him, and he is just a kind young man coming to know the neighborhood."

"I am not as confident as you, Jane. Please, Jane, trust me and take care."

A fond smile came over Jane's countenance and she leaned forward to embrace Elizabeth. "My fierce and protective sister. You do take prodigious care of us, Lizzy, and we all appreciate your determination.

"In this instance, you need not concern yourself for my wellbeing, for I have no intention of opening myself to Mr. Wickham's machinations if he has them. On the contrary — I will not let down my guard enough for Mr. Wickham — or any other man — to take advantage of me."

"That is good," replied Elizabeth. "It is all I wish. You are an eligible woman now — "

"As you have told me many times!"

Elizabeth smiled. "So I have. Please take care to avoid opening yourself to predators looking to get an estate."

"I shall."

Then Jane embraced Elizabeth once more and departed. And with that, Elizabeth was forced to be content.

When the same situation kept playing out in subsequent functions, Elizabeth knew she should inform her father of her suspicions. Jane, dear that she was, would not see the danger until it was too late, though Elizabeth had informed her more than once of what she thought she could see in Mr. Wickham's manners. As the head of the family and one of the leading gentlemen in the neighborhood, Mr. Bennet was in a better position to counter anything the officer might try. At least, Elizabeth hoped he would—sometimes Mr. Bennet tended to laugh off matters as if they were of no importance. Elizabeth hoped this would not be one of those times.

As Elizabeth explained matters from her perspective to her father, Mr. Bennet sat and listened with all the intensity Elizabeth might have hoped. Then, when she finished her recitation, he sat back in his chair and considered the matter for a few moments. Regardless of the gravity of what she had just related to him, Elizabeth was unsurprised when his first inclination was to tease her.

"Are you certain this is not jealousy of your sister speaking?" asked Mr. Bennet with a wink. "Your own actions have not been opaque, Lizzy. More than once these past days I have seen you attempt to draw Mr. Wickham's attention away from your sister."

Gazing skyward for a moment, Elizabeth turned a stern glare back on her father. "Do you think for a moment I would begrudge any measure of happiness Jane might obtain? Please do not make light of this, Papa, for I am in earnest."

Mr. Bennet chuckled and shook his head. "The genuine nature of your concern is not hidden. I will own, however, that I wonder, at times. Though Jane is the elder, you are next to her in age and, if I am to be honest, perhaps the better choice to inherit. It would be understandable if there were times when you resented your sister's good fortune."

"Why should I resent it? And why would you say I am better suited to inherit Longbourn?"

"Because," replied Mr. Bennet, his manner becoming earnest, "it is nothing more than the truth. Should I pass away tomorrow, it is *you* who will take over the estate and its management—not Jane. Your sister is not lacking in ability, but I cannot imagine her collecting rents or negotiating with the other landowners. With you managing matters, I do not doubt you would scold the tenants into harmony and browbeat our neighbors into seeing matters your way. You have taken some interest in how to manage the estate, and would do better than I, should you be forced to take the helm."

Elizabeth had not considered it that way, but she knew her father was correct. Jane would make a poor master of the estate, though she would make an excellent mistress. Shaking her head, Elizabeth banished those thoughts, turning her attention back on her father, curious, in spite of herself.

"There is no room in my heart for envy, Papa. How could there be? Jane is everything good, deserving of every good thing she receives. Having said that, I am curious—if you think I should inherit, why did you not leave the estate to me? Jane would not have protested it. It is more likely she would have understood and supported it."

"It crossed my mind, I assure you," confessed Mr. Bennet. "There were several reasons for it. The first was that it did not seem right to me to pass Jane over—she is the eldest, and by custom, she should inherit. I also knew you would come to her aid if required. It also seems to me that Jane is the most likely among you to choose an amiable man who would not make any remaining daughters feel unwelcome when I am gone.

"The fact of the matter is I can put all the legal requirements into effect with the next master. But if he takes it into his head, he can make life miserable for any daughters of mine who remain at home. A good man would not do this, and I judge it most likely that is the kind of man who would suit her."

"Then what of Mr. Wickham?" asked Elizabeth. "Though I asked after him, particularly to Mr. Denny, no one seems to know much of him, and his behavior in importuning Jane is reason to consider him unsuitable."

Mr. Bennet considered Elizabeth for a moment, then essayed to make a response. "You know I have the highest opinion of your intelligence and discernment, Lizzy. But in this instance, I wonder if you are seeing something which does not exist."

Holding up his hand to forestall Elizabeth's response, Mr. Bennet said: "It speaks well of your character that you take such prodigious care of your sister. Jane is not insensible, Lizzy. She is a clever and capable young woman, and I dare say she is well able to detect a fortune hunter."

"Of course, she is," said Elizabeth. "It has never been my intention to disagree. The issue is not Jane's discernment, rather her perception of others. You know Jane thinks the best of others and is incapable of seeing an ulterior motive in anyone's actions. What I have seen of Mr. Wickham tells me he is capable of less than proper behavior if he thinks his charm is not sufficient to achieve his ends."

Mr. Bennet sighed and sat back again. "It seems you are determined."

"Determined to protect Jane," replied Elizabeth. "I acknowledge I may be seeing more than exists. Can there be any harm in caution? Jane will not behave and act improperly but wonder if Mr. Wickham will."

"There is little I can do when the man has done nothing to deserve censure," said Mr. Bennet. Again he held up his hand to negate her reply. "What I can do is watch him and ensure he does not step beyond propriety. If he gives me reason to suspect him I can speak with his commanding officer."

A tight nod comprised Elizabeth's response. A part of her wished for something far more concrete than a simple promise of vigilance, but she recognized her father was correct. The colonel would deem it an attack on one of his officers if they should raise the matter with him now.

"Then that will need to be sufficient. There should be no need for me to state that I will remain watchful."

A laugh was Mr. Bennet's reply, followed by a jovially spoken: "No need at all!" Then he turned away, grasping a letter which had been laying on the corner of his desk, and addressed Elizabeth again. "This letter will be of interest to you, Lizzy. It is from my cousin, Mr. Collins, who, until I acted to end the entail, would have been my future heir. As you are aware, Mr. Collins was never my heir, as his father was still alive when I acted to end the entail."

"Mr. Collins?" asked Elizabeth, curious in spite of herself. "You have never informed me when you receive a letter from him, though you have shared a few of the contents of many with the family. With great amusement, I might add."

The grin with which Mr. Bennet regarded her spoke to his continued mirth. "Indeed, I have. As I have informed you, his father was a miserly and hamfisted man, uneducated and bitter over his lot in life. The present Mr. Collins is, I suspect, much more ridiculous than bitter. Though you are correct that I have not shared the specifics of his letters in such a fashion before, his previous letters have not had the potential to affect the entire family."

"Affect the entire family?" asked Elizabeth. "How could he affect us? Unless ending the entail was not so legal as you have led us to believe."

"No, that was above the board. Longbourn no longer has an entail, and Jane is my heir. Nothing will change that.

"I shan't bore you with an exact recitation of Mr. Collins's letter, for the man is the most verbose correspondent with whom I have ever exchanged letters. Though his letter is four pages in length, he could have completed it in only one and still conveyed everything he had to say!"

Mr. Bennet chuckled, looking over the pages in his hand. Though Elizabeth knew her father used exaggeration for humorous purposes, Elizabeth thought in this instance he was being candid.

"Why does he wish to visit?"

"It is difficult to divine," replied Mr. Bennet. "Though he spends a great deal of time forgiving me for cheating him of his due and talking of his patroness, who I suspect is a meddling and dictatorial woman, the gist of his letter is that he wishes to visit to 'extend his forgiveness in person and heal the breach between our two branches of the family.' Perhaps he wishes to see if he can reclaim his position as my heir."

Disgusted, Elizabeth huffed her annoyance. "He sounds like an absolute dullard. What did you reply?"

"I allowed his visit, Lizzy," said Mr. Bennet. At her obvious surprise, Mr. Bennet added: "His grievance is understandable. It was my actions that led to the end of his hopes of one day being the master of an estate. It is the least I can do to accept his visit and allow him to say what he will to me."

"I suppose so," said Elizabeth, with more than a little reluctance.

"That is the spirit!" exclaimed Mr. Bennet. Then he leaned forward, as if to impart a secret, and added: "Besides, having such a ridiculous man as a houseguest will provide us ample amusement, do you not think?"

Elizabeth could not help the laugh which escaped. It was so like her father to approve a visit so he could laugh at their guest. After agreeing with him and sharing some thoughts of how the visit might proceed, Elizabeth let herself out of his room.

That morning saw the first visit of the officers to Longbourn. The Bennet family, having paid several visits to other families in the community the day before, were all at home that morning. Thus, when Mr. Hill announced several redcoat visitors into their sitting-room, they were all on hand to greet them. Even Mr. Bennet, who threw Elizabeth an expressive look, was present to welcome their guests.

Besides Mr. Wickham, who took the lead in entering the room and greeting the family, Captain Carter, along with Lieutenants Denny, Sanderson, and Chamberlayn were present, all dressed in their crisp, bright uniforms. They were a fine sight, and Elizabeth hazarded a guess they knew it very well themselves.

A squeal caught Elizabeth's attention, and she turned her head to see Lydia almost quivering with excitement. Though the militia had been there for some weeks, the youngest Bennets had met them but little, and then only on the streets of Meryton. Chamberlayn and Denny were known to them, and they had met Carter and Sanderson, but it would be the first time they had ever met Wickham. With a sigh, Elizabeth pressed her fingers against her temples, hoping they would behave themselves.

"Mr. Bennet, Mrs. Bennet," said Wickham in that easy tone of his, one which suggested effortless civility, "how fortunate we are to find you at home today. How do you do?"

"Very well, Mr. Wickham," replied Mrs. Bennet. The way she looked at them, Elizabeth knew her mind was warring with their status as officers and the reality of their being naught but poor soldiers, none of whom were good enough for her girls. "I thank you for asking. How good of you to visit."

Mrs. Bennet invited the officers to sit, which they all did with alacrity. Sanderson and Denny attended Kitty and Lydia, with Mrs. Garret nearby and looking on like a mother hen watching her chicks. Chamberlayn sat down with Mary, for they were of a similar bent with respect to religion and literature, while Carter approached to pay his respects to Jane and Elizabeth. Mrs. Bennet rang for tea, and they all began the business of a morning visit.

"What a lovely home this is, Mrs. Bennet," began Mr. Wickham. "Though I have never visited Longbourn before, I can understand why your neighbors speak of your home with such reverence."

There were few subjects which could garner Mrs. Bennet's approval like complimenting her on the arrangements of her home. Though Elizabeth was certain her mother did not even think of it any longer, the fact was that she had not been born a gentlewoman. Being reminded of her rise in position was a boost to her vanity, which Mr. Wickham no doubt intended.

"I can see you have done much to it," said Mr. Wickham, when Mrs. Bennet thanked him. "The quality of the home is far superior to any other I have seen in the neighborhood. You must be proud of your work."

While Mr. Wickham continued to flatter her mother, Elizabeth looked at her father, arching an eyebrow when she caught his eye. Mr. Bennet turned his eyes heavenward and shook his head, chuckling to himself. Heartened by his response—for even if he still thought Jane was in no danger, it was clear Mr. Bennet had recognized Mr. Wickham's words for the fawning they were—Elizabeth turned back and attended the conversation.

For a time, Mr. Wickham continued to speak with her mother, his statements never reaching the ridiculous. In fact, they were all measured and delivered with warmth and sincerity. While he was doing this, Elizabeth and Jane were busy speaking with Captain Carter and Mr. Denny, who had joined them in the interim. It was a chance comment by the latter which revealed more than perhaps the speaker intended.

"I see your attention toward Wickham has not abated," said Mr. Denny. Elizabeth, who had been watching Wickham in his attempts to charm her mother, turned to the lieutenant with some surprise. Mr. Denny laughed. "It has been quite marked, Miss Elizabeth."

"Nothing of the sort, Mr. Denny," said Elizabeth. "It is just that Mr. Wickham puzzles me."

Mr. Denny laughed again. "There is no need to dissemble, Miss Elizabeth. In fact, I have seen it more times than I care to count. The man has a gift and no mistake.

"But let me give you some advice," continued he, turning a speculative eye on Elizabeth. "There are many who seek to claim Wickham's attention, but few succeed. When he has made his choice, there is little to stand in his way."

"Is that so?" asked Elizabeth, feeling her temper well up within her.

"I have seen it many times, as I have said." Mr. Denny shrugged and added: "You may test it for yourself, but you are destined for disappointment. Now, if you like a man in a red coat, you are in luck, for there are many others who will fill that requirement."

"Yes, it seems like the neighborhood is swimming with men who wear scarlet," said Elizabeth. The words she flung at him were filled with sarcasm, a fact Mr. Denny did not seem to recognize. "Men often judge their worthiness and desirability by the most trifling measurements. Perhaps you officers boast your prowess with each other, both your ability to attract ladies and the shininess of your buttons, but such matters mean little to me."

"As they should," said Captain Carter, his attention returned to them after being distracted by something her father had said. "It may be best to refrain from speaking of such subjects, Denny, for Miss Elizabeth is correct. Though Wickham's intentions are clear, it seems to me that Miss Bennet's are equally so."

The meaning of his words was not misunderstood, for a glance told Elizabeth Mr. Wickham had come closer while she sparred with Mr. Denny and was now attempting to elicit a response from Jane. His success appeared to be less than inspiring, for Jane was, as her custom, saying little, even when he prompted her.

"I believe it is time we departed," continued Captain Carter, with a glance at his watch. He turned and directed a genuine smile at Elizabeth. "As a member of the militia, I am grateful for the welcome we receive from those of the neighborhood. It would be unwise to tax that welcome by overstaying."

"It is a pleasure to have *you*, Captain Carter," said Elizabeth, certain the captain had received her message. Lieutenant Denny only seemed confused—the man had little understanding of any undertones of the conversation it appeared. "Should the French invade Hertfordshire, I know we can count on the regiment to defend us."

Captain Carter laughed. "We shall do our best. Should Bonny himself stride our streets, I have no doubt we shall make him pay for every inch. And should he come too close, I trust you will do your part by kicking his shins."

"Anything for the support of England, Captain Carter," said Elizabeth.

The captain gathered up his men and departed, though Elizabeth noted that Mr. Wickham was reluctant, throwing more than one reproachful glance at his superior officer. Mr. Denny, on the other hand, appeared lost in thought, as if still trying to understand Elizabeth's comments. The lieutenant, Elizabeth decided, was like a puppy attempting to behave like a wolf. Mr. Wickham, however, was the alpha predator. Perhaps Elizabeth was overstating the danger he posed. That would not keep her from vigilance.

CHAPTER V

ondon in autumn was a dreary sort of place. While it could be said it was not as bad as the summer months when disease sometimes ran rampant and a foul miasma hovered over the city like a plague of locusts, the damp and gloom of gray days, coupled with the lack of any society, left much to be wanted.

Darcy chuckled at his own thoughts. There were many in society who would be shocked if they knew he had repined the lack of association, even in an oblique sense. In fact, Darcy little approved of most society, and being of a reticent nature, one which experienced difficulty in speaking with those he did not know—and those he did, but of whom he did not approve—it was rare he thought of any absence of parties, balls, and the like. When he did, it was more likely to be with relief, or at least indifference.

There was, he supposed, the little season, but there was a dearth of society to be had of the level he inhabited, and what there was, he did not care for. Hertfordshire had been Darcy's destination—he should have been there for almost a month already—but his departure had been delayed unexpectedly. Why the departure had been postponed, Darcy was not certain, as his friend had been rather uncommunicative concerning it. It was some business concern or another, as Bingley had been anticipating his residence in Hertfordshire and the opportunity it provided for him to learn estate management from his experienced friend.

It was fortunate Darcy's cousin, Colonel Fitzwilliam, was also in London for he provided companionship while Darcy waited. That was not without its drawbacks, of course, for Colonel Fitzwilliam, especially when he thought he was being clever, could be difficult to bear. There was also another matter which had been occupying him, a matter which Darcy would much rather had not arisen.

"Still no sign of Wickham," said Colonel Fitzwilliam one evening while they were sitting together in Darcy's study. Fitzwilliam preferred Darcy's company when in town, for it was quieter, and he was allowed to come and go as he pleased. When staying with his parents at the earl's house, that freedom was not guaranteed, for there were immediate family members — particularly his mother — to satisfy.

Darcy grunted, the disdain for his former friend an old acquaintance by now. "Being a snake, Wickham must be at home in the underbelly of London. No doubt it will take you many weeks to discover his lair."

"It would not be necessary if you had listened to my advice even two years ago." Fitzwilliam sipped from his glass. "Wickham should have been hanged from the highest tree or shipped off to Botany Bay before he was allowed to wreak such havoc."

It was an old argument, one Darcy would not repeat. All his life Wickham had plagued him, first with his rough play as a child, then as a young man attempting to goad Darcy into a fight or frame him for some misdemeanor, then as an adult, running up debts, playing false with young maidens' sensibilities, or demanding that which he had not earned. More than once it had been the memory of Darcy's father that had stayed his hand, though he knew Fitzwilliam was correct. Then had come the final betrayal . . . .

"Have you no indication as to a where he may be hiding?" asked Darcy.

"None at present. There have been reports he has left the city, but rumored destinations have been varied, and some are downright nonsensical. I suspect he is skulking around the slums somewhere, though I suppose it is possible he may have fled."

"It is fortunate he did no damage." Darcy paused and stared morosely into the fire. "Georgiana showed some greatness of mind in seeing through his presence in Ramsgate."

"She did so," said Fitzwilliam, "because you informed her of your dealings with the snake. Had you not, we may be coping with a very different outcome."

Darcy shook his head. "I doubt he would have duped her regardless."

"It is difficult to say," replied Fitzwilliam. "Arming her against his schemes was one of the best decisions you ever made, regardless of your speculation now as to what *might* have happened."

"It saved her much heartache. The thought of her attached to George Wickham fills me with disgust."

Fitzwilliam scowled and tossed back the rest of his drink, holding his glass out for more. "Do not even suggest such a thing, Darcy. I shudder to even think of it."

"She is safe," Darcy said with a slight upturn of his lips while he poured for his cousin. "Wickham will never be a threat to her again. I shall make certain of it."

"As will I." Then Fitzwilliam changed the subject. "I understand you are to go to dinner at Bingley's house tomorrow. Were you not to stay at his rented estate for several months?"

"I was, but Bingley was required to stay in London for a time."

A grin settled over his cousin's countenance. "There is one bright side: your time spent with his harpy of a sister under the same roof has been delayed. It also leaves you with more time to devise means of avoiding her certain attempts to compromise you."

"Fitzwilliam, you misjudge her," said Darcy, the mock-sternness of his countenance providing mirth for his cousin. "It is well known that Miss Bingley will never resort to such measures."

"If you think that, you are naïve. That woman will do anything to become the mistress of your estate."

"She would if she had any doubt of her eventual success. To the narcissist, their designs are inevitable. Miss Bingley is nothing if not confident."

"I do not know that I have heard you speak of her in such unflattering terms," said Fitzwilliam. Glass raised, he said, "Bravo!"

Shaking his head, Darcy added: "No, I do not fear for Miss Bingley engineering a compromise. Not only is Snell careful to ensure there is no possibility, but I doubt Miss Bingley believes I would be moved even she should succeed"

"That is well, Cousin. Then I shall leave it to you." Fitzwilliam stood and drained his glass. "As I have an early morning tomorrow, I shall retire. If there are any developments concerning the search for Wickham, I shall inform you."

Though his cousin's portrayal of Miss Bingley was, improper, Darcy could not discount its veracity. Miss Bingley was, in the words of more than one of his friends, the most determined social climber Darcy had ever had the misfortune to meet. Bingley's fortune had originated in trade, his forebears having built their wealth over several generations. It had been Bingley's father's intention to purchase an estate and raise his family above their common origins, but he had passed away without realizing that dream. Thus, it had fallen to Bingley to finish what his ancestors had begun.

It was likely for the best. Though a good man with many sterling qualities, Charles Bingley was not a businessman, though he was not deficient either. Bingley was more prone to becoming distracted, usually by a pretty face, and his attention to detail was lacking at times. While this was an unfortunate lack in a gentleman, it could be remedied by hiring a competent steward to attend to all the minutia of an estate. In a man of business, however, such failing might lead to loss of income and property and possible insolvency. Bingley still had relations who managed the family business, but he had liquidated much of his investment in it, allowing him the opportunity to use that wealth toward the purchase of an estate.

While Miss Bingley was not deficient in understanding and understood the limitations of her descent, she was also adept at ignoring anything she did not like. Having been educated at an expensive seminary, Darcy could confess she was competent and poised, and if her humor was biting, there was nothing overtly amiss in her behavior. Her comportment, that of a high society lady, was not accompanied by the connections and breeding which would make it, in certain circles, acceptable. Then there was her unfortunate tendency to look down on those of her family's level of society, and even those who were their superior by most measurements. She was, in a word, difficult to tolerate.

"Mr. Darcy, dear Georgiana!" exclaimed she as soon as they arrived for dinner the next evening. "How wonderful it is to see you both. Come in, come in, for we have been expecting you."

It took considerable willpower not to grimace at her familiar greeting. To the best of his knowledge, Georgiana had never given the woman permission to address her by her Christian name, making it rude and presumptuous. It was one concession he made to avoid offending his friend and maintaining the connection, though he thought Bingley would not be affronted at all should Darcy profess offense. Still, it seemed best to just ignore the woman altogether.

"We have prepared all your favorites tonight, Georgiana darling," said Miss Bingley, clutching his sister's arm possessively and guiding her to a chair. "It is unfortunate Louisa is not here tonight, for she dotes on you so. But she and Hurst are still at his family estate and will not arrive for some time yet."

"Thank you, Miss Bingley," said Georgiana. Darcy was proud of his sister, for she did not betray a hint of her discomfort.

"Please, Mr. Darcy," added Caroline, while seeing to Georgiana's comfort, "you may sit here."

"Thank you, Miss Bingley," said Darcy, choosing a chair closer to Bingley, intent on avoiding the perception of favor. "I trust you have been well?"

"Yes, I have," replied Miss Bingley. "It is only that town is so dull at present. I am eager to hear of Georgiana's recent adventures."

Amused at having his recent thoughts echoed in her words, Darcy nodded and turned to Bingley, while keeping a close eye on his sister. Georgiana could hold her own against Miss Bingley's intrusive inquisition, but he rarely allowed her to visit with the woman without supervision.

"Are you affected by the same ennui as your sister?" asked Darcy of his friend.

"It is true there has been little amusement for Caroline," replied Bingley. "But my days have been full. I am certain the lack of society has been no burden for you."

Darcy, not about to confess to his own sense of boredom, made an ambiguous comment, before turning to his true interest. "What of going to Hertfordshire? Can I suppose you still intend to go to your estate before long?"

"As soon as I can drag myself away from town," replied Bingley. "I hope you are still planning to accompany me."

"That is the only reason I am still in town," replied Darcy. "Otherwise I would have retired to Pemberley long ago."

Bingley grinned. "I never would have guessed it, old man. I greatly appreciate your willingness to assist."

"Do you know when you will be at liberty to leave?"

"Perhaps within the next few days—perchance as early as next week. Will Miss Darcy join us?"

Darcy looked over at his sister, who was speaking with Miss Bingley. "At present, she is much engaged with my aunt. In the future, perhaps, but I believe she is content to be in London for now."

With a nod, Bingley allowed the matter to rest. His sister, Darcy knew, would not have been so quick to cease pressing him on the matter.

"The true art of managing an estate," said Darcy, turning back to the previous subject, "is learned during the spring planting season and fall harvest. The rest of the year is either waiting for the crops to grow or preparing for the next planting—though preparations for winter are important. I am happy to join you, though I am uncertain how much assistance I will be during the winter months since the estate's steward will do much of the work for the next growing season."

"Then you shall need to join me in the spring!" said the ever-irrepressible Bingley.

Soon after, they were called into dinner. As there were only four diners, the setting was much more intimate than Darcy might have wished, with Bingley at the head of the table, Miss Bingley at the foot, and the Darcy siblings facing each other on the log side of the table. For a time, the conversation, while not to his taste, was at least acceptable.

"It is my understanding you are staying with your aunt, Georgiana," said Miss Bingley. "And how are you finding the countess's house?"

"I have always enjoyed my time with my aunt," replied Georgiana. "Lady Susan is kind to me. She was one of my mother's closest friends."

"You have spoken of her so much that I feel I already know her. It is my hope to make her acquaintance someday."

It had been Miss Bingley's hope to make Lady Susan and Lord Matlock's acquaintance for many months. The reason she had not yet is Darcy did not wish to force her fawning attempts to curry favor with them, and they had no particular desire to become known to her. The Fitzwilliams had met Bingley, and they approved of him. But Darcy judged that Miss Bingley would be a different manner of acquaintance and preferred to keep himself free of the possibility of their censure.

"Perhaps an invitation may be arranged," replied Georgiana, though committing nothing. "At present, I believe my aunt is enjoying the relative lack of her peers in London, for she often tells me the demands of her position can be overwhelming."

"Nothing could overwhelm to her, I am certain!" objected Miss Bingley, unable to understand why a woman of Lady Susan's prominence would not do everything in her power to flaunt it as often as possible.

"I did not say she was overwhelmed, Miss Bingley," was

Georgiana's calm reply. "It is beneficial to rest from such things from time to time, is it not? Regardless, my companion and I are comfortable there."

"Ah, yes—your companion." Miss Bingley peered at Georgiana. "It is curious she did not accompany you tonight."

"She is visiting family this evening," said Georgiana. "As William was to escort me here, I saw no need to include her when she may have the evening to herself."

"Indeed," replied Miss Bingley. "In the future, however, I would suggest you remind her of her place. It is not good for a woman hired for a position to shirk from her duties. You should take her in hand."

The reason Georgiana's companion had not accompanied them tonight was because they knew Miss Bingley would have treated her with contempt, leaving her to herself for the entire evening. It was better she was otherwise occupied, for the woman, while compensated well, was not paid enough to endure Caroline Bingley's barbs.

Later, after they returned to the sitting-room, Darcy rediscovered the more interesting aspects of Miss Bingley's character. At a point when Bingley and Georgiana were speaking of some matter together, she used the opportunity to further her schemes with him and speak of another matter of which she was not happy.

"I must commend you concerning your sister, sir," said she in the simpering tone she used when she wished to impress him. "Georgiana is everything delightful. It is my hope she will consent to entertain us with her skills tonight, for it is some time since I have heard her play."

"Thank you, Miss Bingley," said Darcy. "I will own I am prodigiously proud of her."

"As you should be. It is pleasing they are so comfortable in each other's company. Charles, you know, thinks as highly of Georgiana as I do."

Darcy nearly rolled his eyes. Miss Bingley, it seemed, not only had her eye on the vacant position of mistress of Pemberley but was also eager to bring about a double connection with the Darcy family. Though she considered herself subtle, Darcy had understood her desire for Bingley to marry Georgiana for some time. The woman did not take into account that as a girl of fifteen, Georgiana was not ready for marriage, even if Bingley had looked on her as a more than just a little sister.

"The feeling is mutual, Miss Bingley," said Darcy, refusing to say anything more.

Miss Bingley preened, as if he had just declared his lifelong devotion to her. Then her expression turned sour.

"There was one matter I hoped to discuss with you, Mr. Darcy. It is my hope I may depend on your assistance to help persuade my brother."

"Oh?" asked Darcy. "I cannot imagine what influence you believe I have such that I may contradict him."

"Of course, your influence is profound," said she. "Charles relies on your advice in all matters."

Darcy was not at all certain that was accurate, but he indicated his willingness to hear her regardless.

"It is this business of Hertfordshire." Miss Bingley huffed with exasperated annoyance. "Do you know he determined to lease this estate of which he speaks without consulting me on the matter?"

"Is it not his decision to make? Your brother does not intend to purchase at this time. Netherfield is an opportunity to learn estate management without the risk or responsibility of full ownership. And as the estate is close to London, he may travel here whenever he wishes, whether during the season or otherwise. The prospects are good, in my opinion."

Miss Bingley made a guttural sound in the back of her throat, one Darcy was certain she was not even aware of herself. "Perhaps all that is true. What Charles has told me of the neighborhood tells me, the locals will be positively medieval. How are we to endure a neighborhood with a society it will be a punishment to endure?"

"Perhaps, Miss Bingley, it would be best to meet the locals before pronouncing them unsuitable."

"There is no need," snapped the woman, her impatience impeding her better manners, such as they were. "I know what it will be like, Mr. Darcy. The neighborhood will be full of people of little fashion and less refinement, and every young woman there will set her cap at my brother." Miss Bingley regarded Darcy. "In fact, I have little doubt you will have to fend off determined fortune hunters by the score while residing with us."

"It is nothing less than I have here, Miss Bingley," replied Darcy. Had the woman any inkling she herself was at the top of that list, she would have been mortified. Then again, perhaps she would not care.

"It is clear," said she, and Darcy knew it was clear in her own mind, "we can allow this. I would have much preferred Charles find an estate to lease in Derbyshire. There, at least, we would find people of refinement."

"But you would be three days distant from London."

"A small price to pay."

"Your brother has judged differently. Estates in Derbyshire are no better or worse than those in Hertfordshire, Cornwall, Kent, or any other part of the kingdom, Miss Bingley. It is the diligence of the proprietor which determines their worthiness."

Miss Bingley sniffed with disdain. "That is beyond dispute. But I cannot countenance this neighborhood Charles has seen fit to inflict upon us. No, it will not do. I must have you speak with Charles, convince him of the folly of leasing this Hertfordshire estate. If he refuses the lease, there may still be enough time for him to find an estate in a more proper part of the kingdom."

How Darcy would have loved to indulge in a chuckle! As it was, he had no intention of speaking to Bingley, and he would not, under any circumstances, attempt to persuade his friend. While it was true Bingley relied on him for advice, Darcy had no desire to make Bingley any more dependent on him than he already was. Quite the opposite—everything on which he advised his friend was with the goal of weaning him from Darcy's support. Bingley's learning the management of an estate was also a circumstance which would see him standing more on his own.

"Your brother has signed a lease, Miss Bingley," said Darcy. "To withdraw now would cause him to lose the money he has invested. Besides, as you know, I accompanied your brother to Hertfordshire to inspect the place before he signed the papers. It is a good property, one which will allow your brother to learn without being too difficult. I have no intention of attempting to change his mind."

The look Miss Bingley fixed on him was overflowing with displeasure, though she surely thought he could not read it in her countenance. Regardless, she appeared to come to the correct conclusion, for she did not press her point.

"When you put it that way, I suppose there is nothing to be done."

"I am glad you understand, Miss Bingley."

A rather put-upon sigh was followed by a brightening of her countenance. "I suppose it *is* close to town, which has its advantages. With any luck, we shall be there no longer than a month or two and shall be occupied by the season soon after."

Darcy thought this was a rather vain hope, for he knew Bingley intended to spend some months in Hertfordshire. It would not surprise him if Bingley returned to London for part of the season, but he intended to be in the country during planting season. Knowing this, however, did not lead Darcy to contradict the man's sister—let Bingley do that.

"And I suppose we shall be the leading lights of local society the moment we set foot in it," added Miss Bingley, a distant smile settled on her countenance. "The locals will look to us for guidance in matters fashionable. Though I would not relish moving in such circles, it will do them good. It is unlikely they have had much contact with the civilized world."

"Doubtless they will be rendered speechless."

Miss Bingley missed his barb, instead preening at his perceived compliment. "Yes, well, I shall try not to dazzle them too much." Then she turned to him, her manner becoming serious. "What I said of the locals was not idle commentary, sir. In a small society such as the one we soon shall enter, I am convinced fortune hunters will be on every corner. You must take care not to give encouragement, and I must depend on your help to safeguard my brother."

"Miss Bingley, you should know by now that I am *always* careful. And I am not convinced it shall be as bad as you say, for those living in the neighborhood *are* gentlefolk. While they may not be as polished as those you might meet in town, they will be adequate company while we are there."

The huff with which Miss Bingley responded informed Darcy she did not agree and was not happy, but she subsided and did not speak further on the matter. Bingley, though he was a good man, was prone to having his head turned by a pretty face. What he was not, however, was a man who raised false hopes or allowed an unscrupulous woman to capture him. If he *did* become enamored in Hertfordshire, Darcy would watch the woman to see if she appeared to be a fortune hunter. Other than that, it was Bingley's responsibility to manage his own affairs, and Darcy had every confidence in his friend's ability to do so.

CHAPTER VI

$\mathcal{M}$rs. Bennet's reaction to the imminent visit of the man she once detested as the means of her ruin was everything Elizabeth might have expected. Learning that the man who had, at one time, been in position to inherit the estate would soon darken her doorstep revived the nerves which had been dormant for many years.

"Mr. Collins? Come to visit us?"

It was a mark of her improvement that her incredulous query was not in the form of a screech, as it would have been many years ago. As it was, Elizabeth could hear her tone of rising trepidation.

"Why would that man seek to bother us now? Does he not know you have cut him from inheriting the estate?"

"Given the number of times he has reproached me in recent years," said Mr. Bennet, "I am certain he well knows it."

"Does he have a means of restoring himself?" fretted Mrs. Bennet, continuing with her questions. "Oh, Mr. Bennet! I knew it was too good to be true!"

This last was much more akin to her previous wails, a fact Mr. Bennet noted as clearly as his second eldest daughter. "There is no means of restoring himself," said Mr. Bennet, his sternness catching his wife's attention. "The entail is broken, Mrs. Bennet. The only way

Mr. Collins may become my heir again is if I change my will, naming him to the position. You may rest assured that I shall never do so."

Mrs. Bennet paused and quieted for a moment, eying her husband as if to measure his trustworthiness. After a moment, she began to nod slowly, though she was not content until she had made one last query.

"My brother Phillips is certain of this?"

"There is no doubt, Mrs. Bennet. There is no need to ever fear for Mr. Collins or the entail again."

The tension bled from Mrs. Bennet's shoulders and she straightened, favoring her husband with a smile. "Then I shall endeavor to welcome Mr. Collins as a *visitor* but give him no more deference than what he is due. If he should say anything concerning the entail, I shall not feel myself bound to listen to him."

"That is sensible."

The visit had been scheduled for some few days later, days which were blissfully free of the militia, and Mr. Wickham in particular. The younger girls lamented the officers' failure to visit them again, but the elder sisters stayed close to home. While Jane said no word on the subject and Elizabeth did not raise it, she had the distinct sense that Jane had no more wish to see Mr. Wickham than Elizabeth had herself.

When the day they were to welcome their guest arrived, the elder Bennets gathered together on the front step of Longbourn—in a show of possible disdain for Mr. Collins, Mrs. Bennet had decreed that Kitty and Lydia were too busy with their studies to join them in welcoming their guest. Though it was impossible to misunderstand, none of them said anything to their mother, and Mr. Bennet chuckled and squeezed his wife's hand when she announced it.

The carriage carrying Mr. Collins was a two-wheel gig he had commissioned for the purpose, drawn by a horse, stamping and snorting as it came to halt by the driver. The two men in the carriage stepped down, and while the driver began unloading Mr. Collins's trunks, the man himself stepped toward the waiting family. His nod to them was perfunctory and only barely adequate, as if he considered himself far above the plane his cousin and family inhabited.   "I assume you must be Mr. Bennet?"

"Indeed, I am, Mr. Collins. Welcome to Longbourn."

If any of them had expected thanks, they were destined to be disappointed, for Mr. Collins only sniffed, disdain clear in the curl of his lip. "Yes, well, it seems appropriate, at least for the present. It does no good to bring up old grievances or injustices. You may show me to my room, so I may refresh myself—then I shall attend you."

It was a speech barely civil, and one Elizabeth might not have expected, given her father's tales of his letter writing prowess. While the resentment was evident, his words were not as verbose as she had thought to hear, almost seeming perfunctory. Mr. Bennet did not contradict the parson—instead, he led Mr. Collins inside and commended him to the care of Mrs. Hill, their housekeeper, to be conveyed to his room. If Mr. Collins took Mr. Bennet's unwillingness to do the honor himself as a slight, he did not say so. They saw nothing more than his back as he proceeded to the stairs after Mrs. Hill.

"Well, Lizzy?" said Mr. Bennet, his tone brimming with mirth. "What do you think of our esteemed guest?"

"I think he shall be difficult to tolerate," interrupted Mrs. Bennet. "At the very least, he seems to have little understanding of proper behavior."

"I wonder as to his purpose," said Elizabeth. "Surely he does not think he can change your mind or regain his former position. He must be a rank dullard if he believes his disapproval will do anything other than result in his being banished from the estate forever."

"There is little indication he is anything *other* than a dullard, Lizzy," said Mr. Bennet. "I have great hope he will provide excessive amusement during his stay."

While Mr. Bennet's sense of humor was highly developed and tended toward the absurd, Elizabeth was not sure enduring Mr. Collins's silliness would amuse any of them for long. In fact, she suspected he would grow intolerable before long.

Elizabeth had failed to take Mr. Collins's measure, for he was far more objectionable than she might have imagined. Beginning with his descent after refreshing himself, the man proved himself to be small-minded, resentful, overbearing, and oddly enough, possessing a reverence for his patroness which bordered on worship. Elizabeth had never met someone who disgusted her as much as Mr. Collins, though when she thought on it, if she ever learned the truth about Mr. Wickham, it was possible he might even surpass the parson.

Mr. Collins was in no way appealing to any of the Bennet sisters. He was passably tall, his long, spindly legs protruding from the end of his trousers like a stork's, his dress all in black as befitted a parson. There was a distinct paunch about his midsection and his hair was an oleaginous black, leading Elizabeth to believe he could not be bothered to wash, or even brush it, as it often appeared windblown and unkempt. The sonorous quality of his voice had a soporific effect on his listeners, and he often discounted the opinions of others, especially those of Mrs. Bennet and her daughters. There was altogether an objectionable quality in him which Elizabeth found difficult to endure.

"I hope you experienced a comfortable journey here, Mr. Collins," said Mrs. Bennet when the parson descended. It was an effort to be polite that Elizabeth thought was laudable in her mother.

"It was tolerable," was Mr. Collins's dismissive reply. "Though I am a clergyman and in possession of a valuable living, it is not right for a man to live beyond his means or practice extravagance. Thus, I traveled modestly, as my patroness demands. 'Do not allow yourself to fall into the trap of profligacy, Mr. Collins,' said she on more than one occasion. 'A man in your position cannot be too careful. Your future depends on your frugal nature, and it is a good example to set for the parish.'"

"Wise words," murmured Mr. Bennet. "I find myself curious, sir. There have been many times you have referenced your patroness in your letters in recent months. From what you have said, I must assume she is a woman of prominence in society?"

Finally, there was some warmth in Mr. Collins's manners, though he did not direct it at anyone present. "Lady Catherine de Bourgh. Yes, Mr. Bennet, you are correct, for she is the daughter of an earl and the widow of a knight of the realm. The property she inhabits, called Rosings Park, is a veritable jewel among estates, and Lady Catherine takes prodigious care of it. There is nothing beyond her capacity, and her wisdom is beyond compare. I feel my extreme fortune in having such a guide and mentor. And you all share my fortune in some small way."

"Oh?" asked Mr. Bennet. "I am eager to hear what she has condescended to opine which will lead to our good fortune. What can you mean?"

"Why, it was by her advice I have come to you!" cried Mr. Collins. "It was she who advised me in my conduct. 'Mr. Collins,' said she, 'it is not proper to be estranged from your only living family. Though they have done you grievous harm, it is Christian to forgive. I urge you to do so at the earliest opportunity!'

"Thus, it was by her wise counsel I decided to attempt a rapprochement, though I wondered if you were deserving of my forgiveness. Though I *have* been treated in an infamous manner, I hope we may come together, to share the bonds of family and forge new relationships between us."

"That is quite . . . magnanimous of you," said Mr. Bennet.

"It is—yes, it is, indeed," said Mr. Collins, missing the sarcasm in Mr. Bennet's reply. "It is my hope this visit will be a fruitful one."

Mr. Collins's continually flowery speeches, his praise of his absent patroness, and his self-congratulation for his ability to forgive them all characterized the rest of the time before dinner. Then he turned and requested invitations to the Bennet sisters. Kitty and Lydia, he dismissed as young and foolish, by action if not by word, though Mary seemed to garner greater approval due to her own interest in religious topics. Elizabeth found herself the recipient of his disapproving sneer after she had made a comment he deemed improper. It was to Jane he turned most of his attention.

"I feel myself very fortunate to have made your acquaintance in particular," said Mr. Collins, fixing Jane with an unctuous smile during their dinner. "Can I thank you and your sister Elizabeth for the delightfully prepared meal we are fortunate enough to partake?"

"We can well afford a cook, Mr. Collins," said Mrs. Bennet with more than a little asperity. "My girls are gentlewomen—they do not toil in the kitchen."

"Ah, then I apologize for my unthinking words, Mrs. Bennet!" said the parson, though Mrs. Bennet did not appear at all appeased. "That is excellent news for it shows prosperity to be envied. Perhaps, however, in the interest of economy, you might consider bearing more of the burden of the house yourselves. From what I have seen, Longbourn is not a large estate—certainly nothing to Rosings Park. As my patroness has often said, thrift is a quality to be prized. Perhaps more could be put away in favor of a future crisis if your daughters shared the work in the house."

While Mrs. Bennet was offended to the point of apoplexy, Mr. Bennet seemed about to burst out in laughter. For a moment Elizabeth thought her mother was on the cusp of saying something pointed. But she swallowed whatever she was thinking and only nodded, though in a clipped fashion.

"Thank you for your advice, Mr. Collins. But I am certain my husband and I, having many years of experience, understand what we can afford and what we cannot."

"And perhaps a governess is an inadvisable expense," continued Mr. Collins, oblivious to his hostess's rising anger. "Your youngest daughters are what, seventeen and eighteen years of age?"

"Kitty is seventeen and Lydia is fifteen," supplied Mr. Bennet.

"That is much too old to have a governess!"

"Perhaps it is," replied Mr. Bennet, preventing an explosion of temper from his wife. "But Mrs. Garret does not serve as a governess. She provides the service of a companion and continued tutelage in their education. We are not unable to afford her services, sir."

It was clear what Mrs. Garret thought of Mr. Collins, for she was not in the habit of allowing ridiculous behavior in her charges. Mr. Collins continued to look at her with distaste before something else caught his eye.

"And is this joint of beef not too large? Waste not, want not, as we have been told in the Holy Bible."

"It occurs to me to wonder at this inquisition, Cousin," said Mr. Bennet, his own humor being replaced by annoyance. "Please rest assured everything we do is carefully considered, from the size of our meals to the work I do to care for the estate, to Mrs. Bennet's decisions regarding the house. If it does not meet with your approval, I am sorry for you. Nothing will be changed, however, so there is little point in continuing to criticize."

"If I have offended, I am mortified, Cousin." In fact, Mr. Collins appeared anything but mortified. "It is a subject I should not have raised. I shall refrain from speaking until the occasion demands it."

It was clear to Elizabeth that Mr. Bennet did not know to what Mr. Collins referred, but as the parson turned and spoke to Jane, he decided to leave well enough alone. A moment later Mr. Bennet caught Elizabeth's eye and grinned. But it seemed to her he had realized the possible drawbacks of Mr. Collins's presence outweighed the amusement he provided. Had he asked Elizabeth for her opinion on the matter, she would have informed him of it from the outset.

The truth of Elizabeth's suppositions was proven, as within a day there was no member of the family who could tolerate Mr. Collins's company. Nothing was above his notice, and he criticized everything with equal attention and fervor. The family was given to understand that *his* management would have been so much better, that the estate would have been the picture of paradise had he been the master.

The way he spoke of himself, to the girls, in particular, suggested he thought himself the essence of male attraction. In fact, Kitty and Lydia could not abide his company and stayed with Mrs. Garret as much as they could manage—something they had never done willingly before. Mary seemed able to tolerate him better than the others, though Elizabeth often witnessed a grim set to her mouth or a tightening around her eyes. Mr. and Mrs. Bennet avoided the man as much as possible. As for Elizabeth, she could not avoid him as much as she wished, for she could see what his purpose was in visiting Longbourn.

"Dearest Cousin," said Mr. Collins to Jane the morning after his arrival, "shall we not take a turn around the park? Though it does not compare to Rosings, it seems to be a prettyish sort of wilderness. I should like to become better acquainted with you, and I am certain you wish to know me better."

It appeared Jane did not know what to say. Elizabeth doubted she understood the thrust of Mr. Collins's words, though to Elizabeth herself they were as clear as if he had stood on a chair and announced his attention to wed Jane to the room. It seemed that Mr. Collins had decided if he could not obtain the estate through the entail, he was determined to get it through marriage.

At length, Jane consented and joined him. Mr. Bennet frowned at the gentleman, understanding what Elizabeth had, but he made no objection. When Elizabeth announced her intention to accompany them, Mr. Bennet nodded in approval, though she could see that Mr. Collins did not appreciate her attendance.

Thus commenced Mr. Collins's campaign, one which was punctuated by his singular brand of silliness. The walk outside was followed by his constant attendance on Jane whenever she was available. More than once Elizabeth had to stifle her laughter at the man's inept manner of conducting his wooing.

"I am certain you will apprehend the honor of my homage, Cousin," Mr. Collins would say. "You cannot have been more complimented by any other man, I am sure.

"Shall we not sit and discuss Fordyce? He has informed me as being a man of Godliness, one who instructs us all as if with the voice of the Most High.

"The parsonage, which you will see anon, is perfectly situated in a strand of trees, with a magnificent view of the house at Rosings Park in the distance. It shall be most adequate for you until that unhappy day when you must take up the duty of mistress of this fine estate.

"Ah, I cannot imagine any such bliss as this! My being taken with such a woman as you must be as agreeable as your meeting a man who would suit you in every particular!"

In this, a dull specimen such as Mr. Collins had no inkling of the truth of the matter. Elizabeth was convinced that Jane understood the meaning of Mr. Collins's. Unable to offend anyone, however, Jane had no power to refute the parson's words or induce him to leave her be. Thus, she endured his attentions without protest. Jane was a saint, but

Elizabeth could not think her reticence did her any good in this instance.

By the time two days had passed, every member of the Bennet family was longing for Mr. Collins's absence. Jane and Elizabeth especially wished some distance from the man — even Mr. Wickham's civility did not seem so evil when compared with Mr. Collins. Thus, they determined to walk into Meryton to escape him. But even that was thwarted when Mr. Collins discovered their design.

"A walk would be just the thing! And I shall claim my cousin Jane's hand for the duration, for I am eager to see the scenes of which I have heard so much."

That was a bald-faced lie, and Elizabeth wondered how Mr. Collins could say it with a straight face. No one could speak more than a word or two in the face of the man's ubiquitous conversation.

Thus thwarted, there was no choice but to go regardless. They set off, the three eldest sisters along with their unwelcome guest, walking much quicker than was their wont. As they walked, Elizabeth, striding beside Mary, took the opportunity to whisper to her.

"Take care and watch Mr. Collins, Mary. If there is an opportunity to give Jane a respite, we should seize it."

Mary, who had been watching the parson with increased distaste, nodded. Soon they reached Meryton.

As luck would have it, their sortie into town did not escape the other man Jane had avoided of late. Though Elizabeth could not be certain, it seemed to her like Mr. Wickham had been skulking about, waiting for their appearance. As was their custom, they strolled along the main street, looking into the shops as they walked, and they had not gone a quarter of the distance before the officer made his appearance.

"Miss Bennet!" exclaimed he as he strode up to them, a broad smile on his face. "And Miss Elizabeth and Miss Mary! How fortunate it is to meet you fine ladies today. How do you do?"

"We are well, Mr. Wickham," replied Elizabeth, speaking for her sisters. An idle thought made itself known, and she wondered how the two men would react to each other. She would not need to wait long to discover it.

"Who is this . . . gentleman?" asked Mr. Collins, his lip curled with distaste.

Elizabeth did not know which man had precedence, not knowing much of Mr. Wickham's past or the level of society his family inhabited. Regardless, she decided his question was enough to make the introduction.

"I am pleased to make your acquaintance, sir," said Mr. Wickham, bowing to Mr. Collins.

If he expected the parson to respond in like fashion, Mr. Wickham would be disappointed. Rather than stating his pleasure in return, Mr. Collins regarded the officer with a searching look. When he spoke, it was with little warmth.

"Quite." Then he turned to Jane. "Shall we not continue up the street? I am certain there is much more of interest to see in this charming town."

"It would be my pleasure to accompany you," said Mr. Wickham. "Please, Miss Bennet—allow me to escort you."

"That will not be necessary," said Mr. Collins, clutching Jane's arm as if it was his property. "Miss Bennet is walking with me."

Directing Jane forward, Mr. Collins kept a firm grasp of her hand on his arm, speaking to her as they moved away. While Elizabeth might have expected Mr. Wickham to respond with similar acrimony, she could see he felt nothing but amusement. He offered his arm to Elizabeth with alacrity—Mary had followed Jane, keeping a close eye on Mr. Collins—and turned to follow the rest of the party.

"It seems you have a . . . an interesting houseguest, Miss Elizabeth," said he, hilarity alive in his voice.

"Interesting does not even begin to describe him, Mr. Wickham," said Elizabeth, forgetting for the moment she did not trust the man. "Before he came we had never made his acquaintance. Now we all wish we never had."

Laughter welled up from Mr. Wickham's breast. "I dare say I understand your meaning very well!"

Soon, however, Elizabeth had occasion to remember her antipathy for Mr. Wickham, for he seemed to delight in poking at Mr. Collins. His method of doing so was, of course, to pay his own addresses to Jane. Soon the two men were vying for the greater part of her notice in the middle of Meryton's busiest street.

"Come, Miss Bennet," said Mr. Wickham a few moments later. "I have not spoken to you in several days now. You and your family have been well, I trust?"

"Oh, look!" interrupted Mr. Collins before Jane could respond. "There is a beautifully bound bible in the bookseller's shop. Perhaps I should buy it—would it not make a lovely family heirloom!"

"If such things are to your taste," said Mr. Wickham. "To be honest, I much prefer a more inward form of worship, but I do not think our

Lord puts much stock on flowery pronouncements and finely crafted Bibles."

Having never seen Mr. Wickham express even an ounce of interest in anything religious—and he had not attended church since his arrival—Elizabeth doubted his words. But Mr. Collins considered them an affront.

"Should not every good thing be obtained with an eye toward the glory of God? I would not expect *you* to understand it, sir, but I am a servant of God, and am in a much better position to judge than you."

"You may preach, but you are no better than any other man in God's sight," replied Mr. Wickham. Then he turned to Jane. "Let us walk together, Miss Bennet, for there is a bolt of cloth in the dressmaker's window which I think would suit you well."

Jane looked at Mr. Wickham with skepticism, but she allowed him to lead her way, responding to his words when he spoke. Mr. Collins followed close behind, and Elizabeth thought he might be gnashing his teeth in frustration. When they arrived at the dressmaker's, Wickham proved himself to possess good taste, for it was a color Elizabeth might have chosen for her sister herself. But Mr. Collins inserted himself once again.

"Though I would never dispute a woman's desire to appear to best advantage for her suitor, I do not think Miss Bennet is the sort to be vain. Come, Miss Bennet, let us continue walking."

Jane's hand once again claimed, she allowed herself to be led away, though Elizabeth was certain her sister's distress was building. Acting to prevent continued improprieties, Elizabeth stepped up to Mr. Wickham and scolded him.

"Please desist, Mr. Wickham! Can you not see my sister's misery?"

"Ah, you have my apologies, Miss Elizabeth," said Mr. Wickham, though Elizabeth could see he was not sorry in the slightest. "I did not intend to make your sister feel uncomfortable." Mr. Wickham stopped and winked at her. "I shall yield the field at present and hope for better days."

Though he stated as much, Mr. Wickham again proved himself a liar as he continued with them, making comments designed to provoke Mr. Collins. At least he did not insinuate himself on Jane's person again, which was a relief. Mr. Collins considered Mr. Wickham a threat and treated him accordingly. It was clear to Elizabeth that Mr. Wickham did not return the sentiment, which was the only reason he had ceased importuning Jane for the time being. His behavior once again heightened Elizabeth's disquiet.

"I am afraid I must depart," said Mr. Wickham after following them through the town for a time. "Duty calls, and though I am loath to leave such fair companions, I shall not shirk."

With a bow to them all, Mr. Wickham stepped to Jane, caught up her hand, and bestowed a lingering kiss on its back. "I am grateful to have been in your company again, Miss Bennet. Until next time."

Then with an insolent smirk at the now furious Mr. Collins, he turned and departed, leaving them standing in the middle of the street. The decision to go to Meryton now proven to be a disaster, Elizabeth's only thought was to return to Longbourn before her released the inevitable explosion of anger. She only hoped they would reach their home before Mr. Collins lost control of his temper and embarrassed them all.

CHAPTER VII

"Who was that . . . officer?"

The distaste in Mr. Collins's voice was unmistakable, though Elizabeth detected an equal measure of petulance. A man as wrongly self-confident as Mr. Collins would see no danger to his designs of marrying Jane because of a man ten times as handsome and intelligent. That Mr. Wickham *had* no chance of marrying Jane was not at issue—neither did Mr. Collins, though he pressed forward with all the determination of a zealot.

"I believe we introduced you to him, Mr. Collins."

Mr. Collins scowled at Elizabeth from where he maintained a possessive hold on Jane's arm. "Perhaps you did. It seems to me you should choose your acquaintances rather more carefully, for there is something about him I cannot like." Mr. Collins paused and said: "It comes to my mind I have heard of this Mr. Wickham before, though I cannot remember when."

While Elizabeth could not imagine how Mr. Collins might have come across Mr. Wickham's name in the past, that was not at issue. "If you recall, Mr. Collins," said Elizabeth, continuing to speak for her sisters, "Mr. Wickham approached us—not the reverse. The militia officers are new acquaintances, the regiment having arrived recently.

We cannot be certain of the characters of them all, the acquaintance being new, but when someone known to us approaches on a street, it would be rudeness to refuse to respond."

The glare did not lessen, but Mr. Collins conceded the point. "I suppose you must be correct. In the future, however, it would behoove you all to take greater care in allowing such ruffians into your acquaintance. Especially you, dearest Cousin," Mr. Collins bestowed a tender look on Jane, a look which seemed more like it came from a constipated dog than a suitor, "for a woman in your position must do nothing to jeopardize your good fortune."

"What is your opinion of this verse, Mr. Collins?" asked Mary, attempting to divert his attention. "It is said that we should love others as we do ourselves."

Mr. Collins drew himself up in his self-importance. "Yes, well, charity is the highest virtue we can possess. Lady Catherine has often said we must succor the poor. In doing so, we may ensure they know their place and not attempt to rise above it."

It was such a nonsensical statement that Elizabeth could not help but throw a dumbfounded stare at the man. It succeeded in its purpose, however, which was to distract him from his improper words, and they continued with all three girls silent, though Mary responded to Mr. Collins's grandiose statements whenever the opportunity allowed. That was not often.

So focused was he on imparting his supposed wisdom to his young supplicant that, for a time, he even forgot about insisting on Jane's attendance to his company. While he was distracted, Elizabeth took the opportunity to have a quiet word with her sister.

"Jane, are you well?"

The look her sister gave her in return was filled with more than a little alarm, but she mastered herself and smiled, though it did not reach her eyes. "Do not concern yourself for me, Lizzy."

"But I do concern myself," said Elizabeth, frustrated her sister would not acknowledge the impropriety of Mr. Collins's actions. "When we arrive at Longbourn, we should speak with Papa. If Mr. Collins will not cease proclaiming you as his property, it would be best if Papa were to ask him to leave."

"That is unnecessary, Lizzy," protested Jane. "It is little matter what Mr. Collins says." Then a horror-filled expression came over Jane's countenance, and she turned a little green. "Papa would not insist I marry him, would he?"

"How can you think such a thing, Jane?" demanded Elizabeth,

aghast her sister was uncertain of her father's support. "Of course, he will not! The entail is no more. We need not depend on Mr. Collins's kindness—if such a thing even exists."

"Come, walk with me, Cousin Jane," said Mr. Collins, interrupting their tête-à-tête, "for I have something of which I would speak to you."

The parson directed a suspicious glare at Elizabeth, but he addressed Jane again: "The modesty which you display is pleasing, for it is meet that a parson's wife should be demure in all things. There is little doubt in my mind you will fill my need for a helpmeet in the parish, and I am convinced your beauty and mildness will appeal to Lady Catherine as well. You will, no doubt, wish to defer to her, not only as your superior in every way but because of her extensive experience.

"Having said that, this business of allowing another gentleman such liberties as this Mr. Wickham sought to take is worrisome. To allow other men to dominate your attention, or to rest your hand on their arm, is beyond what any delicate woman should allow. Remember how tender a thing a woman's reputation is, how hard to preserve, and when lost how impossible to recover. I would not have any wife of mine suffer the loss of virtue, no matter how small."

One glance at Jane revealed how terrified she was, looking at Mr. Collins, mouth open, eyes wild with fear. It would be Elizabeth's responsibility to provide a response to the absurd man's comments, and she would not shirk.

"That is enough, Mr. Collins!"

So surprised was the parson he did not immediately reply, a circumstance which Elizabeth used to good effect. "This must stop, sir, for it is most unseemly. You speak of my sister as if you are engaged, and I will not have it. Please desist from speaking in such terms, for you are *not* betrothed, nor, from my knowledge of Jane's feelings and character, will you ever be!"

By the time Elizabeth had finished her speech, Mr. Collins was sporting a fierce scowl. "Though your parents have hired a companion," said he in a lofty tone, "it is apparent her instructions fell on deaf ears in your case. This does not concern you, Cousin. Perhaps you should give heed to the words for Fordyce, which I just quoted, and remember your place." Turning to Jane, he said: "Come, Cousin Jane—let us walk together and discuss our future felicity in marriage."

"Are you witless, Mr. Collins?" demanded Elizabeth, stepping between the parson and her elder sister. "Can you not see how fearful you have made my sister? Can you not understand how she detests the very sight of you?"

"Enough!" roared Mr. Collins. "Cease this objectionable behavior this instant!"

"I might say the same to you, sir," said Elizabeth, her resentment now equal to her abhorrence for his small-minded person. "I will not allow you to compromise my sister by word of mouth. Do a woman's wishes now count for nothing? You have not even proposed to her, you stupid man!"

"If you ever wish to have a home after your father is gone, you will stop now! I will not have one of such indelicacy, such impropriety as you in my home."

"Longbourn is not yours, nor will it ever be," snapped Elizabeth, ignoring Jane's futile effort to have her say.

"It most certainly will be, my *dear* Cousin," sneered the parson. "And I have come to my decision. You will be thrown from Longbourn the instant your father passes, for I will not have you tainting my wife with such indecency."

"I could never have a man who would ban my dear sister from my home!" Jane finally found her voice, and while she did not speak with the forcefulness Elizabeth might have desired, that she spoke up at all was welcome.

"The decision will not be yours, dearest," said Mr. Collins, his angry tone from the previous moments becoming a simpering smirk. "Perhaps you do not understand the laws under which England is governed—and if you are not, perhaps it is for the best, for a delicate creature such as my beautiful flower does not need to know of such matters! Once you are married and your father has passed, Longbourn becomes your husband's possession."

"We are well aware of the law," snapped Elizabeth. "But your thinking is laced with fallacy, Cousin—my father has informed us all he will make provision for all of us in the contract by which he passes Longbourn down to Jane. Should he not be convinced her husband intends to honor the *spirit* of the agreement, rather than just the *letter* of it, he will change the inheritance to one of his other daughters."

"Surely not!"

"He said so himself. Furthermore, he will not force any of his daughters into marriage, and certainly not to a . . . a . . . a malodorous cretin such as you."

"We shall see about that, Cousin Elizabeth," said Mr. Collins, his tone less assured than it was a moment ago.

"Perchance it would be best to end our dispute," interjected Mary.

"For we have been told contention is of the devil, and we would be wise to avoid it."

"Poor, wretched Mary," mocked the parson. "Always speaking of matters of which you know nothing, attempting to portray yourself as a woman of God. There is little difference between you and your elder sister. Be assured that when Longbourn is mine, I will demand your departure, the same as your sister."

"That is enough!" cried Elizabeth. "Jane, Mary, it is time to return to Longbourn. You, sir, are no parson. All you will ever be is a stain upon your profession!"

And with those final words, Elizabeth grasped her sisters' arms and began to propel them back towards the estate. Mr. Collins was not about to be left behind and he followed along behind them, his words a constant stream of abuse at Elizabeth in particular, threats concerning what he would do and admonishments for her to behave better. Elizabeth ignored him. It was a fine irony that a man of Mr. Collins's ilk, one who had little understanding of proper deportment himself, would complain of another's behavior!

The house rose in the distance, and Elizabeth marched toward it, careful to ensure Mr. Collins attempted nothing untoward. The parson was content to continue his criticisms, as he made no move toward anything of a physical nature. When they reached the sanctuary of the house, he stopped long enough to hand his hat and coat to the butler, before he turned a baleful eye on Elizabeth.

"You may be assured I shall speak to your father of this matter. Mayhap he will even understand the necessity of throwing you off now, for your continued presence can only be a detriment to his other daughters."

With those final words, the man turned on his heel and stalked toward Mr. Bennet's study. He threw open the door and entered therein without even the courtesy of a knock.

"Lizzy? Jane? What is happening?" exclaimed Mrs. Bennet as she appeared in the door to the sitting-room.

"Mr. Collins is what is happening," replied Elizabeth. Knowing her mother and expecting this event might bring out her nerves, Elizabeth turned to her sisters. "Please take Mama into the sitting-room. I shall join Papa in his study."

Even in such a distressing situation, her sisters understood the reason to keep their mother calm. The sisters gathered Mrs. Bennet while Elizabeth straightened her shoulders and walked to the open door of her father's room. As she approached, she could hear the raised voice of her father's cousin.

Mr. Bennet had been enjoying a quiet afternoon in his study. The morning had been dedicated to estate business, as there had been a tenant concern to see to and repairs to a fence at one of the estate's borders. After that, Bennet had been at his leisure to return to his room and devote himself to the written word. When he had neglected the estate in the early years of his marriage, Bennet had not realized he could often do the estate business in only part of a day, eager as he was to avoid it altogether. Now that the succession to Jane was secure, he felt a greater urgency to augment his other daughters' dowries. But that did not mean he did not have ample time to indulge his favorite pastime.

The approaching loud voices had not pierced his consciousness for several moments, though subsequent reflection revealed that he had, indeed, heard them. When the outer door was opened, the louder sounds filtered through his door, pulling his attention away from Chaucer. The clear anger in them, and the fact that he could make out the tones of both Elizabeth and Mr. Collins's voices told him something had happened. Bennet stood from behind his desk and had taken his first steps toward the door when the parson's voice had grown louder, and the door was flung open without a by-your-leave.

If it was one thing Bennet had always detested, it was his sanctuary being invaded without a knock or permission being given—his wife had taken some time to learn this simple fact. The ruddiness of Mr. Collins's countenance suggested the man was far too incensed to give any thought to such pleasantries. But it was annoying, nonetheless.

"Cousin!" boomed Mr. Collins. "I cannot even begin to inform you how shameless, how utterly improper her behavior is. I must insist upon your setting your daughters straight, for I shall not countenance such willful contempt for my position as this. You must take them in hand."

"If it is as you say, Collins," said Bennet, "I shall do so with alacrity. As of yet, however, you have not informed me of what, particularly, has angered you so. Shall you not do so?"

"I shall tell you, Papa." Elizabeth entered the room, her glare at his cousin showing her distaste. As for Mr. Collins, the poisonous look he directed at her was enough to alarm Bennet. A man did not look at a woman in such a manner in polite society.

"Mr. Collins has gotten it into his head to speak to and of Jane as if she is already betrothed to him, and he will not moderate his language."

"Is this true, Collins?" asked Bennet, spearing the parson with a look. While Bennet had divined his cousin's interest on that score, it did not seem to him that Collins was behaving inappropriately, despite his ardent and inept attempts to woo Jane. Though Bennet would not have allowed a betrothal, he also did not wish to offend his cousin, their reconciliation being new and fragile, so he had thought to refrain from saying anything until it became a true problem.

"I was merely stating my displeasure for allowing a man of the militia to take up so much of her attention," said Mr. Collins, his righteous indignation betrayed in his posture. "It is a failing in you, I suppose, to allow them such freedom."

"You did, did you?" asked Elizabeth, sarcasm oozing from her voice. "Did you not say I would not be welcome in Longbourn when it was yours? What of your callous words to Mary and your disregard for her feelings? Did we, in any way, misunderstand you?"

The parson attempted to bluster for a moment, but it was clear he had no answer. Bennet looked to Elizabeth, noting her tight nod at his unspoken question, not that he would have disbelieved her account. It appeared the time to disabuse Mr. Collins was upon him, whether he wished it or not.

"It would be best, Cousin, if you approached *me* regarding any of my daughters. Then I may set you straight so you may avoid any misunderstanding concerning their feelings or my opinion on the matter."

"And so I have," replied Mr. Collins with a tight nod. "Furthermore, I ask you to set your daughters straight so there is no misunderstanding. You must know I have come here for this purpose — I am not accustomed to being put off in matters of import."

"I am sorry, Mr. Collins," said Bennet, tiring of the silly man, "but that will have little effect on me. My daughters are all precious to me. Nothing would induce me to engage any of them to a man they did not favor."

Mr. Collins gasped. "No, it cannot be! Miss Bennet *must* be betrothed to me. Every feeling depends on it — honor, mercy, gratitude, justice — all of these must be satisfied."

"You have stated your piece, Mr. Collins. Now let me state mine: my daughters are all free to marry wherever they like. I will not direct them. Considering you have only been here for two days, you cannot have courted my daughter and proposed to her. That is the only way for you to achieve your desire."

"Jane detests the very sight of him," supplied Elizabeth.

"She has never said as much to me!" snapped Mr. Collins.

"When have you ever given her the chance?" demanded Elizabeth. "Had you ever had occasion to dam your continual waterfall of words, you may have heard Jane disavow all interest in you as a husband. But you blather on, speaking of your crone of a mistress and her nonsensical advice, allowing no one else to speak a word. How was Jane to inform you of her disinterest? A man of any intelligence at all would have seen through her eagerness to be out of your company every time she found herself in it!"

"See!" cried Mr. Collins, pointing at Elizabeth. "See what a wild child you have raised? Do you not see how she should be censured and despised?"

"Elizabeth is my most capable and intelligent daughter, Collins," said Bennet, his patience evaporating. "Continuing to slander her will not help your cause — quite the opposite."

"Would it further help my cause to remind you that you have cheated me of my inheritance?" spat Mr. Collins.

"No one was cheated of anything," replied Bennet with a sigh. That he had suspected Collins might have come here for some purpose associated with the entail was nothing less than the truth. This visit was not as amusing as he had expected. "There was a legal proceeding available for my use, and I did so to protect my family. While I recognize how this has affected your own prospects, and I do sympathize, I do not apologize. Longbourn has been in my family for more than two centuries — with God's permission, it shall be so for many years longer."

"Legal proceedings? There is nothing legal about what was done to me." Mr. Collins glared at him with self-righteous indignation. "I have been cheated, sir. Cheated! Stripped of my rightful place as heir to this estate. Shall I stand by and endure this travesty? No, it shall not be! With my patroness's advice, I had thought to try you, to test whether you are a reasonable man, or a thief, as my father always told me you were. By marrying your eldest daughter, both claims may be satisfied — both my claim on the estate and your family's continued association with it."

"There is no legal claim you may make on the estate," replied Bennet. "And I will thank you to avoid using such language."

"My claim is honorable and just!" Mr. Collins stood there, glaring at Bennet, and by this time, Bennet was equally disgusted with his cousin. There would be a break anew over this, and given the specimen standing before him, Bennet could not but welcome it.

"Hear me, Cousin! If you will betroth your daughter to me, this will all be resolved. I will promise to care for any of your remaining daughters and your widow." The parson's gaze found Elizabeth, his contempt a physical entity. "Even your second daughter, though I own that she has offended me grievously."

"And what of the offense you have given us?" demanded Elizabeth. "Jane cannot stand the sight of you!"

"Silence, foul Jezebel! Or I shall throw you out to starve in the hedgerows, promise or no promise!"

"There is no circumstance under which you will be in a position to throw *anyone* out," growled Bennet, drawing the incensed parson's eyes back to him. "Longbourn is *mine* to do with as I wish. I broke the entail to provide for my family. It is unfortunate you feel you have been ill-used, but everything has been done in accordance with the law. You have no complaint."

Mr. Collins glared at him, the muscles in his jaw working. Then he spoke: "If you do not satisfy me, I shall bring suit against you, Mr. Bennet. By betrothing your daughter to me, you keep the estate in the hands of your descendants and provide for your family. If you do not oblige me, I will gain Longbourn through the courts and see you are all removed at once!"

"*If* you feel you have just cause," said Bennet, "I invite you to do so at once. But I warn you, Collins, you will be wasting your time and money. There is nothing you can do. I suggest you resign yourself to your profession."

"You will hear from me again, Mr. Bennet. With my patroness's assistance, we shall cleanse the stain of you and your loathsome progeny from this estate!"

Then with one final contemptuous glance, Mr. Collins turned and strode from the room, brushing past Elizabeth as if she were not there. For a moment, Bennet thought to follow him and give him his richly deserved reward. Instead, he contented himself with striding to the door and calling for the butler. Mr. Hill, good man that he was, had stationed himself nearby, anticipating his master's need of him.

"See that Mr. Collins packs his bags and leaves within the hour. Should he make any more claims or if he importunes my family again, you may throw him from the house."

"Very good, Mr. Bennet," said Hill. There was a fleeting smile of satisfaction on the man's face, then he turned to carry out his orders. Bennet reentered the study and sat heavily in his chair.

"There is no basis for his argument, is that not correct?"

Bennet smiled at the note of worry in his daughter's voice. "No, there is not. Or at least that is what your uncle has informed me. Do not worry, Lizzy. I shall go to Meryton and acquaint him with these events and seek his opinion."

With a nod, Elizabeth rose and left the room. A sigh of annoyance preceded Bennet's departure himself. Though Phillips had been certain, Bennet desired whatever reassurance his brother could provide.

CHAPTER VIII

"*I*gnore him," was Phillips's short reply when Bennet informed
him of Mr. Collins's threats. "Legally speaking he has no case
and will only embarrass himself by bringing suit, and that is
if he finds a solicitor willing to take him on."

"And what of his threat to involve his patroness?"

"Do you know anything of the woman?"

"Only that she is wealthy and the sister to an earl. Though Mr.
Collins praises her to the skies, I suspect she is meddling and
dictatorial, not accustomed to disappointment and eager to direct
everyone she meets. What influence she holds in society is a mystery."

"Women have much less influence in society than men — at least in
matters such as this." Phillips held up his hand when Bennet made to
speak. "I understand your concern, Brother — yes, this talk of an earl is
troubling, for as you know, the peerage often has sway with the courts.

"Again, it is my professional opinion that there is nothing Mr.
Collins can do. Everything was done within the law and within the
boundaries of decades of judicial precedence. While it is possible an
earl might have his way, a case such as this would be difficult to
overturn. Furthermore, I suspect an earl would know better than to
involve himself in a dispute involving naught but his sister's parson.

Such matters must be beneath such a man!"

Relieved his brother had the same opinion he possessed himself, Bennet thanked him and departed. Soon after, he dismounted at Longbourn and entered the house, where he found another kind of madness occurring in his home.

"Oh, Mr. Bennet!" cried his wife as soon as she caught sight of him. "I have heard what that wretched man said to you. Are we to be evicted from our home, forced to rely on my brother for our survival?"

"No, Mrs. Bennet. We are not."

In the years since the entail had been ended, Bennet had found it effective to silence his wife when her nerves got the better of her in such a fashion. Mrs. Bennet, surprised at his abrupt denial, ceased her wailing and looked at him, shock mixed with hope. Bennet did not allow her to wait long for his explanation.

"I have just come from speaking with Mr. Phillips," said he. "In the matter of Mr. Collins's threats, he agrees with me. There is no basis for a lawsuit, and Mr. Collins will only embarrass himself should he persist."

"Then we shall not be forced to leave?" asked Mrs. Bennet, her hopeful tone almost pitiful.

"No, my dear," said Mr. Bennet, stepping forward and sitting by her, taking her hand to provide comfort. "Longbourn is ours. Nothing will change that."

A deflated Mrs. Bennet showed him a shy smile. "Then that is well."

"Indeed, it is. Perhaps a rest would be advisable after this morning's excitement."

"It would," said Mrs. Bennet. "I believe I shall retire for a time."

And that was the end of his wife's hysterics. When she had gone, Bennet was left with his three eldest daughters. Elizabeth, as was her wont, was indignant, while Mary appeared more than a pair for her. Jane, on the other hand, displayed her typical serenity, though a tightness about her eyes spoke to the strain she had endured at the hands of his senseless cousin. Bennet sighed and smiled at them all.

"Though I will own I thought my cousin might make some attempt to persuade me to reinstate him," said Mr. Bennet, "I did not know he intended to marry Jane to gain Longbourn anyway. Regardless, I shall ensure Mr. Collins never importunes us again. And Jane," said he, turning to his eldest, "though you have heard me say it before, let me do so again so there is no ambiguity: I will never require you to marry someone you do not wish to marry if he be Mr. Collins or any other man. Do not concern yourself on that score, my dear, for the choice is yours."

"Thank you, Papa," replied Jane. "I did not doubt it, though I will own Mr. Collins proved to be far more . . . tenacious than I might have imagined."

"That he did," replied Bennet, feeling the urge to chortle. "Well, well, it seems Mr. Collins provided us some excitement, after all. For my part, I will be happy to dispense with odious cousins for the foreseeable future."

Then with a smile for them all, Bennet returned to his study and closed the door, retrieving the book he had been reading when he had been so unceremoniously interrupted. A little peace and quiet would do him a world of good too.

Was it too much to ask for unwanted suitors to leave the Bennet family in peace for a time? It was too much by far, or so it seemed to Elizabeth, for the next day saw the return of the suitor who had been forgotten in the wake of Mr. Collins's sudden arrival and precipitous departure. That he did not come alone did not at all soothe Elizabeth's ire.

As Elizabeth watched the officers enter the room, she noted the composition of the company was altered from the last time they had come. Lieutenants Wickham, Denny, Chamberlayn, and Sanderson were all present as they had been the last time, but Captain Carter's absence was noticeable. The smirk with which Mr. Wickham greeted them suggested a reason, and when Elizabeth reflected on how the captain had cut their visit off the last time, she thought she knew the answer of why he was not with them that day.

Greetings were exchanged, and the visitors sat down with the family, Mr. Wickham claiming the nearest seat to Jane, while the others looked on and snickered. The white-hot flame of anger came over Elizabeth at this latest evidence of the cunning of these men, directed at Mr. Wickham, the instigator of it all. Knowing Jane was not at all disposed to this man, Elizabeth vowed he would not even get an iota of her attention.

"Thank you for your gracious welcome, as always," said Mr. Wickham after a few moments of desultory conversation. "However, I must own to confusion, for I understood you were hosting a houseguest at present. Is Mr. Collins hiding, or is something keeping him from greeting us?"

"Mr. Collins!" exclaimed Mrs. Bennet, the indignation clear in her voice. "That man is gone, and we are all relieved!"

"Ah, then he has left Longbourn." Mr. Wickham shook his head in mock regret. "How unfortunate. I had hoped to converse with him, for you know, there was a time when I thought I might be a member of that venerable profession. Alas, it was not to be."

"*You* may regret his absence if you wish, Mr. Wickham. But I assure you, *we* do not."

"Has he made himself disagreeable?" asked Mr. Wickham. Watching the gentleman, Elizabeth was certain Mr. Wickham was well aware of how Mr. Collins might have worn out his welcome. For some reason, he was taking a perverse measure of enjoyment in learning of his rival's departure.

"Indeed, he has," said Mrs. Bennet. "He importuned my Jane improperly, you see."

Then Mrs. Bennet descended into a long-winded explanation of the events of the previous day, ensuring the assembled officers understood *exactly* the extent of Mr. Collins's crimes against the Bennet family. Several times during her mother's recitation, Elizabeth thought to interrupt, for her indignation had gotten the better of her grasp of proper behavior, leading her to be much more explicit than Elizabeth thought necessary. Elizabeth understood the difficulty of interrupting her mother when she was in this state, however, and thus she stayed quiet. When Mrs. Bennet's words trickled to a halt, Mr. Wickham was quick to fill the void.

"It is unfortunate, Mrs. Bennet, that your family was subjected to such disgraceful conduct." Far from offended on the Bennet family's behalf, Mr. Wickham gave all the signs of glee. "It is unfortunate, but I suppose one cannot choose their relations, can they?"

"No, but they may hold them at arms' length, Mr. Wickham," said Mrs. Bennet. "Mr. Collins was estranged from my family before his coming, and he will be forever unknown to us after. I would not host him here again for any price!"

"Excellent," said Mr. Wickham. "That is likely for the best. Now that I consider the matter, perhaps it is best I do not speak with him. I cannot imagine a man capable of such horrors as you have indicated can have anything at all uplifting to say."

Then Mr. Wickham turned to Jane and the full effect of his charm was unleashed. "You, in particular, must be relieved at Mr. Collins's departure, Miss Bennet, for unless I am mistaken, his attentions were fixed upon you."

"I have no wish for Mr. Collins's presence, Mr. Wickham," said Jane — if Mr. Wickham expected more, there was none forthcoming. It did not daunt him in the slightest.

"Nor would I have thought you would be. An exceptional family such as yours would not wish to associate with a lout. I commend you, Mrs. Bennet, for seeing through his façade to the heart of this man and acting to rid yourselves of him. It shows an uncommon greatness of mind."

After these words of sycophancy, the officers moved in a manner which appeared like a coordinated battle maneuver that might have made the French tyrant proud. Mr. Wickham turned his attention only on Jane and began to speak with her, while Mr. Denny addressed Elizabeth, Chamberlayn spoke to Mary, and Sanderson to Mrs. Bennet. What inane babble Denny said, Elizabeth did not know or care, for her attention was upon her elder sister.

The sudden unleashing of Mr. Wickham's charm was as if he had lit a candle, the flame casting light on the room, illuminating it to remove the blackness of night. It was so pronounced that Elizabeth was instantly suspicious of it—such a sudden change in one's manners spoke to extensive practice, and what could that mean other than to deceive? The longer the man spoke to Jane, the more irritated Elizabeth became. The one saving grace was that Jane appeared as unaffected by Mr. Wickham as she ever had, her answers coming in short sentences or one-word acknowledgments of whatever the man said. Would that she would inform him she was not interested! But the Jane Elizabeth knew would never be so open.

"Tell me, Miss Elizabeth," said Mr. Denny by her side, "is this Mr. Collins so objectionable as this?"

Elizabeth turned to the officer and regarded him, wondering if he would reveal something Mr. Wickham would not wish to become known. "Do you speak of the tale my mother related, or of prior knowledge of our visitor?"

Mr. Denny laughed and said: "The portrait your mother painted was succinct, but Wickham mentioned meeting him in Meryton yesterday. His tale was amusing, but some of us wondered if it was possible for a man to be so ridiculous."

"Ridiculous Mr. Collins was," said Elizabeth, considering how best to elicit the information she wished to obtain. "Jane suffered from his constant attendance more than anyone else in the family. As you can apprehend for yourself, Jane's position is fortunate, one which sometimes brings unwanted attention from those with whom she may not wish to associate."

"Yes, I can well imagine it!" Mr. Denny shook his head, his rueful glance at Jane betraying his own disappointment. "I might have tried my luck with your sister, for she is quite a fine woman. Unfortunately . . ."

Mr. Denny's meaningful glance at Jane told Elizabeth all she needed to know, her own gaze following Mr. Denny's to where Mr. Wickham was still plying her sister with his trade. It was fortunate, she reflected, that Mr. Denny seemed to speak without thinking, for he was a positive fount of information. That he did not mean to be was clear, but Elizabeth did not care for how she had manipulated him into telling her what she needed to know. It was in defense of a beloved sister.

"Thank you, Mr. Denny," said Elizabeth. "I have found our conversation fascinating, as always."

The same as the last time they had spoken, Mr. Denny appeared to have little understanding of her meaning. Elizabeth did not give him an opportunity to reply, however, for she was eager to insert herself between Mr. Wickham and the object of his prey. The incline of her head she gave to excuse herself was less than it should have been, but by this time Elizabeth was tired of all the officers and could only force herself to give him that much deference.

"Jane," said Elizabeth as she stepped up to them, nodding a greeting at Mr. Wickham, perhaps a little tersely. The officer favored her with a bright smile, but Elizabeth was certain it was brittle in nature.

"Miss Elizabeth," responded Mr. Wickham before Jane could speak herself, "we were just speaking of you, and now you appear before us. This is a fortunate happenstance."

"You were?" asked Elizabeth, knowing the skepticism in her voice was reaching his ears. "It is impossible to guess of what you may have been speaking, for I cannot imagine there is anything of interest you can say."

"In fact, your sister was a wellspring of information," said Mr. Wickham, echoing Elizabeth's thoughts of just a few moments before. "In the past few moments, I have learned of your love of walking, your prowess in debating literature, and your loyalty to your family. Why, your sister even informed me of your role in driving off that simpleton Collins!"

When Elizabeth glanced at Jane, she received an apologetic shrug in reply and thought she understood — Jane had been deflecting Mr. Wickham's attention by speaking of her. While Elizabeth was uncertain she wished a man of such an ambiguous character as Mr.

Wickham to know the details of her habits, she could not fault her sister for redirecting his attention.

"It was, in fact, my father who opposed Mr. Collins," replied Elizabeth. "I was only peripherally involved."

"You are too modest, I am sure." Mr. Wickham once again favored her with his devastating smile. "As I have seen your protective nature myself, I know Collins departed terrified of your ability to flay him alive with naught more than mere words!"

"That is an . . . interesting turn of phrase, Mr. Wickham."

"I have always been blessed with the ability to speak in an interesting manner," said Mr. Wickham. Then he became serious. "But I will own that I *do* feel for Mr. Collins's predicament."

The man's eyes widened and he added: "Oh, I would not have you think I disagree with your father's actions, for I understand he proceeded with great integrity and foresight. I would not have you misunderstand me."

Jane did not respond, though Mr. Wickham paused to allow them to state their support. For Elizabeth's part, she watched the man, wondering what manner of falsehood he intended to ply with them next. Their lack of response did not disconcert him in the slightest.

"You see, I had been intended for the church—it was specified in the will of an excellent man, a man who was my godfather and mentor. But after his death, the living which had been designed for me was given elsewhere, leaving me to fend for myself."

"How unfortunate for you, Mr. Wickham," said Elizabeth. "To spend those years in the seminary studying to be a clergyman, and then have it wasted by the actions of a man without scruple. I am surprised you did not find another parish or take a position as a curate."

Mr. Wickham coughed slightly. "I did not study at a seminary."

"Oh?" asked Elizabeth, her tone conveying a wealth of meaning.

"No," replied Mr. Wickham, once more in control of his confidence. "I was still young when he passed, and as I was not to benefit from the living, it did not seem worthwhile to study. Instead, I decided to do something else with my life."

"Then your call to the church was lukewarm."

Again Elizabeth had the distinct impression of Mr. Wickham's annoyance with her. "It was real enough, Miss Elizabeth. But a man must have something upon which to subsist. Not only was there no position available to me and no knowledge of when one might be forthcoming, but my circumstances were depressed, and I needed to go about supporting myself."

"That is understandable, replied Elizabeth. "Then you have been in the militia for some time? I had understood you have only just donned the scarlet."

"Yes, I have. I had other means of supporting myself until I joined the regiment."

"If you were of distressed circumstances, how did you ever have the ability to purchase a commission? Would it not have been beyond your means?"

"God provides, does he not?" asked Mr. Wickham, though she thought his asperity with her questions was growing. "In this case, an acquaintance of mine was willing to assist me. And to him, I am forever grateful."

"That is fortunate," said Elizabeth, her tone indicating she did not quite believe him. Mr. Wickham noted it, for whatever else he was, Elizabeth knew he was not a stupid man.

"What say you, Miss Bennet?" asked Wickham, eager to avoid any further questions on Elizabeth's part. "Do you not think it is reprehensible to deny another man a boon left to him by a generous benefactor?"

"I cannot say," replied Jane quietly.

"Surely your opinion cannot be that powerful men should be allowed to act in whatever manner they please and trample on those who find themselves in their path."

"What Jane means," said Elizabeth, once again pulling the annoyed lieutenant's attention back to her, "is that we cannot judge with no actual knowledge of the events in question."

The man's eyes fixed on Elizabeth and bored into her. "Have I not spoken of it?"

"What is our knowledge of you other than what you have told us yourself?" asked Elizabeth.

"I would hope we have become good friends at least."

"The fact of the matter is we do not know. Perhaps this other man had some good reason for denying you what you believe is your due. If you believe you were treated unfairly, then you should have asked him to explain himself."

"I understand his reasons," snapped Mr. Wickham. "There is no need for me to ask after them."

"That is fortunate for you, Mr. Wickham," replied Elizabeth reasonably. "However, you must consider this matter from our perspective. Our acquaintance with you is of short duration, and we know nothing of this other man—not even his name. It would be improper to pass judgment when we know nothing of the situation.

"Besides," continued Elizabeth, peering at him and attempting to understand him, "what can our opinion matter to you? Why is it so important we give credence to your words? Do you seek our approval by relating irrelevant matters to us in the hopes it will raise you in our estimation?"

"That is exactly it, Lizzy."

The new voice caught her by surprise, and Elizabeth turned to see that her father had entered the room and was now watching Mr. Wickham with some curiosity—and perhaps even suspicion. Mr. Bennet had departed that morning to see one of Longbourn's tenants. He must have returned in the interim.

"I cannot say you are incorrect," replied Mr. Wickham. The nonchalant manner in which he spoke, whereas a moment ago he had seemed eager to be believed, once again whispered to her of his untrustworthy nature.

"Then let us leave such discussions, sir, for they are neither proper nor constructive. And they are certainly not suitable for discussion in sitting-rooms during morning visits."

Mr. Wickham agreed and turned back to Jane. While he had focused on her and attempted to wield his charm as a weapon, Mr. Bennet' presence stifled that intention, and before long the officers excused themselves. Elizabeth and her eldest sister stood close together, watching the officers as they made their goodbyes, accepting their well wishes as they excused themselves. Mr. Wickham attempted to be gallant, but he was clearly still cross at Elizabeth's presence. In the end, he bowed to Jane, though his hand twitched as if he wished to take hers, and he departed. The glare he directed at her while he was turning, however, was enough to freeze water in an instant.

"Their behavior was not improper, was it?" asked Mr. Bennet when they had left the room.

"No, Papa," said Jane. Elizabeth was forced to agree with her sister that their behavior had not been *overtly* improper.

"Very well," said Mr. Bennet. And he turned and departed for his room.

The rest of the day passed the same as many other such days. Feeling a little out of sorts herself, Elizabeth spent some time in her room, considering the matter of Mr. Wickham and Jane. One unwelcome suitor had already decamped in defeat—Elizabeth considered how they might affect the same result with the other. It was unfortunate, but nothing came to Elizabeth's mind. After a time, Elizabeth slept, something she was not accustomed to during the day. She awoke to the sound of a knock on her door.

When the door opened at her call, her sister Mary appeared in the doorframe, peering in as if unsure of her reception. Though surprised, Elizabeth welcomed her sister into the room and rose from her bed to greet her. Mary, belatedly realizing that Elizabeth had just arisen, could only stammer an apology.

"Oh, Lizzy, I did not know you were sleeping."

"It is no trouble," said Elizabeth. "I do not often sleep in the afternoon and was on the verge of rising anyway."

It appeared Mary was unconvinced, but she nodded, though it was tentative. She entered the room and stood for a moment, discomfort radiating from her in her wringing hands and quick glances at Elizabeth. Perplexed at this behavior, Elizabeth beckoned her forward, saying:

"What is it, Mary?"

"I . . . Well, I wished to know . . ." Mary paused and took a breath. "Was what Mr. Collins said about me true?"

Nonplused by the question, Elizabeth stared at her sister. Then Mary seemed to realize her blunder, for she shook her head.

"Mr. Collins said I am silly and that I speak where I know nothing." Mary directed a pleading look at Elizabeth. "Is it true? I have done my best to study the Bible to be a good person. My study of Fordyce has also allowed me to understand how a female should behave. Have I been mistaken?"

All at once understanding her sister's concerns, Elizabeth beckoned Mary again, and this time she came, though not without hesitation. Elizabeth had never felt close to Mary, though she had not disliked her sister. This was an opportunity to share some insights to help Mary grow and become a more active member of society. But Elizabeth knew she needed to tread carefully.

"First, Mary, I believe you should discount everything Mr. Collins says. For a man so little acquainted with proper behavior himself to be commenting on others is hypocrisy of the highest sort. He is a vile, mean sort of man, and I would not wish you to be confused because of him."

Mary regarded her for several moments, her scrutiny suggesting Elizabeth's explanation had not satisfied her. Seeing this, Elizabeth laughed and put an arm around her sister's shoulders.

"We, none of us, are perfect, Mary. There are always weaknesses which we may improve."

"I *have* read the Bible, Lizzy," said Mary with an impatient huff.

"Of course, you have," replied Elizabeth. "The problem is sometimes you quote scripture — or even Fordyce — and those listening take it as a criticism."

"Is it not proper to criticize improper behavior?" asked Mary, her impatience changing to confusion.

"It can be," replied Elizabeth. "But to do so too often and at the least provocation suggests a judgmental attitude. That is also wrong, is it not? Are we not told not to judge others?"

"I had not thought of it that way," said Mary.

"I know. As for Fordyce, it may be best for you to put that book away, Mary." At Mary's questioning glance, Elizabeth replied: "Fordyce's words were considered old-fashioned when he uttered them. While his overall message may be sound and we should behave as properly as we can, do his words not sound judgmental? If Mr. Collins is an adherent of Fordyce's words, do you wish to emulate him?"

Mary's eyes widened such that Elizabeth almost laughed. "I had most certainly *not* thought of it that way!"

"Mr. Collins is not wholly bad," replied Elizabeth. Then she winked at Mary and added: "Just mostly."

This time Mary joined Elizabeth in laughter. "What I would most like to see, Sister dearest, is for you to shed some of your attitude and become more involved in our society. There is no reason for you to sit to the side and be a witness rather than a participant."

"But I am not of an open temperament as you are."

"And you do not need to be. Being more inviting will serve you well, I should think. There is no need to attempt to change your character — just to be more welcoming of others. If you like, I would be willing to assist wherever I can."

A shy smile came over Mary's countenance. "I should like that, Elizabeth."

CHAPTER IX

$\mathscr{S}$everal things happened in the next few days. The first was regarding Mary, who was more often found in the company of her elder sisters than had heretofore been. For a time, she was hesitant when with them, unwilling to share her opinions or even speak much at all. But over time, she lost her reticence, as if reassured that they *did* wish for her company.

While Mary's improved confidence was not immediately seen, there was an improvement in her behavior. The first few times Mary had the opportunity to share the homilies which had been a part of her conversation for some years, she had done so without hesitation. Elizabeth took care in those times not to admonish her, instead encouraging her to stop and consider the matter first before speaking—there were times, after all, when such comments were acceptable and even encouraged. After a few times of this, Elizabeth began to see her sister following her advice, and soon thereafter it began to be noticeable to the other members of the family, as did her change in reading material.

"Have you come again to borrow a book from my study, Mary?" said Mr. Bennet when they went to retrieve a copy of Shakespeare's sonnets. "By my count, this is the second time in as many days. Come to think of it, I have not seen Fordyce in your hands of late."

Mary blushed and looked at Elizabeth, who nodded her encouragement. "I have not been reading it as much of late, Papa," said Mary. "Lizzy is helping me choose other subjects to broaden my mind."

"She is, is she?" asked Mr. Bennet. The wink with which he favored Elizabeth when Mary looked down at her feet belied his serious look. "I am delighted to hear it. Should you desire to speak with me about what you read, I should like to exchange opinions."

With surprise, Mary looked up, and seeing her father's warm smile, she returned a shy one of her own. "I would like that, Papa. Perhaps Lizzy could join us?"

"What, are you afraid of your old Papa?"

It seemed Mary was taken aback until she saw his teasing grin. Relaxed again, serious Mary attempted to return his tease.

"One can only fear you when she does not know you. It seems to me your terrifying qualities fade the closer one approaches."

"I am pleased you see it that way, my dear," replied Mr. Bennet. Then he shooed them on their way. "Please speak to me later, Mary, for I am interested in hearing your opinions."

Later, when Elizabeth was away from Mary's company, Mr. Bennet had occasion to question her on the matter, which he lost no time in doing. Elizabeth explained what had happened, and he remained thoughtful for a moment before nodding.

"Though I am inclined to follow my cousin to Kent and administer some well-deserved chastisement, I believe you have handled it appropriately, Lizzy."

"Mary only wants for confidence, Papa. I only wish I had approached her earlier."

"What you have done is more than sufficient, Lizzy. I commend you for seeing the need."

What shocked Elizabeth was a confession Mary made later that day. It was interesting, Elizabeth thought, but Mary had taken to Shakespeare as if she had been reading it all her life and had hungered for more. Elizabeth suggested she start with the comedies before moving to the more serious of his works. When Mary set the book she was reading aside, Elizabeth thought her sister wished to say something but could not quite find the words. Thus, when she blurted it out a little later, she caught Elizabeth by surprise.

"If Mr. Collins had asked me, I would have accepted him."

Aghast, Elizabeth could not speak for a moment. When she did, she could only demand: "Accept Mr. Collins? Mary are you out of your senses?"

Far from being offended by Elizabeth's outburst, Mary was amused instead. "I suppose it might seem that way. Despite his deficiencies, you must own that Mr. Collins is an eligible match."

"How eligible do you call him, Mary?" Elizabeth could not help the fierce scowl, though she took care not to direct it at her sister. "Mr. Collins is a member of the clergy, which is a respectable profession, but given his . . . limitations, there is no possibility of advancement. This means he will always be a parson. While it would be no scandal to marry such a man, you must consider what marriage to Mr. Collins would entail."

Mary tilted her head to the side. "What do you mean?"

"I cannot imagine him being a good husband," replied Elizabeth. "Think of what he said, how he treated us all. Though he seems to be the essence of servility at times, at others he is brimming with arrogance, especially when he spoke to us. Then he informed me I would *not* be allowed to remain at my home when it became *his*, all because I championed Jane's interests. I suspect he would be uncaring of a wife's feelings and abusive at worst. You cannot consider Mr. Collins eligible."

Nodding her head slowly, Mary said: "Yes, I can see your point."

"Mary," said Elizabeth, grasping her sister's hands and speaking intently, "please do not devalue yourself such as to consider William Collins a good match. You are a gentleman's daughter, and while none of us will be as blessed as Jane, we will have small fortunes of our own. Do not settle for *any* man as a husband, as the years of your life may be long should you choose amiss. Instead, search for a man who will suit you, one who will cherish you for the exceptional woman you are. Make *him* prove he is worthy of *you*, not the reverse."

Though Mary was silent for a moment, Elizabeth was certain her words had found fertile ground, for she was contemplative. When she spoke at length, it was in a voice quiet, yet accepting.

"You have given me much to think on, Lizzy. I believe I shall retire to my room for a time."

Elizabeth squeezed her hands once and allowed her to depart, hoping for her sister's future. Hope for the future was a precious commodity, and Elizabeth now understood Mary had not possessed it. If their time together and Elizabeth's words changed Mary's outlook, she would consider it work well completed.

It would not be accurate to say Jane was not involved in Elizabeth's attempts to assist her younger sister, for Jane was a kind soul, one who accepted others without reserve and loved with all her heart. The unfortunate fact was that Jane was immersed in her own struggles, which often consumed her attention, leading her to sequester herself in her room more often. It was, of course, due to the presence of Mr. Wickham and his continual insistence on paying court to Jane. Though Elizabeth advised her sister to tell him with no hint of ambiguity that his actions were not welcome, Jane—dear sweet Jane—did not have it in her speak so forcefully. Thus, she was reduced to enduring him, without the prospect of his attentions ceasing.

During those days, it hardly seemed two days would pass without the officers visiting Longbourn and imposing themselves on the Bennet family. That, coupled with other events of the area the Bennet family attended and their frequent presence in Meryton, meant it was a rare day when Mr. Wickham was *not* importuning Jane with his ever-increasing ardency. The rest of his friends in the regiment were clearly in his confidence, for they often went to great lengths to separate the other members of the family from Jane's side.

When Elizabeth refused to be corralled into acting the way they wanted, she was often the subject of mirth, which only infuriated her more. She heard them talking on more than one occasion about the futility of her endeavors—they were an insipid bunch, other than the scheming Mr. Wickham.

"What do you think of Miss Elizabeth's attempts to come between Wickham and Miss Bennet?" asked Sanderson one day while at Longbourn. The same four officers had once again visited, and as Elizabeth was moving through the room, having spoken to the housekeeper, they were not aware she was behind them.

Mr. Denny, the man to whom Mr. Sanderson had been speaking, laughed and shook his head. "I have never known Wickham to relinquish that which he wanted. She is a feisty, determined sort of girl to be opposing him in such a manner, but it will all be for naught."

"It is unfortunate she has not allowed herself to be distracted by one of us."

"Oh, aye," agreed Mr. Denny, and with the tone of his voice, Elizabeth could fancy she could see the light of lascivious interest in his eyes. "She is a fine piece, is she not? I might almost think Wickham would favor her instead, had she only been as blessed with an estate as her sister."

A huff almost escaped Elizabeth's lips, which would have alerted them to her presence. With a will of iron, she kept it in, though she was quick in moving away from them and back toward her sister, who was, as ever, the focus of Mr. Wickham. But Elizabeth was certain to show a glare to the two gossiping officers when the chance presented itself, and she had all the satisfaction of seeing their confused looks in response.

Had Mr. Wickham's attentions comprised nothing more than flattery, Elizabeth might have been content with Jane's efforts to remain unaffected by him. But as time wore on, she thought the gentleman had become more than a little impatient with her. Why this might be so, Elizabeth could only speculate, but she thought he had rarely had difficulty charming ladies in the past. His pride was such that he could not fathom a young woman being unaffected by his manners.

This came to a point one day a few days later when he began to show his true character. On this day, Elizabeth had been determined she would not allow any of the other officers to distract her and had stayed steadfast by Jane's side. The acrimonious looks Mr. Wickham had flashed at her, she had ignored, and instead of interrupting him as she had often done in the past, she contented herself with paying close attention and not allowing the man any time alone with Jane.

"Do you not think it is a lovely day outside, Miss Bennet?" asked Mr. Wickham. "Perhaps you would enjoy a walk around the beautiful park in which this estate sits. I should be pleased to escort you."

"Lizzy is the walker, Mr. Wickham," replied Jane. "Though I also go out occasionally, I find it rather too cold for me at present."

Mr. Wickham regarded her with an unreadable expression for several moments. "In fact, the sun is shining, and the day has a warmth rarely seen at this time of year. I am certain it would do you good. We could take a little time together, while the others continue to entertain your sisters."

It had been Elizabeth's opinion that Mr. Wickham was beginning to lose his subtlety in favor of a more direct approach. Though half a dozen retorts sprang into Elizabeth's mind at that moment, she remained silent, instead waiting to see how Jane would respond.

"I am sorry, Mr. Wickham, but I am not inclined to walk."

"Then we shall stay inside if that is what you wish." There was more than a hint of asperity in the man's voice, and Elizabeth smiled, though she thought the expression had more than a hint of grimness inherent in it. Mr. Wickham noticed and frowned at her.

"You appear a little out of sorts this morning, Miss Elizabeth. Perhaps you should lie down for a time."

"On the contrary, Mr. Wickham," replied Elizabeth, favoring him with a serene smile which mimicked Jane's and which she had reason to believe annoyed the officer. "It is rare I suffer from any indisposition. I am well, though I thank you for your solicitous interest in my wellbeing."

Mr. Wickham regarded her for a moment, eyes narrowed imperceptibly. "When we were walking here this morning, Denny mentioned he had something of which he wished to inform you. As he is without a conversation partner at present, perhaps you should take the opportunity to approach him."

"Mr. Denny may approach me if he wishes. I find myself comfortable where I am."

It seemed Mr. Wickham decided trading words with her was fruitless, for he turned his attention back on Jane, and for some time he regaled her with tales of his exploits. Elizabeth thought some of them might even be based on true events, though she was certain they were mostly fabrications. But Jane continued to remain inscrutable, responding only with faint monosyllabic words or with nothing at all. The longer they stood there, the more frustrated Mr. Wickham seemed to become.

"My word, Miss Bennet!" exclaimed Mr. Wickham. "You should have been there to see it! As the challenged, it was up to me to prove that I was the superior horseman, and I did so, beating him by more than five lengths." Mr. Wickham leaned in and said in a low, secretive voice: "Colonel Forster himself has said I have as good a seat as any man in the regiment. As I was trained by the best, I do not think it is any flattery of myself to agree with him."

As he did so, Elizabeth saw the man's gaze fall to Jane's décolletage, then back up to her face again, the despicable light of the lascivious in his eyes. If he expected her to fall down at his feet and beg him to marry her, however, he would be disappointed, for other than the brief look of revulsion—so fleeting that Elizabeth was uncertain she even saw it—she did not reply. It was then the man's carefully held mask, began to slip.

"I declare, Miss Bennet!" said he in a jovial tone, though it was underscored with menace. "You are positively dull today. Why, you have not spoken more than two words together since we arrived."

For a change, Jane's own façade crumbled, and she glared at the man. "On the contrary, Mr. Wickham, I am as I have ever been. I find the company taxing at present."

The officer's eyes glittered. "Ah, cut to the quick! For a man so enamored of a woman to be set down in such a manner, is the cruelest fate. Were you a man, I might demand satisfaction."

"But my daughter is *not* a man, Mr. Wickham," came the sound of her father's voice. "Though I have no notion of how you might have mistaken that fact, there it is all the same."

"It did not say she was, Mr. Bennet," replied Mr. Wickham. "But I must urge you to call the apothecary for your daughter, as she seems out of sorts today."

Mr. Bennet fixed the militiaman with a thin smile. "What is ailing my daughter is not an ague. Your concern is not required."

Then Mr. Bennet looked about the room, noting the presence of the other officers, arching an eyebrow at them. "It is curious, however, that you gentlemen find yourselves in my sitting-room so often. Though I have never been a member of the army myself, I have observed that officers are more often busy with their duties than not. This Colonel Forster must be a lenient man to allow you all such leisure."

The meaning of Mr. Bennet's words was not lost on any of them, though Mr. Wickham attempted to brush them aside with his usual false cheer. "Colonel Forster is an excellent commander! Why, I do not believe I have served under one who is better."

"By your own words," replied Elizabeth, "you joined the militia only a few months ago, Mr. Wickham. Unless I am very much mistaken, I do not believe you have served under *any* other commanding officer."

Surprise did not even begin to describe Mr. Wickham's response, and for a moment he did not seem to know what to say. That moment passed, however, much too quickly, but before he could open his mouth, one of the other officers spoke.

"You are correct, Mr. Bennet," said Chamberlayn, rising and bowing to Mr. Bennet. "There is work to be done, and it is high time we departed." The rest of the officers rose while Chamberlayn turned to Mrs. Bennet. "Once again, we are overcome by your hospitality, Madam. Thank you, but I believe we should be departing."

Mr. Wickham appeared less than pleased to be leaving, but given the other three were arrayed against him, he resigned himself. He could not depart without making one last attempt to pierce Jane's indifference.

"Duty calls, Miss Bennet," said he with a gallant bow, grabbing Jane's hand before she could pull it away. A lingering kiss he bestowed on its back before she could reclaim it, and a smirk appeared on his countenance. "Until next time. I am already breathlessly anticipating it."

The four men took their leave and turned to depart from the sitting-room. Mr. Bennet accompanied them, and given the determined look he was giving them, Elizabeth thought he had something further to say. Thus, she followed them, overhearing the brief instruction he gave them.

"I trust I will not soon see you at Longbourn again?"

It was Mr. Wickham who responded, unsurprising to Elizabeth. "You cannot blame us for wishing to be here! There are wonders to be had at your estate, sir, and your hospitality is unmatched in the neighborhood."

From where she stood, Elizabeth could see the rest of the officers appearing uncomfortable, this display by their leader even beyond what they could countenance. Though her father's back was to her, Elizabeth imagined he was not at all pleased by the facile response.

"Yes, we are pleased by our openness, Mr. Wickham. But believe it must change, for I cannot imagine placing you in a situation where you must be reprimanded by your colonel. Men of the militia must be actively engaged in their professions, and if you spend too much time partaking of my hospitality, you risk censure by your colonel.

"Do not come again, sirs, for you will find my doors barred against you. If you persist, perhaps we shall discover what your colonel thinks of his men neglecting their duties."

Then with a scant bow, Mr. Bennet motioned to the doorway, which Hill was standing beside holding open. The men filed out, quite subdued, followed by Mr. Wickham. For his part, however, he hesitated, glancing at Mr. Bennet and then at Elizabeth beyond, before stalking out the door himself. The sound of it closing behind him was perhaps the most satisfying thing Elizabeth had ever heard.

When he turned, Mr. Bennet caught sight of Elizabeth, and he smiled. "Perhaps I should pay more attention to my family, Lizzy, for these men seem to be abusing our welcome."

"It is my thought," replied Elizabeth, "that they have attempted to time their visits for when they believe you will be occupied by other matters."

"That may be so," acknowledged Mr. Bennet. "For the next few days, however, I believe I shall stay with you all during morning visiting hours. The warning I just gave them should be enough to keep them out of my house for a few days at least, but it is on my mind that Wickham may choose to misunderstand."

Elizabeth considered the matter for a moment. "Will you deny him entrance?"

"I have said I would. But I will not allow him to leave without informing him of my displeasure. At that point, I might need to have a conversation with his commanding officer."

"Yes, I can see that," replied Elizabeth.

Her father turned to go to the sitting-room, but Elizabeth, noticing her sister was no longer there, took herself above stairs and knocked on Jane's door. The invitation came to enter, and Elizabeth did so, noting Jane was laying on her bed, looking up at the ceiling above.

"How are you, Jane?" asked Elizabeth, approaching her sister's bed.

"Weary," was Jane's reply. The look of distress in her eyes pierced Elizabeth's soul. "Can Mr. Wickham not see I do not care for him? Why must he always pester me?"

"Mr. Wickham is capable of seeing your disinterest, Jane. It is simply that he does not care, for he is intent upon his own selfish desires. You must see, Jane, that he has his eye on Longbourn."

"I do," replied Jane, though she spoke as if unwilling to confess to it. "He has made it quite clear."

"Then it would behoove you to refuse to be in his company," said Elizabeth. "You know it only emboldens him when you do not shoo him away."

Jane frowned. "I have made it quite clear I do not welcome his company."

"And that has deterred him, has it?"

The sarcasm in Elizabeth's voice was, perhaps, a little too much, but Elizabeth was beyond caring. It was for Jane to become the primary protector of her own interests, for Wickham was unmoved by her silence. Jane thought for a moment, then looked at Elizabeth yet again.

"I suppose you are correct, Lizzy. In the future, I shall remove myself from his company, should he attempt to impose it on me." Jane paused and then said: "After Mr. Collins's actions, I find I am wary of what he might attempt."

"Good," replied Elizabeth. "That can only be to your benefit. Perhaps we should stay close to home for the next few days. Papa has told the officers not to return, which should protect us for a time."

"That would be no hardship for me," said Jane.

"Then it is settled." Elizabeth leaned forward and kissed her sister's forehead. "Sleep for a time, Jane. It can only do you good."

"I shall."

Soon, Elizabeth heard Jane's breathing even out, then become deeper. Satisfied her beloved sister had found rest and comfort, Elizabeth turned and departed, taking care to close the door quietly. In her mind, she continued to roll the problem of Mr. Wickham about, teasing it this way and that as she attempted to work through it to a solution. Elizabeth was not convinced that Mr. Wickham would surrender — on the contrary, she had every confidence his self-interest would not allow him to yield the field of battle.

Seeking comfort herself, Elizabeth descended the stairs, following the sounds of Mary's practice on the pianoforte. Perhaps they could devise a plan between them to help safeguard their sister.

CHAPTER X

As they had discussed, the Bennet sisters spent the next few days close to Longbourn—the furthest they traveled from the house was the back lawn. And for a time, all was well, for there was no sign of the officers. While Elizabeth had thought Mr. Wickham would not obey her father's instructions, it seemed he had, for the time being, decided not to provoke the estate's master. Or perhaps his fellow officers had understood the anger they were inciting.

Whatever the case, they did not come, and for that Elizabeth felt nothing but gratitude. Jane, too, recovered apace from Mr. Wickham's addresses. Elizabeth was further heartened to see a new wariness about her sister. While she was still open and trusting, whenever anyone made mention of the officers—which was not infrequent, given Kitty and Lydia's characters—a frown would often come over her, and she would attempt to change the subject.

This changed, however, with an invitation to their Aunt Phillips's house for tea and cards one day late that same week. There was some conversation whether to accept or to continue for a few more days in their self-imposed exile.

"The invitation mentions an evening of dinner and cards," said Mr. Bennet. He shook his head and chuckled. "She must be busy preparing for the evening, for usually she brings invitations in person."

"Well, I believe I shall stay at home," said Mrs. Bennet. "Agatha may do without me for the evening, for I believe I have a little headache."

"Papa, may Kitty and I go?" pleaded Lydia.

"We shall be ever so well behaved," promised Kitty.

"A party at your aunt's house would do no harm, I suppose," said Mr. Bennet, giving a fond look to his youngest. "But you must listen to Mrs. Garret and your elder sisters and behave yourselves!"

The two girls promised they would, and looked to Elizabeth and Jane, who shared a glance. When Jane shrugged, Elizabeth turned to Mary, and finding her willing, fixed her gaze upon her youngest sisters.

"We may go to Aunt Phillips's card party, then. I believe we could all do with a little society, and Aunt Phillips's home is not of sufficient size to have invited many others."

"Sometimes you are so strange, Lizzy," said Lydia. "I do not understand why you would wish to avoid company."

The youngest Bennets had remained unaware of the recent intrigues with the officers, and Elizabeth was not about to illuminate their understanding. It was not difficult to distract Lydia to the subject of the upcoming party, and in this way the rest of the day passed until it was time for them to depart.

It was, Elizabeth reflected after the fact, something they should have considered before accepting the invitation. Mrs. Phillips, their aunt, was much like their mother had been before the entail had been ended—delighting in gossip, fond of company, and invariably silly, though not a slave of her nerves as Mrs. Bennet had been. This fondness for company often resulted in parties at her house which boasted more attendees than her small home could easily accommodate. On this occasion, there were many in attendance, including those whom the Bennet sisters—or at least the eldest three—wished least to see.

The first sign of trouble was the sight of several jackets of the brightest scarlet, and Elizabeth soon realized their mistake. The second was the smirking countenance of Mr. Wickham, surrounded by what Elizabeth thought of as his coterie of hangers-on. He must have been lying in wait for them, for as soon as they entered the room, he stepped forward and bowed over Jane's hand.

"Miss Bennet," said he, not reacting in the slightest when Jane retracted the appendage before he could kiss it. "How wonderful it is to see you." His smile at Elizabeth and the rest of the sisters was almost predatory. "And *all* your sisters. I have had little opportunity to come to know the youngest Bennets—I hope to speak to you all before the evening is concluded."

Lydia giggled at the man's forward behavior, but Mary, sensible girl she was, herded them away from the officers and towards her aunt. The look she threw at Elizabeth suggested her intention of staying near them that evening and keeping them out of trouble. It was fortunate the youngest Bennets enjoyed their games as much as they did, for she saw them gazing longingly at any man wearing red before their attention was diverted.

"Shall we join the rest of the company?" asked Mr. Wickham of Jane while extending his arm for her to take. "It seems your aunt has devised amusements for us aplenty."

"It is nothing more than a card party," said Elizabeth, as Jane remained rooted by her side, ignoring Mr. Wickham's offer. "We have been to such parties here many times."

"We almost did not come," said Jane, in what was, for her, a daring statement.

"Then we are all fortunate you did," said Mr. Wickham with his usual gallantry. "It would not be the same had you not."

"Had we known what awaited us," said Elizabeth, looking in the man's eyes, "we would have reconsidered."

Mr. Wickham's eyes glittered though his smile never wavered. "It is my hope the evening turns out better than you expect, Miss Elizabeth. I would not have thought to encounter such reluctance to visit the home of a beloved relation."

"It is not our aunt who causes us pause," said Elizabeth. "Only her choice of company."

Then Elizabeth grasped Jane's arm and pulled her away from the officer, whose smile had turned brittle. She had made an enemy of the man, it seemed, a consequence that did not concern Elizabeth a jot.

The rest of the evening was spent in wariness. Elizabeth was always aware of Jane's position in the room, and she attempted to remain equally apprised of Mr. Wickham's whereabouts, a difficult endeavor, considering he was dressed the same as a quarter of the room. His height was something that marked him, though there were a few others who could boast the same, though his sinuous, yet dangerous, grace was also a feature for which Elizabeth could watch. For the most part, she took the simple expedient of staying close to Jane's side, which by itself foiled the man's designs. That did not mean he was willing to acknowledge defeat.

"Shall we not join this game?" asked Mr. Wickham of Jane not long after their arrival. "I believe your aunt requires a partner, and while there is no other position that I may take, I shall watch and advise you."

"No thank you, Mr. Wickham," said Jane. "I find I am not eager to play cards tonight."

"Then one would wonder why you have attended a card party," said the officer with a laugh. "What else does one do at such a function?"

"Perhaps we come for the company of my aunt and uncle," said Elizabeth. "Or perhaps our aunt has lured us here with the table my aunt sets, which has been called fine."

"Very sensible," said Mr. Wickham. "But hardly what one normally sees. Would you attend a ball and spend the entire time speaking, rather than dancing?" The gentleman turned to Jane. "That is a pleasure I have not had in some time. Do you know when the next assembly will be held? I should dearly love to dance with you again."

"I do not," replied Jane.

"Even if we did," added Elizabeth, "there is every possibility we would not attend. And if we did, the prospect of dancing has lost its lure of late. It would be more rational to stand and talk. As a woman, it is much easier to avoid those with whom you do not wish to associate if conversation is the order of the day rather than dancing."

When they were alone again after this exchange, Jane leaned to Elizabeth and said: "That was bordering on discourteous, Lizzy."

Elizabeth turned an arch look on her sister. "Yes, but the man is deserving, is he not?" Jane's quiet chuckles informed Elizabeth she agreed with the sentiment without reserve. "Mr. Wickham is not deterred by open indifference, so perhaps rudeness will prompt him to reconsider."

The sisters looked across the room to where Mr. Wickham had taken himself—he was now in low conference with Mr. Denny, his glances across the room betraying the subject of his discourse if it had been in doubt. Jane shook her head and turned back to Elizabeth.

"Do you think we might return home early tonight?"

"Kitty and Lydia will complain," replied Elizabeth.

"I can endure their protests," replied Jane. "It is Mr. Wickham's attentions which are becoming intolerable."

Grasping her sister's hand and squeezing it to show solidarity, Elizabeth replied: "I would not wish to offend Aunt Phillips. Perhaps we shall partake of dinner with the company and then make our excuses soon after?"

"Very well," said Jane with a nod.

It might be expected the Bennet sisters' precautions that evening would protect the eldest from the depredations of the rogue officer, and for a time, that prospect was born true. Though Mr. Wickham did not cease his attempts to garner Jane's company for himself, Elizabeth — or Mary — was always nearby. Though Elizabeth thought she saw the man's frustration rising much more quickly than it had in the past, to the gathering, he presented the same façade as he always had.

After some time of this game, the man seemed to think retreat to plan his next move was the best option, for he sat down with several others to a game of lottery. That was also worrisome, as both Kitty and Lydia were also present in the group. After a moment of watching with a critical eye, Elizabeth decided there was little need to concern herself, for there was at least one other player between Wickham and each of her sisters, and they all seemed to concentrate on the game. Elizabeth determined to maintain her vigilance, for she knew the man was slippery as an eel, but for the moment a sense of relief came over her.

"Lizzy," said Charlotte Lucas when she approached only a few moments later. "I have enjoyed your maneuvers this evening, as they have been rather well-coordinated. The reason for them, however, has quite puzzled me, for you seem to be intent on keeping Jane from the company of the officers. How can you account for this behavior?"

A glance to the side told Elizabeth that Jane was still standing nearby, next to another lady of the neighborhood. Confident for the moment there would be no enemy incursions into their territory, she turned back to Charlotte.

"What do you know of Mr. Wickham?"

The question surprised Charlotte. "Only what we all know. He is from the north, joined the regiment recently, and is known to have smooth manners and a charming façade."

"That is exactly what it is, Charlotte — a thin veneer. I am convinced there is nothing genuine about the man, and he is intent upon paying his addresses to Jane."

Charlotte's glance found Jane, much as Elizabeth's had a moment ago, and her friend was of such intelligence that she understood the thrust of Elizabeth's complaint. "Your suspicions of his motives. I understand them, but I was not aware the matter had progressed any further."

"Mr. Wickham will not leave her alone," replied Elizabeth. "The man is a silver-tongued devil. It would not surprise me if he would descend deeper than attempting to court a woman who has no interest in him. That is why Mary and I are always attending Jane—I will not give him the opportunity to hurt her."

"Tell me what has happened," said Charlotte. "I have not seen you in days and have heard nothing of this."

So, Elizabeth did, relating the full of her family's recent experiences with Mr. Wickham, knowing Charlotte could be trusted to keep her confidence. Charlotte was shocked at some of the things she related and had heard little more than rumors of Mr. Collins's visit, which tied into Jane's troubles of recent weeks. What Charlotte had been doing in the intervening time, Elizabeth was uncertain, but her mind was so full of their trouble with Mr. Wickham that she did not ask.

"That is an interesting tale, Lizzy," said Charlotte when Elizabeth had ceased speaking. "There is little enough hint of Mr. Wickham's intentions that had it been anyone other than you, I might have questioned whether you were seeing shadows where none exist." Charlotte gave Elizabeth a fond smile. "Fortunately, I know you and your powers of observation, and I have no doubt of what you say. I do wonder, however, at this Mr. Wickham, and I am concerned. If he is a man intent upon seducing a woman, it does not speak well to his character. What other vices is he hiding?

"I will own I had not considered that," confessed Elizabeth, worrying at her lip in thought. "I have been consumed with thoughts of protecting Jane."

"You should speak with your father," said Charlotte. "Given Mr. Wickham's poor behavior, he can bring the matter to the colonel's attention and see that Mr. Wickham is controlled."

"I have already done so," said Elizabeth. "Papa is watchful, but he has not seen enough yet to give him true alarm."

"Lizzy!" hissed a voice close by, and Elizabeth turned to Mary, who was white and agitated. "Look!"

Following Mary's gesture, Elizabeth looked to the side of the room, noting that Jane had moved away, and was now in a corner, Mr. Wickham looming over her and speaking intently. Mr. Denny had taken Mr. Wickham's place at the lottery table. Jane's distress was unmistakable, as she caught Elizabeth's eyes, her gaze beseeching her for rescue from the man's wiles. While distracted speaking with Charlotte, it seemed Elizabeth had allowed her vigilance to lapse.

"Come," commanded Elizabeth to each of her companions, her

determined stride taking her toward the pair. The only word to describe Mr. Wickham's posture was menacing, and Elizabeth decided the only thing to do was to intervene directly.

Mr. Wickham jumped back with surprise when Elizabeth wormed her way between him and Jane, an oath almost escaping his lips. When he saw who it was, his mouth changed to the rictus of a frown, then disappeared altogether in favor of his customary pleasant smile. But his eyes — oh, his eyes! They rested on Elizabeth, hard as diamond, and about as forgiving.

"Miss Elizabeth!" said he with a jovial note in his voice. "I see you have discovered us. Your sister and I were just exchanging some thoughts regarding the evening. I very much enjoy speaking with her, for I know no one so kind and gentle as your sister."

"There is no need to speak of my sister's qualities to me, for I am aware of them."

"Ah, yes, I suppose you must be. Given your constant attendance on her whenever in company, one might be excused for mistaking your diligence for lack of knowledge. Your sister does not require such constant supervision."

"Perhaps she does not," said Elizabeth, her eyes boring into the man before her. "But there are, unfortunately, many who would take advantage of her good and caring nature. If they would leave her be, I would be well-pleased."

Mr. Wickham did not miss the innuendo in Elizabeth's words, for his jaw became slightly tighter. "It may be best if you take care, Miss Elizabeth," said he. "Young ladies who insert themselves into matters of no concern to them often find themselves mired in situations detrimental to their wellbeing. If you put your hand in the fire, you cannot be surprised when it is burnt."

Mr. Wickham turned and departed, his contempt for her shown in his failure to even take his leave. Silence descended on the four women remaining behind, Charlotte in shock, the other two Bennets in slight fear, and Elizabeth in blazing anger. Then she turned to Jane.

"What was he saying to you, Jane?"

Though shaken, Jane essayed to respond. "He was making some improper statements to me."

"What statements?" demanded Elizabeth. "What were they?"

"Comments about his intentions toward me," replied Jane, still speaking slowly. "He said I would not be allowed to escape from him; that he intended to make me his wife. Then he pressed me to state my love for him, and when I would not, he began to demand it, saying I owed it to him."

"A short time ago he warned me to stay out of his way," added Mary. "His manner was intimidating."

"What is the nature of this man?" asked Charlotte, bewildered. "Does he believe he can issue threats and insinuations and not be challenged?"

Elizabeth, so angry she could hardly reply, found Mr. Wickham where he was sitting across the room, speaking with Kitty, who was blathering away without a care. The mocking smile with which he favored Elizabeth, and the way his eyes darted to the girl by his side, seemed a warning—if she tried to interfere the consequences would be dire. But he had not reckoned with Elizabeth Bennet. Not by half.

"Mary, go sit beside Kitty," commanded Elizabeth, startling her sister. Mary, good girl that she was, obeyed with alacrity. Elizabeth turned one more disdainful glare at Mr. Wickham and turned away, beckoning her remaining companions to follow her. Their object was her uncle.

"Uncle, there is a situation of which you must be aware," said Elizabeth when they had reached him.

"Yes? What is it, Lizzy?"

Their uncle was a portly man, affable and pleasant. But he and his wife had never produced any children, and as a result, they were protective of all their nephews and nieces, though more especially of the Bennet sisters, by virtue of their home being much closer than the Gardiners, who lived in London. Elizabeth endeavored to explain in as brief a fashion as possible what had occurred, including a little background of their history with Mr. Wickham. The more she spoke, the darker became Mr. Phillips's countenance.

"Your father has informed me of some of this, Lizzy," said Uncle Phillips, "but I had not heard to what extent this man has carried his actions. He shall do so no longer in my house."

Motioning them to stay where they were, Mr. Phillips turned and marched to where Mr. Wickham was still plying Kitty with his false charm, Mary sitting close by observing them. Though he appeared to have fixed his attention on her, Elizabeth was certain Mr. Wickham knew what was happening in the room. At her uncle's approach, Mr. Wickham shot her a glare, looking more murderous than ever.

"Kitty, Mary," said Uncle Phillips, interrupting whatever was being said, "go join your sisters while I speak with this *gentleman*."

Though Kitty appeared startled, Mary nodded with grim satisfaction, and took her sister's hand, leading her away. Mr.

Wickham rose, his movements indicating a certain lazy confidence which seemed to infuriate her uncle all that much more.

"It seems you have been busy, Lieutenant Wickham," said Mr. Phillips. "Tell me, do you make it a habit of insulting, offending, and *threatening* young ladies in their uncle's home?"

The frown with which Mr. Wickham responded was equal parts surprised and aggrieved. "There must be some misunderstanding, sir, for I have issued no threats."

"Do you think me witless, young man?" Mr. Phillips's voice cracked like a whip. "I have complete confidence in my nieces' honesty, and I have noted your attempts to approach Jane. You are a man who is seeking a comfortable situation for himself, and it becomes increasingly evident you have no scruples as to how you obtain it.

"I am a man who will protect my nieces, and you may be assured their father is the same." Mr. Phillips glared at the man before looking about. "You all have my apologies, but tonight's entertainment is at an end. Mrs. Phillips, the rest of your guests may stay for dinner, but I require the officers to depart at once."

While Elizabeth might have expected to hear Mrs. Phillips's protests, the only comment she made was to the effect that the officers were not so gentlemanly as those to whom she had been introduced when she was a girl. Uncertain what to do, the men in scarlet gathered together, and as there was no one of greater rank than Mr. Wickham present, no one seemed inclined to act as spokesman. Under Mr. Phillips's watchful eye, they made to depart, most seeming bewildered.

"And Mr. Wickham," said Mr. Phillips. The lieutenant looked back with disdain and anger. "Do not return, for you—and any who call you friend—are no longer welcome in my house. I shall ensure you are not admitted to Longbourn either, or at any of the other estates, If I can manage it."

Mr. Wickham did not respond, instead taking the simple expedient of turning on his heel and departing. But as he was turning, Elizabeth saw his eyes rake over her. She had made an enemy that evening if she had not already done so.

The rest of the evening—what there remained of it—was subdued. Not even their aunt, who could be counted on to express her displeasure in the loudest possible voice, had much to say, other than a few comments concerning the poor standard of men in the regiment. They partook of their dinner, as Mr. Phillips had promised, but most conversation was undertaken in low voices. Word of what happened there that night would be all over Meryton by first light tomorrow—of this, Elizabeth was certain.

"I am worried, Lizzy," said Charlotte as they sat to dinner. "It seems to me that Mr. Wickham is an implacable enemy once aroused."

"Perhaps he is," replied Elizabeth, her anger still ruling her reply. "But he will discover that I am also an enemy he does not wish to make."

Charlotte laughed and embraced Elizabeth. "You are all that is fierce, Lizzy. Only take care, for with what has happened tonight, he may be prompted to act against you."

Though she did not say it, Elizabeth was determined to take Charlotte's warning seriously. They had already curtailed many of their activities because of Mr. Wickham's presence, so she had little idea of being hurt by him. But taking care was prudent.

When the evening ended, the Bennet sisters gathered together to depart. Lydia, who had not been part of the excitement, complained loudly, but Mrs. Garret silenced her and shepherded her toward the carriage which waited out front, pulling Kitty along with her. Before they left the house, Mr. Phillips took Elizabeth aside to speak to her.

"I do not know of what this Mr. Wickham is capable, but I believe we should act before it becomes clear. I have sent a man on to Longbourn with news of the evening's excitement. Make him aware of all the facts and tell him to visit me tomorrow morning. Together we can approach Colonel Forster concerning the behavior of his officers."

"I will," said Elizabeth. That she had already determined she would speak to her father, she did not mention. Mr. Phillips farewelled them and saw them all to their carriage, and soon they were off.

Their arrival home saw Mr. Bennet waiting for them, having been alerted by the servant. Kitty and Lydia were taken above stairs by their companion—Lydia still complaining as she went—while Mr. Bennet invited the three eldest into his study to discuss the matter at hand. Soon they were sitting comfortably in his study, Jane appearing weary, while Mary had gained a measure of anger similar to that which Elizabeth felt.

"Your mother has retired," said Mr. Bennet in response to Elizabeth's query. "Now, girls, your uncle's servant informed me of the quick dissolution of the party this evening, but he was not explicit. Please explain what happened."

In a quick and concise manner, Elizabeth did so, with occasional help from Mary. Jane remained silent, as Elizabeth might have expected. When the explanation was complete, Mr. Bennet's ire had also been raised.

"It seems you were correct about this Mr. Wickham, Lizzy," said he with a tight nod. "It is past time I spoke with the commanding officer of the regiment."

Mr. Bennet's countenance softened as he regarded his eldest. "Are you well, Jane?"

"I am," was her simple reply. "For I have the best sisters in the world, sisters who will not allow any harm to come to me."

A chuckle comprised Mr. Bennet's response. "I cannot agree more. You should all retire. By tomorrow, I hope this will all be resolved."

The girls filed from his room, returning above stairs. Their disquiet and anger were such that none of them wished to be alone that evening, and after preparing for bed in their separate rooms, they gathered together in Jane's and all snuggled together under the counterpane.

But sleep was difficult to attain for Elizabeth, though she thought her sisters were not similarly afflicted. In her mind, she kept running over Charlotte's words, and she was forced to agree. Mr. Wickham was a dangerous man to have as an enemy.

CHAPTER XI

*A*nger had not been a constant companion to Henry Bennet. In fact, he was judged to be a mild-mannered man, one who delighted in laughter, loved his children, and dealt with all of his fellows with fairness. Rarely did Bennet find his dander raised to the point of fury. The morning after his girls returned from the Phillipses' party, full of tales of insistent soldiers and improper threats, found him as angry as he could ever remember being in his life.

It was with a sense of impatience he waited for the hour to progress enough that he could reasonably depart for Phillips's office. In that, however, he was surprised when the man himself arrived on his doorstep long before visiting hours began.

"Bennet," said Phillips, his gruffness a testament to his own state of mind. "I might have thought you would beat on my door as soon as it was first light."

"Trust me, Brother," replied Bennet, "I considered it. But I thought to maintain some semblance of my status as a gentleman rather than rushing in with guns blazing."

Phillips barked a laugh. "Then you are much more patient than I am. Mrs. Phillips finally demanded I depart, for she accused me of wearing a hole in her parlor floor."

"Did you note anything of Wickham's behavior during the evening?"

"Not enough, it seems," said Mr. Phillips with disgust. "His attempts to speak with Jane I easily marked, though Lizzy and Mary's constant attendance seemed to deter him. The confrontation in question escaped my notice, though there were several others present who saw something of it."

Phillips paused and grimaced. "Though I have heard nothing but rumors, it seems this Wickham and his coterie have attained something of a reputation in the community. No other young lady rivals Jane's position as heiress of Longbourn which appears to have protected them, but the manners of these officers are overly familiar, it seems. As I was passing by the blacksmith this morning, the man said he had heard something of what had happened. A few days ago he banished Wickham from his shop and threatened him should he ever speak to his daughter again."

"The arrogance of this man is beyond belief," said Mr. Bennet with a disgusted shake of his head. "Do you think the colonel will be up and about by now?"

Phillips flashed him a sardonic grin. "If he is not, he is no military man worth his salt. Let us wake him if he is still abed."

As it turned out, Colonel Forster *was* awake, and if the expression with which he greeted them was any indication, he had heard something of what happened the previous night and was unhappy because of it. While Bennet did not know much of the colonel, he had wondered if he was nothing more than a man eager to avoid active duty, entered into the militia for a life of leisure and society with no real work, his first words disabused Bennet of that thought.

"I expected you to visit me, Mr. Bennet, though if you had not, I would have waited on you at your estate." Then the colonel turned a questioning glance at Phillips.

"My brother by marriage," said Bennet, introducing him. "It seems obvious you have heard something of what happened last night. Phillips's wife was hosting the party in question."

"Ah," said Colonel Forster. "You were next on my list to visit, sir. It is not often several of my officers return to quarters long before they are expected. I could pull little explanation from them, though I noted several dark looks at one of their number. Then Mrs. Forster heard something of the matter in the village and brought those reports back to me."

Bennet gave him a tight nod. "Are you aware of the recent behavior of several of your officers?"

Colonel Forster sighed. "The militia, as you are no doubt aware, is populated by lesser men than the regulars. Most are good men, but they are not, as a rule, a diligent bunch. There are many I would say are not eager to see to their duties, and as such, no one of them stands out. I have been attempting to instill greater discipline, but there are still issues to resolve."

"The officers of which I speak are led by Mr. Wickham, and they include Mr. Denny, Mr. Chamberlayn, and Mr. Sanderson."

Colonel Forster's jaw worked, indicating annoyance. "I am not surprised. Wickham is the leader of the most troublesome group, which includes the names you have mentioned. Please, Mr. Bennet — tell me what you came to say, for thus far I only have fragmented accounts which make little sense."

Bennet complied as the colonel asked, informing him of the officers' visits to his home and how Wickham pressed his attention on Jane for what he believed were mercenary purposes. He informed the colonel of his actions in banning them from the estate the last time they visited and, finally, of what had happened the previous night. No detail was spared in the interest of ensuring the colonel knew the situation without cause for misunderstanding. As he spoke, the colonel's gaze became flintier, his manner angrier, and by the time Bennet concluded, he thought the man was ready to chew rocks.

"I thank you for bringing this to my attention, Mr. Bennet." The colonel paused and shook his head. "In the past, I have been a member of regiments that wore out their welcome in certain towns because of the behavior of the men. As colonel, I have always striven to uphold a certain standard. Meryton has been very welcoming, indeed, and I would not have you turn against us.

"Unfortunately, I have heard something of this behavior of Wickham's in the past."

"Oh?" asked Bennet.

The colonel nodded, an abrupt motion. "In our last location, a man accused Wickham of similar behavior. As he had only been a member of the regiment for a few weeks at the time and claimed it was a misunderstanding, I allowed the matter to rest with a reprimand. Until recently, I thought his behavior was much better."

"You refer to the blacksmith's daughter?" asked Phillips.

Colonel Forster glanced at him and grimaced. "That is one account I have heard. There is one more."

Though Bennet was curious, he decided it did not signify. "Does

Mr. Wickham not think word of his actions will not become known? Even if my daughter was inclined toward him, I would not approve of a betrothal—which is obviously his aim—with such accounts of his behavior."

"That is his fatal flaw, I believe," said Phillips. "He seems to think we will all be charmed by his manners."

"He has certainly seemed frustrated by his lack of success with Jane, according to Lizzy." Bennet barked a laugh. "I must own that Lizzy has shown her typical good judgment, for she saw through him from the beginning. It was I who said there was no harm in him. More the fool was I, it seems."

"Please wait," said Colonel Forster, rising to his feet. "I shall have Wickham summoned and we shall confront him together."

The colonel stepped out of his office into the room beyond and spoke a few words to the junior officer waiting there. Within a few moments, the lieutenant arrived and was admitted to the office. As he entered, Bennet watched him, looking for any hint of embarrassment or remorse. There was nothing to be had. In fact, the man appeared to possess an arrogant confidence, much as Phillips had described him only moments before. Bennet could not help but shake his head in disgust.

"Do you know why you have been summoned, Wickham?" asked the colonel, leaving the man standing at attention.

"The reason quite escapes me, sir," said Mr. Wickham.

"It does?" said Colonel Forster, his voice more of a snarl. "Do you not recall being removed from Mr. Phillips's house last night, of making veiled threats to the Bennet sisters, neglecting your duties to impose upon a young woman who has no interest in you?"

Though he continued to look straight ahead, the muscles at Mr. Wickham's temple flexed. "That was nothing more than a misunderstanding."

"A misunderstanding?" demanded the incredulous colonel. He turned to look at Bennet and Phillips, shaking his head. Phillips appeared about to plant a facer on the man where he stood, and for Bennet's part, he was not certain he would not hold Wickham down while Phillips pummeled him.

"Just like Brighton was a misunderstanding?" spat Colonel Forster. "I begin to think nothing you say should be believed. There was no misunderstanding, Wickham, not with the woman in Brighton, and not with Miss Bennet. You should also know I have accounts from the blacksmith and the innkeeper which provide additional evidence against you. Are *they* also misunderstandings?"

Though Bennet might have expected Mr. Wickham to further attempt to extricate himself, he seemed to understand the dangerous note in the colonel's voice. While fury roiled within him, he remained silent. The colonel himself appeared to have enough knowledge of Wickham's character that he did not expect him to remain silent either, for he waited to see if Wickham would make some other comment. He did not.

"Very well," said Colonel Forster after a moment. "You are hereby docked two month's pay and are ordered to stay away from the Bennet sisters. If I hear anything more of your escapades regarding them, or anyone else in the neighborhood, it will be fifty lashes and the loss of your commission. Do I make myself clear?"

It was then Wickham made some reaction, for he turned to look at the colonel, fury smoldering in his eyes. Had he been any more belligerent, Bennet though he might have induced the promised future punishment at that moment. It seemed, however, that he retained some measure of discretion. The expected defense finally arrived.

"There is no need for that," said Mr. Wickham. "If Miss Bennet does not wish to speak to me, she should have said something to me. I have rarely had more than a few words from her. From what everyone in the neighborhood says, she is reticent. How was I to know she did not welcome my presence?"

"That does not cover your actions last night," said Bennet. "Can you explain your threats to my daughters without resorting to the unbelievable claim it was all a *misunderstanding*?"

Wickham's mouth clamped shut yet again.

"You knew she did not wish for your presence," said Bennet. "It did not make any difference, for you wished to gain control of her future inheritance. It was Lizzy's vigilance which prevented any further misbehavior from you.

"You should know, Lieutenant, that I would never allow my family's estate to fall into the hands of one such as you. Even if you did somehow force my daughter into a marriage, there are safeguards in my will which would prevent you from ever gaining control of the estate. I have four other daughters who can inherit in their sister's stead."

Wickham glared at Bennet. "It seems you think little of your daughter if you would disinherit her with so little provocation."

A snort was Bennet's response. "As you are nothing more than a selfish, grasping sort of man, I would not expect you to understand. It would bring me no joy to cut my eldest daughter off, but she would understand my reasons. Though you know nothing of my past struggles to ensure the estate is protected, I did not save it for my family's posterity only to have a man such as you bleed it dry."

There was little to be said in response, and Wickham made no attempt to reply. Colonel Forster nodded and took control of the conversation again.

"It seems we are finished here. I will say it once again, Wickham—do not approach the Bennet sisters, and do not go to Mr. Bennet's estate. And you should tell your cohorts the same, for you have all become persona non grata to the Bennet family."

"And I will publish your untrustworthiness far and wide," added Bennet. "Though I would not besmirch the colonel's reputation, for he has proven himself to be a good and decent man, I will not have any of my neighbors taken in by you. The events of last night have permanently stained your name—when I am through with you, no one of the neighborhood will admit you to their homes."

"Dismissed, Wickham," said the colonel. "Do not go far from the encampment, for I want to keep my eye on you."

Wickham turned on his heel and stalked from the room. After he had gone, the colonel sighed and turned back to Bennet and Phillips.

"Thank you, gentlemen. I am sorry that it has come to this. Given what has happened here, it is obvious Wickham cannot remain in Meryton. I shall inquire as to the possibility of transferring him to another regiment. Perhaps when he goes, we can regain our honor."

"In my eyes, you have lost no honor," replied Bennet. He clasped the colonel's hand tightly. "There is little you can do to ensure men of only the highest moral fabric are admitted to your regiment. I thank you for hearing us and acting accordingly."

"It was the least I could do."

Bennet and his brother soon took their leave. But as he farewelled his brother and rode toward his home, he could not help but speculate that Mr. Wickham was a vindictive man. The girls would need to be warned to take care until he was gone from the area for good.

While Elizabeth was gratified by what her father revealed of the conversation with Colonel Forster, she could not help but suppose the matter was not at all closed. For the present, Mr. Wickham remained in the area, and she could only conjecture he was not a man who was apt to surrender that which he wanted.

"What do you think, Papa?" asked Elizabeth.

Mr. Bennet grimaced. "It is my hope Wickham will be transferred quickly. But until that happens, I consider him to be a danger. As such, it would be best if you all stay close to Longbourn and not tempt him."

"Of course, Papa," said Jane in her agreeable way.

"What if Jane were to go to town?" asked Elizabeth. When her two companions turned questioning glances on her, Elizabeth said: "Aunt and Uncle Gardiner would be happy to host Jane for a time, and it would remove her from the influence of Mr. Wickham."

Jane, whom the suggestion most concerned, fell silent, thinking about it for a time. Mr. Bennet exchanged a glance with Elizabeth, and though he did not speak, she thought certain he approved of the suggestion. At length, Jane spoke.

"That is a possibility. But I think I would prefer to remain at Longbourn for the moment. I would not wish to give Mr. Wickham the impression he has chased me away."

"Upon my word!" said Elizabeth. "Of all the times for you to be more like me, now is most inconvenient, Jane."

Mr. Bennet laughed and Jane swatted at Elizabeth, displaying a glare. Elizabeth only grinned back, for Jane's displeasure was not at all a fearsome sight.

"If it should become necessary, I will go to Uncle Gardiner," repeated Jane. "But I prefer to remain in my home at present. Mr. Wickham does not have as much influence as he believes."

"Very well, Jane," said Mr. Bennet. "For the present, we shall abide by your wishes. However, you must both take great care until he is gone." Mr. Bennet directed a significant glance at Elizabeth, who shrugged her willingness to follow her father's instructions. "If you leave Longbourn for any reason, do not go alone — go together or take a footman with you."

"We will, Papa," chorused the sisters.

As it happened, Elizabeth could never have guessed trouble would find them so soon. The rest of the day was spent quietly at home with their mother and younger sister. Mary, though she had not been privy to what had happened since the party at Aunt Phillips's house, was astute, and she quickly pulled the matter from Elizabeth's lips. Though she did not say much thereafter, it was clear Mary approved of their precautions and her father's confrontation with Mr. Wickham. Mrs. Bennet was informed of the matter, assured everything was well, and then refused to speak of it again. As for Kitty and Lydia, as they were ensconced with Mrs. Garret, no one thought to bring it to their attention. It was likely for the best.

The day after, however, Elizabeth felt the familiar longing to be out of doors walking in the groves near their home, and while she did not voice her desire, it must have been clear. Jane, dear sister that she was, offered to be her companion that morning.

"You will be out of sorts all day if you do not have at least a short walk, Lizzy," said Jane. "As I am feeling a little restless myself, I would be happy to accompany you, as long as you do not walk halfway to London as you often do."

"I do *not* walk halfway to London," said Elizabeth, glaring at her sister. "Rarely do I walk more than a quarter of the way."

The two sisters laughed together and decided that was what they would do. Mary's opinion was canvassed, and she elected to go with them. Therefore, fifteen minutes later the three sisters had informed their father of their plans and departed. Mr. Bennet was working with his books and waved them from the room when they informed him they would all go together.

It was not Elizabeth's intention to walk far at all that morning, so after consulting with her sisters, she led them down Longbourn's drive and down the little path which led away from Longbourn to the west, skirting Longbourn Village, but keeping the town close within their view. This was a good compromise, in Elizabeth's opinion—the path was not a long one, and it would keep them close to civilization while giving her the illusion of the bounty of nature she craved.

That was when trouble arrived at their doorstep. Out of the calmness of the still woods surrounding the path, and as Longbourn fell below the line of the trees, a man stepped out onto the path and confronted them, his scarlet coat marking his identity. Surprised, the three sisters halted and stared at him in astonishment, and for a moment no one spoke.

"I might wonder why," said Mr. Wickham, his voice grinding with anger, "my heartfelt overtures are rejected and tossed underfoot. Did I not show you the highest favor?"

There was room to retreat from the man, as they could return back the way they had come. The spire of the church was visible to the right, and if she strained, Elizabeth could hear the sounds of the small village, a dog barking, and someone calling to an acquaintance. Given Mr. Wickham's position and from whence he had come, Elizabeth thought he had lain in wait for them. He had likely marked their departure from Longbourn, seen the path they meant to take, and hurried on ahead to a position where he could waylay them.

All these thoughts passed through Elizabeth's mind in an instant, and she wondered how they could extricate themselves from the situation. Then again, she had long suspected that Mr. Wickham was much more the brute than he revealed in public. Such actions as accosting young women on deserted paths was not the mark of a gentleman.

"Honeyed words seasoned with threats?" asked Jane, surprising Elizabeth with her daring. "You would have us believe that you meant only to make love to me?" Jane laughed, a bitter, harsh sound. "There is no need to speak such platitudes, Mr. Wickham, for I am well aware you care far more for my future inheritance than my person."

"Had you taken the opportunity to discover my feelings, you would not have been disappointed"

"So, a spurned lover warns a woman's sister what will happen if she does not stay away?" said Mary. "That is an odd way to go about wooing, Mr. Wickham."

"Ah, the awkward, wallflower sister speaks," sneered Mr. Wickham. "As I doubt you have ever been the object of a man for longer than you took to bore him to tears, I suggest you remain quiet."

"Do not speak to my sister so!" exclaimed Jane. "You are not worthy to so much as say her name!"

Mr. Wickham's scorn never abated as his gaze turned to Elizabeth. "What has infected your sisters? I might have expected you to take the lead in castigating me, and yet you stand there, witless while they cry their ineffectual insults."

"Oh, I am quite capable of speaking, Mr. Wickham." Elizabeth smiled thinly. "At present, I am enjoying their dressing down of a worthless excuse for a man."

"I might have known some of your impertinence would infect them." Mr. Wickham took a step toward them, a motion which caused all three sisters to stiffen. "It seems you must be taught a lesson in what happens to those who interfere with my designs, my dear Miss Elizabeth. It would have been better had you kept silent, for I am not a man who allows interference."

"Then you mean to assault us?" demanded Elizabeth, moving in front of her two sisters to confront the cad. "How heroic of you, sir, to brave the likes of defenseless women. Shall you draw your sword to protect you against the fiery contempt from this coterie of enraged females, or shall you slink away in fear and shame?"

"You are about to discover what I shall do," spat Mr. Wickham.

Elizabeth poised herself to defend her sisters by whatever means she possessed. She turned her head to tell her sisters to flee back to

Longbourn to summon their father when a shout rang from down the path beyond Mr. Wickham.

A glance beyond the libertine, who had stopped and turned to look at who had interrupted them, revealed the approach of a rider on a horse. The man was tall, dressed in the clothing of a gentleman, his steed a powerful stallion. As he reined in before them, Elizabeth heard a gasp from their tormentor as he stiffened in recognition. The rider drew his mount to a halt before them and vaulted down from the saddle, reaching them in a few short strides. From his mouth issued a single word, though its meaning was amplified by the utter scorn and derision it contained.

"Wickham!"

CHAPTER XII

"*Y*ou seem to be slipping, Wickham," snarled the gentleman into the silence which had ensued after his coming. "With three ladies arrayed against you, it seems they have not been taken in by your charm and smooth manners. Or perhaps you have been here long enough they now know of your proclivities."

"I knew him for what he was within a few days of his coming," said Elizabeth. Mr. Wickham started as if he had forgotten of their presence.

"Well, Wickham, explain yourself! What do you mean by accosting these young women? Is your usual method so unsuccessful you must now resort to intimidation?"

"D-Darcy," said Mr. Wickham, his voice bleeding with fear. "I had not thought to see you in such a place as this!"

"That much is clear, worm! It is fortunate that I have caught up with you. Fitzwilliam will be interested to hear of your whereabouts, for I believe you owe us for your misdeeds."

This was too much for Mr. Wickham. Turning, he fled past them and into the woods which lay to the side of Longbourn Village, never once looking back over his shoulder. The gentleman took a step forward as if to pursue him, and then paused, looking at Elizabeth and her sisters. Jane and Mary were now standing close together, their hands clasped in mutual comfort, while Elizabeth still stood before them, though the danger had now passed.

For the first time, Elizabeth possessed the presence of mind to take stock of the man who had been their protection. As her first impression had indicated, he was tall, broad of shoulder and slender of build. On his head, he wore a fine black top hat, and from underneath on all sides, she could see his curly dark hair sticking out, his eyes a light and piercing blue. The man was formidable, his jaw strong and clenched tightly as if due to some great anger. Had he smiled, Elizabeth might have thought him the most handsome man she had ever seen.

The gentleman hesitated, and though he appeared torn, he turned and sketched a bow. "My apologies, Miss, but I had not meant to appear so abrupt. Do you require an escort to return to your home?"

"I thank you, sir, but I believe we are well," said Elizabeth, speaking for her sisters. "Though we have no one here to perform our introduction, might I know the name of our rescuer?"

A smile, though strained, fell over the gentleman's countenance. "Of course," said he. "My name is Fitzwilliam Darcy. I would ask how you know Wickham, but given his mode of dress, might I assume he has joined a regiment of militia encamped close by?"

"Yes, sir," replied Elizabeth. "It was in early October that the regiment arrived. Mr. Wickham has been doing his best to insinuate himself into the neighborhood, and, into Jane's good graces."

Elizabeth gestured to Jane and Mary before catching herself. "Oh! You have my apologies, for I have not introduced myself. I am Elizabeth Bennet, and these are my sisters Jane and Mary."

"I wish we had met under better circumstances," replied Mr. Darcy. "In fact, my cousin and I—my cousin is a member of the dragoons— have been looking for Mr. Wickham for some time. I cannot stress enough how important it is to stay away from him, for there is no more worthless man in all of England."

"It seems we are of similar opinions, Mr. Darcy, for Mr. Wickham has made himself unwelcome here."

The man smiled, but again it did not reach his eyes. Though she thought him a rational man, at present he fidgeted, his eyes darting away through the woods where Mr. Wickham had fled. At once, Elizabeth understood his predicament.

"My sisters and I can return to our home alone, Mr. Darcy. If you wish to pursue Mr. Wickham, please do not concern yourself for us. I can only wish you luck in apprehending him."

Mr. Darcy grinned. "Thank you, Miss Bennet. It is clear you are a woman of much perspicacity." Pausing, Mr. Darcy added: "Do you live nearby? I should like to speak with your father when I return."

"We live at Longbourn, Mr. Darcy." Turning, Elizabeth motioned toward the west, saying: "Our home lies on the other side of these trees. Please visit, for I know my father would like to speak with you. I shall inform him to expect your arrival."

"Excellent," said Mr. Darcy. Then he turned and mounted his steed again in one smooth motion. "Can I ask for directions to the encampment? I have business with the colonel of the regiment."

"It is in Meryton, on the far side of town. Colonel Forster has his office in a large building at the end of the street on the right."

"Thank you," replied Mr. Darcy. "Until I return."

Then he spurred his horse into motion and galloped from sight, leaving the three sisters staring after him. For a moment, none of them spoke a word.

"Well, that was fortuitous," said Mary. "I believe Mr. Wickham meant to assault us, though it is difficult to believe him capable of such audacity."

"I think he is capable of just about any audacity," said Jane quietly.

Though Elizabeth agreed, she thought it would be best for them to return to Longbourn as quickly as possible. Thus, she began to shepherd her sisters back toward their home.

"I agree with you, Jane, but should Mr. Wickham elude Mr. Darcy, it is possible he may return. We should seek the safety of Longbourn."

It was clear neither of her sisters had considered the possibility, for they soon turned with a will, hurrying back toward their home. But as they walked, Elizabeth could not concentrate on what had just occurred, for her thoughts were focused on the gentleman they had just met. Though she did not know him and thought it may be because of his rescue in the face of Mr. Wickham's belligerence, Elizabeth felt that she could trust him. She hoped he would also be willing to tell them more of Mr. Wickham.

Wickham here near Netherfield! Darcy could hardly believe the chance that had brought him across the accursed man so close to where he was visiting. After months of searching for Wickham's whereabouts, Darcy had begun to wonder if the man had left England, even knowing Wickham did not have the funds to make such a journey. To see him in Hertfordshire, of all places, was something he would not have expected in his wildest dreams!

However the fortunate circumstance had come about, Darcy was determined to prevent him from running yet again. As Wickham was on foot, he would be slower than Darcy, and if Darcy could arrive and speak with his commanding officer before he could flee, they could take Wickham into custody and deal with him once and for all. Wickham would never importune anyone close to Darcy again!

Though unfamiliar yet with the neighborhood—Darcy was not even certain how he had come to be on the neighboring estate—he found his way to the town without trouble, for the instructions the young lady had given him were excellent. The town was small, and the one main street was busy, horses mingled with townsfolk and gentlefolk walking in small groups, their conversation fleeting as he rode by. Once again, the lady's directions were sufficient, for soon Darcy found himself in front of a nondescript building he was certain must be his destination. Dismounting, he tied the reins to a post and entered the building.

A junior officer, by the look of him, hailed him from where he sat behind a desk. "Good morning. How may I help you, sir?"

"I am here to see the commander of the regiment regarding a matter of some urgency. It is concerning an officer of his by the name of Wickham."

Though Darcy thought the man was not inclined to be of service, the moment he mentioned the miscreant's name, it appeared a door was opened. With a nod, the officer stepped to a door set in the far wall, opened it, and stuck his head in, the low hum of voices reaching Darcy's ears. Then he turned and beckoned Darcy forward.

"The colonel will see you, sir."

When Darcy entered, he noted the sparse and utilitarian nature of the office and the scarlet-clad man sitting behind the desk, scribbling furiously as he worked. The man was perhaps a few years older than Darcy's cousin, though still a man of action and vigor. It appeared he was busy, as his greeting, when he rose, was perfunctory, almost harried.

"I do not believe I have met you, sir. Are you from one of the outlying estates?"

"I am not a resident of these parts," replied Darcy, feeling more than a little impatient. "Fitzwilliam Darcy, at your service. My friend, Mr. Bingley, has just taken possession of Netherfield Park. In fact, I have come to speak to you of Mr. Wickham and request you take him into custody at once."

"What has he done now?" asked the colonel without preamble.

"My cousin, a colonel in the regulars, and I have been looking for him for months because of some... previous difficulties we experienced with him. I did not even know Wickham was in the area until I happened to come across him confronting three young ladies of the neighborhood."

The colonel's expression, which had been grim, changed in the blink of an eye to one forbidding. Looking past Darcy, he bellowed for his aide.

"Have Lieutenant Wickham brought to me, *at once!*"

"You will have to be quick about it," said Darcy. "I believe I returned first, as he was on foot, but I suspect he will flee, now he knows I am staying in the neighborhood."

The colonel scowled again. "Please wait here, Mr. Darcy. I will see to this matter personally."

For the next several agonizing minutes, Darcy waited in the colonel's office for word of what was happening. Unable to sit, he occupied his time with stalking the floor like a caged lion, alternately berating himself for not following Wickham at once, knowing his honor as a gentleman required that he offer his assistance to the three ladies. When Colonel Forster returned, Darcy had worked himself into quite a state.

"Wickham is not in the camp," said the colonel shortly as soon as he entered. "If he is as afraid of you as you suggest, he is likely hiding somewhere, or he has already attempted to flee. I have sent searchers out to apprehend him."

Darcy swore. "He should not get far, unless he steals a horse, for he was on foot when I saw him."

"I would not have thought Wickham was a horse thief."

A grim smile was Darcy's response. "Where his own wellbeing is concerned, Wickham is capable of anything. There is ample reason for him to fear me and even more for him to fear my cousin. I might have followed him and apprehended him myself, but his confrontation with the ladies was tense, and I judged it proper to see to them first."

"Might I assume the three ladies in question were the three eldest Bennet sisters?"

For a moment, Darcy was bemused, despite the situation. If the colonel referred to the three *eldest*, Darcy wondered how many there were, and if they were all as pretty as those he had met this morning.

"That was what they called themselves," replied Darcy, forcing his thoughts back to the task at hand. "I did not see the genesis of the disagreement, but I cannot imagine it began with any cordiality."

The colonel looked at him with some appraisal. "If you were only in their company for a few minutes, they would not have had time to inform you of their recent trials with Wickham. If you are willing, I will share the story of the matter with you. Since it is known throughout the neighborhood, I cannot imagine there is any harm in doing so."

With a nod, Darcy sat in the chair in front of the desk while the colonel positioned himself behind it. It was not a long story, but the contents were of no surprise to Darcy. As he sat back and considered what he had been told, Darcy reflected there were certain aspects of it which did not seem like the Wickham he had always known. But perhaps there were reasons for that change.

"Though you have not spoken," said Colonel Forster, "I can see you have heard something similar of this man in the past."

"In fact, I have heard little of Wickham's attempts to gain a fortune for himself, though I can well imagine to what lengths he might descend." Then Darcy paused and shook his head in rueful regret. "I am far more knowledgeable of Wickham than I wish, but it has just occurred to me that I have not explained my connection with him. Let me do so briefly so you understand a little more of what you are dealing with in this man."

And so, Darcy did, relating his experiences with Wickham, from his childhood at Pemberley to university. He spent more time on Wickham's character as he knew it rather than the specific events, and he did not touch the matter of Georgiana, except to say that Wickham had attempted to induce a young girl of his acquaintance to elope to obtain her dowry. The colonel listened to what Darcy was telling him, and when his account was complete, he sat back in his chair.

"That is quite the tale, Mr. Darcy."

"And every word is true."

Colonel Forster put his hand up in surrender. "I do not doubt it, sir. Even if I did not already have Wickham's recent behavior to inform me of his character, I doubt I could put your account aside."

"Thank you." Darcy paused and then returned his attention to his previous thoughts. "The one part of Wickham's actions in Hertfordshire which contradicts what I know of him is how he became impatient with the Bennet sisters. The Wickham I know is unruffled, at least by a woman. If he was not getting what he wanted from her, I would have thought he would move on to the next target with little regret."

"Perhaps being a member of the militia tied his hands," suggested Colonel Forster. "Deserting, even from the militia, is not a matter to be undertaken lightly."

Darcy considered it and nodded. "That is possible. However, of greater import is my continued search for him, and his repeated failures to obtain a fortune. The frustration has likely been mounting, especially after he failed with the young woman of my acquaintance. It is also possible he has convinced himself a marriage to the daughter of a landowner will protect him, should we find him."

"Would it?" asked the colonel.

"Perhaps from me," replied Darcy, though he was uncertain that was even true. "But my cousin is another matter entirely."

Colonel Forster nodded his head in approval. "Yes, I can see how that may be."

A knock sounded on the door, and the colonel called out permission to enter. On the other side stood a tall man, his scarlet jacket bearing the insignia of a captain's commission.

"Captain Carter," said Colonel Forster. "May I assume you have no good news of our missing lieutenant?"

"Wickham cannot be found," said Captain Carter. "The entire village has been searched, and I have canvassed the local estates. In addition, there is a horse missing from the stables."

"Damnation!" thundered the colonel, rising and pacing the room. "When was the last time he was seen?"

"Denny reports having seen him not long after rising this morning, but no one has seen him since. Since his reprimand yesterday, the regiment has been informed of your instructions for him to remain close to camp. But somehow he gave us the slip and departed."

"Do you believe Denny?" asked Colonel Forster. "Since Wickham's arrival, he and Denny have been thick as thieves, as have Chamberlayn and Sanderson."

"It is unlikely, and equally unlikely they are still close friends," replied the captain. "After the excitement at the Phillips home, the men had a falling out. Though it did not come to blows, several of the other men reported a loud argument among the four men, which resulted in Wickham returning to camp alone."

"Then I begin to see something different from what I thought I saw this morning," said Darcy. "I expected he would return to camp after escaping from me, but I suspect now he had a horse nearby and was intending to leave after accosting the Bennet sisters."

"Because his plans in Meryton were in ruins," said Colonel Forster with a curt nod. "Why confront the Bennet sisters? It would have increased the chances of his capture and had he hurt them, he would have become wanted by more than just you and your cousin."

"The Wickham I know has never been violent," replied Darcy, speaking slowly while thinking. "However that may be, it seems he has changed over the years since I have associated with him. There may be a measure of vindictiveness in his character which was not present before—he always relied on his manners and charm when I knew him."

Colonel Forster nodded. "Despite our conjecture, it seems our quarry has flown. Do you have any suggestion of where he has gone?"

"London," was Darcy's short reply. "There is no other place in which he can conceal himself with so little effort, and his knowledge of the dark underbelly of the city is extensive. If you have a pen and paper, I shall write a letter to my cousin and send it by express."

"If you provide the directions, I shall have one of my men deliver it."

Darcy nodded and sat down at the desk when the required implements were produced. The letter was short and to the point and was soon passed to the captain, who left to see to its disposition. When he had left, Darcy turned back to Colonel Forster.

"I should have prevented Wickham from leaving. If I had, he would be in our custody right now."

"Do not blame yourself, sir. Wickham might have been armed, and any attempt at capturing him might have resulted in the loss of life."

It was a factor Darcy had not considered. "I suspect my cousin will come to Meryton to see if he can learn anything of Wickham's time here or his future plans."

Colonel Forster grimaced but nodded. "There is little for him to discover, I fear, for Wickham has spoken little of himself. Even his group of friends know little of him, and Denny, who was acquainted with him before, has told me Wickham was closemouthed about his history. With his manners and his bearing, he had always impressed us as a gentleman's son, though his behavior often proved such suppositions a lie."

"That is his greatest asset," said Darcy with a nod. "He wishes to be a gentleman, but even more, he wishes for unending riches. The manners he displays to the world are nothing more than a pretense he can use to forward his selfish desires."

"I hope we find him, Mr. Darcy, for a man such as he does great damage to our society."

"I cannot agree more," said Darcy, reaching out his hand and grasping the colonel's in a tight grip. "But I should leave you now, for

I suspect you have much to do, and I promised I would return to speak
to Mr. Bennet."

"And I shall set in motion a further search for Wickham. It may be
futile, but we should make the attempt."

Darcy nodded and turned to depart. Perhaps he had missed the
chance to capture Wickham, but he was much closer to it now than he
had been yesterday. Oh, yes—they were now so close Darcy could
almost imagine the expression on the face of the cur as he languished
behind bars where he belonged.

Near the outskirts of London, a rider whipped his horse ever faster,
caring little for the hard blowing of the beast. George Wickham had no
thought in mind but escaping the wrath of the colonel of the regiment
and, even more importantly, putting himself beyond the reach of
Darcy and his vengeful cousin.

Darcy! The name filled Wickham's mouth with bile, the revulsion
of it causing his eyesight to turn a murderous red. How had rotten
chance brought the man to the location in which he had concealed
himself? Would that he had remembered his pistol at that moment and
shot the sanctimonious bastard, forever putting him out of Wickham's
misery!

But, no, it was best he had not allowed his passions to rule him.
Though he would like nothing more than to repay Darcy for all the
misery he had caused over the years, the killing would forever put
Fitzwilliam on his scent like a bloodhound. Had he killed Darcy, he
knew he would never be free of the man's cousin, and if there was one
man in all the world that Wickham feared, it was the burly cavalry
colonel. Furthermore, Wickham had resolved to leave the regiment
before Darcy had even arrived, and though vengeance on those insipid
Bennet sisters would have been satisfying, it was better he had not
given another angry father reason to pursue him.

The anger still simmered, but with these thoughts, Wickham was
better able to put it in perspective, and he allowed his laboring mount
to slow as a result. Wickham had underestimated Darcy. The man had
always been eager to wash his hands of Wickham in the past, and he
had thought he would do the same this time, notwithstanding
Wickham's knowledge of Fitzwilliam's search for him. It was also
evident that marriage to the daughter of a gentleman would no longer
be any protection.

The question was then what Wickham's next move should be. If
Wickham managed to make a marriage to a woman in possession of

an estate, he would still come to Darcy and Fitzwilliam's attention, even if he married a woman with the smallest estate in the remotest part of the kingdom. That suggested the only choice was to leave England forever. The notion of leaving England did not distress Wickham as much as he might have thought it would. While playing the part of a gentleman was amusing, Wickham could get along well in any society where there was ample money, amusement, and the chance to gamble occasionally. Willing young females were plentiful wherever one went, after all.

But Wickham would not go into exile with nothing to sustain him. The chances of wealth in the New World were better than they were in England, he thought, but he still did not wish to go without something. Fortunately, Wickham was a clever, devious sort of man, and the first glimmers of a plan had begun to burn in his mind. The details were as yet unclear, but a little thought would flesh them out nicely.

As the first order of business, he would need to stop somewhere and rid himself of the blasted uniform which would make him an easy target of anyone searching for him, and then sell the horse he had ridden to exhaustion. That infusion of funds would sustain him while he waited for his plans to come to fruition. Then, he could make the rest of his way to London, where he could stay where he usually did. A few contacts later, and his plans would be set, waiting for the correct time to spring his trap. Then he would have what he needed to begin a new life in a new place. And Fitzwilliam Darcy would pay for interfering in his life.

CHAPTER XIII

$\mathcal{T}$he estate of Longbourn was no more than a mile from Meryton, and Darcy's mount made short work of it at a swift canter. It was a pleasant country, he decided, though in his view, it could not be the equal of Derbyshire and Pemberley. But the land was good here, and it was fertile, the landowners of the area coaxing the bounty of their estates with a gentle hand, unlike the wrestling which was often required in the rockier north.

Longbourn itself seemed to be a small estate, likely comprising the home farm and perhaps two or three tenants. But as he rode up the drive and inspected the house before him, Darcy noted how everything was kept in good repair, the pastoral nature of the scene and the trees, now bereft of their summer greenery, gently waving in the breeze, spoke of the solidity of those who called it their home. His impression was of a neighborhood populated by country squires and no one of any prominence. Despite his expectation of their countrified manners, Darcy was not fooled into thinking like Caroline Bingley, for he knew people such as these were salt of the earth.

It was a little surprising that one of the young ladies was already waiting for him on the portico, watching him with expressive eyes, seasoned with gratitude. Though thoughts of vengeance had occupied him at their first meeting, Darcy studied her, noting the diminutive stature, the lightness of her figure, the mahogany of her locks tied behind her head, and the intelligence which shone from her expressive eyes. Those eyes were fine, as fine as any Darcy had ever seen. She was, altogether a picture of youthful hope and happiness, though tempered with a sure knowledge of the nature of the world. Given her family's recent association, Darcy suspected they had learned that lesson painfully.

"Miss Bennet," greeted Darcy when he dismounted. "I see you have anticipated my coming."

The woman regarded him, cataloguing him unless Darcy missed his guess. There seemed to be a measure of instinctive trust between them, no doubt a result of the circumstances of their meeting. But she did not trust him implicitly — Darcy knew he would be required to prove his constancy to this exquisite woman.

"I have been watching the drive for your arrival," said she at length. Then she directed an impish smile at him, her eyes sparkling. "But I must correct your misapprehension — the title 'Miss Bennet' belongs to my sister Jane. I am naught but the second daughter of the house, while my sister Mary is the third. Should you wish to flee, I suggest you do so at once, for I have *two more* younger sisters!"

A delighted laugh escaped Darcy's lips. An exquisite woman? A rare gem? It was becoming clear to him she was all of that and more.

"Shall you protect me from your predatory sisters, Miss Elizabeth? If so, I shall be content to take my chances."

The laughter in her eyes never abated. "I can make no promises, sir. Though Jane will inherit this estate and is thus secure, the rest of us must shift for ourselves. You seem to be a man of such substance — it would be foolhardy for me to allow you to escape."

In the past, the mercenary attitudes of young ladies had always disgusted Darcy — not to mention similar behavior from not a few young men. This woman, jesting of the subject openly, informed Darcy she was not one of their ilk. An idle thought crossed his mind, and he wondered what it would be like to earn her regard. Akin to the sweetest ambrosia, he imagined.

"I have informed My father of what happened on the path with Mr. Wickham, sir. Perhaps I should take you to him?"

The reminder of the business at hand refocused Darcy's attention, and he pushed thoughts of this woman to the side for the moment. As he did so, he could not help but marvel they had entered his mind at all. Their acquaintance was only a few minutes old, after all!

Darcy agreed, and a stable hand appeared, taking charge of his mount. The vestibule, to which she led him, was also clean and tidy, a few treasured items displayed with great care. It was a home, one lovingly maintained and tended to, one which spoke to pride in one's possessions and responsibility for one's stewardship. The door to which the young lady led him was situated a short distance down a hall, away from the entrance, and after Miss Elizabeth knocked, she led him into a spacious room, decorated with a large desk and several bookshelves, stuffed with a bounty of books Darcy had never seen at such a small estate.

"Mr. Darcy, I presume?" asked the gentleman who stood and rounded the desk. He reached out his hand, which Darcy clasped in greeting. "I am Henry Bennet, Elizabeth's father and proprietor of Longbourn."

"Mr. Bennet," said Darcy. "I am Fitzwilliam Darcy of Pemberley in Derbyshire. It is a pleasure to meet you."

"The feeling is mutual and doubly so," replied Mr. Bennet. "Having heard my daughters' accounts of what occurred this morning, I suspect I am in your debt for having prevented their harm."

"It is nothing, Mr. Bennet. I am relieved I could provide assistance, for I know much of Wickham and have been searching for him for some time now."

"Yes, Lizzy mentioned as much." Mr. Bennet's eyes found his daughter and he smiled. "I suspect we will learn as much as we wish concerning Mr. Wickham, Lizzy. Perhaps you would prefer to stay, rather than hearing it from me later?"

"If that is acceptable," said Miss Elizabeth, her eyes finding Darcy.

"I have no objection," replied Darcy, interested to see how this man included his daughter in their discussions. Most men would have sent her away.

While Darcy and Miss Elizabeth were settling themselves on chairs in front of the desk, Mr. Bennet stepped from the room, returning a moment later. He took his own seat behind his desk and regarded Darcy with a speculative eye. It appeared Miss Bennet had received her intelligence from this man.

"I have ordered a tea service, Mr. Darcy, for I expect your revelations will be a dry and dusty business. Perhaps it would be best if you inform us of what you know of Mr. Wickham, after which we will reciprocate by relating the events of the last few months."

Darcy nodded, saying: "I believe I understand Wickham's activities in Meryton from Colonel Forster. But I am willing to share what I know of Wickham."

Marshaling his thoughts, Darcy fell silent for a moment, before he said: "George Wickham has long been known to me. In fact, he is the son of my late father's steward, Mr. Wickham's father having passed on five years ago, within a month of my own father's passing. Living at an estate with few close neighbors, I found myself often in company with Wickham when I was young. We were once the closest of friends.

"While I began to notice Wickham's want of character at a young age and drifted away from him, my father remained his steadfast supporter until his death." Darcy paused and grimaced. "When I look back, I realize I should have informed my father of Wickham's character. I chose not to because my father was already lost in grief because of my mother's untimely death a decade earlier, and Wickham's sunny manners provided him some measure of happiness. Much might have been different if I had not remained silent."

"It is clear you feel it keenly, sir," said Mr. Bennet. "While perhaps you might have judged better and the matter might have had a different ending, I do not know you acted improperly. I might have done the same in your place."

Darcy nodded and continued: "I shall not be explicit as to his vices. Knowing something of him, I suspect you have some knowledge of this already. The material point is that Wickham was educated under my father's auspices and received a bequest after my father's death of one thousand pounds. At the same time, my father recommended in his will that Wickham receive a valuable family living when it became available. I am sure you must apprehend that I had little desire to install a man such as Wickham as a spiritual leader of anyone, let alone those nearest my estate."

When both his companions nodded, Darcy shook his head. "It is fortunate that Wickham had his sights set much higher, for he had no interest in the living. I negotiated an amount in lieu of the preferment which was substantial—far too substantial, to be honest, though it was much less than he demanded."

"How much was it?" asked Mr. Bennet. "If you do not think the question impertinent."

"Three thousand pounds," said Darcy.

The lady by his side gasped. "Four thousand pounds? In the hands of the son of a steward, that must have been a veritable fortune."

"And yet I believe he depleted it in a matter of months," replied Darcy. "You are correct—a single man of prudence could live off the interest if he so chose. A man of diligence, character, and ingenuity could have used it to fund his own future wealth. Wickham did none of these things. His life was one of idleness and dissipation, and I suspect certain illegal activities.

"That is, I believe, where his true depravities began to appear. Though I kept track of him for some time, he has been secretive, and I have never had any proof of his dealings in his quest to acquire a fortune. I believe, however, that gambling four thousand pounds away in a matter of months is the least of his sins."

Darcy paused, painful memories intruding, and considered ending is recitation. But the earnest empathy with which they were both regarding him convinced him they needed to know all, and he was convinced, even on so short an acquaintance, of their trustworthy natures. Thus, he did not shirk and pressed forward.

"Of Wickham's depravities there is not much I can say. But an incident occurred last summer which, if he had succeeded in his designs, would have been injurious to myself and those closest to me. I have in my care a young sister, a dozen years my junior, who became the target of Mr. Wickham's schemes."

Miss Elizabeth gasped again, her hand flying to her mouth as she looked at him in horror. "Why, that is Lydia's age. Surely he would not be so lost to all decency as to take advantage of her!"

"I assure you he was, Miss Elizabeth." Darcy clenched his hand into a fist to control his anger. "To this day, I still do not know what he planned, though I can guess. My sister, you see, was holidaying in Ramsgate with her companion when Mr. Wickham came upon her, seemingly by chance. There was, however, little chance involved – of that I am certain, though I do not know how he discovered her location.

"It is fortunate I had warned my sister of Wickham's character, for she was not taken in by his smooth manners or silver tongue. That day when she returned to the house after meeting him, she dispatched an express to me. That night, however, Wickham was discovered inside the house by a footman. We do not know how he gained access or what he planned, but the footman is one with whom Wickham shares a mutual dislike."

Darcy paused and grinned, though he was certain it was little more than baring his teeth. "Thompson has reason to resent Wickham and gave him a good beating when he discovered him in the house. Even so, Wickham succeeded in escaping. Though I have no direct knowledge, I suspect Wickham's object was my sister's bedchamber, his intentions such that I could only shudder at the thought of her fortunate escape."

"Oh, Mr. Darcy," said Miss Elizabeth, shaking her head, her distress unfeigned. "I hope your sister has not been affected by this betrayal?"

Touched by her concern, Darcy directed a smile at her. "I will not say it was not a shock, for Georgiana possessed fond memories of her childhood when Wickham would play with her. It has been difficult, but she was not hurt, and her recovery has been swift. Georgiana has become warier of those she meets, as a consequence, but in the end, I think she will be well."

"I am happy to hear it," murmured Miss Elizabeth.

"And you have been looking for Wickham ever since," said Mr. Bennet.

"Yes," replied Darcy. "Today was the first time I have set eyes on him since long before the day he accosted my sister at Ramsgate and the first direct knowledge I have had of him since the summer. Though the memory of my father's regard for him induced me to leniency, I can no longer ignore such perfidy. It has been my thought when he is apprehended, I would see him transported to the penal colony at Botany Bay. My uncle, you see, is an earl, and knows of Wickham from both myself and my cousin. With his assistance, Wickham can be shipped away from England within days of his capture."

It had long been Darcy's habit to watch those to whom he revealed his connections to determine their reactions—an uncle who was an earl was not an insignificant relation, after all. Mr. Bennet and Miss Elizabeth made no response to his disclosure. On the contrary, they turned the conversation to other matters.

"Given your presence here and your failure to mention Mr. Wickham's current disposition," said Mr. Bennet, "might I assume he has eluded you?"

"He did," replied Darcy shortly. "It appears he was already planning his escape, for he did not return to the encampment after he ran. Moreover, a horse belonging to the regiment was reported missing." Darcy's eyes darted to Miss Elizabeth. "It seemed he planned to decamp soon after he had accosted your daughters."

By this time Darcy felt he had enough measure of this woman to understand the extent of her mettle. Though the tightness of her lips suggested she understood what he did not say, she made no other response.

"The question is, will he return?"

Mr. Bennet's words seemed to hover in the air, his concern evident in his furrowed brow. Upon thinking on it for a moment, Darcy shook his head.

"I do not believe so, Mr. Bennet. In fact, now that the chance of catching your daughter in his net has failed, my presence here will ensure that he will avoid the neighborhood. Though I would counsel prudence, I do not believe there is any danger to your family at present."

With a shaken head Mr. Bennet turned a mournful look on his daughter. "The strands of life are woven in such a manner that it is impossible to know how a change in one of them may affect the rest. If I had not ended the entail and made Jane the heir of this estate, Mr. Wickham would not have paid any heed to any of you."

"That may be true, Papa," said Miss Elizabeth, "but we are secure because Jane will inherit. Her birthright may bring unwelcome attention, it is true, yet I do not think we are the worse off because of it."

The fond look Mr. Bennet gave on his daughter displayed the man's regard for her, warranted, in Darcy's opinion. "Dearest Lizzy. You always see through to the heart of the matter."

"You ended an entail?" asked Darcy with some interest. "Entails are rarely used because of their vulnerability."

A laugh was followed with a jovial: "A backwater neighborhood, are we not? I dislike town and do not go there, a trait inherited from my father, and he, from his father. As my brother, who serves as my solicitor for most matters, has been a small-town attorney all his life, none of us knew this until he discovered it about seven years ago. As I have no sons, the support of my family was always a concern—now, I know I can ensure their care when I am gone, which gives me much relief."

"That is understandable," replied Darcy. The information confirmed Darcy's supposition that the Bennet sisters would not have much dowry, other than the eldest. The thought wormed through his head that this woman, at least, was worth much more than a dowry might have provided. As it was, Darcy knew it was premature in the extreme to be harboring such thoughts, so he shunted them to the side.

"Then I confess to curiosity about one more matter, Mr. Darcy," said Mr. Bennet. "Though you have been of great assistance to us today, I still have no knowledge of you or from whence you came. How did you happen to be here, sir?"

Darcy startled and began to laugh. "That is a great jest, Mr. Bennet! I am amazed you have credited my tale, though you still do not even know who I am."

"It was easy to believe," said Miss Elizabeth, though he noted her interested glance.

"I thank you, Miss Elizabeth. At present, I am staying at Netherfield Park, which I believe borders your estate to the east. My close friend, Charles Bingley, has leased the property. We arrived in the area only yesterday."

"Indeed?" asked Mr. Bennet. "Then you have my congratulations, Mr. Darcy, for effecting your arrival without exciting the gossip of the neighborhood. As my wife is foremost among their number, I know she has not heard a whisper of it, for she has not mentioned it to me!"

Darcy laughed. "In fact, we planned to avoid detection. Bingley, you see, was delayed by a matter of important business which arose, else we would have come before Michaelmas."

"That was the rumor at the time, yes," replied Mr. Bennet.

"Then did you set out without sending word and without the housekeeper preparing for your arrival?" Miss Elizabeth clucked her disapproval. "Mrs. Nichols must have been put out with you all."

"When you meet my friend, you will agree he is capable of just such impulsive behavior. But, in fact, he sent word the night before, and as the house was previously made ready, we deemed it likely it would be no imposition. Given the usual state of gossip in the country, I think it is making its way through the neighborhood even now."

As if on cue, the sound of a loud knocking on the door interrupted their discussion, and Mrs. Bennet bustled into the room when Mr. Bennet gave his permission. It seemed she did not notice the presence of the unknown gentleman, for she addressed her husband.

"Mr. Bennet!" said she. "I have just had it from Mrs. Long that the new tenant of Netherfield has finally come. It is said they arrived, almost as thieves in the night, and that Mr. Bingley has brought a large party of friends."

"Only one friend, Madam," said Darcy, rising to bow to the matron.

The gentleman and his daughter chuckled at the expression of stupefaction with which she greeted him. At the same time, Mr. Bennet arose and greeted his wife with affection, turning and gesturing at Darcy.

"Please allow me to introduce Mr. Fitzwilliam Darcy to your acquaintance, Mrs. Bennet. Mr. Darcy is a friend to Mr. Bingley, who is the new tenant at Netherfield."

"I am pleased to make your acquaintance, Mrs. Bennet," said Darcy, speaking kindly to put her at ease while bowing to her hasty curtsey. "In fact, at present, I am Bingley's only guest, though his sister is also in residence. At some later time, I believe he expects his elder sister and her husband to join us."

"Oh!" said Mrs. Bennet, with somewhat less than full coherence. "But if you are all only just arrived, it must be difficult for Mr. Bingley's sister. Shall you not come to dinner at Longbourn? Tomorrow evening would be perfect if you are not otherwise engaged."

Darcy was charmed. Her reaction to his unexpected presence suggested she was flighty, unlike the obviously intelligent Mr. Bennet. While procuring two single gentlemen for her daughters might interest her, he thought she was more genuinely interested in knowing them, and perhaps being of service. As such, Darcy had little difficulty in conditionally accepting her invitation.

"I shall speak with Bingley when I return to Netherfield. However, as we know no one in the neighborhood, I cannot imagine we are engaged for tomorrow evening. After consulting with my friend, we shall be certain to send a reply."

"Then I shall look forward to it," said Mrs. Bennet. "But now I should leave you again. I am pleased to make your acquaintance, Mr. Darcy."

The woman curtseyed and let herself from the room, though the look she shot at her daughter was questioning. Miss Elizabeth smiled and nodded at her mother, which seemed to satisfy the elder woman — she did not attempt to induce her daughter to depart with her.

"In fact," said Darcy, turning to Mr. Bennet, "if *you* are not engaged, perhaps you will ride to Netherfield with me? Bingley is a good man, and eager to make the acquaintance of all and sundry. I should be happy to perform the office."

"An excellent notion, Mr. Darcy," said Mr. Bennet. "I would be delighted. If you will wait for a few moments, I will join you directly."

What Elizabeth thought of Mr. Darcy she could not quite determine. It was clear, given his reaction to Mr. Wickham, his assistance, and his subsequent return to Longbourn, that he was a good man and a conscientious one. Reserve appeared to be a facet of his character, though he had spoken without hesitation to all the Bennets to whom he had been introduced.

It was also clear he was a prominent man, for if his clothing and bearing did not mark him as such, the revelation of his uncle being an earl would have removed all doubt. Though Elizabeth knew something of what happened between men and women, the feelings and sensations coursing through her provoked by this tall and handsome man were new and confusing.

"I hope you and your sisters are quite recovered from this morning's confrontation with Wickham," said Mr. Darcy as they were waiting together for Mr. Bennet to return.

"Yes, we are," said Elizabeth. "My eldest sister found it fatiguing and retired to her room soon after our return. Mary, however, you can hear playing the pianoforte."

Darcy nodded, having noted the sound of the instrument. "It sounds like she is proficient."

"You may have not judged so had you come two years earlier," said Elizabeth with a laugh. "Mary is technically proficient, but she used to have an unfortunate tendency to choose pieces which were beyond her level of skill. My father sent her to London to my uncle's house, where she was provided with a master, who assisted not only her feeling for the music but also what it was appropriate for her to play. She has improved very much."

"And do you play, Miss Elizabeth?"

"I do not play so well as Mary." Again Elizabeth laughed. "There are far too many activities I enjoy to allow me the practice time I require. Consequently, while I play, I would not wish to excite your anticipation, when the reality will be much less than you expect."

"You must be much too modest," said Mr. Darcy. "Perhaps I shall have the pleasure of hearing you tomorrow evening?"

"We shall see," said Elizabeth. "Does your sister play?"

Mr. Darcy showed her a fond smile. "Sometimes I think Georgiana does little else. There are few things she enjoys more than music, and though I will confess to bias, I must say she is quite skilled."

"Then I shall hope to make her acquaintance, Mr. Darcy. She sounds delightful. Mary, in particular, would appreciate making her acquaintance, for music is one of her passions too."

Mr. Bennet's arrival prevented Mr. Darcy from responding, but his smile informed her he was not displeased with her suggestion. The horses were soon brought around, and the gentlemen departed for Netherfield, leaving the second daughter of the house full of thoughts of Mr. Darcy.

CHAPTER XIV

*B*ingley was his usual self when introduced to Mr. Bennet. A gregarious and friendly man, Bingley was eager to meet and approve of everyone he met and bask in their returned friendship. Though this trait had sometimes irked Darcy in the past, in this instance he approved without reserve, for he favored the Bennet family himself. The meeting was brief, as Mr. Bennet informed them he could not stay long, but they met long enough for each man's friendship for the other to be assured.

"We would be pleased to accept your invitation to dine at your home," said Bingley as Mr. Bennet delivered the request in person. "It is good of you to invite us on so short an acquaintance."

"Not at all," said Mr. Bennet with evident pleasure. "In fact, I believe it will cause great joy in my home. My wife and daughters will, I am sure you apprehend, take great pleasure in informing their friends of their early intelligence of your party."

Bingley laughed, as did Darcy, appreciating the wry sense of humor Mr. Bennet had displayed. "Then we could not possibly decline. You may tell your family we will be delighted to attend."

"Excellent!" said Mr. Bennet. He rose to his feet and extended his hand, which Bingley accepted. "Until tomorrow."

When Mr. Bennet had mounted his horse and departed, Darcy indicated to Bingley he still had a matter to discuss with him. Miss Bingley was not in evidence—Darcy did not even know if she was aware of their visitor—so it seemed like an opportune moment. Thus, Bingley led the way back to his study, where Darcy informed him of the morning's excitement.

"Wickham in Hertfordshire!" exclaimed Bingley. "That is a strange coincidence, my friend. I would wager you had no notion of seeing him here."

"I did not," replied Darcy. "Had I met him with no others present, I would have chased him down and turned him over to the magistrate. As it was, I was forced to ensure the ladies' disposition before I could see to Wickham, and he fled in the interim."

Though Bingley appeared interested at the mention of the ladies, he concentrated his attention on the subject at hand. "What can be done about him?"

Darcy sighed and leaned back in his chair. "At present, I do not think anything can be done. Wickham is slippery and adept at eluding us, it appears. Colonel Forster dispatched one of his men to London with a letter for my cousin, but I suspect it will anger Fitzwilliam rather than assist. Wickham has been in Hertfordshire for more than a month, and in Brighton for some time before, and all the while Fitzwilliam was searching for him in London."

"Do you expect him to come to Hertfordshire?"

"Perhaps," replied Darcy. "It is possible he will wish to interview Wickham's friends in the regiment. There is little to be found, but Fitzwilliam is stubborn."

"I believe he would prefer to call it meticulous," said Bingley with a grin.

"Whatever you call it, I doubt it will allow him to ignore this news of Wickham's whereabouts. I do not know when he will join us here, but I believe we will see him before long."

"Then perhaps I should inform Caroline, so she may have a room prepared."

Though he had not intended it, Darcy grimaced at the mention of Bingley's sister, which prompted a laugh from his friend. "What a pickle this is! It is less than two days since we have come to the country, and yet you are already eager to be out of my sister's company."

"I offer my apologies, Bingley," said Darcy, embarrassed at being so caught out.

"There is no need," said Bingley, waving away his concern. "You forget, my friend—though you have only known Caroline for about two years, I have had the pleasure of her acquaintance for over twenty. My sister's character is not a mystery, I assure you."

"Perhaps, but I would not insult your sister, and that means controlling myself, even when not in her company."

Bingley shook his head. "It is just like you, Darcy, to blame yourself for reacting, when it is my sister who provokes it by her behavior whenever she is in your company."

"Do you know when the Hursts will arrive?"

"Hurst has not been explicit as to their plans," replied Bingley. "But I expect it should not be long. He and his father only tolerate each other's company, and I expect they will reach the limits of their patience before long. But I would not count on them for relief—Louisa agrees with everything Caroline says, you know."

"Well do I know it, my friend. But at least she will provide a buffer, and another person in residence who can absorb a little of your sister's attention."

"I hope you will not retreat from her," said Bingley. "I have been anticipating our residence here and would not wish you to depart early."

"No," replied Darcy. "I can manage your sister." In his mind's eye, he was thinking of a pretty, vivacious miss he had met only that day. It was unlike Darcy to think of a woman in such a manner, but there was little desire in him to retreat from Hertfordshire before learning more of her, even if he was required to fend off Miss Bingley as a consequence.

"Doubtless you can," replied Bingley. The man hesitated, his manner introspective, until he voiced his thoughts: "Tell me, what were your impressions of the Bennets?"

"Or perhaps more accurately, you wish to know what I thought of the daughters!" Darcy laughed when Bingley appeared shamefaced. "I know you, my friend. In answer to your question, they appeared to be pretty, genteel sort of ladies. The eldest and the third daughter I met only briefly and was preoccupied at the time, though I can tell you the eldest was pretty and blonde, while the youngest was smaller of stature and dark of hair.

"Miss Elizabeth—the second daughter—was present when I spoke to her father, allowing me to gain more of an impression of her. The resemblance is striking between them, though Miss Elizabeth is not so tall as her sister and, like the youngest, possesses darker hair. She also impressed me with her intelligence and courage. The family, I believe, will be well worth knowing."

Bingley regarded at him and seemed to have some inkling of Darcy's unstated admiration for Miss Elizabeth, but he chose not to say anything. "Then we should inform Caroline of our new acquaintances. Should you possess the stomach for it, I should appreciate your support, for I have little idea of her approbation."

Darcy agreed, and they departed from Bingley's study. A quick question to the housekeeper revealed Miss Bingley's location to the two men, who made their way to the main sitting-room. As they entered, Darcy noted how Miss Bingley's gaze slid past her brother to rest upon Darcy, as it always did when he was present. The sensation of being a side of beef or a haunch of venison was always present, for Darcy well understood the woman's desires and knew they had everything to do with his position in society and wealth and little to do with his person.

"I see you have returned, Mr. Darcy," said Miss Bingley. "The country in this neighborhood cannot be agreeable after the beauties of Derbyshire, but I hope it was tolerable."

"Quite acceptable, Miss Bingley," replied Darcy. "In fact, the district is pleasant and pleasing."

"But you must confess it is nothing to Pemberley."

Darcy could not help but wonder why it was so important to Miss Bingley that he disapprove of the neighborhood. Or perhaps he did— her stated desire for her brother to lease or purchase an estate in Derbyshire would bring her closer to *him* and Pemberley, in her mind. How that would bring her closer to eliciting a proposal, when he had given her no inclination toward her in the last two years, he could not quite understand.

"Is one not always convinced of the superiority of his own home?" asked Darcy, the rhetorical note, he hoped, would not invite reply. "Yes, I prefer Derbyshire. But there is nothing objectionable in what I saw this morning. Quite the contrary."

Before Miss Bingley could respond, and Darcy was uncertain she would, Bingley spoke up. "It seems, Caroline, you will get your first taste of what the neighborhood has to offer, for we have received an invitation to dinner."

"An invitation to dinner!" echoed Miss Bingley, her surprise turning to a sneer. "I am all astonishment. In fact, I had little notion you had made any acquaintances."

"It was Darcy's doing," said Bingley, her focus once again on Darcy providing Bingley with amusement. It was all Darcy could do to avoid shaking his head — Bingley did enjoy provoking his sister thus.

"*Your* doing, sir?" asked Miss Bingley, a definite note of disbelief in her tone. "Might I suppose someone of the neighborhood accosted you as you rode through the fields?"

"I was not put upon, Miss Bingley," replied Darcy. "I met one of the locals during my ride and was introduced to his wife and certain members of his family. Seeing we are newly arrived in the neighborhood, the family was good enough to invite us to dine with them, hoping to assist us in settling in."

Miss Bingley sniffed with her usual disdain. "Though I would not call the staff here adequate, I have brought the servants and meals up to an acceptable level — it is more than we will find anywhere else. It will not be possible to expect the level of cuisine we would find at Pemberley, but I hope it will be sufficient."

"More than sufficient," replied Darcy.

His compliment provoked an unwarranted measure of preening as if he had praised her culinary skills to the sky. Bingley noted it too, for Darcy saw his friend's grin. Perhaps it was not proper for him to take such amusement from his sister's continual attempts to impress, but with a sister such as Miss Bingley, Darcy supposed Bingley must take his amusement where he could.

Then Miss Bingley's expression altered, like the sudden change of wind from a soft westerly spring breeze to a cold northern gale. The frown she sported was fixed upon him, and Darcy could sense a hint of speculation behind it.

"It *is* curious how you made the acquaintance of a local family so quickly." She paused and sniffed. "Though I would hesitate to dignify any of them with a discernment necessary to the task, I suppose they must have seen you for the prominent man you are and imposed upon you."

"Nothing could be further from the truth, Miss Bingley," replied Darcy. "It was a pleasure to make their acquaintance."

"It was?" asked she, her tone and narrowed eyes informing him she thought him to be dissembling. "And how did this fortuitous meeting come to pass?"

"In the usual manner, Miss Bingley," replied Darcy, keeping his tone and manner bland. Under no circumstances would Darcy share his intrigues with George Wickham, nor did he wish her to know of Wickham's interest in Georgiana.

"Does it matter how Darcy met them?" asked Bingley, deflecting his sister's attention. "What matters is that he has met them, and as we came without fanfare, these are the first locals we have met. I, for one, am eager to accept their invitation. It shows an affability which bodes well for the future."

"As always," was Miss Bingley's derisive rejoinder, "you are far too apt to associate with anyone you meet, Charles. We know nothing of these people. How can you be certain they measure up to our standards?"

"Darcy has met them," said Bingley, almost causing Darcy to break out in laughter. "Or do you question his judgment?"

Miss Bingley's eyes flicked to Darcy and then away. When she spoke again, Darcy was unsurprised she chose to ignore her brother's statement.

"No, it will not do, Charles. You must send a reply to these people declining the invitation. It would not do for us to encourage intimacy with those who may be little more than lowborn louts."

"Would you insult our closest neighbors?" asked Bingley. While Bingley's tone was reasonable, Darcy—who apparently knew the man better than his sister—knew he was not about to give way to her condescending dismissal of his new neighbors. Miss Bingley thought she ruled her brother, that he was weak-willed and easily led. But Darcy knew that Bingley did not often give way to his sister when he felt he was correct.

"I care not if they are insulted," snapped Miss Bingley. "The material point is we cannot be seen to associate with those who are not acceptable."

"Perhaps you should meet them before you pronounce them unacceptable."

"There is no need for me to meet them. I am highly conscious of the quality of people who inhabit such neighborhoods as this. If you are not careful, they will entrap you, seeking to attach you to their insipid daughters to raise them from the squalor in which they live. A connection to you would be quite a feather in the cap of anyone living in this neighborhood."

Though her words were ostensibly directed at her brother, Miss Bingley's eyes flicked to Darcy for an instant, one so quick he might have missed it had he not been looking for it. It was all the reason Darcy needed to insert himself once again into the conversation.

"There is no reason to fear the family I met, Miss Bingley. While they are not among the wealthy of society, they were quite acceptable."

"How could you know it on such a short acquaintance?" challenged Miss Bingley.

"Do you suspect me of lacking discernment?" asked Darcy.

Darcy's statement was uttered with a disinterested air in the certainty she would backtrack. He was correct, for she assumed that false smile and syrupy sweet tone she used when attempting to cajole him to her way of thinking. That it had not yet worked had not penetrated her conscious—Darcy found it more than a little patronizing.

"Of course not, Mr. Darcy, for there is no more discriminating man than you. It is merely my thought that those possessing of baser natures, or even less refined manners, will attempt to hide what they truly are. After nothing more than one morning's acquaintance, we cannot be certain, and thus, we should step back a little, force them to prove to us what quality of people they are."

When she finished her pretty little speech, Miss Bingley sat back and regarded him, a half smirk playing about her lips, thinking she had won the argument. Though Darcy did not consider it an argument—for there was no chance of her persuading him—he was not about to allow her the upper hand.

"One can learn much of others if the opportunity to observe is truly taken, Miss Bingley." Darcy paused, noting the smile which had run away from her face, enjoying the opportunity to pierce her conceit. "Regarding the Bennet family, the estate is well maintained and prosperous, the master diligent and welcoming, the mistress gracious, and the daughters I met were everything proper and lovely."

"*Daughters*, you say?"

"Yes," replied Darcy. "I was introduced to the eldest three, all of whom are demure and interesting women, and though I did not meet them, there are also two younger girls."

"*Five* daughters?" demanded Miss Bingley, her eyebrows rising in disbelief. "That is singular. If there is no son to inherit, what will happen to the estate when this Mr. Bennet is gone?"

"That is hardly a question I could ask, given the newness of my acquaintance with the family," said Darcy, though knowing well who was to be the next heir. "It is not uncommon for a man to pass an estate down to one of his daughters."

"I suppose," said Miss Bingley. "But I still think we should allow our knowledge of the family to develop naturally, without a precipitous invitation which will tie us to an acquaintance too early."

"There is nothing more to discuss, Caroline," said Bingley, though it was clear he was enjoying how Darcy had overcome all Miss Bingley's objections. "We have been invited, and we will not offend them by rejecting their kindness. We shall go to dinner tomorrow."

Miss Bingley, however, ignored her brother, continuing to look at Darcy, as if she thought he could overrule him. Thus, it seemed to Darcy that it was time to deliver the coup de grâce.

"Again, Miss Bingley, I would remind you the Bennet family *are* gentlefolk. Whatever their situation in life, they own land, and while I do not know the extent of their history, it has been of several generations at the very least. In matters such as this, their *birth* gives them legitimacy, as do their present circumstances. There are many in society who pretend to be more than they are, but I am confident the Bennets are not among their number."

Miss Bingley could not misunderstand Darcy's inference. The unfortunate thing about it was that Darcy was certain she would convince herself he had meant something else before the end of the evening. In the end, it seemed her objections had been quelled by his final words, which was all he wanted.

"Then it seems as if we have no choice." Miss Bingley rose and gave him a brazen look. "As always, we shall trust in your judgment, Mr. Darcy. For now, however, I must see to the servants to ensure my instructions regarding tonight's dinner have been followed."

When she had exited the room and the door closed behind her, Bingley turned to Darcy and regarded him with a grin. "You know she has gone to ensure a stupendous dinner. It will be a competition to ensure the fare we receive tonight is far superior to what our hosts will provide tomorrow."

Darcy shook his head, knowing his friend was correct. "She may as well not bother. I have sat at her table before and have no expectation it is anything other than worthy of praise. Should tomorrow's meal be excellent, it will be no reflection on your sister."

"But she will not see it that way."

"No, I suppose she will not."

It had long been Mr. Bennet's custom to tease his wife and children about certain matters of which they had an interest but Bennet possessed the knowledge. The game was not malicious and, instead, forced them to use whatever wiles they possessed to cajole the information out of him. While it provided him much amusement, he thought they considered it more of an exasperation, even while they played along with it. Eventually, however, the information would be vouchsafed, and they would be satisfied.

The knowledge of Mr. Bingley was an example of this, for the moment he returned, his family subjected him to the inquisition. Even Lizzy, who had the most knowledge of their morning visitor, was interested to hear of his friend. It was when the family sat down to dinner that Bennet relented.

"Is he tall?" asked Jane

"Is he handsome?" asked Lydia.

"Does he wear a blue jacket?" asked Kitty.

Finally, Mr. Bennet was convinced to acknowledge his defeat, for he laughed and set his knife and fork down on the table. "I am sure I am unable to discern whether Mr. Bingley his handsome, Lydia," Lydia frowned at his response, "but he seemed pleasantly featured to me."

Turning to Kitty, he said: "Today he was wearing a green jacket—I am sorry to disappoint you, Kitty. And, yes, he is tall, Jane, though not as tall as his friend Darcy."

Lydia leaned back and crossed her arms, throwing vexed looks at her father and eldest sisters. "I am still quite put out that I was not introduced to this Mr. Darcy. It sounds as if he is a very handsome man."

"There, there, Lydia," said Mrs. Bennet. "We shall all be known to Mr. Darcy and his friends before long."

"Your mother is correct, Lydia, for we have invited Mr. Darcy and his friends to supper with us tomorrow night."

This news was still unknown to all the sisters except Elizabeth, and there was great rejoicing between the two youngest. The older sisters took the news in stride, though Elizabeth's lack of reaction resulted in Jane throwing her a mock glare.

"He shall bring *all* of his friends?" demanded Lydia.

"There are rumored to be many," fretted Kitty. "How shall we accommodate them all?"

"Oh, stuff and nonsense, Kitty!" exclaimed Mrs. Bennet. "There is little truth to be had in such gossip. Mr. Darcy—and a gentlemanly man he is—informed me himself that there is only Mr. Bingley, Mr. Darcy himself, and Mr. Bingley's sister, though he mentioned that another sister and her husband would join them soon after."

"Papa, since they are new to the neighborhood, you *must* allow us to attend," said Lydia. "How else are we to make their acquaintance?"

"There is nothing your father *must* do, Lydia," said Mrs. Garret, who had remained silent until that point.

"But surely *you* think we are ready to attend a simple dinner party with neighbors," said Lydia, Kitty nodding by her side."

"What *I* think is immaterial," said Mrs. Garret, fixing Lydia with a pointed look. "Your father will decide."

Though both girls turned to Bennet with beseeching eyes, he did not immediately respond, instead considering all that had come to pass. It seemed only the day before that Lydia had been a girl following after her elder sisters, and now she was on the cusp of being a young woman. Though the years had seemed to pass with idyllic slowness when Bennet had been a boy, the cares of an adult hastened the passage of time, such that he often wondered where it had all gone. Bennet found he missed those times when the girls had been just that—girls whose greatest concerns were the games they would play, their dolls and other toys, and the pretty dresses and ribbons they wore. Some of those concerns persisted but now they were becoming focused on young men. Bennet did not know how he would withstand losing them all.

"Let us table this discussion for another time," said Bennet, smiling at his youngest. "If you attend to your studies tomorrow, perhaps we might find a place for you at the table."

Both youngest girls gave their solemn promise to learn well the following day, though Bennet well knew how promises could fade in the face of whatever interesting matter crossed their minds. Both girls were social, and would do as they promised if only to ensure they were allowed the amusement. High-spirited they were, but their training had given them a sense of what was proper and what was not. They only needed some opportunity to practice that which they already knew.

CHAPTER XV

A morning of study, it seemed, was nothing less than a punishment for young girls intent upon taking part in the imagined wonders of an evening in company. Being of a social disposition herself, Elizabeth could well understand their desire to meet new and interesting people, though she thought it was also due to their desire to sigh and bat their eyelashes at handsome young gentlemen. Unfortunately, the application of their excitement which manifested in continuous chatter designed to avoid returning to their studies was ill-judged.

"I cannot wait to meet our new neighbors," said Lydia with a sigh. It was during the morning meeting, both girls had made themselves comfortable at the breakfast table long after it would normally have been time for them to retreat from it. "How farcical would it be if Mr. Darcy were to fall in love with me and that I, the youngest, were to marry first?"

Kitty followed along with Lydia's subsequent giggles and exclaimed: "Or if Mr. Bingley should fall at *my* feet!"

"It seems to me," said Mr. Bennet, "that you should both reconsider this eagerness to marry early. After all, I should think you would prefer to come out in due time and be the center of attention, as your elder sisters were before you."

Mr. Bennet looked kindly at the two youngest, who appeared contemplative, and added: "Besides, given what I saw of Mr. Darcy, I suspect he might prefer your elder sister." When Elizabeth regarded him, surprised he would make such a declaration, Mr. Bennet said: "I detected a great deal of interest in you, Lizzy, though he is a reticent man who does not display his emotions openly."

"I saw nothing of the kind," said Elizabeth. "Mr. Darcy was being polite."

"If you are to marry Mr. Darcy," said Lydia, ignoring Elizabeth's protests, "you must promise me a season in town. I am sure I shall have hundreds of beaux, should I only be introduced to society!"

"Lydia!" snapped Elizabeth. "Do not say such foolish things, for we would not wish Mr. Darcy to come to the wrong conclusion about our family."

It was all for naught. With Mr. Bennet's words, the entire family joined in the teasing, speculating on how long it would be before Mr. Darcy proposed and when she could expect to be married. Knowing they were teasing her in good humor, Elizabeth allowed it, responding with a few comments designed to deflect the fun to others, but with little success.

Mrs. Garret watched this all with no comment, her gaze resting on the youngest Bennets. Having had the woman as a companion and voice of instruction herself, Elizabeth knew she possessed an innate sense of when to take young girls in hand and direct them and when to step back and allow them to make their own mistakes. Kitty and Lydia, in attempting to avoid their lessons, were inviting their father to forbid them from attending that night by their actions. And Elizabeth noted her father looking at the two girls more the longer they stayed.

"This morning's breakfast has gone on longer than usual," said Mr. Bennet a few moments later. While the youngest girls attempted to ignore his words, Elizabeth was certain they were in no doubt of his meaning. Mrs. Garret continued to sip her tea in seeming unconcern.

"Yes, is it not grand to spend such a lovely time in the company of those we love the most?" said Lydia.

"It is," said Mr. Bennet. "But time spent in company *now* may inhibit that which is available later."

Elizabeth was convinced it was Mr. Bennet's offhand tone coupled with how he did not even lower his newspaper which informed the girls he was serious. And suddenly they were eager to retreat above stairs for their morning lessons.

"It *is* grand to sit in this attitude," said Lydia, "but mayhap we should be about our daily tasks."

"We are all awed by your diligence," said Mr. Bennet, again not lowering his newspaper. Within a few moments, the girls had exited the room, accompanied by their companion, who was shaking her head, though in fond amusement. Soon after, the rest of the family went their separate ways.

Though Elizabeth did not find herself as easily distracted as her younger sisters, she might have found the hours remaining until the Netherfield party arrived to be long, indeed. Elizabeth had not thought much about men or her status as an eligible woman, except to note, with some despair, there were few men in the area who interested her and none who would consider her a potential wife. But somehow the meeting with Mr. Darcy had her climbing the heights of imagination, though she was always careful to rein it in.

Thus, when she spied Charlotte walking up the drive to Longbourn, Elizabeth was relieved she would have a visitor with whom she was friendly to keep her occupied for a time. Since Charlotte was interested in speaking of their new neighbors at Netherfield, Elizabeth was uncertain how much relief she was to obtain.

"You have met the new residents of Netherfield?" asked Charlotte with some interest when Mrs. Bennet made some comment to that effect. "That is curious, for my father has only become aware of their presence in the neighborhood this morning, and you know how he is always the first to greet new neighbors. He will be quite put out with you."

Charlotte's words, though perhaps a little more apropos than Sir William might confess, were spoken with a hint of irony which provoked laughter in them all. Mrs. Bennet felt a little satisfaction for finally gaining an acquaintance before Sir William managed it, and Elizabeth was certain Charlotte understood.

"It was my girls who first met our new neighbor," said Mrs. Bennet. They had all agreed to avoid mention of the confrontation with Mr. Wickham, though Elizabeth would inform Charlotte herself before she left today. "What a gentlemanly man! Upon making their acquaintance, he accompanied them back to Longbourn and greeted Mr. Bennet. And when I invited his party to Longbourn to dinner, he was quick to accept."

"And what is the composition of the party?" asked Charlotte. "There have been so many rumors, I might expect a veritable army of friends in attendance."

"The rumors are roundly overstated," said Elizabeth as her sisters laughed at Charlotte's question, so like the family's previous conversation. "There is only Mr. Bingley and his sister and Mr. Darcy."

"And what did you think of him?" asked Charlotte.

"As Mama said," replied Elizabeth, "He was a very gentlemanly man. If Mr. Bingley is anything like he, I am certain they will be charming neighbors."

Charlotte's gaze lingered on Elizabeth for a moment, and Elizabeth wondered what her friend saw. She made no comment and did not tease as Elizabeth might have expected, choosing instead to pursue general conversation. Elizabeth promised to give her friend the first intelligence of the entire family on the morrow, and the subject was dropped for other matters.

When Charlotte sat with them for some time, she rose to leave, Elizabeth accompanying her. They made their way to the back lawn, where Elizabeth informed her friend of the truth of the previous day's events, much to Charlotte's interest. When she finished her tale, Charlotte shook her head.

"It had become obvious that Mr. Wickham was not a good man, but I would not have expected him to be so depraved." Charlotte paused. "Then again, this event only reinforces what we learned of him at your aunt's party."

"That seems to be true. At least Mr. Wickham has now fled, and we shall not be required to concern ourselves with him any longer."

Charlotte turned to give Elizabeth a pointed glance. "There is little to stop Mr. Wickham from returning, Lizzy. I know your habits. If he should come upon you while you are out walking in some remote corner of your father's estate, I shudder to think of what will happen."

"I considered that," said Elizabeth, though not without a little vexation. "As loath as I am to curtail my activities, I suppose I have little choice, as to do otherwise is to invite disaster."

"A sensible approach to this situation is the best approach, Lizzy," replied Charlotte seeming relieved. "I should have thought you would dig in your heels and insist you would not be intimidated."

"I have not said I would not walk, Charlotte," replied Elizabeth, showing her friend a wry smile. "Only that I will take care."

"However you take care, do so with an eye toward not allowing him an opportunity to harm you."

Elizabeth shot a warning look at her friend, who laughed and allowed the matter to drop. When Charlotte spoke again, however,

Elizabeth was not any better pleased by her choice of subject.

"What of this Mr. Darcy?"

"What of him?" asked Elizabeth.

The teasing smile and raised eyebrow with which she looked on Elizabeth provoked an exasperated shake of Elizabeth's head.

"Come now, Lizzy," said Charlotte. "I have always thought you had the best chance to snare any eligible man who came into the area. Have you succeeded in turning his head toward you?"

"More than Jane?" asked Elizabeth.

Regarding Elizabeth with a level look, Charlotte said: "Yes, I know Jane is acclaimed as the most beautiful Bennet daughter, but Jane is also quiet and reticent, while you are *interesting*. While a man may be enamored of Jane's face and figure, a man would be sooner drawn to your wit and vivacity."

"But one only has to look at Jane to see her worth," said Elizabeth. "By your estimation, a gentleman must engage me to understand mine."

A laugh was Charlotte's response, Elizabeth joining her, diverted by their silly conversation. "You may laugh at me if you like. But I have always thought you have your own share of admirers, though you deflect attention to Jane. Now, tell me, Lizzy—what was your impression of this Mr. Darcy?"

"A gentlemanly man to be sure," said Elizabeth. "In other circumstances, I believe I might have found myself drawn to him as you have suggested, though he has given me no indication of returning the sentiment. There is something dignified in his air, but not in any pompous or arrogant way, as if he is every inch the gentleman and will not settle for anything less than the best behavior in himself. In his account of himself, he informed us a little of his family his connection to an earl, which must be in his favor.

"Even in so doing, he did not state it with the intent to impress— instead it was nothing more than a fact. The gentleman is tall and handsome, listens when others speak and responds in a manner which shows his understanding of another's viewpoint, his opinions well-founded and rational. My father thinks highly of him after only one meeting, and not only because he was the means of our protection against whatever devilry Mr. Wickham had in mind. I found him an altogether estimable sort of gentleman.

"There. Will that do?"

Elizabeth had intended her account as a means of silencing her friend's questions and giving her everything she knew of Mr. Darcy.

Far from rendering Charlotte mute, however, the way her friend looked at her told Elizabeth she had much to say. Even so, Charlotte did not speak for several moments.

"It will do nicely, Elizabeth. I had not expected you to be so open. I do so hope I shall receive an invitation to the wedding."

Then, patting Elizabeth's cheek as she turned, Charlotte departed, Elizabeth watching her as she made her way down the drive and from thence to the road which led back toward Lucas Lodge. Left to her thoughts, Elizabeth indulged them for some time after, wandering the wilderness behind the house, though ensuring she did not go far from it. And she wondered about Charlotte's words. More than this, she wondered about her own reaction to Mr. Darcy, though they had only met twice.

The day of the dinner at Longbourn, Darcy found himself pensive. Having been so close to capturing Wickham and ensuring he was gone from Darcy's life forever, he felt the mantle of failure settle over him. More than once he wondered if he should have acted. Now Wickham was on the loose again, secreted somewhere in the slums of London, the situation was the same as it had been before, and Darcy could not but wonder where he might strike next.

Then he would be reminded of the sisters who had captured his attention, allowing Wickham to escape, and he knew his duty was to see to them first, before taking his vengeance. The niggling thought of Wickham, possibly armed and always dangerous, gave him pause, and he knew Bingley was correct. That Wickham would be so depraved as to harm the man whose father he claimed to revere was difficult to fathom, but Darcy could not help but think Wickham had gone far enough down his path of selfishness and infamy that anything was possible.

It was not Darcy's intention to ignore his hosts that day. Bingley, eager to avoid conflict which would arise if his sister continued her campaign to garner Darcy's attention unchecked, suggested a ride that morning. Miss Bingley had shown ill-concealed impatience when they returned, but at least it had allowed him to be away from her company for a time. Then when in the sitting-room with the Bingley siblings, Darcy found himself again distracted, something the woman in question did not fail to notice.

"I wonder at your inattention today, Mr. Darcy," said she after some time of this. Darcy had been sitting with a book in his lap, albeit forgotten, while Miss Bingley chattered on about something. Though he would not confess it aloud, Darcy neither knew nor cared what she had been saying. "One might think your thoughts were miles away from Netherfield."

"You have my apologies, Miss Bingley," said Mr. Darcy. "I have been preoccupied today about some matters of importance."

Miss Bingley suppressed a huff. "Well, at least you are not imagining the delights that await us at our neighbor's estate this evening. Then again, I hardly think delight will be our companion this evening."

The titter which followed her statement irritated Darcy, and he turned back to his book to avoid replying. But Miss Bingley was not willing to allow his attention to slip away again.

"What do you think we shall do to protect our sensibilities, Mr. Darcy? Perhaps a short stay would be advisable."

"My sensibilities are not so fragile that I require preparation to protect them, Miss Bingley. They can well withstand an evening in company with your brother's new neighbors."

"And *my* sensibilities will never be offended by good and honest people, no matter their position in society," said Bingley. "Perhaps we should turn our conversation to other matters."

Though Miss Bingley sniffed, she did not continue with that subject and began to speak of other matters. Once again, Darcy focused more on his thoughts than the woman's prattle, and though he noted her growing frustration at his inattention, it was akin to something seen out of the corner of his eye, noted, but not with any thought.

Later in the afternoon, Miss Bingley's continual attempts to gain his attention began to grate on Darcy's nerves. The woman was persistent—this Darcy could acknowledge, little though it pleased him. After a time, he began to consider the relative merits of returning to his room until they were to depart for their neighbor's home. Then an interruption was provided which allowed Darcy's escape.

"Cousin!" boomed the voice of Colonel Anthony Fitzwilliam, as he was shown to the sitting-room by the housekeeper. "And Mr. and Miss Bingley, of course. I hope you do not mind, Bingley, old chap, but after receiving Darcy's letter, I thought it prudent to verify for myself you are treating my cousin well."

"You are always welcome, Fitzwilliam!" said Bingley, jumping to his feet and pumping Fitzwilliam's hand. "I informed Darcy to include the invitation for this purpose. Caroline, please see to a room for our new guest."

Caroline Bingley had never liked Fitzwilliam. Though the woman was eager to prostrate herself to anyone she felt above her in society, particularly those with ties to the highest echelons, something about Fitzwilliam had always irked her. Whether it was his flippant manners, his tendency toward amusement — especially of her attempts to capture Darcy — or his often boisterous and sometimes satirical humor, Darcy did not know. The animosity she held for him Darcy had long understood, though the woman would not do or say anything to give this feeling voice. At present, she must resent his unannounced appearance, for though the trouble of preparing a room would fall on the servants, it was her time in Darcy's company which was to be curtailed.

"Of course, Charles. I shall see to it directly." Miss Bingley turned to Fitzwilliam and gave him a credible smile, though its effect was undone by the hardness of her eyes. "Welcome, Colonel Fitzwilliam, to my brother's estate. If you gentlemen will excuse me, I shall instruct the housekeeper regarding Colonel Fitzwilliam's room and retire to my chambers to prepare for this evening."

The curtsey she dipped at the gentlemen was perfunctory, matched by Fitzwilliam's rather insouciant bow. It was with pursed lips the woman departed, leaving the room and lightening the atmosphere all in one fell swoop. Fitzwilliam, as was his wont, greeted her departure with little gravity.

"It seems your sister still does not care much for me, Bingley," said Fitzwilliam with a sigh. "It is unfortunate, as she possesses a dowry almost enough to tempt me into matrimony, and she is a handsome woman besides."

"I would be willing to augment it, should you wish to take her off my hands."

Fitzwilliam's roar of laughter informed them both his views of the offer. "Unfortunately, I will have to refuse your kind off. Your sister is fixed on my cousin, here, and I doubt she would take kindly to my competing for her attention."

"But Darcy is not interested in her," was Bingley's plaintive reply.

"Then perhaps you should ensure he is married off. She can hardly pursue a married man."

Bingley muttered something which sounded suspiciously like disagreement, but he did not respond otherwise. This allowed Darcy to change the subject, much to his relief.

"I had not expected you to come here so soon, Cousin. To what do we owe the pleasure of your company?"

The shrug with which Fitzwilliam responded was so like him.

"There is little to hold me in town at present, and I am interested to see if I can discover anything about our friend Wickham."

Fitzwilliam turned a baleful eye on Darcy. "From what your letter said, I suspect you allowed him to escape."

"There were others involved," said Darcy. "I came upon Wickham accosting three sisters. Given his belligerence and the raised voices, I thought it best to ensure their wellbeing and protection rather than chasing after Wickham. I thought I could cut him off before he disappeared again."

"With you in the area," grumbled Fitzwilliam, "I doubt he remained after he escaped from you. He would run as far and as fast as his legs could carry him."

"In my discussions with Colonel Forster, it seems likely he was already prepared to decamp," replied Darcy. "Be that as it may, I could not do other than what I did."

"Perhaps not. But it complicates the situation. For myself, I should as soon put a bullet in his head as capture him, for I have not your attachment to him."

It was the cold and casual manner in which Fitzwilliam spoke of killing Wickham which reminded Darcy that his cousin, though everything gentlemanly and good, was an implacable enemy. Darcy did not *think* his cousin would murder Wickham without a second thought, but if he should have the opportunity to face him across a field of honor, Darcy knew Fitzwilliam would have little compunction in ending the man's life. Bingley, it seemed, was shocked, for his stare showed the whites of his eyes.

"Do not worry, Bingley," said Fitzwilliam, noting Bingley's consternation. "I shall not descend to murder, even for the worthless likes of George Wickham. But he shall not escape me—if it takes me the next fifty years, I will find him and see he pays for his crimes."

"And I cannot blame you," replied Bingley.

"Then I shall go to the town tomorrow and speak to this colonel of the regiment." Fitzwilliam turned to Darcy. "Do you know if Wickham had any confederates in the corps?"

"There are three men with whom he was friendly," replied Darcy.

"Wickham does not have friends," said Fitzwilliam, his tone ominous. "He has nothing more than those he uses and then discards when they are no longer useful. Though these men might have considered themselves to be his friends, I am certain he left gaming debts among them. I doubt they understand how he used them."

"I do not disagree," said Darcy, knowing his cousin's assessment was accurate. "The colonel will inform you of what he has learned, but I doubt you will pull much more from them."

"In all honesty, I doubt it myself," said Fitzwilliam with a shrug. "All it costs me to make the attempt is a day's travel and a little time with bland militia officers. If there is any chance it will lead me to Wickham, I will seize it."

Fitzwilliam then clapped his hands and rubbed them together. "Now, what is this I hear about a function of some kind tonight? And what of these sisters of whom you spoke? Are they pretty? Possessing huge fortunes? Desperately in need of a dashing husband?"

"Well, if they are, they would not be looking for you."

Bingley guffawed at Darcy's jest and Fitzwilliam grinned. "Oh, I do not know. Give me a moment or three in their company, a few tales of my exploits, and I shall have them eating out of the palm of my hand.

"As always, you are far more confident in your charm than you should be," replied Darcy.

"I could send a message to Longbourn to inform them of your presence," supplied Bingley helpfully. "They would readily include you in the invitation, I am sure."

"Excellent!" cried Fitzwilliam. "An evening in lovely and charming company is just what I need to fortify myself before braving a bunch of dull militia officers tomorrow. Send word, Bingley, and I shall attend."

Fitzwilliam then excused himself to wash, and Bingley sent a note. As they had expected, the Bennets included Fitzwilliam in their invitation without delay. Thus, when the time arose, the four residents of Netherfield — one unhappy about the presence of the fourth, which she thought would restrict her struggle to attract the notice of the third. The fourth, however, paid no notice. Instead, he regaled them with tales of his exploits the entire three-mile distance to their neighbors' home, prompting daggers from Miss Bingley and ill-concealed hilarity from the remaining two.

CHAPTER XVI

Colonel Fitzwilliam of the dragoons was a man larger than life. Mr. Darcy had spoken of his cousin, but his words had consisted of little more than a mention of him. Elizabeth might have expected to meet a man much like Mr. Darcy in essentials given their close connection, but it was evident within moments of his arrival that nothing could be further from the truth.

The Netherfield party arrived, and those who had not been introduced were soon acquainted with each other. Mr. Bingley was, as Mr. Darcy had described, an amiable man, eager to meet, to converse, to approve and be approved of in turn. His sister, Miss Caroline Bingley, was a large contrast to the gentleman, being both superior in attitude and condescending when she spoke. The difference between siblings was striking.

"Mrs. Bennet," said Colonel Fitzwilliam expansively when they were all known to each other. "I wish to thank you for including me in your kind invitation on such short notice. It is an imposition, I know, but I was not anticipating the wait for my cousin and my hosts while they enjoyed your hospitality this evening."

"It is no imposition, Colonel Fitzwilliam," said Mrs. Bennet, flattered by his pretty words. "There is no difficulty in setting one extra place at dinner, and to be introduced to any of Mr. Darcy's relations is our pleasure."

The quiet snort with which Miss Bingley greeted Mrs. Bennet's words was politely ignored by them all. Then Kitty and Lydia made their presence known, for an actual colonel in their mother's sitting-room was all they had ever wished.

"Are you a real colonel?" asked Lydia, appraising the man as frankly as any woman of twice her age. "My sisters have told me of Colonel Forster, but I suspect he is a stuffy man, and I hear he is ancient!"

"I am, indeed," replied Colonel Fitzwilliam, not put off at all by her forwardness. "And though I do not know this Colonel Forster, I can assure you that *I* am not ancient by any means. *And,* whereas *he* is merely of the militia, *I* have fought for king and country."

The girls could not reply, staring at him with wide eyes, which Colonel Fitzwilliam seemed to enjoy if Elizabeth was any judge of the matter. Though he did not need to focus on her sisters' amusement, Colonel Fitzwilliam led them to a sofa nearby, saying:

"Come, ladies. I shall regale you with tales of my exploits, though I warn you that not all of soldiering is adventure and romance. But I shall do my best to avoid injuring young ears with my tales."

The two girls went willingly, and for a time they were quiet, except for the occasional gasp or giggle his words elicited. Elizabeth, though curious to know what he was telling them, decided it was best to leave well enough alone. Besides, there were other interesting conversations to be had and other events to witness.

Within moments of entering the room, Mr. Bingley had commandeered Jane's attention for his own, and soon they were seated together, speaking cordially, with Mary in attendance. The way he spoke to her, gave her all of his attention, hung off her every word, was a sight Elizabeth had seen many times in the past. A look passed between Elizabeth and Mary, one fraught with amusement and meaning. It seemed Jane had gained herself another admirer and this within minutes of his arrival.

It was unfortunate, but Elizabeth's introduction to the final member of the party with whom she had previously been unacquainted was not as pleasurable as the others. Having heard her reaction to Colonel Fitzwilliam's earlier words had given Elizabeth an initial insight into the woman's character. An overheard comment from the woman further reinforced Elizabeth's opinion of her as superior, impressed with herself, and disdainful of others.

"I know you assured me of our safety, Mr. Darcy, but I must own that I am not so convinced."

The sound of the grating voice pulled Elizabeth's attention to her, and as she was standing nearby, it was unsurprising Elizabeth could hear every word she said. It was a further mark against her that she did not seem to care who she was insulting.

"My brother, in particular, may be in great danger," continued the woman, glaring at the man who sat close by Elizabeth's sister. "I believe I shall be required to intervene to protect him once again."

"Anyone who considers my sister a threat of any kind must not know her, Miss Bingley," said Elizabeth before Mr. Darcy could make a reply. "She is the kindest, gentlest, most beautiful soul I have ever met in my life. As for my family, you may be assured you will escape our home unscathed—we do not bite, Miss Bingley."

Then, not allowing the woman to respond, Elizabeth turned and walked away, joining Jane and her sisters. Elizabeth neither knew nor cared about what Miss Bingley thought of her rebuke, but as Mr. Darcy was soon standing with her father speaking, and Miss Bingley's glare seemed to be directed more at Elizabeth thereafter, she assumed the woman had no taste for it.

The party was called into dinner soon after and they went in to partake of the meal. Mrs. Bennet had long been acknowledged to be one of the premier hostesses in the neighborhood—invitations to dine at her table were highly prized. That evening did no damage to her reputation, for by their guests praised the dinner, and conversation flowed effortlessly. If the youngest Bennets still hung onto every word which proceeded forth from the mouth of the colonel or Miss Bingley cast a pall over her part of the table, overall, it was a success, Elizabeth thought.

After dinner, they retired once more to the sitting-room, and that is when matters became a little more interesting. Mr. Bingley was not to be moved from Jane's side, for the two sat together throughout the course of the evening. That Jane appeared to be as pleased with Mr. Bingley as the reverse was a matter which gave Elizabeth some satisfaction—many a more promising inclination had begun with less.

For her part, Elizabeth found her attention being more captured by Mr. Darcy, who seemed eager to speak to her again. That Miss Bingley did not like this attention attested to her interest in the man. It was of no concern to Elizabeth, however—as a new acquaintance, and one she found interesting, Elizabeth had no notion of anything beyond conversation and character sketching. Let Miss Bingley be offended by the man's attention to her if she chose.

"Might I assume your cousin has come to investigate this matter of Mr. Wickham?" asked Elizabeth of Mr. Darcy.

"He has," replied the gentleman. "Though there is to be little more that can be learned, he thinks it is worth his while."

Elizabeth nodded. "A friend reminded me this morning that Mr. Wickham is still on the loose and may return to Hertfordshire at any time. As he blames me for his failure to attract my sister, I have resolved to be more careful in my habits."

"Do you mean something in particular?"

"It is obvious you are new to the neighborhood, Mr. Darcy," said Elizabeth, directing a warm smile at him. "My love of walking is well known throughout the neighborhood. With the uncertainty concerning Mr. Wickham's whereabouts, however, I must exercise greater care and diligence, and that means restricting my walks."

The gentleman's nod was followed by an oblique change of subject. "My sister is also inclined to walking, though I suspect she has not the stamina or range you possess. If you are this much of a lover of nature, you would love Pemberley, my estate in Derbyshire."

"I have often heard others speak of Derbyshire, but I have never been there," said Elizabeth. "Is it much different from Hertfordshire?"

"In some respects, it is quite different. My home, you see, is near to Dove Dale and the Peaks, which can be seen in the distance on a clear day. Derbyshire is rockier and less tamed than the counties to the south, though there are many similarities. Pemberley is situated in a long valley and features long strands of trees and the fertile farmlands which comprise the bulk of its prosperity."

Mr. Darcy continued to regale Elizabeth with tales of his home, and while he did not brag or boast, she could feel his love for it in every word, in every gesture punctuating his words. Furthermore, Elizabeth could almost see the estate in her mind's eye due to the picture he painted, an estate she thought dwarfed Longbourn in consequence and grandeur. And while Mr. Darcy did not boast, there was another who had no qualms in boasting on his behalf.

"Are you speaking of Pemberley, Mr. Darcy?" Miss Bingley directed a thin smile at Elizabeth. "A lovely place, indeed. It is, Miss Elizabeth, the most tranquil place I have ever had the fortune to visit. Such beauty! Such sheer esthetic pleasure in every line, every stone which forms its foundation! It is, you see, accounted as one of the great estates in all the land—I dare anyone to name a more pleasing place than Pemberley."

"Miss Bingley, of course, exaggerates," said Mr. Darcy, appearing faintly uncomfortable. "It is a fine estate to me and my family, but it is also a home, and I regard it as such."

"To your credit, sir," said Miss Bingley, the coquettish lilt in her voice causing him to stiffen. "No one could blame you if you should proclaim the greatness of your estate from the rooftops, and yet you prefer modesty to conceit."

"Have you ever been to the north?" asked Mr. Darcy of Elizabeth. Though she could not claim he was changing the subject due to his discomfort with Miss Bingley's praise, she felt confident that was a motivating factor.

"I have not, though I should love to visit someday," said Elizabeth. "My uncle and aunt have spoken of traveling to the north, perhaps as far as the lakes. At present, however, I have little more than the promise of such future delights to sustain me. But I have often heard of the wonders of Derbyshire, for my aunt lived there when she was a girl."

"In what part?" asked Mr. Darcy with interest unfeigned.

"I do not know where it is situated, but the town in which she lived is called Lambton."

"Why, that is not five miles from Pemberley!" exclaimed Mr. Darcy.

This new discovery of a shared connection made their conversation flow ever easier, and much of Mr. Darcy's words concerning Lambton were similar to what she had heard from Aunt Gardiner. This discussion had the unfortunate effect of excluding Miss Bingley, for though she had, by her own words, visited Pemberley, the mention of the market town provoked a rolling of her eyes — Elizabeth doubted she had never visited when she had been at Mr. Darcy's estate.

After a few moments of this, Miss Bingley huffed and looked around the room, settling on Mrs. Bennet. It was to the Bennet matron that the woman directed her next efforts, though her opinion of Mrs. Bennet appeared set in the hardness of her eyes. Still, she put on a sickeningly sweet smile and took herself to sit nearby. For some time Elizabeth did not know of what they spoke, as she was too focused on Mr. Darcy's conversation to pay such an objectionable woman any heed. During a lull in their conversation, however, she overheard some little part of it.

"We are from the north, in Yorkshire," Miss Bingley was saying in response to some query by Mrs. Bennet. "But of late our residence has been in London, though it is my brother's intent to obtain an estate of his own. Netherfield is only a temporary stop along the way — I suspect my brother will wish to purchase in the north."

"Do you have any other siblings?"

Miss Bingley looked at Mrs. Bennet as if trying to discern if her question was anything more than the polite query it seemed. "One sister," said Miss Bingley at length. "Louisa is our eldest sibling and is married to a Mr. Hurst, whose family owns an estate in Norfolk. Soon we expect them to join us at Netherfield."

"It is always wonderful to have family nearby," said Mrs. Bennet.

"Are you from the area, Mrs. Bennet?"

"I am," replied Elizabeth's mother.

"And your family estate? Where is it located?"

Mrs. Bennet regarded Miss Bingley for a moment before answering, clearly not liking something in the woman's manners. "My sister is the wife of an attorney, and my brother lives in London. If you stay here long enough, I shall introduce you to my brother, for he always visits us a Christmastide."

Miss Bingley pursed her lips, but while she gazed at Mrs. Bennet for a moment, wishing to ask further, it seemed as if she possessed some well of discretion. Knowing her mother had the woman well in hand, Elizabeth turned back to Mr. Darcy, noting how he watched her with interest.

"Is something amiss, Miss Bennet?"

"Not precisely amiss," was Elizabeth's slow reply.

Hesitating for a moment, Elizabeth wondered if she ought to make any comment about Miss Bingley—Mr. Darcy was staying at a house her brother was leasing, so any perceived criticism of the woman might be ill received. It was the smile playing around the corners of Mr. Darcy's mouth which settled it and convinced Elizabeth that the gentleman was not blind to the woman's improprieties.

"Perhaps I am speaking out of turn, Mr. Darcy, but Miss Bingley has given me the impression she does not think much of my family. The way she is questioning my mother suggests suspicion."

"I shall not say your impression is incorrect, Miss Bennet." Mr. Darcy paused and then said: "It is not proper to speak of her. Let me only say you are correct to suspect her motives and any professions of friendship she may make."

"Thank you, sir," replied Elizabeth. "Though I do not rejoice in being correct, I would not have my family taken in, either."

Having canvassed the disagreeable subject, neither felt any compulsion to continue to speak of Miss Bingley. Thus, they spoke of other matters and stayed together for some time, speaking of items of much substance, and Elizabeth's opinion of Mr. Darcy's worth was quickly confirmed. The gentleman was intelligent and could speak to his opinions in a confident, yet respectful manner. And Elizabeth soon realized the danger this man presented — it would be as easy falling in love with him as it might be to fall from a horse. The ramifications of developing feelings for him, Elizabeth did not wish to consider, for men of his consequence and position did not fall in love with women of hers.

Elizabeth shunted those thoughts to the side, instead content to enjoy his company. Thus, it was some time later when she became aware of an issue which had arisen, namely that her sisters were becoming a little excited and loud as a result. A glance around the room showed that Colonel Fitzwilliam was now speaking with her father and Mrs. Garret was nowhere in evidence — it seemed she had stepped from the room for a moment, possibly on an errand for Elizabeth's mother. Her sisters were whispering and giggling, looking in the colonel's direction, and it was up to Elizabeth to settle them.

"If you will excuse me, Mr. Darcy. It seems my sisters are in need of a guiding hand."

Stating it was no trouble, Mr. Darcy bowed to Elizabeth's curtsy, and when she turned away, she noted him following her. Elizabeth tried not to notice his presence and concentrated on her sisters instead.

"Kitty, Lydia," said Elizabeth as she drew near, "I believe that is enough, girls."

"Oh, Lizzy!" exclaimed Lydia, her voice still too loud. "Have you ever seen such a man as Colonel Fitzwilliam? Next to him, the officers of the militia are nothing at all!"

The snort Elizabeth heard behind her told her Mr. Darcy's amusement at hearing his cousin referred to in such terms. The urge to smile was strong, but Elizabeth suppressed it in favor of regarding her sisters with as much firmness as possible.

"Yes, Liddy, Colonel Fitzwilliam appears to be a good man. But let us have some decorum, shall we not?"

"You always curb our fun, Lizzy," grumped Lydia, Kitty nodding beside her.

Then Mrs. Garret appeared to take her sisters in hand, and Elizabeth retreated after giving them a smile. Mr. Darcy was grinning at her, still amused with Lydia's comment of Colonel Fitzwilliam, she was sure. Unfortunately, the event had caught attention of another.

"What . . . *interesting* younger sisters you have, Miss Elizabeth," said Miss Bingley, the sneer setting fire to Elizabeth's temper. "Perhaps your father should consider sending them to school, for surely they could use some seasoning." Miss Bingley laughed, a cruel sound designed to offend. "Then again, as they shall never have a London season, I suppose it is of little matter. Such manners must be normal *here*."

Elizabeth kept herself from gasping by force of will. There was little of subtlety in Mrs. Bingley's ill-bred attack, and Elizabeth's immediate instinct was to respond in a like fashion. But as Mr. Darcy was standing nearby—though the gentleman appeared startled and annoyed by Miss Bingley's words—and Mr. Bingley was a guest in their home, Elizabeth would not descend to Miss Bingley's level. Then again, she could not allow the insult to pass without some response.

"I thank you for the advice, Miss Bingley," said Elizabeth. "But Mrs. Garret has matters well in hand. Besides, it is not the practice of families such as ours to send their daughters to school when a governess's instruction is much more effective. At a school, one never knows to what influence they will be subject."

Miss Bingley looked down at Elizabeth, the image of a vulture peering at its prey entering Elizabeth's mind. "If your father chooses the proper seminary, Miss Elizabeth, a young woman may attain an education without worry for unwelcome influences. *I* attended a *very* well-regarded seminary, so I have knowledge of these things."

"That much is obvious, Miss Bingley."

Mr. Darcy cleared his throat, sounding suspiciously like he was about to break out into laughter. Though Miss Bingley did not like what Elizabeth said, it was obvious she considered nothing Elizabeth said to be of consequence, given the superior way in which she continued to look down on her. Instead, she turned to Mr. Darcy, and while she was speaking to Elizabeth, she continued to look at the gentleman.

"Should you wish for an example beyond reproach, your sisters should take the likeness of Miss Georgiana Darcy." Miss Bingley laughed. "Then again, I suppose your sisters will never be acquainted with her, for Mr. Darcy is discriminating regarding her acquaintances. But I assure you, Miss Elizabeth, Miss Darcy would never behave like your sisters."

"All young ladies have high spirits at one time or another, Miss Bingley," replied Mr. Darcy. "It is not unexpected. That is why children are taught the proper way to behave and young ladies are not allowed in society until they are prepared. I am certain that Miss Kitty and Miss Lydia will improve with experience, and with the examples of their excellent elder sisters and their companion's instruction, they will be acceptable as companions for Georgiana if they are introduced."

Miss Bingley regarded Mr. Darcy without betraying her feelings on the matter, not that Elizabeth required any clues about how the woman felt. In the end, it seemed she took him at his word — or was not willing to contradict him — for she did not protest.

"Quite," was all she said before she turned and made her way back to the chair she had recently occupied. For the rest of the evening, she said little, staring at them all with ill-concealed disdain.

"Thank you for your support, Mr. Darcy," said Elizabeth quietly.

"It is nothing less than the truth, Miss Elizabeth," replied he in a similar fashion. "There is nothing wrong with your sisters that a little experience will not resolve."

Then they left the objectionable subject behind and spoke of other matters for the rest of the evening. And by the end, Elizabeth was convinced that Mr. Darcy was a dangerous man. In many ways, he was far more dangerous than even Mr. Wickham.

"So, you have found nothing?"

Fitzwilliam scowled, a sight Darcy found rather amusing, though the subject most certainly was not. "Not a thing," replied Fitzwilliam. "I have interviewed all of Wickham's supporters with the regiment, but he has told them as little of his past as he could manage." Fitzwilliam paused and barked a laugh. "Given his reticence, I find myself surprised that Wickham did not invent some alias to use, though I suppose falsifying one's identity when joining the army might come back to haunt him."

"Is it any worse than deserting?" asked Darcy.

"Touché."

Darcy was less than surprised at his cousin's words, for his own knowledge of the situation from Colonel Forster had informed him the same. It had often been a pattern with Wickham to inform his so-called friends little of himself, for Darcy had long known the man's skill at making friends was far superior to his ability to keep them. As for an alias, Darcy thought his erstwhile friend was far too arrogant to stoop to something so weak as to hide his identity.

Still, Fitzwilliam had determined to make the inquiries, and as his cousin was a skilled interrogator, the possibility of something of use being discovered had been something they could not forgo. Darcy had not accompanied Fitzwilliam that morning, as his cousin had been firm in asserting Darcy's presence would only be detrimental.

"You loom, Cousin," said Fitzwilliam when Darcy asked if he should attend. "It would be better to speak to these men as friends than to intimidate them into telling what they know. They are more likely to be honest if treated well."

"I *am* capable of discretion, Cousin," said Darcy, though not offended by Fitzwilliam's words.

"Perhaps," replied Fitzwilliam. "But I think I should take care of the matter myself all the same."

"Then what is our next move," asked Darcy, returning his thoughts to the present.

"There is nothing to be done except to return to London to continue the search there." Fitzwilliam rubbed his chin in thought. "Our George has been adept at concealing himself, but eventually he will make a mistake and I shall have him. Then he will pay for his misdeeds."

Fitzwilliam paused, a frown settling over his countenance. Knowing his cousin was considering something important, Darcy did not respond, preferring to allow him to speak in his own time. That moment took longer than Darcy would have thought.

"I do not know," said Fitzwilliam at length, "but something about this whole situation bothers me, and I do not know what to make of it."

"What is that?"

"That is just it," growled Fitzwilliam, his frustration evident. "I cannot quite place my finger on it. But something bothers me, and I know it is important to unraveling this mystery." Fitzwilliam paused and then spoke slowly: "You know we have long suspected there is someone in London harboring Wickham, someone who assists him and is willing to provide him shelter."

Darcy nodded. "That could be anyone. There are plenty of people in London who do not care for those of our status, and any of them might be hiding him. For that matter, there are many he might have charmed, plying them with false tales, or even a false identity. That would be easiest for him to accomplish."

"It is possible," said Fitzwilliam, albeit grudgingly. "It has been on my mind, however, that it might be something more. Though I have no proof, I suspect whoever he has turned to for aid, it is someone known to us. He has driven away all of his friends, even those who despise you now know what he is and know he would turn on them without compunction if it gained him a copper. Even so, something tells me this person is known to us."

"I do not know how to advise you, Cousin," said Darcy. "In matters such as this, I suspect your instincts are more highly honed than my own."

"Not to worry," said Fitzwilliam, his tone dismissive. "It will come to me eventually. And when it does, I shall find Wickham and exact vengeance from his hide. Then the prison ship can have him, and I will stand on the pier and wish him a swift journey to hell."

Fitzwilliam laughed at his own words. "Either way," he continued, "I shall return to London. Should anything arise, you know where to find me."

Chapter XVII

"*I* had not thought you would leave us again so soon after your arrival," said Bingley to Fitzwilliam when informed of his imminent departure. "Duty calls you back to your regiment?"

"Duty, yes," replied Fitzwilliam. "Though, as always, the regiment calls, it is also our friend Wickham who provides the main impetus for my return. Once again, our friend has made himself into a nuisance, and that is one boil I intend to lance at the earliest opportunity."

Bingley frowned. "Do you have any more idea of where he may be hiding now than you had before?"

"Unfortunately, he remains elusive." Fitzwilliam bared his teeth, the rictus of a grin making him appear devilish. "It is only a matter of time, though I suspect Wickham believes he may evade us indefinitely. But I have no doubt I shall find him at some time or another, and God help him when I do. Dear Wicky has much for which he must atone."

"Then I wish you every fortune in your search," replied Bingley. "And should your presence be required again in Meryton, you may be sure of your welcome."

"My thanks, Bingley," said Fitzwilliam, slapping Bingley's back. "There is every possibility you will see me again, and likely far sooner than you might wish."

It was fortunate Darcy had much with which to distract him, or his continued worry for whatever Wickham was planning might have caused him to be irritable, to lose much sleep in thinking of it without cessation. As it was, however, life in Hertfordshire was pleasant, though not in all matters. Miss Bingley was a continued thorn in Darcy's side, as the woman had redoubled her efforts to ensnare him. When he continued to ignore her efforts, it made her angrier than had Darcy rebuffed them. But he was rapidly coming to lose all interest in her feelings, and as such, he was not concerned for her state of mind.

The other aspects of his stay, however, were fine, to the point where Darcy found himself eager to continue his time in Hertfordshire, whereas otherwise, he might have wished to be at Pemberley. While the people were the same as those he might meet in any other corner of the kingdom, there was one who was far beyond them, and was the means of the bulk of Darcy's contentment: Miss Elizabeth Bennet.

The day after Fitzwilliam's return to London, Darcy, together with Bingley, found himself drawn once again to Longbourn. Had Miss Bingley known of it, she would have been disgusted with them, but neither saw fit to inform her. Soon, Darcy found himself in the company of the family, and before long, Miss Elizabeth suggested they walk out to the back lawn. The three elder sisters agreed and were shooed from the room by the mother in the company of Darcy and Bingley. And there, Darcy was pleased to engage in conversation with the fascinating Miss Elizabeth.

"I must congratulate your father, Miss Elizabeth," said Darcy after they had engaged in desultory conversation for several moments. "Though I should be pleased to one day have daughters, I do not know I could withstand five without a son to even matters a little."

Miss Elizabeth laughed. "It should be no surprise that my father quite agrees with you, Mr. Darcy. He has often lamented as much."

"It is well you have a governess. Your mother might not have had any time for anything other than seeing to the education of you and your sisters otherwise."

"Mr. Garret has not always been with us," said Elizabeth. "In fact, she came to the estate only six years ago."

That surprised Darcy. "She was not your governess when you were young?"

"No, Mr. Darcy. When we were young, my father tutored Jane and me, and we spent much time with my uncle in London, who assisted with our education."

"Then the arrival of your sisters' companion coincided with the ending of the entail your father mentioned?"

"That is correct." Miss Elizabeth paused and smiled. "When our futures were secured and my father set in place new measures to save dowries for myself and my younger sisters, he noted that Kitty and Lydia do not . . . Well, let us say they do not always behave with perfect propriety. As none of us will have great fortunes, he began to take some thought to ensuring we are well mannered, for while we will have dowries, most of what we will bring to marriage is ourselves."

"A prudent conclusion," said Darcy. "I imagine it was difficult for Mr. Bennet to manage an estate he would not be in a position to pass on to his own family."

"While it does not speak well to my father's character, I cannot say you are incorrect."

"Perhaps it does not," replied Darcy. "However, your father is diligent now, and that is the most important consideration, is it not?"

"Indeed, it is," replied Miss Elizabeth.

"Then let us speak of other matters."

And speak they did, then and on other occasions. No subject was barred, allowing each to obtain a greater understanding of the other, for as they both possessed many interests, their discussions were varied and interesting. In addition, their conversations proceeded in an easy, effortless manner, as if they had known each other for many years and could predict what the other would say. At times, their conversation became rather personal, but it did not feel awkward in any way—quite the contrary, in fact.

"It seems to me your father often allows you and your elder sister to reprimand your youngest sisters," said Mr. Darcy on a day when Kitty and Lydia had been more than usually rambunctious. "That is an interesting tactic, as it is usually the father who has the final authority."

"And you would be correct," said Elizabeth. "If he feels it to be necessary, Papa will assume responsibility, and he has done so on many occasions. But he also believes my sisters and I are better positioned to understand young girls and guide them accordingly. Mrs. Garret has much to say in directing their behavior." Miss Elizabeth paused and seemed a little embarrassed, before she pressed on, saying: "My mother, you see, is not in a position to provide much guidance, as she was not raised a gentlewoman herself."

"And yet your mother behaves like one." Darcy smiled. "Believe me, Miss Elizabeth, I have met women of much higher standing whose behavior leaves much more to be desired."

"I thank you for your words, sir," said Miss Elizabeth, and the way she glanced over at her mother—who was sitting with some needlework in hand but watching over her brood with a keen eye—Darcy thought she held Mrs. Bennet in high esteem. "If you had known my mother before the entail was ended, you might have judged differently."

"Was she fearful for her future?"

Miss Elizabeth's eyes found him, reflecting the truth of his statement within. "Terrified would be closer to the mark. Though Jane was naught but fifteen, Mama had already begun to talk about bringing her out in society, for it was Mama's opinion that our futures could only be assured if we were married, which would, in turn, assure *her* future."

The grin with which Darcy regarded her was quickly mirrored by his companion. "I would imagine that Bingley and I would have been highly sought-after commodities, in that case."

"I cannot say you are incorrect."

With those words, they released their mirth, though quietly enough they did not garner the attention of the room. For a moment, Darcy regarded Mrs. Bennet, wondering at her daughter's words, trying to imagine what she might have been as a matchmaking mother and a desperate one at that. There was something about her behavior, he supposed, which suggested such tendencies, particularly the day he had met the Bennets when she had burst into her husband's study to speak of Bingley's arrival. But even then, she had seemed more interested than covetous, and it was difficult for Darcy to imagine it.

"And you, Miss Elizabeth?" asked Darcy, turning back to his companion. "If your mother had been intent upon marrying her daughters off to save the family, would you have been willing to marry for convenience?"

Miss Elizabeth looked away in embarrassment, though why she might feel shame, he could not fathom. It did not last long, however, for she soon turned to him, her posture filled with assurance, her tone firm when she spoke.

"When I was young, Mr. Darcy, I could see the discord between my parents. He regretted marrying her, for I believe he proposed in a moment of infatuation, and the time since their marriage had been a torturous journey in the company of her nerves. For my mother's part, she was consumed by her fears, so much so that she rarely could spare the time to focus on their marriage.

"My father has said many times that the woman he married was returned to him when the fear of the entail was removed, and they are much happier. For myself, however, I would much rather achieve a meeting of minds and hearts with my future husband, and I had determined so almost from the time I understood something of what it meant to share my life with another. So, while I cannot be certain of the answer to your question, at present I am determined to achieve something more than what my parents have. That may be imprudent, but I have never learned to doubt my convictions."

"It is not imprudent, Miss Elizabeth," said Darcy, his heart becoming fuller by the moment. "In fact, I think it shows some greatness of mind."

"Do you have a similar experience, Mr. Darcy?"

Darcy chuckled and nodded. "As always, you have seen to the heart of the matter, Miss Elizabeth. The situation of my parents, while different in essentials, was not that dissimilar.

"My father was a creature of duty, his every action guided by the desire to honor the family name and increase our consequence. As my mother was the daughter of an earl, as she brought a handsome dowry and connections to the peerage to the union." Darcy paused and smiled. "My mother was not my family's first connection to the peerage, but my father felt he was living up to the legacy of those who had gone before."

"Were your parents unhappy together?"

"Not unhappy, no," replied Darcy. "But my father was too immersed in his obligation to the family legacy to possess much ability to declare his feelings. My mother, I believe, loved my father, but forever lived without the knowledge of his feelings, which were profound, I suspect. My father's distress upon my mother's passing was deep and abiding, and I believe he never recovered from the sorrow. Thus, I can state that my own wishes regarding my future felicity align well with yours."

Perhaps it was a statement Darcy should not have made. The acquaintance with Miss Elizabeth was far too new for any declaration to be possible. It nevertheless felt right in saying it, as if it was something that was meant to be, that a higher power had declared that he was destined to find a bride in this, the most unlikely of places. It was as if he already knew he would offer for Miss Elizabeth, as if fate had drawn them together. Darcy could not state with any surety that any of these fanciful thoughts were the truth, but he could not say the opposite either. Soon, however, he hoped certainty would come.

*   *   *

As time passed, Elizabeth experienced her own heady feelings and stirrings deep within her heart. It was not long before she thought Mr. Darcy to be the best man she knew, and not long after that when she began to realize he was exactly what she wished for in a husband. Though a romantic young woman by nature, she had never expected to meet a man and develop an attachment with such swiftness. Before long, however, she began to long for his presence at all times, though she knew it was irrational.

Through these near-daily meetings, Elizabeth was quick to notice that Mr. Bingley was taking an ardent interest in her eldest sister. It was likewise important that Jane was not at all averse to the company of the gentleman. If Mr. Wickham or Mr. Collins had seen even half the enthusiasm for themselves as she was now showing for Mr. Bingley, they might well have proposed on the spot! What was even more gratifying was Mr. Darcy seemed to welcome his friend's interest in Jane.

"I have often seen Bingley's infatuation, Miss Elizabeth," said he on one occasion, giving rise to Elizabeth's fears. "One common thread to every other time I have seen him in such straits was my disapproval of the woman on some grounds or another."

"And have you set yourself judge over Mr. Bingley's future matrimonial prospects?" asked Elizabeth archly, prompting mirth from her companion.

"No," replied Mr. Darcy. "Bingley is his own man and capable of making his own decisions. I have never spoken to him or tried to interfere. It is to Bingley's credit he came to the same conclusion, as for some his wealth was their primary interest, for some he was a pleasant diversion, and some were not interested in him for whatever reason. Your sister, however, is different, for not only is there nothing of artifice in her, but she seems to have a true affection for him."

"And now you have shown your discernment, Mr. Darcy," said Elizabeth. "There is nothing of pretense in Jane, and she will not show an affection she does not possess. What you see is the true Jane."

"I am glad to hear it." Mr. Darcy edged a little closer, and when he spoke, there was something of secrecy in his manner. "Bingley and I have always spoken of the possibility of being brothers, but it has never seemed possible, given my lack of interest in his sister and the youth of mine. Now, however, I begin to wonder at the prospect."

Though Elizabeth felt the thrill of his words set her heart to fluttering, she stifled it, knowing it was still premature, despite his words. Instead, she smiled to let him know she was not at all averse to the notion and said with a voice full of irony:

"Poor Miss Bingley."

Miss Bingley was, indeed, a problem. The woman was no friend to her brother's interest in Jane, but she was certain Miss Bingley was even less of a friend to Mr. Darcy's attentions to her. While the woman often came to Longbourn when the gentlemen visited, she said but little and maintained a close watch on every interaction between Mr. Darcy and Elizabeth. And she never visited herself, though the Bennet sisters often visited Netherfield, and a return visit would have been nothing more than politeness.

Until, that was, one day more than two weeks after the Bingley party's arrival in Hertfordshire. On that day, the Bennet sisters had been at home, Elizabeth having entertained Charlotte for a time, and when the Bingley carriage arrived and Miss Bingley entered the room, it was revealed to the surprise of them all that the gentlemen had not come.

"A matter arose on the estate," said Miss Bingley, her manner making it clear she knew little of the problem and cared less. "As Mr. Darcy and my brother rode out to investigate, I decided I should like to come to know our dear friends better. And here I am."

As Miss Bingley had directed her words toward Jane, Elizabeth had the opportunity to look on the woman without being observed. There was a shifty look about her, one suggesting she had come for a different purpose than she had stated and was attempting to obfuscate.

For a time, the conversation was pleasant, proving Miss Bingley could behave in a friendly manner when she thought it worth her while. It was Jane who spoke for the Bennets, Elizabeth being too watchful and Mary not having much interest — Mrs. Bennet had greeted Miss Bingley and announced there were matters which needed her attention, surmising Miss Bingley saw her daughters. In this, Elizabeth was not certain Mrs. Bennet was correct; whatever Miss Bingley wished to accomplish, any of them would do.

After a time, Miss Bingley's questions became more probing in nature and more intrusive. Jane, dear woman she was, noticed nothing, which played into Miss Bingley's hands. Even Mary, who had not been paying attention, began to take notice of the woman's inquiry.

"I have heard it said you have few relations, Miss Bennet," said Miss Bingley, in what Elizabeth thought was the true thrust of her visit.

"We are not a large family, it is true," replied Jane.

"Then you differ greatly from the Bingleys!" exclaimed Miss Bingley in what Elizabeth suspected was a false air of joviality. "There are so many of us—it is difficult to keep all our relations straight."

"It has always been my opinion that a larger family would be a fine thing," interjected Elizabeth. "Though I can understand the drawbacks as you describe them."

"Yes, well, I suppose having a large family has its benefits." The woman paused then looked back at Jane. "Are you close with your extended family?"

"To some, yes," replied Jane. "On my father's side, we have an aunt who lives in a distant part of England, and no other closer relations than a distant cousin from whom we have long been estranged."

Elizabeth was gratified Jane mentioned nothing of the entail, nor of Mr. Collins's recent disastrous visit. Though she spoke calmly, Elizabeth thought she detected a hint of reserve in her sister which exceeded that which was normally present. Perhaps Jane had learned something from the debacles surrounding Mr. Collins and Mr. Wickham.

"And your mother's family?"

"My mother has one brother and one sister," replied Jane. "There are others of a more distant nature, but they are too many generations removed to be deemed connections."

"And where are their estates?"

Jane's brow furrowed, for she was as aware as Elizabeth that Mrs. Bennet had already vouchsafed this information—or a portion of it at least—to Miss Bingley. Though she thought to speak again, Elizabeth waited to see how Jane handled the questions, for even if Miss Bingley *did* look down on their relations, the Bennets had never been ashamed of them.

"As I believe we have said before," said Jane, as close to censure as she could ever bring herself to be, "my aunt is the wife of the town's solicitor."

"And a respectable *profession* it is," replied Miss Bingley, the sneer evident in her voice. "What of your uncle?"

"Our uncle lives in London and owns a very successful business," replied Jane.

It appeared Miss Bingley had found what she had been seeking, for her manner became abruptly cold. "A man of business, is he? In what part of London does your uncle reside?"

"On Gracechurch Street," interjected Elizabeth, having had enough of the woman's supercilious questions. "It is my understanding it has not been long since your father passed, has it? Perhaps he was acquainted with my uncle, for Mr. Gardiner is well known in London and possesses connections to all levels of society."

Cold did not even begin to describe the look Miss Bingley fixed upon Elizabeth. However, she kept her composure, though Elizabeth suspected it was a near thing. The only words she spoke in response were:

"We are not connected to trade."

The visit deteriorated from there and little more was said. Miss Bingley appeared to have little interest in speaking further with any Bennets, for she said little, and what she did say was perfunctory. For her part, Elizabeth did not care to speak to her again and, therefore, she made no effort to do so. Jane attempted to maintain the pretense of friendliness, but it appeared her efforts were in vain. After the requisite time had passed, Miss Bingley rose to go, her parting less than polite in her haste to depart.

"That was unkind, Lizzy," said Jane when their unwelcome guest had departed.

"So were her intrusive questions and her arrogance after she learned of the Gardiners," rejoined Elizabeth. "Please do not tell me you have been taken in by her."

"No," replied Jane with a sigh. "It appears she is no friend of the Bennets."

"Nor of her brother's interest in you, Jane," said Mary.

Jane smiled, then turned a raised eyebrow on Elizabeth. "Nor perhaps of Mr. Darcy's addresses to Elizabeth?"

Mary laughed. "I think that must be the greatest of her concerns, though I have seen no sign that Mr. Darcy gives her any more than the most grudging of his civility."

"No, he does not," said Elizabeth, not embarrassed at all by their banter. "Mr. Darcy himself has informed me he has no interest in her, not that it deters her in the slightest."

"It does not," replied Jane, rising to her feet. "But let us speak no further of Miss Bingley, for I would not belittle her when she is not present to defend herself."

So saying, Jane excused herself and left the room. Elizabeth and Mary exchanged a look and laughed. "Jane is correct, I suppose," said Elizabeth. "But there is so much material for us to use to make sport with her. It is hard to have a perfect sister, for one must always strive to live up to her example."

Miss Bingley waylaid Darcy and Bingley as soon as they entered the house. Her actions were little removed from the truth, though had he had spoken out loud, Darcy knew some might have protested it. In fact, when they climbed the stairs, dusty from the road and still smelling of horses, the way she appeared from a side door, Darcy had the impression of highwaymen, waiting in ambush for some unwary traveler.

"You will never guess what I have just learned, Brother," said she, her manner all triumphant.

"It is likely I will not," said Bingley, "but I believe I should like to divest myself of these clothes before you inform me."

"The Bennets are connected to trade!" crowed the woman, taking no heed to his words. "I have had it from Miss Bennet's own mouth. We already knew of the *country attorney*," the woman spat the words with open contempt, "but this matter of the man of *business* they have successfully hidden until this moment."

Bingley eyed his sister. "Miss Bennet visited Netherfield while we were on the estate?"

"No!" cried Miss Bingley, clearly frustrated. "I paid a visit to Longbourn and was entertained, if you may call it that, by the eldest sisters." Miss Bingley paused to titter, her dark amusement was most unpleasant. "Then again, I suppose it is correct to say I was very *entertained*, indeed! Imagine! An uncle actively involved in trade and not even hiding the fact. Do you know Miss Elizabeth had the temerity to suggest my father may have been known to her odious uncle?"

"What of it?" asked Bingley. "While I am sorry to disappoint you, Caroline, I could not find the Bennets any less agreeable had they tradesman uncles enough to fill all the British Isles."

Miss Bingley glared at her brother and then turned to Darcy. "What of you, Mr. Darcy. Are you able to countenance such unsuitable connections my brother seems to welcome?"

Darcy suppressed an ungentlemanly sigh, but before he could reply, her brother interjected. "I know not Darcy's opinion—though I can guess—but you asked *me*, Caroline. Why you find the Bennets' connections distasteful, I cannot imagine, if you only remember from whence our own fortune was derived. If you think of it, we still have some relations who manage their own businesses."

"Distant relations," spat Miss Bingley. "Those who are closer have all disavowed all association with such improper pursuits."

It was an overstatement—of that much Darcy was aware. Though he was not at all acquainted with Bingley's family, Bingley had informed him of them. His immediate uncles had profited from the sale of the family business such that they were no longer active participants, but many still kept interests in certain enterprises. Miss Bingley might be aghast to know it, but Darcy himself possessed many investments, for he was well aware the future wealth of the merchant class would outstrip that which the landed families had amassed.

"Be that as it may," replied Bingley, declining to correct her, "I see no reason why the existence of an uncle in trade should affect our friendship with the Bennets."

"Brother," said Miss Bingley in that tone she used when she thought he was a child who needed correcting, "for our family to rise in society, we must take great care in choosing those with whom we associate. Our friendship with Mr. Darcy has done wonders for our standing."

The woman paused and directed a coquettish smile at Darcy, one he thought approximated an expression which might be worn by a mastiff with a stomach upset. Darcy made no response, and she turned back to her brother.

"The Bennets are unsuitable, especially given the attention you are paying to Miss Bennet. It would not do to raise the girl's hopes, expectations you can never fulfill. It would be best if we returned to London, sell the lease, and search for an estate in a more appropriate neighborhood."

"I am quite settled at Netherfield, Caroline," said Bingley.

"And if you choose to give up the Bennets' friendship," added Darcy, "you will do so without me. I find that I esteem the family greatly. If your brother intends to give up this estate, it is not my concern. But as I enjoy the neighborhood, I shall stay."

Darcy turned to Bingley, noting the grin showing his concealed mirth. "In fact, old man, if you are intent upon giving up the lease, I believe I will take it off your hands."

"That is kind of you, to be sure, Darcy," replied Bingley, a hint of a chuckle accompanying his words. "It is unnecessary, however, for I am quite settled here."

Then Bingley turned back to his sister who was regarding them with astonishment. "There — we are both comfortable here for the time being. And as you know, Louisa and Hurst are due to arrive tomorrow. I know we shall be a merry party, and I expect Louisa and Hurst will enjoy the society as much as we have.

"Now, if you will excuse us, I believe Darcy and I require a change of clothing."

Following his friend, Darcy turned and walked toward the stairs, not daring to look back at the woman they had left behind. If he had possessed the fortitude, he was certain he would have seen her staring open-mouthed at their retreating backs. It was not in any way gentlemanly, but he found a savage sense of satisfaction welling up in his breast at the thought of Miss Bingley's consternation.

"I thank you for your support, Darcy," said Bingley as they gained the upper level. "But I will own to some curiosity. I might have thought you would balk at a connection to a tradesman."

"Nothing could be further from the truth," replied Darcy, forbearing to mention his friendship with Bingley himself. "Should this tradesman uncle be as estimable as the Bennets themselves, he must be an excellent man."

"I cannot agree more. However, you know that my sister will not surrender."

"Of course not," murmured Darcy. "I would never have suspected her of it."

CHAPTER XVIII

$\mathcal{L}$ ouisa Hurst anticipated the coming stay at her brother's leased estate in Hertfordshire. The previous months, she and her husband had been staying at his family's estate, a picturesque plot of land near to the coast of Norfolk. While Louisa had always found the estate to be beautiful, she could not say the same of the time they spent there. There was a simple reason which could be summed up in a single name: Aloysius Hurst.

Aloysius Hurst was her husband's father, Gerald Hurst, and a more cantankerous man she had never had the misfortune to meet. Having married at an already advanced age, her father-in-law was an aged man, though in excellent health, showing no signs of infirmity, other than perhaps that of the mind. Though he had always been a difficult man, according to her husband, the elder Hurst was also disapproving of his son's choice of wife and was not hesitant to share his opinion. The Bingleys were, Louisa knew, descended from tradesmen, though her brother had sold his portion of the family business, but to listen to Mr. Hurst, his family were higher than the dukes. Thus, while he tolerated Louisa, he was not friendly, and the time they spent there had always seemed akin to a prison sentence.

Hertfordshire was a beautiful county, full of pastoral landscapes, gently rolling hills, and small neighborhoods, allowing Louisa to realize the rest she so desperately needed. The anticipation was not hers alone, however, for her husband had mentioned more than once how happy he was to leave Norfolk.

"With any luck," said Hurst as the carriage rolled toward the country manor in the distance, "with Darcy in residence, there will not be much society."

"I have no objection to taking part in society," replied Louisa. "It is the quietude in the house I crave. Though I offer my apologies for speaking so, living with your father is not restful in any way."

Hurst chuckled and grasped her hand. "There is little for me to do but agree. Let us hope, then, we have left our trials behind us."

In their eagerness to reach Netherfield, however, neither Louisa nor Hurst had considered what might have happened in their absence. They were to learn soon after their arrival.

The greetings were exchanged as they ever were, Charles his usually happy and gregarious self, while Mr. Darcy, reserved, yet pleased to see them. Louisa knew Darcy considered her husband to be more than a little dull, and at times she was forced to agree with him, though Hurst was a good man. The final member of the welcoming party greeted them, and Louisa's guard rose in an instant, for behind Caroline's façade of welcome, discontent and anger seethed.

"Is it just my imagination or is Caroline angry?" asked Hurst as they made their escape and go to their rooms.

"I am surprised you noticed it, Husband," replied Louisa.

"Believe me, my dear, I am well enough acquainted with Caroline's moods to know when she is discontented." Hurst paused and snorted, stopping to open the doors to their chambers and allow her to walk through. "Then again, I can always tell when Caroline is unhappy — when she is awake, she is almost always in that state."

Louisa could not help the laugh which escaped, and she swatted at him in mock affront. The man grinned, unaffected by her show of displeasure. "Do not allow Caroline to hear you speak so. You know you and she do not get on at the best of times."

"I find I am unconcerned for your sister's resentment," replied Hurst. "It would be best if your brother were to curb her excesses. Darcy has warned him several times she will shame him in society if he does not, and I agree with him."

"Yet Charles is not a man to be firm with her," replied Louisa with a sigh.

"No, he is not. But if Darcy and I keep speaking to him of it, perhaps he will do something. Regardless, let us change and attend your brother. I hope he has something stronger than tea at hand, for I need it after Norfolk."

They parted, Louisa shaking her head at her husband with true amusement. There was little he liked so well as good food and smooth brandy, and as there was little of either at his father's estate, it did not help his mood when they stayed there. Louisa turned her steps to her own chamber, calling for her maid and eager to change into something less dusty. With any luck, she would avoid her sister that day at least. Luck, however, was not with Louisa Hurst.

"Louisa!" the strident tones of her sister announced her presence before even the opening of the door could. "Why did you wait so long before joining us?"

"Hello, Caroline," said Louisa, as the maid was making the last few adjustments to the repair of her coiffeur. "Our visit to my father-in-law's estate was scheduled for two months—I am certain I informed you of this before we departed."

"I know not why you go there at all," said Caroline with her customary sneer. "A pitiful little plot in the middle of nowhere, and an argumentative old man who makes your life miserable. Besides, I had need of you here!"

While Louisa could not dispute her sister's account of the elder Hurst, she did not appreciate her characterization of the estate her husband would inherit. Dunton Heath was not the greatest estate in the land, but it was respectable, with an income approaching five thousand a year. Then again, Caroline always had considered anything smaller than London itself to be a rustic country setting with no redeeming qualities. Louisa wondered why her sister was so intent upon marrying into the higher echelons of society—did she not understand they spent half the year at their country estates?

"I cannot imagine why you might have had need of me," replied Louisa, smiling at her maid to allow her to depart.

"Then let me inform you," hissed Caroline. "Not only is this neighborhood bucolic and rough, peopled with savages who have no notion of proper behavior, but Charles has once again had his head turned by a young woman. Not only that, Mr. Darcy seems to find the country tolerable, and he has been paying attention to one of the barbarians himself. This is not to be endured!"

The news of Charles was unsurprising—Louisa had seen her brother's infatuation frequently. He would lose interest like he had so many other times. Mr. Darcy, on the other hand, had never so much as looked at another woman, except to find something to criticize. If it was something more than Caroline's intense interest in the man for herself speaking, it explained her sister's pique.

"Is he?" asked Louisa. "That is unusual."

"We must do something," said Caroline, beginning to pace the room. "If we can persuade Charles and Mr. Darcy we would be better in town—or even Pemberley!—we could leave this behind. I shall not have my brother marrying a country nobody."

In the past, Louisa had always supported her sister. Of the three, Caroline was the most forceful, the most determined to have her way, and as Charles was as he was and Louisa of a quieter disposition, it had always seemed like the path of least resistance. Now, after a long journey, having spent the past two months in company with a man who saw fault in everything she did, the last thing Louisa wished was to be drawn into her sister's schemes with respect to Mr. Darcy.

What Caroline would not acknowledge was Mr. Darcy's lack of anything resembling interest in her. The mere mention of it would send Caroline into a rage, so Louisa usually avoided speaking of it where her sister could overhear. Mr. Darcy was a man capable of seeing to his own interests, having fended off every determined fortune hunter in society since he had inherited his estate five years before. On that day, however, fatigue, coupled with Caroline's tiresome insistence wore on Louisa, and she was not as circumspect as she usually endeavored to be with her difficult sibling.

"Oh, Caroline," said Louisa, sinking back into the chair from which she had just arisen. "There is little you can do to direct Mr. Darcy. Has he not proven it many times in the past? I cannot imagine the gentleman has any true intentions toward a woman of the country."

"You have not seen them together." Caroline growled and continued to pace. "Though I would not have credited him with such interest in a woman so unsuitable, his attentions have been unmistakable. Something must be done to stop it."

Louisa made no reply, and she did not need to, for Caroline was deep in her own thoughts. For several moments she paced, the sound of her slippered feet striking the floor tiles providing a soporific effect, lulling Louisa to a sense of complacency. When Caroline spoke, it roused Louisa, though she remained in a state of lowered awareness.

"Perhaps a letter to that aunt of his—Lady Catherine de Bourgh. She would be no friend of Mr. Darcy's attentions to this country nobody."

"I do not think that would serve," replied Louisa. "Not only are you unacquainted with the woman—a letter would be presumptuous—but by all accounts, Lady Catherine covets Mr. Darcy for her own daughter."

"Perhaps she does. It seems she hopes in vain, however, for Mr. Darcy has not seen fit to offer for her."

Lady Catherine is not the only one who hopes in vain, thought Louisa, though she would not say it aloud. "Informing her would do little. Unless you wish her to insist he marry her daughter."

"I doubt he would. Lady Catherine would put a stop to his infatuation and then leave. With any luck, she would persuade him that leaving Hertfordshire is for the best, which would allow us to convince Charles of the same."

"I am sorry, Caroline," said Louisa, "but while you might not credit it, I have been eager for this holiday in the country, after two months with Hurst's father. I do not wish to return to London."

"Oh, do be serious, Louisa," said Caroline, her tone dismissive and distracted. "Hurst may become soused on our brother's brandy in town as easily as he may do it here. The important matter is to ensure we remove Charles and Mr. Darcy from these country temptresses."

The slight directed toward her husband raised Louisa's ire, but she forced down any number of retorts which would only set her sister off. Watching Caroline pace proved anything but calming, but a moment of holding her tongue eased the desire to bark back at her sister.

"I must find a way to do it," muttered Caroline. "This cannot be allowed to stand. I had thought to prove my qualities to Mr. Darcy, to show him what an excellent mistress of his estate I can be. To be shunted aside by some country adventuress is not to be borne!"

"Perhaps you should allow the matter to rest," said Louisa, fatigued by her sister's ranting. Caroline turned a dangerous glare on her, but Louisa could not bring herself to care. "It has been two years, Caroline. If Mr. Darcy meant to make you an offer, do you not think he would have done so already? It would be best if you returned to London for the season with the intention of finding a husband who wishes to have you for a wife."

"Mr. Darcy is *mine!*" hissed Caroline. "I shall not allow another woman to steal him from me!"

"It seems he is *not* yours. Else he would have offered for you. Find yourself a husband, Caroline—it will make you happier than scheming to entrap a man who does not wish you for a wife."

"Perhaps you are content to resign yourself to a sodden bore for a husband, but I am not. I *will* be mistress of Pemberley!"

"That sodden bore is our only family connection to the gentry," said Louisa, standing and glaring at her sister. "I will thank you to remember that he is my husband and deserving of your respect."

Caroline snorted. "Respect, dear sister, is reserved for those who earn it."

"Then perhaps you should leave," said Louisa. "I have little desire to hear you disparage my husband. And as for your doomed campaign to tempt Mr. Darcy, I shall have you know that I am little inclined to assist you, given your unkind words about my husband. I should not wish such a wife as you on Mr. Darcy."

"Traitor!" spat Caroline. "Is this how you treat me?"

"It is when you are so insulting and unreasonable."

"Then so be it. I shall deal with it myself." Caroline stalked to the door and flung it open, before turning and fixing Louisa with a baleful look. "When I am mistress of Pemberley, you should not expect any notice from me. It will be long before I will forget your betrayal."

With those final words, Caroline stalked from the room, the sound of the door to the sitting-room slamming reverberated through the room and served to give Louisa a headache. Sitting in her chair again, Louisa reached up to massage her temples, wondering what she had done to deserve such a sister as Caroline. The sound of her husband entering the room was welcome after the argument.

"It seems your sister has a bee in her bonnet," said Hurst.

With a single look, he exited, returning a few moments later with a glass of sherry. Hurst placed it in her hand, urging her to drink, which she did in small sips, while he placed his hands on her shoulders and massaged them gently. Louisa felt she could sleep at his ministrations, so heavenly did they feel at that moment.

"Now, perhaps you should tell me what has prompted your sister to anger."

"What is always the matter with Caroline?" asked Louisa with an uncaring shrug. She sipped at her drink again, appreciating the sweet liquid as it lingered on her tongue. "Charles is infatuated, the country is unsuitable, and Mr. Darcy has not yet fallen at her feet."

The derisive snort with which Hurst replied informed Louisa what he thought. "Your sister is delusional," said he. "Darcy will never make her an offer. The sooner she acknowledges it the greater chance she possesses of finding a husband. At this rate, she will never marry."

Louisa nodded but did not reply. The glass she set aside, as she did not wish to dull her senses further, given the difficult evening she expected in Caroline's company. Hurst squeezed her shoulders once more and stepped around her, pulling a nearby chair closer so he could sit with her and speak, his manner as serious as she had ever seen.

"It is good you put her off, Louisa," said he. "It will not be a surprise to learn I dislike your sister. She is demanding and selfish, contemptuous of you and our marriage, and thinks entirely too well of herself in my opinion. While my father is difficult to endure, the fact is that your sister is intolerable—while my father refuses to leave the estate, your sister is, in fact, with us whenever we are not there. Her presence is not only ubiquitous, but it is disruptive and puts a strain upon our marriage which would not exist if she was not present."

"I . . . I had not thought of it that way." Louisa paused, looking down in embarrassment. "Caroline is my sister, and I, as the eldest, have always thought it my responsibility to care for her."

"It is your brother who has the responsibility for her," said Hurst. "Bingley holds her dowry in trust, provides her with an allowance— which she routinely exceeds, I might add—and your brother will approve of any suitors for her hand. Should there be any, of course. It is commendable you wish to see to her needs, but her selfishness makes it difficult."

Thoughtful, Louisa nodded slowly, thinking of all the times Caroline put her own desires before those of anyone else. As there were no instances of the opposite which readily came to Louisa's mind, many such events flashed across her mind, filling Louisa with a resentment toward Caroline she had never felt before. It was, perhaps, not laudable to feel that way for another, but Caroline did not invite sympathy, and the loyalty Louisa had always offered her sister had never been reciprocated. Now all Louisa could feel was fatigue, colored by a hefty measure of affront.

"Thank you for speaking, Husband," said Louisa, focusing her attention once again on the man before her. He was not the most handsome or the most interesting, intelligent, or industrious man—but he cared for her and had always endured her sister for her sake. It was time she gave her support to *him* instead of Caroline.

"I believe I shall take your words into consideration. Caroline has ruled us too long."

"I am happy you agree," said Hurst, once again squeezing her hand. "Come, let us join your brother and learn more of this young lady who has caught his fancy. You never know—she might be the one to catch and hold his devotion."

"Perhaps she will," said Louisa, allowing Hurst to pull her to her feet. "Suddenly, I am eager to make her acquaintance."

*   *   *

As Mr. Bingley's sister was expected that day, Elizabeth had little notion of seeing either gentleman at Longbourn, and while she might repine the loss of Mr. Darcy's company, the visit of a dear friend amply distracted her. And Elizabeth was to learn of a new development which was a surprise to her, as much because she had not heard it before as that the gossips of Meryton had, it seemed, not heard of it either.

"Well, Lizzy, are you still happy with your suitor?" Charlotte turned to Jane. "And you too, Jane. I suppose they visit daily, and you have come to expect them!"

"That is near to the truth," inserted Mary with a grin for her elder sisters. "They seem to be quite pleased with my sisters, though I doubt Miss Bingley is similarly happy."

Elizabeth laughed. "The woman is as sour as a lemon and not as sweet."

"It is sad, in my opinion," said Jane quietly. "Mr. Darcy shows no interest in her, but she is desperate to become his wife. One can only assume it is for his wealth and position in society, which, as I understand, are to be envied."

"That is the most unforgiving statement I have ever heard you make!" exclaimed Charlotte. "Good for you! It seems the troubles with Mr. Wickham and Mr. Collins have taught you something, Jane."

Embarrassed, Jane looked to the floor. "They have. I have learned to be more cautious."

"Does this caution extend to the interest Mr. Bingley to have in you?" asked Charlotte.

"If you mean whether his sister will influence any overtures Mr. Bingley makes, it is possible," replied Jane. "But it will depend on the gentleman himself. It is not a crime to have a difficult sister—it is far more important to determine how he handles her. I will note, however, that it is still premature for expectations to be raised, for Mr. Bingley has made no mention of any such sentiments."

"Nor should he," said Elizabeth. "It is still early in your acquaintance, after all. While I would assert we understand Mr. Bingley's character well, I should prefer to see you become more comfortable with him before you take such a momentous step."

Jane flashed her a smile. "If I am not very much mistaken, I believe *you* are closer to an impulsive decision than I am."

"Decisive, dear Jane. It is not impulsive, only decisive."

They all laughed at Elizabeth's jest, their mirth flowing freely for several moments. When it had run its course, Charlotte was the first to speak.

"You may call it what you like, Lizzy. It is not a calm and rational decision, not one you are urging your sister to make."

"When is love rational?" asked Elizabeth. "If Jane should feel for Mr. Bingley as much as I suspect she can *and* be certain of his character and ability to support her, I should not advise her to delay."

"This is the first time any of us have mentioned love, Lizzy," said Jane, Mary chortling by her side.

"Is that not what we have determined we shall have?" asked Elizabeth. "Just because I have said the word does not mean I am caught in its throes."

"It is likely you are not," said Mary. "It is equally likely you are not far off."

"Speaking of love," said Charlotte, "I have news I would share with you, first, of all the neighborhood."

"Oh?" asked Elizabeth, curiously resting her eyes on Charlotte. "Has someone caught your eye?"

"You need not show such disbelief!" cried Charlotte, swatting at Elizabeth. "Am I not able to attract a gentleman?"

"Eminently capable," replied Elizabeth, meaning every word. "Your words have always betrayed you to be a practical woman. Have you not always informed me that a good home with a respectable man is all you desire?"

"And that has not changed," replied Charlotte. "My practicality has not wavered, Lizzy, but I must own that being the object of a gentleman's attentions is far pleasanter than I might have expected."

"Who, Charlotte?" asked Elizabeth, her sisters clamoring for details.

"Mr. Pearce," said Charlotte, a look of satisfaction displayed for them.

"Why, he is Longbourn's neighbor to the north!" said Elizabeth. "Papa does not have many dealings with him, but I understand his estate is a little larger than Longbourn."

"He is also the father of two daughters and wishes for an heir, and a mother for his daughters. Last week he called at Lucas Lodge and has been calling on me ever since." Charlotte paused and smiled, a self-deprecating display. "Though he is not the master of a great estate in the north, I find I am happy with him, for he is gentlemanly and appears to esteem me greatly."

"Of course, he does," said Elizabeth warmly, grasping her friend's hands. "Any man must be a fool if he does not. And wealth is all relative, in my opinion—compatibility and happiness with one's partner is a much greater concern."

"Though I might have disagreed with you not long ago, I can now see the merits of your position."

The ladies continued to speak in a lively fashion, thereafter, sharing their hopes and dreams and expectations for the future. As she had informed her friend, Elizabeth was pleased for Charlotte, having thought for many years that Charlotte's disposition, along with her practicality and intelligence, would make her a good wife. That someone had seen that potential was all Elizabeth had ever wished for her friend.

When Charlotte rose to depart, Elizabeth accompanied her to the vestibule to see her off. As she was donning her hat and gloves, Charlotte turned to Elizabeth with a question.

"Lizzy, our conversation today consisted of much merriment, but I wish to be serious at present. This Mr. Darcy—if he should offer for you, are you inclined to accept him?"

"At present, I hardly know," replied Elizabeth. "I will, however, inform you I like Mr. Darcy very much. A better man I do not think I have ever met."

"Then that is all I wish for you. With your romantic nature, I always thought it would be difficult for you to find a partner who would meet your standards, and your tendency toward cynicism does not help. If he is a man who will answer every question of your future happiness, I am well content."

Then Charlotte squeezed her hand and departed. How long Elizabeth stood there considering her friend's words and the man of whom they had spoken, Elizabeth did not know. Eventually, the cold of the room prompted her to seek the warmth of the hearth in the sitting-room. The thoughts of Mr. Darcy, however, did not subside.

CHAPTER XIX

*H*aving heard, albeit briefly, from Hurst concerning the disagreement between sisters and his subsequent words with his wife, Darcy found himself relieved that Miss Bingley could not count on her sister for support. Mrs. Hurst was not a bad sort at heart, but the two sisters united often made Darcy uncomfortable, especially when they praised Georgiana to elicit his favor or schemed to recommend Miss Bingley to him. Long had Darcy known the elder sister deferred to the younger—should this new dynamic between them persist, he thought he could expect a more restful stay in Bingley's company.

When they left for Longbourn the next morning, Bingley eager to introduce his sister to the family of the woman who seemed to have caught his fancy, Darcy might not have known there had been a disagreement had he not heard of it. Miss Bingley, it seemed, still considered her sister a supporter and confederate, given the words which punctuated the short journey.

"I would not prejudice your opinion before meeting our new neighbors," said she, her next words giving the lie to the first. "But there is little of sophistication—or even proper behavior—to be found among them. While the eldest is tolerably well behaved, the younger are not, particularly the two youngest, who are positively wild. Mr. Bennet shows an astonishing sardonic contempt of everyone he meets, and Mrs. Bennet is uncouth and uncultured.

"And the entire neighborhood is the same!" exclaimed she, professing disappointment. "I had high hopes for our brother's home, but there is little of worth any of them.

"Why, did you know Mrs. Bennet actually asked me concerning the lace on my gown?" Miss Bingley gave an indelicate snort. "Then again, I suppose French lace is a luxury which cannot ever have made its way to this backwater community."

"Thank you, Caroline, for your interesting commentary," interrupted Bingley. "I am certain Louisa may take the Bennets' likeness without your commentary."

Hurst grunted in amusement while his wife remained carefully noncommittal. If Bingley thought for one moment his rebuke would silence his sister, he would soon be disappointed.

"I would not have her enter Longbourn without preparing her first, Charles," replied Miss Bingley. "It is a country home, an attempt having been made at its gentrification, I suppose, but small and dingy, compared with some of the great houses we have seen."

Miss Bingley's eyes flicked to Darcy, betraying her meaning to them all. "There is little difference between it and the other hovels this unfortunate neighborhood boasts, making Netherfield, as inadequate as it is, a veritable palace by comparison. If Mrs. Bennet has redecorated her sitting-room in the past fifteen years, I am certain I can see nothing of it, not that I would trust her taste regardless, for I am sure she has none.

"And perhaps the most shocking thing you will see is how much our brother and Mr. Darcy treat the Bennets as if they were veritable nobility. I cannot account for it, for Mr. Darcy, in particular, has always shown his discerning and discriminating nature. Perhaps the Bennets are practitioners of the occult, for I know no other way in which he could be misled in such a fashion."

"Oh, look!" exclaimed Mrs. Hurst, neatly cutting her sister off. "What a perfectly charming little church."

"That is Longbourn church," said Bingley with a sly look at his other sister, while Miss Bingley sat mouth agape. "It is where we have attended church while we are in the neighborhood."

"And I suppose that is Longbourn beyond?" asked Mrs. Hurst, pointing out the front of the carriage. "It seems delightful. In the summer, when the blossoms are blooming, I can imagine the rose gardens must be divine."

Between them, Mrs. Hurst and Bingley carried the conversation, their sister glaring at them both as if betrayed. While Darcy had never had any great opinion of Mrs. Hurst, in this instance he could only tip his cap to her, for she had disarmed Miss Bingley's crass ridicule of the neighborhood and the Bennets and all without provoking an argument. Bingley had been on the verge of commanding his sister to be silent, so it was all the more diplomatic of her to have diffused the situation.

When they entered into the sitting-room, the Bennets regarded them with curiosity for the new members of the party, though Darcy thought he detected a hint of wariness. It was understandable since it was reasonable to assume that in Mrs. Hurst, they were about to meet another lady of Miss Bingley's ilk. Within moments, however, the tension lessened, as Mrs. Hurst proved both friendly and eager to meet them, much to her sister's disgust. Then, she was seated with the two eldest Bennet daughters, speaking of matters of interest to young ladies. Then, a few moments later, she spoke loudly, the pièce de résistance, in Darcy's opinion.

"Oh, Mrs. Bennet, that is lovely French lace on your gown. You must tell me where you found it, for I should love to procure some."

Though Mrs. Bennet did not understand Mrs. Hurst's significant glance at her sister — nor the scowl with which Miss Bingley replied — she was clearly pleased to speak of it.

"It is from my brother. He is an importer, and his warehouse is filled with such treasures as this." Mrs. Bennet swept her hand out, indicating her eldest three daughters who were sitting nearby. "All our fabrics come from my brother's warehouse, for he obtains the most beautiful materials I have ever seen."

"Yes, I can see your dresses are made of the most excellent fabrics," said Mrs. Hurst. She then turned back to Mrs. Bennet. "Please, tell me more, Mrs. Bennet. I am eager to make your brother's acquaintance."

"Of course, you are!" said Miss Elizabeth, her eyes dancing with laughter. "For what woman can refuse the promise of fine dresses?"

The ladies all laughed together and fell into further conversation, and had Darcy been more conversant regarding ladies' fashions, he might have attempted to follow it. As it was, his knowledge was limited, though he had found of late that his approval was more often given to whatever Miss Elizabeth Bennet wore that day. And so he might have continued to observe her, had Mr. Bennet not spoken, drawing the attention of all the men.

"I hope you do not mind my wife spending your money, Mr. Hurst," said he, nodding at the womenfolk. "Though my wife has learned some measure of economy, she still succeeds in spending much of my income on dresses, lace, and other feminine fripperies."

"Anything to keep the ladies happy," replied Hurst. "Though it could be said my wife possesses expensive tastes, I am eager to indulge her." Hurst paused and grimaced. "Or do when I possess the means. My father, you understand, keeps a tight hold on the purse strings."

Mr. Bennet laughed. "I was fortunately spared the indignity of depending on my father for funds, as I inherited the estate before I married."

The conversation continued from there, the two men speaking of estate matters and the foibles of miserly fathers, Bingley chiming in from time to time with various observations from his own experiences. It seemed to Darcy that Mr. Bennet was becoming friendly with Hurst, for it seemed their senses of humor were similar in many respects, as were their general outlooks on life.

Darcy listened with half an ear and ventured opinions when he thought it least likely he would be required to elaborate. Instead, he concentrated on watching Miss Elizabeth, noting with pleasure how animated she became when speaking, her great joy in good company, and how she put others at ease with such effortless and instinctive good cheer. She was unlike any other woman Darcy had ever met.

As the visit passed, Darcy found the opportunity to once again bask in her presence, unsurprised when he heard the first subject she raised between them. "It seems, Mr. Darcy, that we may have quite misjudged Mrs. Hurst without meeting her. I was convinced she would be nothing more than an image of her sister, though as the elder, I suppose it may be more correct to say that *Miss Bingley* would be an image of *her*."

"In the past, you might not have been incorrect," replied Darcy.

"Indeed?" asked Miss Elizabeth.

"Since I have known them," replied Darcy, "they have always been close, their opinions aligned. While I cannot say what brought about this alteration, it seems Mrs. Hurst has decided not to support her sister any longer."

Miss Elizabeth laughed. "That must be a relief for you, sir, given what I have seen of Miss Bingley's ambitions."

"I can neither confirm nor deny your supposition, Miss Elizabeth," said Darcy with a wink.

"Then I shall not press you further," said Miss Elizabeth, still chuckling. "Let us simply say that for whatever it is worth, we find Mrs. Hurst to be an admirable woman and look forward to coming to know her better."

"It is worth much, Miss Elizabeth," replied Darcy.

Their conversation wound on from there, touching on many subjects, as was their wont. Darcy found himself becoming more and more entranced by the woman's manners and the sheer allure of her person. He could not have resisted her if he had been of a mind to try — and *that* he most certainly was not.

It was not long before they began to attract attention from a most unwelcome source. Miss Bingley, it seemed, was not willing to yield the field to the superior combatant.

"Of what are you speaking, Mr. Darcy?" said the woman in a loud voice as she approached them.

"We are talking of the subject of the Luddite unrest in the north, Miss Bingley," said Miss Elizabeth, an expressive look at Darcy showing her amusement at the woman's actions.

"You are?" asked Miss Bingley, her eyebrow lifted in skepticism. "That is a singular topic, Miss Bennet, and not a subject gentle ladies should be discussing."

"Should ladies not be aware of the world in which we live?" asked Elizabeth. "In fact, I suspect there is little of which ladies should not talk, especially if we believe our opinions have merit."

"There is little to be said," replied Miss Bingley, her manner condescending. "The leaders should be rounded up and hanged. The next time the rabble considers such rebellion, perhaps they shall think twice of it."

"Would you have England go the way of France? Was the kind of oppression you propose not directly responsible for the revolution there? Where will we all be if the lower classes of England rise against us?"

"England is not France, Miss Elizabeth," said Miss Bingley, her nose firmly thrust into the air.

"No, but people are people, wherever one may find them. It seems to me the workers have a legitimate grievance — they are fighting for their livelihoods, their means of feeding their families. That is something we cannot ignore."

Miss Bingley fixed a cold glare on Elizabeth. "Then you agree with their methods and support the threat of violence."

"Violence should, of course, always be condemned," said Miss Elizabeth, keeping her composure admirably. "My remarks were neither praise for their methods, nor did I applaud anything done with evil intent. All I suggested is that when a man's livelihood is at stake, it is hardly surprising he would wish to defend it. Take, for example, your brother—should his income be threatened, would he not act, knowing his ability to provide for his future family might be compromised?"

"That is in no way analogous," snapped Miss Bingley. "Or are you suggesting my brother works in a factory?"

"Of course not!" was Miss Elizabeth's equally short reply. "But the principle is sound. More and more machines are taking the place of workers, and any rational thinker can see the machines are both more efficient and cost the factory owners less money than paying workers to do the same jobs, more slowly, and with a greater chance of error. That is not in dispute. What is in dispute is what those workers who are replaced by machines can do to continue to ensure their families have homes, to put food on the table and to provide other necessities. Ignoring these concerns is not only short-sighted but dangerous. If you corner a wild animal, so it cannot flee, does it not turn and fight for its life? That is what these workers are facing—it is no surprise there is hostility."

"And are *you* the one to save them all? Shall we all listen to the great Miss Elizabeth Bennet, the guardian of justice for all beings?"

"I never said that, Miss Bingley," said Miss Elizabeth. "Mr. Darcy and I were only discussing the problem—I neither know enough of the industries affected nor those who work in them to suggest a solution."

"Perhaps you do not," said Miss Bingley, her haughtiness once again on display. "Mr. Darcy, however, most assuredly does. It would be best if you allow great men to think about such things, rather than concerning yourself with them."

"There is little harm in discussing such matters," said Darcy, finally speaking. "I consider it a mark of an accomplished woman that she takes an interest in the world around her, even when society might not consider it exactly proper."

"Miss Bingley," said another voice, and turning, Darcy noted that it was Mrs. Bennet. "Can I ask you to advise me? I have a question about London fashion which I would very much like you to answer."

Though Miss Bingley did not wish to allow Mrs. Bennet any of her time, it was also evident she relished the notion of sharing her superior knowledge. Thus, she curtseyed to Darcy, gave Miss Elizabeth a disdainful sneer, and left to attend the Bennet matron. A sigh of relief welled up in Darcy's breast, and he suppressed it, though he suspected

Miss Elizabeth was in complete agreement with him.

"Well thought out and argued, Miss Elizabeth," said Darcy, smiling warmly at her. In a debate, I can see you are a formidable opponent."

"I was taught by the best, Mr. Darcy." Miss Elizabeth shot a fond look at her father, who was still speaking with Hurst. "Papa encouraged my curiosity and taught me how to think and speak critically. I suppose, in some ways, I was the son he never had."

"No one would ever confuse you for a son, Miss Elizabeth," said Darcy, earning her laughter.

With the disruptive presence of Miss Bingley departed, they continued their conversation. A powerful feeling was welling up in Darcy's heart, and he wondered at the vagaries of life, the strange twists and turns it often took. The thought of meeting a woman he could imagine as his future wife in such a place after searching for years had never crossed his mind. Now that the reality was before him, he was coming to the conclusion he must act to secure his future happiness.

Mrs. Bennet was not blind, nor was she bereft of sense. The end of the entail had dispensed with the fear with which she had lived daily, and with it, the urgent imperative to marry her daughters as soon as possible had also died. While she remained of the opinion that their interests were best protected in marriage, the immediate need was gone, and as such, Mrs. Bennet was content to allow her daughters to find their own partners in life.

Having said that, Mrs. Bennet possessed a keen sense of when a gentleman was interested in one of her daughters, a talent she had honed for many years. Not only was Jane in Mr. Bingley's sights, but it seemed Mr. Darcy was interested in Elizabeth. Her second daughter was so dissimilar to what Mrs. Bennet had always thought a man wanted in a wife, she had wondered if Elizabeth would ever find a husband. The emergence of Mr. Darcy as a potential suitor was a relief in more ways than one.

While Mrs. Bennet could see the interest of the two gentlemen, it was also clear that Miss Bingley was not a friend of either of the developing romances, her brother's because she did not consider the Bennets good enough for her, and Mr. Darcy because she wished him for herself. Mrs. Bennet's decision to allow her daughters to find their own paths in life did not extend to allowing Miss Bingley to interfere in something that would bring her daughter much happiness.

When Miss Bingley followed her away from Lizzy and Mr. Darcy,

Mrs. Bennet could see the contempt in which the woman held her. It did not bother her so much as amuse her. Then when they sat down together, Miss Bingley expected her to speak, but Mrs. Bennet only regarded her, wondering if the presence of a mother in this woman's life might have made her more tolerable. Then again, Mrs. Bennet's own mother had died when she was young, and she had not ended proud and haughty. It seemed Miss Bingley's disposition was naturally born. Regardless, Mrs. Bennet hoped Mr. Bingley would be strong enough to control his sister, should he take the step of offering for Jane.

"Yes, Mrs. Bennet?" asked Miss Bingley when they had sat for a few moments. "You said you had a question to ask of me?"

"I offer my apologies, Miss Bingley, for I have no need of your fashion sense. My brother's wife keeps me informed, and as we acquire the best fabrics from his stores, there is little we cannot do for ourselves from the standpoint of fashion."

Miss Bingley frowned, glaring at her with haughty contempt. "Then what is the purpose of your interruption?"

"Only to prevent you from making a fool of yourself."

The affront Miss Bingley betrayed at that moment rendered her incapable of speaking. Knowing the woman would turn away in a moment, Mrs. Bennet used that time to impart the message she wished to relay.

"What you do is your own business, but please allow me to advise against it, Miss Bingley. Mr. Darcy seems like a man of determination. Should he wish my daughter for a wife, and should she return the sentiment, I doubt there is anything you may do to prevent it. Regardless, Mr. Darcy shows no inclination for you, and continuing to pursue him in such circumstances suggests you are desperate or blind. Please desist."

Miss Bingley shot to her feet, her glower turned on Mrs. Bennet with all the force of her displeasure. "You know nothing! Mr. Darcy will never forget himself enough to offer for your insipid daughter."

"We shall see, Miss Bingley. We shall see."

The woman turned on her heel and stalked to an uninhabited corner of the room, muttering imprecations at them all. From across the room, Mrs. Bennet caught her husband's eyes, noting his laughter and the way he directed an expressive look at her. Miss Bingley's quick retreat and position by herself had not escaped his attention, and it seemed he approved of her actions. Mrs. Bennet felt warm all over — she deeply esteemed her husband as an intelligent man, one who had provided a home and a good life to her. Times like these, when she felt his approbation, she treasured.

Though she could not quite determine what it was, something had happened at Longbourn, something which vexed Caroline enough to make her moody and uncommunicative. Louisa could well bear her sister's silence, for she had little notion that Caroline would say anything she wished to hear. The concern was that Caroline would not hold her tongue when they returned and would seek a moment alone with Louisa to release her pent-up vitriol. Louisa's suppositions were not without merit.

Upon gaining the house at Netherfield, Louisa decided to keep herself in the company of the others, to prevent Caroline's designs, and for a time she was successful. Charles, it seemed, was eager to wax eloquent on the subject of his chosen lady and did so for at length as the company remained in the sitting-room. And while Mr. Darcy was much more reserved, Louisa felt it likely that had he been only a little more inclined to speak, he might have done the same. No wonder Caroline was fit to be tied.

The moment her sister struck was not a surprise to Louisa. How Caroline had watched them all, her temper seething below the surface, was something Louisa had seen many times before. When the company broke apart early that afternoon, Louisa found that she could no longer put off the inevitable, much though she wished to postpone it indefinitely.

"Louisa!" hissed Caroline as she stepped into Louisa's bedchamber. The maid, who had been working around the room, started at the sudden entrance, and Louisa shooed her away, resulting in her quick flight. There was no one in the employ of her brother or husband's households who were unaware of Caroline's temper.

"Do you see the danger now?" demanded Caroline.

"If by danger you mean Charles's attentions to Miss Bennet, I can only say from a short observation that there may be something to your suspicions. In Miss Bennet, however, I can find little to criticize — she is a lovely woman, and if I might be so bold to say it, perfectly suitable for our brother."

"How can you speak such rubbish?" demanded Caroline. "She is in no way suitable to be Charles's wife. Can you imagine having *Mrs. Bennet* as a connection? It is in every way intolerable!"

"If Charles chooses her, then you can have nothing to say. The choice is his."

Caroline's eyes narrowed for a moment, then she stepped forward, attempting to use her greater height to intimidate Louisa by looming over her. "Let me make this clear, *dearest sister*—I shall have your support in ensuring Charles never offers for Miss Bennet. We shall convince him to return to London along with Mr. Darcy."

"We shall, shall we?" asked Louisa, her scorn matching her sister's vitriol. "Your words betray you, sister, for I realize your primary concern is Mr. Darcy's attentions to Miss Bennet's sister. And well you should be concerned—had Mr. Darcy shown such favor to you, I have no doubt you would have shouted it from the rooftops."

The fury in her sister's stance was unmistakable, and for a moment Louisa thought Caroline might raise a hand against her. "I will have your aid, Louisa," spat Caroline.

"Or?" asked Louisa, unimpressed by her sister's show of rage.

"Or I shall make your life miserable."

"That is enough!"

The sisters sprang apart, both so focused on their confrontation they had not detected the entrance of another. That other turned out to be Hurst, and from the way he glared at Caroline, he was not amused by the threats she had uttered.

"In case you have forgotten, Caroline, I shall remind you," said Hurst, striding forward to stand at Louisa's side. "Your brother controls your dowry and provides you with your home. It would not do to anger him."

Caroline laughed, her scorn cracking like a whip. "I fear nothing Charles may do."

"Then you are a fool," said Hurst. "Though he chooses not to challenge you, he knows of your excesses. I suspect that this business with Miss Bennet may be his breaking point, should you choose to push him too far. Leave it alone, Caroline—you have never convinced your brother in matters of importance to him. Furthermore, I require you to refrain from threatening my wife—Louisa will be of no assistance to you in this matter, for I am determined Bingley shall act in a manner which suits his own conscience. Now, get out."

For a moment, Caroline glared at Hurst, attempting to determine the extent of his resolve. Then she apparently came to the correct conclusion, for she sniffed and turned to depart. Louisa could not help but wonder if her relationship with her sister had been irreparably damaged; then she remembered there had been little enough relationship and more of Caroline's demands, and she realized it was no great loss. In fact, it was rather liberating.

CHAPTER XX

❧⊱⊰❧

"*S*urely you did not, Mama!" exclaimed Elizabeth.

"I did, Lizzy," said Mrs. Bennet, unconcerned with Elizabeth's horror. "Rarely have I seen the like of Miss Bingley's brand of arrogance, and I wanted to let her know that all her pretensions would be for naught. Mr. Darcy is not the kind of man to allow her to interfere with his designs, and you, Lizzy, are no more forgiving when it comes to such nonsense."

"But to say such things! What will Mr. Darcy think of me?"

Mr. Bennet, who had been laughing at Elizabeth's consternation—quite unhelpfully, in her opinion—stepped in and gave his wife an affectionate glance before turning back to Elizabeth. "However precipitous your mother's words were, I doubt Mr. Darcy will be put off by anything anyone in this family says. Given how he dotes on you whenever he is present, I wonder if he so much as recognizes when anyone else speaks."

Exasperation did not even begin to describe what Elizabeth was feeling at that moment when her sisters—traitors that they were—laughed at Mr. Bennet's words. In the end, Elizabeth did not know if she should laugh or cry, but the thought of laughing was much more appealing, so she joined in with them.

"Do not concern yourself, Lizzy," said Mrs. Bennet, her smile of satisfaction an echo of the old, less proper Mrs. Bennet. "Though I doubt the woman will desist, there is little chance of her turning Mr. Darcy's head. If you like him, I see little wrong with protecting your interests against her."

"But you just claimed she will have no success with Mr. Darcy!" exclaimed Elizabeth, her father and sisters still looking on with amusement.

"Anyone with any wit at all can see that," was Mrs. Bennet's unconcerned reply. "Even so, there is little harm in ensuring a favorable outcome, now, is there? You cannot be too careful about these things."

This was more than an echo of the previous Mrs. Bennet—it was as if her mother had suddenly reverted to the woman she had been seven years before. Had Elizabeth not been able to see the humor in her mother's shedding so many years of improvement, she might have thrown up her hands and stalked from the room. As it was, she had no desire to allow her family any more amusement at her expense.

"What did you all think of Mrs. Hurst?" asked Elizabeth, knowing all too well her voice was not as steady as she might have wished.

"She seemed to be a lovely woman," said Mary. "Unlike her sister."

"Miss Bingley is not *too* bad," replied Jane.

"Oh, she is not?" asked Mary, shooting her sister an incredulous glare. "In fact, by my account, she shows a contemptuous disdain for us all, though she is the daughter of a tradesman, and is no friend of either her brother's or her guest's interest in my elder sisters. What is there to admire in such a woman?"

"Miss Bingley is an intolerable woman," said Mrs. Bennet with a sniff. "If you were not so enamored with Mr. Bingley, I would suggest you send him on his way, ensuring he understood it was because of the disadvantage of having such a sister as she."

"Mama!" cried Jane, scandalized her mother would say such a thing.

"I am well aware it would not be proper, Jane," said Mrs. Bennet, patting her daughter's hand. "*And* I understand your attraction for Mr. Bingley. If it was not so, however, it would be the least of what the woman would deserve. To think of it! She, a woman as low in polite society as it is possible to be, considering herself higher than my daughters, who are the scions of a long line of gentlemen. How is such misplaced pride to be endured?"

"How, indeed, Mrs. Bennet," said Mr. Bennet. "It is unfortunate,

204 *❧ Jann Rowland*

but there are many such Miss Bingleys in society today, and it is our misfortune that one of them has taken up residence in the neighborhood."

"And such a contrast with Mr. Bingley! He is everything amiable and obliging, and to be cursed with such a sister!"

"Just so, Mrs. Bennet. Whatever she might do or say, however, we need not care for it, need not give consequence to her nonsensical statements. In the future, should she speak in such a fashion, allow her to do so, for her silliness shall redound back on her. If she makes a fool of herself, it is nothing to us."

"I cannot say you are incorrect." Mrs. Bennet turned back to Elizabeth. "As for Mrs. Hurst, I found her a very elegant woman, very obliging and kind. Let us foster friendship with her and with Mr. Bingley. We need not care for Miss Bingley's airs."

Elizabeth glanced at her father, seeing his satisfaction, and she was filled with appreciation for his words. When she was a girl, he might have responded to such excesses on her mother's part with a caustic remark that Mrs. Bennet might not even understand. Now, he guided gently, and many times without telling Mrs. Bennet what she should do, allowing her to come to the correct conclusion herself. It was a mark of how a man should deal with his wife, especially, as in the Bennet family, when the wife was of a more limited understanding. It was an example of what she wished for in a marriage—a meeting of minds, someone who would respect her, would speak kindly and show his affection in everything he did. Her parents' marriage was by no means perfect, but it was harmonious.

In the back of Elizabeth's mind, she whispered to herself she might have already found such a man. And her heart grew ever fuller because of it.

"Of all the insubordinate, selfish, contemptible actions you have taken over the years, this has to be the worst! I am ashamed to have you as a sister, Caroline, for you care only for yourself—your wants, your desires, your ambitions. Does it not matter to you what *my* feelings are? Do I mean nothing to you?"

"Charles—"

"Of course, she cares not," interjected Hurst.

The look Caroline shot at Hurst was pure poison, laced with contempt. Bingley watched the interplay with a detachment he had never before felt, pushed to it by his sister's continued attempts to have her own way. She was like a spider in its web, weaving, lying in wait, plotting to catch unwary flies in her unholy schemes. Well, Bingley did not intend to ever be that fly again, for he had had enough of her machinations, her need to order their lives as she saw fit, to push him toward a woman of *her* choosing, which met all *her* needs for advancement in society.

"There is nothing in your sister's mind," continued Hurst, "but grasping, artful scheming. If she cared about you, she would not threaten my wife."

"You misunderstood," said Caroline, sitting stiff-backed in the chair, anger radiating out in waves.

"Do you consider me witless, Caroline?" asked Bingley, his own fury a match for hers. "You may not respect me — you may think I am nothing more than a man perpetually in love with the next pretty woman I meet. To be frank, I care nothing for your respect and doubt you have any affection for anyone but yourself.

"Let me be rightly understood," growled Bingley, leaning on his desk and peering at her with all the determination he could muster, "I will tolerate no interference in my affairs, particularly those with respect to my choice in a marriage partner. If I choose Miss Bennet as that partner, it can be nothing to you."

"Nothing to me?" screeched Caroline. "It affects *me* in every way, for choosing so unsuitable a woman will make it more difficult for me to marry. The Bennets can do nothing for us — they have nothing, they are connected to no one. Is this how you will betray our father's sacrifice, his memory?"

"Do not speak to me of my father," spat Bingley. "Father did not care for society any more than I do. His wish was for us to become landed, to become that which he could not in his lifetime. But he was not so foolish as to believe the Bingleys would be acceptable to high society, for he understood our history is an impediment to our acceptance. I shall not continue to shift in the wind for that which I cannot acquire. I prefer to be happy."

"Happy with a woman so far down on the scale of gentry she may as well not even be on it!"

"Is she not a gentleman's daughter?" demanded Bingley. "Have the Bennets not lived on their land for generations? Is Miss Bennet's dowry not the estate itself?"

"A mere pittance," was Caroline's dismissive reply.

"And yet they have the one thing we Bingleys have *never* had. Even Netherfield, which is a fine estate for a man of my wealth, is not *mine*. I only lease it, as you should understand."

"Netherfield is larger than Dunton Heath," interjected Hurst. When Caroline opened her mouth to speak, Hurst leaned forward and looked her in the eye, saying: "And before you say it, the Hursts have owned our land for as long as the Bennets. My father did not consider your sister a suitable wife—that is one reason he is so difficult at present. But I married her because of my affection for her. This business of you disparaging those above you in society would be laughable if it was not so very pathetic."

"And so is your pursuit of Darcy," said Bingley as Caroline glared and seethed at Hurst. "I have it on good authority—that of the man himself—that he does not consider you a prospective bride, and while I am eager to cede your responsibility to another, I cannot blame him!"

"You know nothing!" rasped Caroline. "I am everything he could ever wish for in a wife."

"There is no reasoning with her, Bingley," said Hurst. "She will believe what she wants to believe, and nothing you say will change her mind."

Bingley grunted in agreement. He cared little what Caroline thought—his concern was her interference in matters of importance to him. *That* he would not tolerate.

"Let me say it again, Caroline," said Bingley, drawing her attention back to him. "It is of no concern to you if I look at Miss Bennet as a prospective bride. There is nothing about her that is objectionable, and a connection to another landed family will only do the Bingleys good, especially if her sister marries Darcy, which I consider likely."

Holding up his hand, Bingley forestalled Caroline's angry retort, looking at her with pity. "If you will not cease this objectionable behavior, then I shall have no choice but to put you out of my house. And before you protest, you should remember that you are of age, and are not my ward. I have kept you here, offered you an allowance, paid your overages, and squired you around in society longer than any man should endure, all without a jot of thanks—you continue to demand more! It is well within my right to release your dowry to you, set you up in an establishment with a companion, paid from the interest of your dowry, and wash my hands of you."

Caroline listened with growing alarm, exclaiming: "You would not dare!"

"Try me, Sister," said Bingley, glaring at her with pitiless determination. "Father only charged me to see to your care—in setting you up in your own establishment, I would consider that charge well fulfilled."

For a moment longer, Caroline gazed at him, calculating, attempting to see how strong his will, how firm his determination. It seemed she did not like what she saw, for it was she who looked away a moment later. Bingley nodded with grim satisfaction.

"You may continue as mistress of this house at present, but let me inform you that any objectionable behavior on your part will lead to Louisa's assuming the position. Do not test me, Caroline, for you will find that Darcy's admonitions all these years have borne fruit. You will not bully me into doing as you wish."

"May I be excused?"

"Yes, please leave," said Bingley. "Do not rejoin us until you can act properly."

Caroline's nostrils flared at his sarcastic words, but she did not reply. Instead, she rose and glided from the room, the door impacting with the wall behind it with less force than he might have expected. Bingley sank wearily into his chair—he had never liked confrontation, but Caroline had driven him beyond what any man could be expected to endure. Though he could not predict her future actions, he hoped he would not be forced to cast her off. Little though she deserved his affection, she *was* still his sister.

As the woman stalked down the hall in high dudgeon, Darcy waited until she disappeared from sight and the sound of her footsteps on the stairs echoed away before he strode to the door she had left open. Turning, he closed it, moving to a chair beside Hurst, noting Bingley's still agitated state. A sudden thought entered his mind, and he instead moved to the sideboard, poured three measures of the brandy Bingley kept there, and handed one to each of his companions, noting with amusement how Bingley drained his in one swallow.

"My cousin would abuse you for treating this fine brandy in such a cavalier fashion, Bingley," said Darcy with some amusement while he sipped from his own glass. "Brandy is to be savored, not devoured."

"Then he may make his complaints to my sister," said Bingley shortly. "I would wager even he could be driven to sacrilege by Caroline's ways."

Darcy smiled and sipped again, while Hurst snorted around his own glass. It was Hurst who spoke next.

"Thank you for your support, Bingley. Louisa, as you know, is not as forceful as her sister, and I would not have her upset." Hurst paused and thought for a moment, before adding: "In fact, I believe Louisa may be with child."

Bingley looked up. "Has she informed you of this yourself?"

With a shaken head and an amused smile, Hurst said: "I am uncertain she has made the connection herself, though it is possible she might. It is not customary for a wife to inform her husband until she feels the quickening."

"Then how do you know?"

"I maintain enough knowledge of my wife to know when certain things happen. While I should not wish to injure the virgin ears of two unmarried men, suffice it to say the cessation of certain . . . functions of a woman's body indicate the possibility of a child, which leads me to suspect—and hope—that an heir is on the way." Hurst snorted again. "With any luck, the birth of a grandson will satisfy my father, and he will slip off into the ether and cease to bedevil me!"

Darcy could only shake his head at Hurst's irreverent words about his sire. Hurst, he knew, did not dislike the irascible old man, but he longed for his own independence. It was something Darcy could not understand himself—he would have been happy if his own father had lived for thirty more years!

"If it is true, then you have my congratulations," said Bingley, as Darcy murmured his own as well. Then Bingley paused and stared morosely into his own glass. "Would that I had something similar to anticipate. Instead, I am weighed down by a bitter shrew with delusions of grandeur."

"I may be incorrect," said Darcy, "but I believe you must first marry a woman before siring an heir—at least if you wish the child to be accepted in polite society."

A bark of laughter was Hurst's response, and even Bingley grinned, his mood seeming to lighten. "Yes, well I think I might have that matter in hand if I can keep my sister from offending the woman I am considering. And what a woman she is! Tall, elegant, beautiful, blonde, and in every way perfect. I doubt I could find her like if I searched the entirety of my life."

"Perhaps it is time to leave," said Hurst *sotto voce*. "Now he has begun reminiscing about his lover, I have no doubt he will continue for hours."

"I have half a mind to join him," said Darcy. "Though I will own that Miss Bennet is a fine woman, it is, in my opinion, daft for anyone to suggest any woman could be to her sister."

"Ha!" cried Bingley. "Do my ears betray me? Has the great Fitzwilliam Darcy owned to being captivated by a mere woman?"

"Completely," replied Darcy. "It was inevitable, old man—I was not willing to settle for a woman of society, one who can net purses, paint tables, embroider, play the pianoforte, and sing like an angel, but who is dull enough to put a man to sleep the minute they are alone together."

The two men laughed, but Hurst, who was not willing to be inundated with such talk, drained his glass and rose. "I can see this is about to turn into a discussion of lovely young ladies—unwed young ladies. Since I have one I married, I believe I shall go to her and inform her of this morning's discussion with her sister, if you will excuse me."

When Hurst left the room, closing the door behind him, Bingley turned to look at Darcy, a questioning quality in his gaze. "Are you set on Miss Elizabeth?"

Darcy demurred. "I do not know I am set on her, for I have not yet known her long enough to make that determination. But I *am* interested, enough to further my acquaintance with her to decide whether I *can* be set on her."

"Then perhaps we shall be brothers after all," said Bingley with a wide grin. "It will not be in the way *my* sister desires, but I find myself less concerned with *her* desires than I have ever been before."

"It shall most certainly *not* be in the way your sister desires," replied Darcy. "As for the Bennet sisters—we shall wait and see. At present, I find I am prepared to acknowledge the possibility and more than a mere possibility."

"Excellent!" said Bingley. "Now, unless I am very much mistaken, I seem to remember hearing you claim that *your* Bennet sister is superior to *mine*. I must disabuse you of that notion, old man, for no one can possibly be any better than *Jane* Bennet."

"You may think that—if it brings you comfort. But while Miss Bennet may bring an estate with her, I am certain I shall receive the better bargain, for Miss Elizabeth is incandescent. There is no other way to describe her!"

They debated the virtues of their chosen ladies for a time, much laughter and amusement passing between them. Though Darcy knew there were many in his circle who would consider him daft, he welcomed the thought of Bingley as a brother, for he was one of the best men Darcy had ever met. Society could disapprove all they wished—Darcy had never had any care for society and did not intend to start now.

That was one facet of Miss Bingley's desire to be his wife that had always confused Darcy. The woman was not stupid, just eager to see the world in a way she wished, ignoring that which she did not like.

Even so, she could not be in any doubt as to his opinion of society, for she had often witnessed his discomfort, his eagerness to withdraw, the downright disdain for many members of whom he did not approve. It must be her propensity to see things as she wished, for any rational person could not help but understand that marriage to Darcy would not be an endless progression of balls, parties, dinners, and the adulation of the masses, which was what Miss Bingley wanted. Darcy much preferred to be at Pemberley — if he could, he would be there always.

After a time of this, they were interrupted when the door opened and in stepped the larger than life person of his cousin, grinning at them as he entered. Bingley, as was his wont, stood and welcomed Fitzwilliam with a hearty shake of his hand.

"Fitzwilliam! We did not expect you back so soon. How do you do, man?"

"Very well!" said Fitzwilliam, greeting Darcy in a similar manner. "If I informed you of my coming, it would deprive me of the pleasure of seeing you surprised by my entry, would it not?"

"One of these days your glib tongue will land you in trouble, Fitzwilliam," said Darcy, shaking his head at his cousin's antics.

"I have every confidence your conjecture is correct," said Fitzwilliam. "But I dare say that will not be today." Then his manner turned more serious. "I apologize for arriving unannounced, Bingley. I have come to ask a few further questions of Wickham's friends in the militia and shall not stay long."

"Still no sign of Wickham?" asked Darcy.

"There has been a sighting or two of him, though unconfirmed," said Fitzwilliam. "The man continues to evade us, though I am convinced the noose has tightened. It is only a matter of time before we shall have him."

"I hope you are not spending all the hours of the day and night looking for him. It would not do to anger your general."

"Ah," said Fitzwilliam with a laugh, "but you forget this is now a matter which concerns the military since our friend Wickham was so good as to desert from his regiment. I have kept up with my duties, but they have been largely superseded by the search for Wickham and a few other deserters. As Wickham is the only one suspected to be hiding in London, I have concentrated most of my efforts there."

Fitzwilliam paused and put his hand on the desk, tapping his fingers against the surface, an absence of mind, as he continued to consider the matter at hand. "There is also this matter of Wickham's supporter. There has been little success in determining who that may be, though, again, I believe I am getting closer to discovering the identity of the individual. I hope you do not mind, Darcy, but I took the liberty of interviewing some of the staff at your house."

"Oh?" asked Darcy with a frown. "Why would they know anything?"

"Somehow Wickham must have had access to the house at Ramsgate," replied Fitzwilliam. "The housekeeper and butler were not there, of course, but they know the staff, and know what goes on below stairs. On the other hand, Georgiana's companion was also there, though I found the woman had little she could tell me."

"And what of Georgiana?" asked Darcy. "Is she still busy with my aunt?"

"There are other matters which have consumed my mother's attention of late, though I believe they still meet regularly." Fitzwilliam grinned and shook his head. "Do not concern yourself, Darcy. Thompson is always in close attendance, and the staff is alerted to the possibility of nefarious activity on the part of our dear friend Wickham. With all these safeguards, I doubt Wickham will make the attempt. At present, she is immersed in her studies with her companion, and I have no doubt Mrs. Younge will keep her from harm."

CHAPTER XXI

Colonel Fitzwilliam's return was welcome by the Longbourn family, as he routinely visited with Mr. Darcy and Mr. Bingley and was often in evidence when the Bennets returned the visits to Netherfield. That there was much congress between the families was welcome to most, though there was a notable exception. What Miss Bingley's behavior in those days presaged, Elizabeth could not be certain, for she was much altered from what she had been before. The visits to Longbourn were usually conducted without her presence, a circumstance for which Elizabeth could not repine. When the Bennets were at Netherfield, however, Miss Bingley attended them, though with evident reluctance. But unlike before, she did not talk to anyone, watched them all with disdain (which was no alteration), but made no attempt to disparage them.

What Elizabeth did see was an increase in both Mr. Bingley's attentions to Jane and Mr. Darcy's eagerness to engage her. As convinced as she was of Mr. Darcy's worth, Elizabeth was thrilled at the sight of his ardency, and several times, she felt almost like Lydia, required to regulate her excitement lest she embarrass herself. It seemed they could speak of anything, and they often did. Matters were proceeding as she might have hoped and dreamed, making her wonder if it was all imagined.

The one matter which was not as idyllic as Elizabeth might have liked was the reason for Colonel Fitzwilliam's presence and the news Mr. Darcy brought of Mr. Wickham. Or perhaps it was more correct to call it the lack of news.

"That is why he has come," said Mr. Darcy the day after Colonel Fitzwilliam's unannounced arrival. "It seems he believes he can pull something of use from Wickham's former associates in the regiment."

"But you have a different opinion," replied Elizabeth.

Mr. Darcy shrugged. "If Wickham followed his usual pattern — and it seems he did — he will have told them little of himself or his activities. To be honest, I suspect Fitzwilliam is looking for an excuse to spend leisure time in the country."

This last was spoken with a grin, one which Elizabeth returned. "It does not speak well to his character if that is his purpose."

"Whatever gave you the idea that Fitzwilliam was of good character?" asked Mr. Darcy.

They laughed together, drawing the eyes of more than one of the company and Colonel Fitzwilliam in particular. He glared at Mr. Darcy as if suspecting the conversation was regarding him and then turned back to Elizabeth's youngest sisters whom he was entertaining at present. As for Elizabeth, she turned the conversation to other matters and was well diverted for the rest of the visit.

In this way, matters continued for some days. While nothing of overt import was said or done in those days, everything took on a new meaning for Elizabeth as her feelings grew ever more ardent for Mr. Darcy. Then in the middle of the week, something happened which threw Longbourn into chaos.

"The post, Mr. Bennet," said Mrs. Hill, placing a stack of letters on the table beside Mr. Bennet that morning while the family was at dinner. Mr. Bennet thanked their housekeeper and left the letters for a few moments. Then, after he had assuaged his immediate hunger, he turned to them, inspecting them with a disinterested eye. That was until he picked up the last.

"What is this?" asked Mr. Bennet, murmuring to himself as he raised the letter and inspected the writing. Then he frowned and broke the seal, opening it and reading, and as he read, his expression became more forbidding.

"What is it, Mr. Bennet?' asked Mrs. Bennet.

As if startled, Mr. Bennet looked up at his wife. For a moment he was silent, and if Elizabeth was to guess, she thought he was not certain what to say. Then Mr. Bennet rose abruptly, grasping all the letters.

"It is a matter of business I must see to at once, Mrs. Bennet. If you will excuse me."

Mr. Bennet walked from the room, the eyes of his family on him as he left. For a moment, no one said anything.

"Well, what was that about?" asked Mrs. Bennet. "Your father usually is not this secretive."

It was a stretch of the truth, Elizabeth knew—Mr. Bennet was not in the habit of sharing the details of his correspondence with his family. It was odd, Elizabeth decided, as he had seemed shocked and more than a little worried. There were few things that had the power to discompose her father, for he was usually more inclined to be amused or dismissive when a problem presented itself.

"Papa was almost rude when he left the room," said Lydia, seeming to believe she had scored a significant point against her father.

"Whatever the case, it is not your concern, young lady." Mrs. Garret frowned at Lydia, daring her to speak, and when she did not, the companion nodded with satisfaction. "Come—finish your breakfast, and perhaps we may walk to Meryton this morning."

The possibility of amusement did the trick, and soon Mrs. Garret shepherded the younger girls from the room for their lessons. Mary and Jane went their separate ways and Mrs. Bennet, to the sitting-room, but Elizabeth found she could not rest until she learned of what had discomposed her father so. A few moments later, she was admitted to his study, noting the concern he was not attempting to hide.

"What is it, Papa?" asked Elizabeth.

Mr. Bennet shook his head. "I do not know whether to tend to amusement or worry, Lizzy, but it seems my cousin has struck."

"Mr. Collins?" asked Elizabeth.

"Indeed," said Mr. Bennet. He threw the offending letter on the desk before her and added: "Here, you may read it if you like. The letter is not from my foolish cousin, but from his patroness. The gist of it is that she intends to support Collins in filing suit against me to wrest possession of Longbourn from my control."

With a scowl, Elizabeth retrieved the letter and skimmed over it, her anger growing as she read the senseless woman's words. The letter was written in an elegant hand, the only positive thing which could be said of it, for the rest was no less than a diatribe of demands and threats of legal action. One particular passage caught Elizabeth's attention.

I have never in my life encountered such wantonly selfish acts as those my parson — your cousin — has related to me. Do you not understand that it is by my advice that Mr. Collins offered you the olive branch you not only spurned but threw back in his face? How can you justify such perfidy, such malignant betrayal as this? Mr. Collins is the rightful heir of your estate, and I think it a kindness he was willing to overlook your offenses against him and offer for your insipid daughter, allowing you to retain Longbourn for your eldest daughter's progeny. Have you no decency?

That you rebuffed his more than generous offer ensures the estate shall not be yours for future generations, for Mr. Collins has no intention of renewing his offer. Let me be rightly understood, Mr. Bennet — this betrayal to which you have descended is beyond the pale and shall not go unpunished. If you act to reinstate Mr. Collins to his proper position, I shall take no further action against you, though I hope you will apprehend that Mr. Collins will do nothing for your widow or remaining unwed children. If you do not, however, know that the full force of the law shall be brought against you. I will spare no expense in ensuring you are thrown from the estate immediately, that it is put in the hands of Mr. Collins, rendering you homeless.

Avoid this calamity on your family, sir. Do what is proper and give your cousin his due. I await your response. Should you decline to reply within one week, I shall know how to act.

"Is the woman daft?" demanded Elizabeth, holding the offending letter between one finger and thumb as if it was a snake. "What manner of woman involves herself to such an extent when she is not connected to the principals of the dispute?"

Mr. Bennet snorted. "Lady Catherine strikes me as a woman who expects to order the world as she decrees. Though I cannot imagine what my cousin told her, I am sure she believes the matter of Longbourn's inheritance will be changed because she has said it must be so. I presume you read the part where she insinuates the support of her brother, the earl."

Though Elizabeth had not read that part carefully, she did remember something of that nature. Mr. Bennet grimaced and turned away to look out the window.

"This business of her promising to see us evicted is nothing more than bluster — the estate is mine until my death, and nothing she says or does will change that."

"And the entail?" asked Elizabeth.

Mr. Bennet remained silent for several moments, drawing out Elizabeth's concern. When he spoke, his manner was hesitant, as if testing the words for their veracity, but remaining uncertain.

"Your Uncle Phillips assures me we worked within the law and above reproach." Mr. Bennet paused and chuckled. "Or I suppose that while it was entirely within the law, it could not be termed, strictly speaking, to be above reproach. I *did* disinherit my cousin in direct contravention of the initial intent of the entail.

"Having said that," said Mr. Bennet with a smile, "I believe my ancestor would have understood and agreed with my reasons, especially if he was introduced to Mr. Collins. A less likely master of an estate would be difficult to find."

"And yet . . ." prompted Elizabeth.

"Powerful men have a habit of getting what they want in our society," said Mr. Bennet. He shrugged, conveying a wealth of meaning. "This reference in Lady Catherine's letter concerns me. The law is on our side, but will it be if a peer becomes involved? That I cannot answer."

When Elizabeth opened her mouth to answer, a sound from behind her alerted her to the presence of another. Turning at the same time as her father, she noted the presence of her mother and could see she had overheard something of what they had been discussing, for she was staring at her husband, mouth open, eyes large. For a moment, no one spoke, the two in the room shocked to see her, while Mrs. Bennet was struggling to voice her feelings.

Then, in a small voice, Mrs. Bennet said: "Are we to lose our home, Mr. Bennet?"

It was a rational question, the subject one about which Mrs. Bennet had *never* been rational, and as such, it caught Elizabeth by surprise, when she might have expected hysterics. As a result, Mr. Bennet was slow to respond, which brought about Mrs. Bennet's nerves, such as they had not seen in more than half a decade.

"Oh, Mr. Bennet!" wailed she. "I knew it was too good to be true! Mr. Collins shall bring suit against us, and that awful Lady Catherine will see we are thrust from our home to freeze in the hedgerows! It is all too much! We should have left well enough alone!"

Mr. Bennet rose at once and approached his wife, taking her by the arm and leading her from the room, saying: "Nothing is wrong, Mrs. Bennet. Yes, Mr. Collins has made threats, but under the law, there is nothing he can do. We shall not lose our home."

"But I heard you!" screeched Mrs. Bennet. "Now what shall we do?" Mrs. Bennet paused and looked back at Elizabeth, who was walking behind them, and said in a loud voice: "Mr. Bingley and Mr. Darcy! They shall be our salvation! You must induce a proposal as soon as possible, Lizzy, for if you do not, I do not know what we shall do!"

"Calm yourself, Mrs. Bennet!" said Mr. Bennet in a louder voice. "No one shall take our home away from us!"

Before he could say anything more, they entered the sitting-room to see that guests had arrived in the interim. With shock, Elizabeth looked on the grim countenance of Mr. Darcy, noted the shock Mr. Bingley displayed, and most of all, the arrogant amusement and contempt direct at them by Miss Bingley. And the reality of their situation settled in on her, pinking her cheeks and drawing her gaze to the ground. Elizabeth wished she could be swallowed up in the depths of the earth, for Mr. she was sure Darcy had heard every word Mrs. Bennet had said. What must he think of her?

"Well, it seems the polish has rubbed off, leaving nothing more than a pig behind. Typical. There can be no thoughts of alliances with these people now."

Though Miss Bingley spoke with her usual venom, Darcy could not spare a moment for her, as his attention could not be moved from Miss Elizabeth. Darcy had heard the same words Miss Bingley had, but his interpretation could not be more different from that of the supercilious woman. As Mr. Bennet greeted them with a few terse words and focused instead on his wife, who seemed to realize she had made a social gaffe, speaking softly to her, controlling her outbursts for the moment.

Mrs. Bennet had always seemed soft-spoken in the time Darcy had known her, though he had seen her more animated at times. It seemed there was a more excitable part of her character, though what had occurred to bring it out he could not say. The notion that anyone would take the estate Mr. Bennet had inherited, that his family had owned for centuries, was preposterous in the extreme. Yet the memory of Mr. Bennet and his daughter speaking of the previous entail welled up within Darcy, and he wondered if Mr. Collins had, against all reason, made a play for the estate. It was not something with which Darcy should concern himself, but his esteem for the family, and for the second daughter, in particular, would not allow him to rest without offering his aid. Since Mr. Bennet was still engaged in comforting his wife, Miss Elizabeth was the likeliest source of information.

"Miss Elizabeth," said he, stepping toward her. "Has something happened regarding the previous entail?"

"I apologize, Mr. Darcy," said Miss Elizabeth, still refusing to raise her gaze from the floor at her feet. "My mother meant no harm. The entail has long been a fear of hers, and times like these bring those fears back to her mind."

"Miss Elizabeth," repeated Darcy in a much gentler tone. Though it could be considered a breach of propriety, he reached out, putting a finger under Miss Elizabeth's chin, and tilting her head until her eyes met his. "Nothing your mother said offended me, as it is clear that something has upset her composure. I assure you, Miss Elizabeth, that I can spot a fortune hunter from one hundred paces. Had I seen mercenary tendencies in you or anyone in your family, I would have fled long ago."

Had she not been made of the sternest blend of determination and willpower, Darcy might have thought she would collapse as the relief flowed through her. As it was, she only smiled, peering up at him through watery eyes, then nodding and standing straighter with determination. Darcy allowed his hand to fall to his side, loath though he was to lose the precious contact with her porcelain skin which was, he decided, as soft as it looked. But there were important matters at hand, so he thrust such thoughts to the side.

"Now, Miss Elizabeth, if it is not too much to ask, will you explain to me what has happened?"

"Father's cousin sent him a letter." Miss Elizabeth paused and shook her head. "Actually, it was his cousin's patroness who sent him the letter. In it, amid insulting language and condescending demands, she threatened to bring suit against my father if he does not reinstate Mr. Collins as his heir."

"But that is preposterous, Miss Elizabeth," said Darcy. "Though I am not a solicitor, I know of the worthlessness of entails. This Mr. Collins must be a dullard if he thinks he may prevail in such a case. Your father must understand this."

"Papa is of the same opinion," replied Miss Elizabeth. "But there is a factor of which you are not aware, for Mr. Collins's patroness referenced peer who is a relation. I have no notion of who it might be, but Lady Catherine sounds like a woman accustomed to having her own way. Will the law stand if a peer involves himself in this dispute?"

Darcy started at the name which slipped from Miss Elizabeth's lips, and he gawked at her, wondering if he had heard correctly. "I am sorry, Miss Elizabeth, but did you say Lady Catherine? Lady Catherine de Bourgh of Rosings Park in Kent? *She* is your cousin's patroness?"

Now it was Miss Elizabeth's turn to be shocked. "You know of her?"

"This is unbelievable," muttered Darcy, wondering at the vagary which had led him to a family whose relation was Lady Catherine's parson. Turning, Darcy caught Fitzwilliam's eye and beckoned him over from where he was standing in awkward conversation with the Hursts. Fitzwilliam did not hesitate, coming with eagerness, while Mrs. Hurst sat with Miss Bennet and Miss Mary. Some semblance of order was returning to the room, though he could see Mrs. Bennet was still distressed.

"We have a heretofore undiscovered connection with the Bennet family, Fitzwilliam," said Darcy when his cousin stepped close. "Miss Elizabeth, will you do me the honor of informing my cousin of the situation with the estate and recent actions of your father's cousin, including exactly whom he claims as his patroness."

Though Miss Elizabeth still appeared mystified, she complied, laying the whole of the history before them, but in a short and concise fashion, not given to verbosity or recriminations. As Darcy listened, he noted Fitzwilliam's concentration, not betraying anything, like any good soldier. That all changed when Miss Elizabeth mentioned the name Lady Catherine de Bourgh.

"But Lady Catherine de Bourgh is our aunt, Miss Elizabeth!" exclaimed he. "She is sister to my father and sister to Darcy's late mother."

Miss Elizabeth appeared even less comfortable now that the connection was made known to her, but Darcy hastened to reassure.

"Do not concern yourself with anything you say of my aunt, Miss Elizabeth."

"It will be nothing we have not thought ourselves," added Fitzwilliam.

Though seeming surprised at their words, Miss Elizabeth nodded and said: "My father believes they acted according to the law, but if Mr. Collins calls on the assistance of a peer, he fears for what may happen."

"Then let me set your fears to rest, Miss Elizabeth," said Fitzwilliam. "Whatever Lady Catherine has said to your father, *mine* will never involve himself in a matter such as this, and to be honest, I am shocked that Lady Catherine has chosen to do so."

"Do you think this Mr. Collins is misleading her?"

Fitzwilliam shrugged. "It is possible, though Lady Catherine needs little incentive to impose herself on the lives of others. What confuses me is she has always concerned herself but little for what happens beyond her domain—I would not have thought she would care two figs about her parson's dispute with his cousin."

"Perchance she wishes to be rid of him," said Miss Elizabeth with a scowl. "Mr. Collins is the stupidest, most ridiculous man I have ever had the misfortune to meet. If your aunt should wish to see the last of him, I would not blame her in the slightest."

"Be that as it may," said Darcy, amused at her characterization of the parson, "this is a matter with which Lady Catherine should not become engaged."

A look around the room informed Darcy that Mrs. Bennet was now calm and was now speaking with Mrs. Hurst in placid tones, though her agitation was still bubbling under the surface. Mr. Bennet was sitting close at hand, ready to assist his wife should she need it. Of the gentleman, however, Darcy had need, and he asked Miss Elizabeth if she could persuade him to join them.

When Mr. Bennet approached them a few moments later, it was with concern and no little curiosity. Darcy attempted to put the man at ease while relating their interest in the matter.

"Lady Catherine is your aunt?" asked Mr. Bennet, surprised.

"It seems to be so unless there is another Lady Catherine de Bourgh of Rosings Park in Kent."

"Please, Darcy," said Fitzwilliam in a pained voice, "one is entirely enough, thank you!"

Mr. Bennet grinned and said: "A difficult woman, is she?"

"You have no idea, sir," replied Fitzwilliam. "There are few in the family who can tolerate her, and only my father can control her to any extent." Fitzwilliam paused and laughed, pointing a thumb at Darcy. "And my cousin here, I suppose, since she has always wished for a union between Darcy and her daughter."

"She claims it is an agreement made between herself and her sister," said Darcy, eager to avoid any misunderstanding. "As my father informed me there was no such agreement, I have never considered myself bound. My uncle agrees."

"That is all very interesting, gentlemen," said Mr. Bennet. "Is there some reason to speak of your relationship with this woman?"

"There is," replied Darcy. "I would like to be of some use to you, Mr. Bennet, and I propose that I journey to Kent on the morrow to speak to my aunt. Though I do not know why she has chosen to champion Mr. Collins's cause, I believe when she is informed of the truth of the matter, she will rescind her support."

"It was my plan to return to London soon, regardless," added Fitzwilliam. "I would be pleased to join Darcy and add my voice to his."

"You have my thanks, gentlemen," said Mr. Bennet. "If your father will not join Lady Catherine in supporting Mr. Collins, I doubt there is anything she can do."

"It is not only altruism that motivates us, Mr. Bennet," said Darcy. "Lady Catherine's imprudent support raises the possibility of damaging our family's good name, for this cause could lead to her ridicule."

"My father's name might be connected to it too," said Fitzwilliam. "The lady is not above invoking his name without his consent."

"It may also be that Mr. Collins is misleading Lady Catherine. If that is true, it is imperative to set her straight."

"Then I thank you, gentlemen," said Mr. Bennet, seeming easier than he had before. "If there is a way to dispense with this business in a way that does not result in a court battle, I am eager for it to be done."

"Leave it with us, Mr. Bennet," said Darcy, offering his hand, which Mr. Bennet grasped.

The visit which proceeded thereafter was the most disjointed Darcy had ever experienced at that house. The Bennets had always been excellent hosts, whether for dinner or just a morning visit. That morning, however, the conversation was forced, and the atmosphere was tense. After they had stayed for a few more moments, Darcy motioned to Bingley that it was time to leave, and Bingley, though uncomprehending and wishing for more time in Miss Bennet's company, agreed and rose. Preparing for departure the following day was paramount, but Darcy did not wish to leave without speaking with Miss Elizabeth once again.

Arranging it was not difficult, as their leave-taking was chaotic, but Miss Elizabeth surprised him by speaking before he could address her.

"You are a good man, Mr. Darcy. I know you need not involve yourself in this mess, but I am thankful you shall, nonetheless."

"It is nothing, Miss Elizabeth," replied Darcy, though he felt warmth flood him at this sure sign of her regard. "There are many reasons for my actions beyond wishing to be of use to you and your family."

"I think you devalue your contribution and goodness, sir," said she, placing her hand on his arm.

"Miss Elizabeth," said Darcy, struggling to find the words in his heart, "I am not an eloquent man and often struggle to know what to say, specifically to vibrant young ladies."

"It does not seem to have been a problem these past weeks," said Miss Elizabeth.

Darcy could not help but grin. "If it has not, then it is the first such experience of my life. I shall only be away for a few days, for I think there is little that can induce me to stay away. What I wished to ask is whether you think there is a possibility for something more between us."

The way in which Miss Elizabeth blushed and ducked her head charmed Darcy, for it was so unlike the self-possessed young woman he had come to know. But then she raised her gaze back to his, her confidence returning, and said: "I have no doubt of it, sir."

"Excellent," said Darcy. He reached out and squeezed her hand once, bowing over it and kissing it. "Until I return, then."

They made their farewells, and the Netherfield party boarded Darcy's carriage for the return to Bingley's leased estate. From the grins to which they subjected him, Darcy thought his short interlude with Miss Elizabeth had not been missed by any of them. Most of his companions were content to do nothing more than grin. There was, of course, one who could not hold her tongue.

"So, shall I arrange for the packing of our effects?" asked Miss Bingley in an all too cheerful tone. "Since there is nothing left for us here, I have a great longing to be back in town again."

"I shall depart for a few days," replied Darcy, "but you have my assurance I will return when my business has been completed. If you wish to quit Netherfield, that is your choice—I shall either stay in the inn or find an estate of my own to lease in the area."

"There is no need for that," said Bingley, glaring at his sister. "I have no intention of leaving Hertfordshire." Bingley turned to Darcy and frowned, saying: "Might I assume that whatever is causing the Bennets' distress is of a serious nature?"

"It is not that serious at all!" said Fitzwilliam in his irrepressible manner. "But as the matter is one that concerns *my* family, Darcy and I must resolve it in an expeditious manner."

"Concerns your family?" demanded Caroline. "I cannot imagine how the Bennets of Hertfordshire would be of any interest whatsoever to the great family of Matlock."

"And yet it is," said Darcy, his tone short as he did not wish to trade words with the objectionable woman.

"Do you require my help?"

"Thank you, Bingley, but in this instance, I believe it is not required. You had best remain here and keep an eye on the situation — as I say, I shall return before long."

"Excellent," replied Bingley. "In that case, I wish you luck."

The rest of the journey passed in merciful silence, for even Miss Bingley did not speak. Her offense Darcy did not give a moment's thought, for her habit of speaking out of turn and trying to direct them, Darcy found difficult to bear. Of more importance was the coming confrontation with his aunt. Darcy did not relish the prospect, though he knew it was necessary. There was no telling what damage Lady Catherine might do to the family name with nary a thought, and thoughtlessness was one of the hallmarks of her character.

CHAPTER XXII

$\mathcal{I}$t may be deemed impetuous, but the following morning Elizabeth felt compelled to witness for herself the gentlemen's departure from Netherfield. Thoughts of Mr. Wickham and how he might be lurking nearby vanished in the face of Elizabeth's desires, and therefore she dressed early and made her way from the house, feeling the freedom of a long walk calling her again after a long cessation of such activities.

The paths of Longbourn were well known to Elizabeth, and she knew that if she followed a small track which skirted Meryton and wound generally east, she would emerge through the forest at a point higher than the manor house, and from whence she could see to the entrance itself. Accustomed to walking as she was, Elizabeth lengthened her stride, her pace eating the distance as if it was nothing more than a stroll in a nearby park. Soon she reached her destination, taking in the view with the eagerness of a small child.

There was, indeed, activity around the entrance at Netherfield, for a large coach had been drawn up to the door, around which was a bustle of activity. Before her eager eyes she saw men running this way and that, leading horses to their place in front of the conveyance, or women carrying baskets, likely the gentlemen's luncheon to be consumed during their journey. Elizabeth could even discern the tall forms of Mr. Darcy and Colonel Fitzwilliam as they exited the estate, stood for some moments speaking to another man who Elizabeth assumed was Mr. Bingley. Then the gentlemen entered the coach, and it departed in a cloud of dust, making its way down the long road which led to Meryton, soon disappearing in the trees. Elizabeth could not help but feel bereft.

Not one made for melancholy thoughts, Elizabeth turned away from the scene, deep in her reflections as the path led her around the edge of her father's estate to the north. It was a cool day, though at this time of year most days held the chill presaging the oncoming winter months. The trees were now bare of their summer mantles, and the wind, as it blew softly, kissing her cheeks like a lover's caress, stirred the blanket of leaves, sending them careening across the path, or swirling up in a funnel, only to drift back down to the ground when the wind found somewhere else to play.

As she walked, Elizabeth's mind fixed on the events of the past few weeks, in particular, dwelling on the gentleman who had been at the center of her thoughts since his coming. The request he had made of her still possessed the power to thrill Elizabeth, to send her soaring through the clouds with the wind. Though Elizabeth had never been in love, she was certain she was already in a fair way of being in love with Mr. Darcy. It was beyond doubt he was the best gentleman she had ever known.

A sudden flight of birds, winging their way into the sky, startled Elizabeth and brought her swift march to a halt. The flock wheeled and cried, circling the place in the trees from where they had arisen, then turned and winged toward the east and Netherfield, leaving Elizabeth alone again in the quiet woods. A glance at the grove revealed nothing — it seemed they had been startled by some animal, perhaps a fox. Thus unconcerned, Elizabeth began to walk again.

It was only a few moments later when two things happened at once. As she was walking, she heard a loud snap, as if a branch in the underbrush had been stepped on. Turning, Elizabeth looked back the way she had come, while at the same time hearing someone hailing her from the opposite direction. Once again, she turned and noted the approach of one of Longbourn's tenants.

"Miss Elizabeth," said the man with a bow. "I did not think I would see you this morning. Tis a little cold for walking about the estate."

"Come now, Mr. Campbell," said Elizabeth. "You know me better than that."

"Aye, I suppose I do!" replied he with an amused smile. "The missus mentioned your visit the other day—we appreciate the basket you brought to us. We had a good harvest this year, but we are still grateful for the assistance."

"It is no bother, Mr. Campbell," replied Elizabeth. "I hope your daughters enjoyed the apple butter."

Once again Mr. Campbell guffawed. "Indeed, they did. But you already know that."

"Of course," replied Elizabeth. "I know of no one in the district who does not enjoy Longbourn's apple butter."

The tenant shook his head. "Well, I thank you all the same. Please take care as you make your way home."

Then the man tipped his hat and strode off, Elizabeth watching him go. The thought of the sound which had caught her attention before his arrival crossed her mind, and Elizabeth looked back to the woods. There was nothing other than the sound of the wind, which had picked up a little, whistling through the bare branches.

Shrugging, Elizabeth turned her steps back to Longbourn, eager to reach the warmth of her home. The rest of her walk passed without incident, and by the time she joined her family at the breakfast table, she had quite forgotten the matter altogether.

Travel was something the cousins did not enjoy, though Fitzwilliam, due to his years in the army, was inured to the discomfort. Darcy had made the journey many times himself, for Pemberley was three days from London, necessitating hours cramped in a carriage, which always seemed small, no matter how large or well-appointed it was. When the façade of Rosings Park rose in the distance, Darcy found himself almost grateful, though he knew the visit would not be pleasant.

"You know Lady Catherine will not be easy to convince," said Fitzwilliam, his eyes fixed on the distant building, showing he too had been alerted to their imminent arrival.

"When is she?" asked Darcy. "I have never met a woman so convinced of her own infallibility, particularly about matters of which she is ill-informed or lacks knowledge altogether."

Fitzwilliam snorted. "Come now, Darcy. Do you think, for example, that a lack of any skill or training in any way lessens her knowledge of music? Why, she has told us many times how she would be a true proficient if she had only learned."

Shaking his head, Darcy decided against responding—his cousin needed no encouragement.

"Do you think you will escape mention of Anne? She will take our visit as a compliment to her daughter."

"Yes, I know it very well. It is my intention to procure her agreement to drop her support of Mr. Collins and leave as soon as possible. If she pushes me to it, I will remind her I will not offer for her daughter."

"Then 'lay on, MacDuff,'" said Fitzwilliam, though mercifully he did not speak on the subject again.

As the carriage approached the manor, a tall figure dressed all in black came into view by the side of the road. The man was tall and portly, had a distinct bald patch on his head, and wore the collar of a cleric, little though it did him any distinction. When the carriage passed him by, he made an obeisance, for that was the only word for his low bow—his knuckles might have dragged on the gravel beneath his feat, had he allowed them to fall from his side.

"And *that* I suppose is Mr. Bennet's cousin." Fitzwilliam chortled, adding: "I had wondered if they were not exaggerating, but I see now they have downplayed his silliness if anything!"

"It seems to be so," murmured Darcy. "Given his groveling, I suspect we could put the fear of God into him and induce him to desist without even applying to Lady Catherine."

"Now he has brought it to her attention, it would not work."

"That is true," replied Darcy. "But perhaps, should the opportunity present itself, I shall do so regardless."

"Take pity on the dullard, Darcy," said Fitzwilliam. "He cannot help it if he does not possess the wits God gave a goose."

Darcy shot his cousin a grin but did not reply, for the carriage had turned onto the drive before Rosings. When the carriage stopped, Darcy allowed his cousin to step down before following him, noting a stable boy was approaching them along with the cadaverous butler. The horses had been changed in London, meaning they were still good for a time. Thus, Darcy addressed the driver, instructing him to feed them a few oats sparingly, but to leave them in their traces. That completed, Darcy turned toward the butler.

"Mr. Darcy," said the man in a gravelly voice. "We have had no word of your coming. Shall I have the housekeeper prepare rooms for you and the colonel?"

"That will not be necessary. Is Lady Catherine within?"

"The lady is in the drawing room, but Miss Anne has retired for the afternoon."

"Excellent," said Fitzwilliam, shooting Darcy an expressive look.

"Do not concern yourself for us, for we know the way."

The butler bowed, but Fitzwilliam was already bounding up the stairs, Darcy close on his heels. As always, Rosings was quiet, more akin to a mausoleum than the home of a wealthy and privileged English woman. Of the garish décor Darcy took no note—he knew Lady Catherine's preferences and her desire to display her wealth to all who passed through the door. It was one of the many reasons he had no interest in marrying Anne—Darcy had no desire to allow Lady Catherine to make Pemberley into a copy of Rosings.

The footman stationed at the side of the door opened it to Fitzwilliam's signal, though he had likely been told the mistress was not to be disturbed. As her attention was about to be taken by their arrival, there would be no repercussions for the unfortunate man. Unless Lady Catherine was rendered angry by the coming discussion. This was a distinct possibility . . . .

"Fitzwilliam!" said the lady, shock coloring her voice. "And Darcy!"

While the greeting had been for them both, as soon as she caught sight of Darcy, Lady Catherine's gaze remained on him, considering. It was always thus, and Darcy had often felt like the woman was a wolf, crouching in the long grass of a meadow, waiting to catch the unwary. Or, more particularly, Darcy himself.

"Why did you not send me word of your coming? I have nothing prepared for your comfort." Lady Catherine paused and then said in her usually haughty tone: "Of course, I always keep rooms at the ready, regardless, for my staff is instructed in all these details. Since you are here, you must stay for a fortnight. Anne is eager to see you too."

It took all of Darcy's considerable willpower to refrain from rolling his eyes, and Fitzwilliam's large grin did not help matters. Instead of replying, Darcy greeted his aunt, asking after her health before rejecting the offer of shelter.

"A stay, even for the night, is impossible, Aunt, for I have other matters to attend to. Fitzwilliam, I believe, is expected back at his regiment before long."

"Tomorrow, actually," said Fitzwilliam. Darcy could not say if his cousin's assertion was truthful, but if it was not, he could not blame him.

"Oh, then I suppose you must go," said Lady Catherine with a dismissive wave at Fitzwilliam. "But Darcy may stay. It is late autumn, and I know there is nothing calling you away at present."

"Again, I am not at liberty to stay at Rosings, Lady Catherine—not even for the night. A matter of great importance has brought us here, and we must depart once we discuss it with you."

Annoyance at his recalcitrance warred with curiosity on Lady Catherine's visage. For a moment, Darcy thought annoyance would win the day, but then Lady Catherine huffed in irritation.

"A matter of importance? I know of no such matter. Of what are you talking?"

"Your parson," said Darcy, sitting on a nearby sofa, allowing Fitzwilliam to take the other. "Mr. Collins has approached you with a concern regarding his cousin's estate, I believe. Is this not so?"

"How did you know about that?" demanded Lady Catherine. When Darcy said nothing, giving every indication of waiting for her to speak, Lady Catherine sniffed with annoyance. "Yes, he brought a matter to me, one of grave importance. His cousin, you see, has cheated him out of his inheritance, claims to have removed him in favor of his daughter! Can you imagine such a thing?"

"It was an entail, Lady Catherine," said Darcy, his eyes boring into her. "You are aware, are you not, that entails no longer have much force in the law? For Mr. Collins to be secure in his status as heir to Mr. Bennet's estate, he would have needed Mr. Bennet to approach him—not the opposite!—and work out an agreement of strict settlement. An entailment by itself is not worth the paper on which it is printed."

"Then why was it implemented at all?" demanded Lady Catherine. "If that is so, why did Mr. Bennet not change the entail long ago?"

"Many of these small neighborhoods are not always up to date on certain legalities, Lady Catherine," said Fitzwilliam. "It matters not *when* the business was completed. It only matters it was done according to the law."

Lady Catherine glared at them, a mutinous glint in her eyes. "I do not see that at all. It seems to me a man is cheating another for his own family's gain and after his own failure to provide for them. Do you think Mr. Collins did not ensure I know every detail?"

"From what I understand," replied Darcy, "Mr. Collins was at Longbourn for less than two days complete. Is he of such experience and intelligence that the workings of an estate are an open book? He has never trained to manage a property and has not even had the benefit of being raised where he may have gained some insight through simple observation. Is his account to be trusted?"

"What is the meaning of this inquisition?" asked Lady Catherine, looking at them through narrowed eyes. "What can it mean to you?"

"I am asking you the same question, Lady Catherine. What is it to you whether Mr. Collins inherits an estate or remains at Hunsford for the rest of his life as your parson?"

"What matters is I am attentive to all such injustices as that which is being perpetrated on Mr. Collins." Lady Catherine glared at them each in turn, and for a moment Darcy thought she would once again challenge him on his own interest in the matter. In the end, she did not, saying: "How could I not assist when I heard his cousin's betrayal?"

"Then let me clarify matters for you, Lady Catherine," said Darcy. "In fact, though it is unfortunate that Mr. Collins is now not in a position to inherit an estate, Mr. Bennet has acted as was his right, and nothing was done in contravention of the law. I am acquainted with the Bennets and know every detail of these transactions. Mr. Collins can win no appeal to the law—his suit would be dismissed in an instant, and he would be left a laughingstock, as would all those who support him."

"Are you suggesting I am not familiar with the law?" demanded Lady Catherine.

"We believe you lack the facts," said Fitzwilliam. "If you were aware of the great disadvantage which must come of the imprudent decision to support Mr. Collins, you would judge different."

Lady Catherine paused and considered them, and Darcy held a smirk in check. There was no better way to induce Lady Catherine to desist than to insinuate harm to the family, for whatever else she was, Lady Catherine was proud of their position and reputation in society. When she did not speak to press her point, Darcy knew she had been persuaded. It was just as well, for Darcy had been prepared to pit himself against her, to support the Bennets against Lady Catherine and the fool of a parson. *That*, he knew, she would not have received well.

"It may be I have been hasty in agreeing to support Mr. Collins," confessed Lady Catherine. It sounded like it was being unwillingly drawn from her lips. "This Mr. Bennet has a strong case in the law?"

"The strongest," replied Darcy. "The papers for the common recovery of his property were submitted and executed by his solicitor to a judge. There is little Mr. Collins can do except make a fool of himself."

"What of this business of a daughter inheriting?"

"Come now, Lady Catherine," said Darcy, annoyed she would even bring up such an objection. "Was Anne not set up as your late husband's heir? There is nothing in the law that prevents a woman from inheriting property—the only stipulation is the property becomes her husband's when she marries."

Lady Catherine glared at him, suspicion radiating from her agate-hard eyes. "Can I assume *you* have no interest in this matter? I presume you understand to what I refer."

As it happened, Darcy well understood the thrust of her comment. "No, Lady Catherine, I have no interest in Miss Bennet, or at least in the manner you are suggesting." It was true, even if Darcy omitted the interest he had in Miss Bennet's *sister*. Lady Catherine did not need to know that.

"Then I shall cease to support Mr. Collins," said Lady Catherine.

"That is for the best," replied Darcy. "It is a mark of your intelligence you have seen the sense of our arguments."

Lady Catherine nodded tightly. "Now I have agreed to withdraw my support to Mr. Collins, perhaps you would be so kind as to explain what interest *you* have in this matter."

"The Bennet family are friends," replied Darcy with a dismissive shrug. "I would not see them ill-used, nor would I wish our family to be pulled into his dispute under false pretenses. If Mr. Collins persists, it will not end well for him, and it would not reflect well upon you if you continued to support him."

Lady Catherine grunted, and while she desisted, she continued to regard him with open suspicion. "Yes, well, perhaps it is best you warned me. I shall have strong words with my parson—of that you may be assured.

"Now, this business of leaving at once is nonsense," said she, shifting the topic. "You must stay at least two weeks. Anne will be so happy to see you, as she always is. Let me have the housekeeper show you to your rooms, for Anne will arise before long."

"As I stated, Lady Catherine," said Darcy, "I must return to town today, as I have business waiting for my attention."

"No business can be as important as obliging your family! Come, Darcy, I insist!"

"You may insist all you like," replied Darcy, rising to his feet, pulling Fitzwilliam along with him. "But we shall depart at once. I thank you for your time and commend you for making the right decision regarding Mr. Collins—I suggest you warn him against any future actions on the matter of the estate, for he shall not prevail."

Lady Catherine rose along with them, though by this time her expression was most unfriendly. The scathing look she directed at them suggested she knew something, and Darcy wondered what stories her stupid parson had been spreading about the Bennets.

"Are you to return to Hertfordshire?" asked she, her bluntness more acute than usual.

"Yes, though there are matters in town which require my attention before I do," replied Darcy.

"Then I shall bring Anne to London. It is high time you announce your engagement. Though it is not the height of the season, I believe it will still be a matter of much interest—we shall announce it before Christmas."

Darcy suppressed a weary sigh. It had been foolish, he supposed, to hope to escape Rosings without having this conversation. Then again, given his ardent attentions to Miss Elizabeth, he supposed now would be as good a time as any to have it. Darcy would not put it past her to journey to Hertfordshire to set him to rights or to abuse Miss Elizabeth into refusing his proposal.

"There will be no need for you to go to London," said Darcy. "I have already stated I will not be there long. Furthermore, though I have told you many times before, you have not heard me, so I will say it one last time: I will not marry Anne."

"Yes, you shall," said Lady Catherine, her voice laced with steel. "It was the favorite wish of your mother and hers. It is your duty, and I shall see it done."

"Lady Catherine is a break between my house and yours what you wish?" asked Darcy. He could be every bit as blunt as she. "For let me state without disguise: if you push me on this subject, that is what will happen."

The glare with which she regarded him might have frozen a lesser man into a block of ice. "You would not dare."

"I most assuredly would."

The two combatants stood eye to eye, neither giving an inch. For Darcy's part, he was entirely calm, for he knew there was little Lady Catherine could do to force him into acting as she wished. It was up to her to determine how this confrontation would end, for good or ill, and while she might *think* she could bend him to his will, she would soon know disappointment. In the end, she attempted conciliation.

"Come, Darcy, you know this is what your mother wished. Let me show you to a room so you can consider the matter before making a hasty decision."

"My decision is not a hasty one," replied Darcy. "It is the work of many years. I am not bound by so irrational a demand as yours in the most important choice of my life."

"You behave like a spoiled child," spat Lady Catherine. "Do you think I will recede? If you do, you know me less than I might have expected."

"And you know less of me if you believe I will give way, no matter how long you insist."

"And, thus, you have proved yourself a weak man, tempted by thoughts of pretty young gentlewoman on the hunt for a wealthy man. Do you think Mr. Collins has not informed me of his cousin's family? It is obvious you have allowed your head to be turned toward one of the man's daughters, for otherwise you would not be so hard-headed."

"On the contrary, Lady Catherine," replied Darcy, "I made this decision long ago. I have not insisted you accept my determination because I knew what your response would be. I am no longer willing to listen to your diatribes on the subject, nor will I allow you to crow to all and sundry of my future as your son-in-law. If you cannot accept this, all connection between our families is dissolved until you are more reasonable."

Sketching the woman a perfunctory bow, Darcy turned and stalked from the room, eager to be away from Rosings as soon as possible. It was a surprise she did not follow him, haranguing him as he went, but Darcy was grateful for her forbearance, however it had been achieved. When he entered the carriage, it became apparent why, for Fitzwilliam had not followed him. His cousin came striding out of the house and entered the carriage soon after.

"You have stirred up the hornets' nest, Cousin," said Fitzwilliam as he gave the driver the command to depart. "Had I not stopped her, I might have thought she would follow you and bury a dagger in your back."

Darcy arched an eyebrow at his cousin and said: "Et tu, Brutè?"

Fitzwilliam laughed and shook his head. "Lady Catherine will not allow this to rest unchallenged."

"Then I shall have a word with your father. As for myself, I will not allow Lady Catherine into any property I own until she begins to behave in a rational manner."

"Then her banishment will be permanent," replied Fitzwilliam. "I would not expect her to ever relent."

The mood Darcy was in, the need to lash out at someone or something was nigh overpowering. Thus, when the carriage attained the main road and swept past the parsonage, the sight of the rotund parson filled Darcy with a cold determination, and he gave the command to halt the vehicle. Then he stepped out and confronted the man, who was clearly astonished by his actions.

"Mr. Collins, I presume?"

It was not polite in any way, but Mr. Collins seemed to take no notice, for he bowed low and began to babble. "You must be Lady Catherine's nephews. Never would I have imagined I would be so fortunate as to make your august acquaintances so soon, for it is my understanding you visit but once a year. Please allow me to take the opportunity to — "

"A simple yes or no will suffice!" spat Darcy, silencing the stupid man's ineffectual mutterings.

But Mr. Collins had no way to respond, as he straightened and stared at Darcy, his mouth hanging open. Darcy glared at him, but it seemed to make no difference.

"You had best say something, Cousin," said Fitzwilliam, "for if you do not, I fear a bird will take up residence in his mouth."

Mr. Collins's mouth snapped shut, and for the first time, he showed a little spirit in the glare with which he responded. Darcy was not about to allow him to speak.

"I know who you are, so you need not reply. Heed me well, Mr. Collins, for I will not repeat myself. If you have any notion of suing Mr. Bennet for control of Longbourn, I suggest you drop it at once, for not only will you bankrupt yourself, but you will make yourself a laughingstock. And you should know that I will support the Bennets in their fight against you. My influence is not insignificant, sir, and you would do well to take note."

By this time the parson had recovered his wits — what there were of them — and he essayed to reply: "I have secured the support of Lady Catherine in my fight against the wrong done to me."

"You will find Lady Catherine is less eager to lend her assistance now and distracted by other matters." Darcy stepped closer to the silly man, prompting him to cringe away, and hissed: "Stand down, Mr. Collins. I will ruin you if you persist."

Then Darcy turned on his heel and walked back to the coach with Fitzwilliam following behind. When the carriage departed, Darcy looked back to see the parson hurrying toward Rosings, no doubt to discover for himself the truth of Darcy's words. A snort alerted him to Fitzwilliam's dark amusement.

"Do you not think Lady Catherine will support him if only to spite you?"

"No," was Darcy's short reply. "This cradle betrothal Lady Catherine has concocted in her mind is of utmost importance, beside which Mr. Collins's concerns are nothing more than an infant's mewling. When I speak to your father, I shall ensure he knows to warn Lady Catherine away from such a disastrous course."

"A wise plan, Cousin. I would put nothing past the old bat, and you have made her angry enough to provoke her to anything."

Darcy did not reply. Instead, he glared out the window at the passing scenery. The visit with his aunt had been as bad as he had expected, and now it was past, he longed for the comfort of Miss Elizabeth's smiles, her laughter, and above all, her sympathetic ear. He could not return to Hertfordshire soon enough.

CHAPTER XXIII

*T*hough unfortunate, the return to Hertfordshire was to be delayed, at least until the following afternoon. When the cousins arrived in London, both were ready to seek their beds, though their hunger was such that a small meal taken in their rooms was necessary. The following morning, having recovered from the long journey the day before, Darcy and his cousin approached Lord Matlock.

The earl was a good man, in Darcy's opinion, who, though perhaps proud of his position in society, was nevertheless kind and genuine, one who did not look down on others. Tall and aristocratic in bearing, Lord Matlock was a man of more than sixty years, still hale and active, blessed with excellent health and a keen intellect. He was also little disposed to enduring his sister's tantrums and determined to prevent her from staining the family name.

"Darcy, Anthony," said he when the cousins entered his study that morning. "I suppose I might have expected to see you some time or another, Darcy, given what my son has told me of your exploits in Hertfordshire."

"Exploits?" drawled Darcy, turning a hard eye on his cousin. It had as little effect on him as usual.

"A poor term, perhaps," said Fitzwilliam. "There are matters of interest to the family occurring in Hertfordshire, you must own."

"I had not thought my private actions were bandied about the entire family."

"Oh, do be reasonable, Darcy," said Lord Matlock. "Anthony informs me of the general state of matters, and I make my own inferences from there. Even you must own that any attention you pay to a young woman must be a subject of interest for us all, given your usual practice of keeping them at arms' length."

"Be that as it may," said Darcy, deciding it was best to come to the point, "we have just come from Rosings last night and have some tidings of Lady Catherine of which you ought to be aware."

That caught Lord Matlock by surprise. "The last I heard of you, you were in Hertfordshire—it must have been a matter of some import to take you to Rosings. Please, let me know what my sister has done now."

And so, Darcy shared his knowledge with his uncle, informing him of the entire matter without holding back. When he was finished speaking, his uncle was shaking his head with disgust.

"It is just like Catherine to stick her nose into matters like this with no thought of the consequences." Lord Matlock paused and then eyed Darcy. "This neighborhood in which your friend has leased his estate must be backwater if they use entails to ensure the solvency of their estates."

Darcy shrugged and said: "It is not uncommon for small neighborhoods to be less versed in such matters."

"Strict settlements have been in use for many years."

"Yes, they have," replied Darcy. "But the state of the neighborhood's knowledge of present events are not the point. Mr. Bennet did nothing that was not done many times in the past. For Lady Catherine to support Mr. Collins in his mad quest to overturn it would lead to nothing more than infamy for her, for she would be ridiculed by society."

"As Lady Catherine rarely leaves Rosings," added Fitzwilliam, "she would not bear the shame of it. We would."

"Have no fear," said Lord Matlock. "I have no intention of allowing Catherine to have her way in this matter." Lord Matlock paused in thought for several moments, before continuing slowly. "Though it may be best if I should visit Rosings to rein her in, this business of you rejecting Anne once and for all will almost certainly bring her to my doorstep soon enough anyway. Thus, I think I shall spare myself the inconvenience of going into Kent and wait for her."

Having said that, Lord Matlock again turned a discerning eye on Darcy. "This matter of you refusing to offer for Anne, however, is a change from your previous practice of avoiding the subject at all costs. Do you care to share the exact reason with me? I knew you were interested in a young lady of the country, but I did not know your interest was that far advanced. Perhaps my sister's suspicions are correct for a change—God knows she must be right occasionally."

Fitzwilliam laughed, while Darcy could only shake his head. "A stopped clock is correct twice a day."

"Exactly," said his uncle. "So? Will you share it with me?"

"There is nothing to share at present."

"Oho! But there will be something in the near future?"

"She is a lovely young lady," said Fitzwilliam, unhelpfully in Darcy's opinion.

"I was expecting it, but I must own to some surprise." When Darcy fixed him with a questioning glance, Lord Matlock shrugged. "As I said before, you avoid young debutantes like they carry the plague. As a young man in your position, you could have the pick of any young lady in society, perhaps even as high as the daughter of a duke, if you set your mind to it. To turn your nose up to all these and instead choose a young woman of the country, no matter how capable or suitable she may be, will set tongues wagging and earn you enmity in some quarters."

"Quarters for which I have no concern at all," replied Darcy.

"Of course, you do not, and I cannot fault you for it. Please tell me one thing: she is suitable, is she not? Entering a world of which she has no knowledge, being a target for every jealous young lady and their mothers—and perhaps even some of their fathers—would be a daunting task for anyone. She will bear up under the scrutiny?"

"I dare say there is nothing that Miss Elizabeth could not do if she set her mind to it. The thought of her intimidated by society is laughable—I suspect she will have them eating out of the palm of her hand in a trice and will soften all but the hardest of hearts."

"Well, then," said Lord Matlock, smiling slightly, "it seems you may have chosen well after all, for I trust your judgment. Since I cannot imagine any young woman of the country refusing you, I shall consider it a fait accompli."

"This is not *any* young woman, Father," said Fitzwilliam. "As I have also made her acquaintance, I can say she will not accept Darcy for his wealth or position. He will have to convince her—as he has never found himself in such a position before, it might concern me. But I think he will muddle through in the end."

Lord Matlock guffawed with his son. Darcy, knowing they would tease regardless, allowed them their mirth and waited for his uncle to speak again.

"Then when you have secured her — *if* you secure her — bring her to London to meet us. Catherine will have no thought of supporting her, and we cannot allow her vitriol to affect us. If Susan and I publicly give you our support, it will go a long way to securing her acceptance. And if what you say is correct, your young lady will do the rest."

Their return to Darcy's house coincided with a surprise visit from Bingley, who bounded in with his usual energy not long after Darcy and Fitzwilliam arrived themselves. "Darcy, I was hoping I would catch you before you departed for Hertfordshire."

"Bingley!" exclaimed Darcy. "What the deuce are you doing in London?"

"My banker called me into town on an important matter of business. It should take me no longer than this afternoon to complete, and I should be ready to depart tomorrow morning if you care to wait."

Darcy did not care to wait, but another concern was of more importance. "It was my understanding you were to wait in Hertfordshire and watch the situation there."

Bingley shrugged and replied: "Hurst is there, and I was only to be gone for a day. And before you say anything about trusting Hurst," added Bingley with a laugh, "since he came to Hertfordshire and Louisa has thrown off Caroline's shackles, he has been much more alert and engaged. I dare say it has almost made a new man out of him!"

"I would suggest that is a bit of an exaggeration, Bingley," said Fitzwilliam.

"Perhaps it is," said Bingley, his grin never dimming a jot, "but there it is, all the same."

"Delaying your return may be beneficial," said Fitzwilliam. "You have not seen Georgiana for some time — I believe she would appreciate the opportunity to visit with you."

While Darcy did not like the delay, he could only agree with his cousin. The decision was made, and Bingley left for his appointment with his banker, while Darcy went in search of his sister.

It had not been Darcy's intention to ignore Georgiana, and it seemed to him his sister had not taken it in such a way. They had met briefly that morning, Darcy stating his need to speak to their uncle before Georgiana began her lessons, and while he had thought to see her again before departing, Darcy's attention had been fixed on the return to Hertfordshire. The delay chafed, but the opportunity to see his sister was one Darcy always relished.

Georgiana was in the music room that morning, a place Darcy could always find her if she was given the choice. Mrs. Younge, though she could play, was not a superior performer, and she allowed Georgiana to play or allowed the master to do his job when the situation demanded it. That morning, she noted his arrival and nodded in deference, but did not speak when Darcy approached his sister, noting the sweet flow of notes as guided by her supple hands. When she finished playing, Darcy clapped, prompting her to turn to regard him. The smile which swept over her countenance was a testament to their shared affection.

"Are you not to return to Hertfordshire this afternoon, Brother?"

"I was," replied Darcy. "Bingley arrived only a few moments ago, informing me he has been called here on a matter of business which was to occupy his time today. I decided to accommodate him and delay my departure until tomorrow."

"Then I am please I shall have some of your time." She paused and gave him a sly grin. "Or shall you spend the day in morose contemplation, wishing you were in the company of your lady friend?"

Though Darcy could not help his responding grin, he was curious. "What do you know of the matter?"

"Only what Anthony has told me and what I have gleaned from our correspondence. You never mentioned a woman in your letters until recently and having done so with such frequency suggests there is something about her you feel is important."

Darcy nodded. It had been a priority for him to teach her to read between the lines, not only in the written word but also when listening to another speak. A skill made necessary due to her position in society, not to mention their unfortunate connection with George Wickham, Darcy thought she had made excellent progress.

"Then let us sit and I shall tell you of her. I do not think you will be disappointed."

They spent a pleasant morning in each other's company, beginning with Darcy informing Georgiana of everything about Miss Elizabeth, to which she listened, showing her interest in her eager questions and expressions of delight. When he tried to speak of her doings,

Georgiana's answers were superficial, and her questions always directed the conversation back to Miss Elizabeth. After a time, Darcy did not even bother to attempt to induce her to speak of anything else.

"This Miss Elizabeth sounds wonderful," said Georgiana with a sigh some time later. "To think I shall soon have a sister! I cannot wait!"

"Nothing has been settled yet, Georgiana," said Darcy. "In all honesty, I have not even decided to offer for her."

"Given everything I am hearing, I cannot imagine you will *not* offer for her," said Georgiana with a dismissive wave of her hand. "If even half of what you say of her is true, I cannot imagine she will fail to understand your worth."

His sister, in saying that, was referring to his worth as a man, Darcy knew. To a man who had often heard himself summed up by the size of his fortune, hearing such words was gratifying. Georgiana was as unpretentious as a young woman could be—both Darcy's father and he himself had attempted to instill a sense of humility in her—and Darcy knew she meant every word, regardless of their familial relation.

"If you like, you may come to Hertfordshire to meet her," said Darcy. "Bingley would be willing to host you, and Miss Elizabeth would be eager to make your acquaintance."

Georgiana thought about it for a moment. "I *would* like to meet her, but at present, I should like to remain in town." Georgiana shot him a grin. "I am still engaged with Aunt Susan, and I hardly think a man needs his younger sister underfoot while he is conducting his courting."

"You have never been underfoot, Georgiana."

"I thank you for that. But at present, I believe I shall stay here with Mrs. Younge. Perhaps in a week or two I shall come to Hertfordshire."

"Very well. Send me a note and speak to Fitzwilliam. He will escort you here."

"Of course, William," replied Georgiana. "I look forward to it."

With a final smile, Georgiana turned back to her pianoforte and Darcy rose to leave the room. Before he left, however, a thought occurred to him and he approached Mrs. Younge, noting how the woman watched him.

"Has anything of note occurred of late?" asked he of the companion. "Anything out of the ordinary?"

"If you refer to what happened in Ramsgate, I have seen nothing of that sort in London, Mr. Darcy. Everything has been quiet."

Darcy nodded. "I am entrusting you with Georgiana's care, with the assistance of Mr. Thompson and the staff. Please ensure my sister is protected to the best of your ability. When you go out, Thompson is to be with Georgiana at all times."

A frown graced the woman's countenance. "Do you expect Mr. Wickham to make another attempt?"

"It is difficult to say," replied Darcy. "He is still at large, and his audacity is such that he might believe he can succeed where before he failed."

"Then I will remain vigilant, sir."

"Thank you," replied Darcy. Then he removed himself from the room. As long as he was stuck in London for another day, he may as well see to some correspondence. The time before he might expect to see Miss Elizabeth again was beginning to seem like a lifetime.

The second day of Mr. Darcy's absence from Hertfordshire, the Bennet sisters paid a morning visit to Netherfield. While Elizabeth could have cheerfully forgone the visit altogether, she went for Jane's sake, though she would readily confess that Mrs. Hurst was a good woman. Miss Bingley, however, was not, leading Elizabeth to wish to avoid her. But attend her sister she did, along with Mary, who dutifully embraced their social responsibilities, despite her preference for spending the morning at the pianoforte.

When they entered the sitting-room, it surprised Elizabeth to see only Miss Bingley and the Hursts in attendance. While the thought of Mr. Darcy having hurried back had crossed Elizabeth's mind, she had not expected to see him, and as a result, she was not disheartened by it. Mr. Bingley's absence, however, was quickly noted by Jane, who frowned, earning a satisfied smirk from the ever-detestable Miss Bingley.

"Charles was obliged to go to town today on a matter of business," said Mrs. Hurst, noting Jane's expression. "Before he left, he informed us he would return on the morrow."

Miss Bingley frowned at her sister, but Jane nodded her acceptance of Mrs. Hurst's assertion, and for a time all was well. Mrs. Hurst called for tea, earning a sharp look from her sister again, and they sat down to their visit. Conversation flowed with ease and interest, and even Mr. Hurst, the lone man in a room of woman, was induced to make a few remarks on occasion.

To Elizabeth's surprise, it was not long before Mr. Hurst moved, it appeared to address Elizabeth in particular. Not having spoken to the gentleman much before, Elizabeth was uncertain what to make of his apparent interest in her, but he soon revealed it with his words.

"Miss Elizabeth," said Mr. Hurst, "is everything well at Longbourn?"

Surprised, Elizabeth paused for a moment before responding. "As well as can be expected, Mr. Hurst. Was there something specific you wished to hear?"

Mr. Hurst smiled and sipped from his teacup. "To be honest, I am not certain. But when Darcy went away, he charged my brother to keep watch, and when Bingley left, he passed the responsibility down to me. It is my understanding you have had some difficulties with a past associate of Darcy's?"

"Mr. Wickham," replied Elizabeth. "But he left soon after your brother arrived in Hertfordshire and has not been here since."

"Aye, I have heard of this Mr. Wickham before. He is a bad sort and no mistake." Mr. Hurst paused and considered her. "I do not suppose Darcy to be inclined to hysteria with no reason for it, as he is a most rational sort of man. Though I cannot say what manner of devilry this Mr. Wickham is capable of perpetrating, you will take care, will you not?"

"I have been doing exactly that," replied Elizabeth. "Though I have not ceased my walks altogether, I have curtailed then to a great extent and take care when I do go out."

"Then that is well. As I said, Miss Bennet, Darcy is not the kind to worry with no cause. If he is concerned there is danger, you should heed his warning."

With those final words, Mr. Hurst rose and excused himself. "While a man finds himself alone amidst a bevy of lovely ladies but rarely, I find this talk is not to my taste. Enjoy your visit."

When he had gone, the ladies resumed their conversation, and after a time, Mrs. Hurst rose to retrieve an item of which she had been speaking with Jane, returning soon after. Mary drew in close to the other women, and while Elizabeth thought to join them, a look at Miss Bingley showed her to be glaring at them all with disdain. To that point, Miss Bingley had not been part of the company, preferring to sit to the side like a sulking child. Feeling it incumbent upon her to at least attempt civility Elizabeth nodded in her direction.

"The weather has been fine of late, has it not?"

While a discussion of the weather was among the most banal, Elizabeth was uncertain the woman would not take offense if she said anything else. Offense, however, was not what Elizabeth prompted, though she supposed she might have guessed in advance.

"It is tolerable, I suppose, but I care little for the dreary months of winter."

"Oh, I agree," said Elizabeth, grateful at finding a subject about which they were not at odds. "I understand you are from the north. It does not become too cold in Hertfordshire, and there is often little snow, but I imagine it must be different there."

"It is," said Miss Bingley. "Sometimes there is enough snow to make travel difficult and dangerous. Why, I have heard Mr. Darcy say he has been snowed in at Pemberley many times."

The mention of Mr. Darcy seemed to recall to her mind to whom she was speaking, and she scowled. The congenial moment lost, the woman fell silent, and Elizabeth, in part due to desperation, turned the subject.

"Since the weather is excellent, I assume your brother will travel without difficulty. I hope he will return soon."

It seemed that was the wrong comment to make, for Miss Bingley sneered at Elizabeth and affected an uncommon haughtiness seen. "Yes, I am certain he arrived in London without difficulty. His return, however, is less certain."

"I am sorry, Miss Bingley, but I do not understand your meaning," replied Elizabeth with a frown.

"It is simple, Miss Elizabeth," replied Miss Bingley. "This business which drew Charles to town might be more complicated than he expected—it is a similar matter which delayed our arrival in Hertfordshire, you understand. And once Charles is in town, with the amusements available there, I doubt he will be eager to return."

"He will not?" asked Elizabeth, the skepticism in her voice prompting a further glower from Miss Bingley.

"Nothing is certain, of course. But I know my brother as well as anyone in the world, and I suspect his return will be delayed. It is possible he might even call us to town. While our time has been *interesting* here in Hertfordshire, I will not pretend to miss it. Town is far pleasanter than the country.

"Furthermore," said Miss Bingley, leaning closer as if to impart a secret, "I suspect Mr. Darcy's absence will lessen the chances of my brother's return."

"Is that so?" asked Elizabeth. "That would suggest that Mr. Darcy has no intention of returning himself, and I had it from him before he left that he plans to return as soon as possible."

"I am sorry, Miss Elizabeth, but you must bow to my superior knowledge of him. Mr. Darcy, you see, is a good and amiable gentleman, but he also takes great care in choosing his associates and a prodigious deal of care of his affairs, and particularly his sister. Leaving Hertfordshire will, I have no doubt, recall to his mind the need to hold himself to his strict standards, and there is nothing in Hertfordshire to meet his exacting requirements. Mark my words, he will not return."

It was more with amusement than anger that Elizabeth listened to Miss Bingley's attempts to convince herself. It was why she resisted the urge to throw Mr. Darcy's promise to her in Miss Bingley's face or abuse her lack of knowledge of the gentleman. In the end, she knew to do so would be to infuriate her, drawing her into a confrontation. Elizabeth had no intention of allowing such unpleasantness to occur.

Instead, she rose and looked down at Miss Bingley, saying: "Thank you for this interesting conversation, Miss Bingley. With respect to Mr. Darcy or your brother's return, I suppose time shall tell the truth of the matter. I shall choose to believe Mr. Darcy's words to me and not this portrait you paint of a fickle man."

Then she left the woman fuming behind her, instead, approaching her sisters and Mrs. Hurst, who were speaking of whatever item Mrs. Hurst had left to retrieve. If Elizabeth never spent another minute in Miss Caroline Bingley's company again, she would be well pleased.

CHAPTER XXIV

*I*t is the fate of all men to feel incomplete when the company of the woman they admire is denied them, and Darcy found he was no exception to this rule. Though it was only two days since he had last seen Miss Elizabeth, it seemed like an age, so much that he spent much of the previous night in quiet contemplation of her perfection, rather than sleeping as he ought. His eagerness to return, however, was such that fatigue did not plague him as he arose and prepared. In fact, he felt nothing but energetic and impatient to set off.

The final preparations for the departure were completed with his staff's usual efficiency, and soon the carriage was ready to depart. Georgiana, though usually not an early riser, was on hand to see him off—Fitzwilliam had already departed for his barracks.

"Whenever you wish to come to Hertfordshire," reminded Darcy, " send me a note and inform Fitzwilliam. I should like to have you with me again."

"Thank you, Brother," replied Georgiana, giving him a warm embrace. "I shall anticipate it keenly."

With a few more words of farewell, Darcy soon seated himself within his conveyance, which proceeded down the street. Bingley had traveled to London on his horse for the sake of speed and expediency, so they were to return together. Thus, Darcy made his way to his friend's house, pulling up some time later and entering the house in search of his friend.

"You are right on time, as usual," greeted Bingley. "If you will give me a moment, I shall join you directly."

Darcy nodded while Bingley gave a final few instructions to his butler, and soon he was ready to go. His friend, Darcy noted, was as eager as he felt, for Bingley was not usually one to arise as early as this. Thoughts of his own Bennet sister must dominate his mind to rouse him to movement this early. Whatever the case, Darcy was grateful for it, for he did not think he possessed the patience that morning to roust his friend from his bed.

It was as they were preparing to leave the house that the fly in the ointment of the apothecary presented itself in a person Darcy least wished to see. The outside door opened, and before either man could make any comment, Miss Bingley breezed in as if floating on air. Her predatory gaze fell on them, and she donned a smile, which Darcy instantly determined was false, and approached them, a spring in her step.

"Oh, how good it is to be back in our home! I see you are on hand to greet me, Charles, Mr. Darcy. I thank you for this warm reception."

"Warm reception?" demanded Bingley, finding his tongue sooner than Darcy might have thought. "We were about to depart for Hertfordshire. What in the blazes are you doing here? And where are Louisa and Hurst?"

Miss Bingley sniffed in disdain. "I left them in Hertfordshire, though I know they will be eager to return themselves before long. As for my presence, you know I care nothing for Netherfield."

"Perhaps you do not," said Bingley, an icy note in his voice. "But I most certainly do."

"It will still be there *if* we decide to return," said Miss Bingley with an airy wave of her hand. "Now, I shall go change and take charge of the house, and we shall settle in. Though there is a dearth of acceptable society during the little season, I am certain we have invitations aplenty. And I wish to visit the London museum and perhaps attend a play and an opera. I am certain we shall have no difficulty in finding amusements with which to occupy ourselves.

"Mr. Darcy, is your sister still in town? I long to once again be in her company, for I consider her to be the most wonderful young girl in all of England. She, I am sure, would be pleased if you stayed to attend her."

Darcy exchanged a look with Bingley. It was no more than a glance, but Darcy thought his friend understood the meaning it conveyed, for Darcy was prepared to return to Hertfordshire and live in the inn, if necessary. Bingley nodded in understanding, no more prepared to stay and cater to his sister's whims than Darcy.

"I must confess, Caroline," said Bingley, interrupting her constant stream of words, "you have done many senseless, selfish things before, but this might be the worst."

"What are you saying, Charles?" asked she, a nervous glance at Darcy revealing her anxiety. Her worries must not have been assuaged at all, for Darcy felt nothing but contempt for her transparent machinations.

"What time did you leave this morning? It must have been early, given the time it is now. To force our servants to attend to you at such an early hour, to travel in the darkness when it is unnecessary—and all for what? To keep Darcy and me in town? You have failed, Sister, for we have no intention of being held here against our will."

"Charles," said Miss Bingley, speaking as if he was a small child, "it would be better to stay in London, so you may regain your perspective. There is nothing for you in Hertfordshire at present. Why," the woman continued, "when Miss Bennet was informed of your departure, she said nothing. Nothing! The only reason she has accepted your attentions at all is to obtain your fortune."

"I doubt that since she is independent and need not respond with anything other than inclination."

"And you, Mr. Darcy," said Miss Bingley, ignoring her brother's words, "I know Miss Eliza has impressed you with her impertinent tongue and witty rejoinders, but she is not the sort of woman with whom the Bingley and Darcy families should be associating. If you stay in town for a time, I am certain you will see this too."

"Your certainty is misplaced," was Darcy's short reply. "And let me inform you, Miss Bingley, so there is no mistake—*I* am the only one who may determine the suitability of the Darcy family's acquaintances, and I will thank you not to suggest otherwise."

Miss Bingley opened her mouth to say something else, but Bingley did not allow it. "Caroline, my offer to set up your own establishment is still in force. However, I shall not do it now, for I am expected back in Hertfordshire. If you cannot tolerate the neighborhood in which I make my home, you may visit Aunt Esther in Scarborough."

That put an end to the woman's complaining, for as Darcy knew, she despised the place of her origins, would not visit her family unless under duress, and particularly loathed visiting her aunt's house. Miss Bingley glared at Bingley, but he took no notice, instead stepping outside and giving directions for his sister's items — it appeared like she had brought everything she owned with her — to be moved to Darcy's carriage.

"I hope you do not mind, Darcy. Since my horses were put to use very early this morning, I prefer to leave them here to rest a day or two." Bingley's dark look at his sister was followed by: "Luckily, we shall not be without means of traveling in Hertfordshire, as Hurst's carriage will be there too."

"Oh, I cannot possibly return to Hertfordshire now," said Caroline. "The journey this morning has rendered me fatigued. Let us return tomorrow."

"Your fatigue does not concern me a jot," growled Bingley. "Your actions led to it, which leaves me unmoved. Either return to Hertfordshire this instant or return to Hertfordshire this instant and continue on to Scarborough tomorrow. It is your choice, Caroline."

It was no surprise when Miss Bingley chose the former option, though with as little grace as she ever displayed. Soon, Bingley's carriage was making its way to the carriage house, and Darcy's, with two more passengers than expected — Miss Bingley and her maid — departed for Hertfordshire. It took little discernment to perceive Miss Bingley's pique. Had she deigned to look, she would have understood neither gentleman cared for her anger.

The morning of Mr. Darcy's expected return to Hertfordshire, the Bennet sisters received a note, once again inviting them to Netherfield for the morning. Though they had visited the day before and did not wish to impose, Mrs. Bennet pointed out an invitation precluded the notion of imposition.

"Mrs. Hurst would not have invited you if she did not wish for your company," said the lady. "Go and visit with her — I am certain you will enjoy yourselves."

Thus, it was settled, and once the carriage arrived, they entered for the short journey to their friend's home. The carriage trundled along the road toward Meryton, past Lucas Lodge and into the town itself, before taking the northeast road toward Netherfield. While they were passing through, Elizabeth, who had been looking out the window, happened to notice Lieutenants Denny and Sanderson in the town, speaking with the Long sisters. The former looked up as they passed and sketched a bow at the carriage, and Elizabeth, who was the only one watching, returned his greeting with a nod of her head. The Bennets had seen little of the officers of late, and Elizabeth could not repine their loss. While Mr. Denny was not the level of despicable man that Mr. Wickham was, their friendship did not speak well to his character.

A few minutes later, they sighted manor house in the distance, and they approached the front doors, seeing Mrs. Hurst standing on the stairs waiting for them. They alighted and exchanged greetings all around, Mrs. Hurst inviting them inside with pleasure and eagerness. It was only when they had reached the comforts of the sitting-room that Elizabeth realized Miss Bingley's absence, rather than not wishing to meet them at the door, was a matter of more significance.

"Will Miss Bingley be joining us?" asked Jane after they had sat and visited for several moments.

The way Mrs. Hurst's color rose at the mention of her sister was not missed by any of them, but the woman responded in a creditable manner. "My sister left for London very early this morning."

Jane frowned, but Mary and Elizabeth exchanged a glance, each understanding the reason for Miss Bingley's sudden departure. Though dearly wishing she could indulge in a laugh, Elizabeth kept her composure, if only to spare Mrs. Hurst any further mortification.

"I hope her journey is pleasant and safe," replied Jane not knowing how to respond. "Do you expect her return before long?"

"It is uncertain," replied Mrs. Hurst. "However, I believe it will not be long. Charles sent us a note yesterday confirming his presence in London for the night and his return today in Mr. Darcy's company."

"You must be eager to have everyone back, Mrs. Hurst," said Elizabeth. "You were a party of five, and now you are only two."

Mrs. Hurst smiled with gratitude. "Yes, that is exactly it. I do not suppose Caroline's business will take much time to complete, so I would almost expect her to return with the gentlemen this morning."

"Then we shall hope for their safe arrival," replied Elizabeth.

While Elizabeth could not find it in her heart to wish Miss Bingley ill and longed for the gentlemen's return—or at least that of *one* gentleman—a little further thought on the matter informed her it may not be best for the Bennet sisters to be on hand should Miss Bingley return in her brother's company. How she would behave was uncertain but given what Elizabeth thought was a desperate attempt to keep them away from Hertfordshire, she did not think the woman would be pleasant. Thus, it would behoove them to absent themselves before any chance of meeting her could come to pass.

The problem, as Elizabeth saw it, was that Mrs. Hurst enjoyed their company. Watching as she was, while Mrs. Hurst spoke in an animated fashion with Jane, her hands gesturing to make some point or another, Elizabeth knew whatever confidence had subsisted between the sisters in the past had been set aside. Whatever opinion Caroline Bingley had of the neighborhood, it did not appear that Mrs. Hurst shared it—or she did not share Miss Bingley's opinion of the Bennets. Thus, Elizabeth had no wish to offend her or give her the wrong impression of their early retreat.

It was with these thoughts Elizabeth took part in their morning visit in the company of Mrs. Hurst, though Mr. Hurst made an appearance for a few moments. The ladies spoke of fashion and local society, they played and sang and laughed together, and spent some time walking the paths of Netherfield's gardens, talking and laughing. It was a visit much like Elizabeth might have experienced with a friend of longstanding. And when luncheon approached, Mrs. Hurst pressed them to stay.

"We expect my brother and sister after luncheon," said the lady, "and I would appreciate your presence for the noon repast. Then perhaps it would be best if you returned to Longbourn."

Elizabeth smiled at her hostess and answered for her sisters: "I believe we would like that very much, Mrs. Hurst. We thank you for your invitation. You must wish to greet your absent family members without an audience."

It seemed Mrs. Hurst was as relieved that they had understood her wishes, and Elizabeth thought the woman had shown some greatness of mind in recognizing the need. Thus, when called into luncheon they joined their host and hostess and spent another delightful hour in their company. Then, when they were preparing to leave, and the carriage had been called, Mrs. Hurst approached Elizabeth with a tentative smile.

"Thank you, Miss Elizabeth, for understanding the situation and responding accordingly."

"It did not take much insight to understand, Mrs. Hurst. Though you are little acquainted with my younger sisters, they can be a trial. I understand completely."

"Perhaps that is a bond that connects us," replied Mrs. Hurst with a nod. "Regardless, I would not wish you to think the opinions I hold in any way resemble my sister's. Though I am now the wife of a gentleman, I do not forget my origins, nor do I look down on others whose background is different."

"I believe, Mrs. Hurst, that a person's character is much more important than their history. History, of course, has a large influence in character, but I put much more stock in kindness, generosity, and all other virtues, rather than who one's father was or in what circumstance one was raised."

"That is exactly it," said Mrs. Hurst, grasping Elizabeth's hands and squeezing them. Then she spoke to all three sisters: "I should like to take this opportunity to invite your entire family to dinner. Would three nights hence be acceptable?"

"While I am uncertain," replied Jane for the sisters, "I do not believe we have any other engagements that day. I shall inform my mother and ask her to respond."

"Excellent. Now, I believe your carriage awaits. I hope to see you all again soon."

The sisters offered similar sentiments and soon departed. As the carriage rumbled down the drive, Elizabeth happened to look back, seeing Mrs. Hurst as she watched them go, her husband having emerged to stand by her side.

"After meeting Miss Bingley, I was not certain it would be possible," said Mary, "but I like Mrs. Hurst very well, indeed."

"Perhaps Miss Bingley will return from London having realized her manners require mending," said Jane, ever the optimist.

Though Elizabeth and Mary glanced at each other, both declined to say anything, for they knew Jane would not be moved in her opinion. It was fortunate that Jane was looking out the window at that moment, for her two sisters could not quite suppress their grins.

A more miserable journey Darcy had never experienced: not even the long, wearing journeys of three days from Pemberley to London, or the week-long odyssey which took him to the Scotland estate. In those instances, Darcy contended with the cramped confines of carriages not built for his height, bone weariness which set in after many days on the road, or rain or cold or whatever weather nature could conjure. But he had never had to endure a vengeful sister intent upon persuading those who did not wish to be persuaded.

It was an interesting dichotomy, he supposed, as Miss Bingley droned on about how backward Meryton society was and how awful its people were. Bingley, who was one of the most genial and easy men Darcy had ever known had been cursed with the worst shrew of a sister, while Darcy, who was usually branded as cold and unfeeling, was blessed with a complying and sweet sister, one whom any man would feel fortunate to have. Darcy had endured Bingley's sister for the sake of their friendship, but his forbearance was coming to an end.

All might have been ignored, had Miss Bingley chosen to confine her comments to those general to her displeasure. Ignoring her had become something of an art. When she chose to attack one, in particular, who was becoming dear to Darcy's heart, he was not about to sit in silence and allow her to denigrate at will.

"You do know, do you not, that Miss Bennet has no inclination toward you, Charles."

"Oh?" demanded Bingley, clearly becoming as annoyed with his sister as Darcy. "And how would *you* know, Caroline? It seems to me you are rarely induced to be civil enough to speak to her."

"All anyone requires is a dram of observation," replied Miss Bingley with a superior sniff. "She smiles, but there is nothing in her eyes, nothing in her posture to suggest she has any affection for you."

"You astonish me, Caroline," said Bingley, his tone dripping with sarcasm. "Did you not previously assert that she wished to attach herself to me for those reasons you now think she is indifferent? Is Longbourn not a hovel she wishes to escape for a larger fortune and access to society?"

Miss Bingley glared at her brother, but when she spoke it was with a flippant tone. "Further reflection and observation have forced me to reevaluate my opinion. Mark my word, Charles—if you offer for her, she may be prevailed upon to accept by her awful mother, but she will do so only unwillingly."

"I thank you for your insight, Caroline," said Bingley. "It is unfortunate for you, but I believe I shall trust my own judgment in this matter."

With a sniff, Miss Bingley's eyes flicked to Darcy, and she paused to consider. Darcy, who had been watching her, was unsurprised when she then turned her vitriol on the one who must be a greater impediment to her plans.

"As for the rest of the family, why there is nothing to recommend them. The girls are all silly and insipid, Mary Bennet a bluestocking, and Miss Eliza, though perhaps she may *wish* to be a bluestocking, her opinions are not intelligent enough for the designation. The father is sardonic and indifferent, and the mother, a harpy. Lord, I do not know why you favor them so!"

"I wonder if we are speaking of the same family, Caroline," rejoined Bingley. "In fact, I find them delightful, their lack of artifice refreshing, and Miss Elizabeth and Miss Mary unlike your description. Were your eyes at all open when meeting them?"

A cold fire burned in Miss Bingley's eyes. "I never thought my brother could be so blind as this, though you have paid attention to many unsuitable ladies before." Then her eyes swung to Darcy. "And you, sir. Have you not always striven to uphold the highest standard of behavior? Or perhaps you have been so bewitched, you wish your sister to emulate Kitty and Lydia Bennet." Miss Bingley snorted, unladylike and disdainful. "Or perhaps she should emulate Eliza Bennet. Heaven knows if you wish her to be a hoyden of the worst sort that last would be the best."

"In fact, Miss Bingley," said Darcy, his temper snapping, "I think Georgiana could not find a better example than Miss Elizabeth Bennet, for she is confident and open, two traits with which Georgiana struggles. Like your brother, I have nothing but respect for the Bennets and eagerness to continue my association with them. I would ask you not to continue this, for I have no desire to hear you.

"And let me make one more thing clear," said Darcy, leaning forward and gazing into her fearful eyes. "If she will have me, I intend to make Miss Elizabeth my wife. Though you have long aspired to that position, let me state and here and now so there is no misunderstanding—nothing could ever have induced me to offer for you. You are wasting your time attempting to pull me to your way of thinking, for I will not be moved. I would be highly gratified if you would cease this improper display and leave me in peace."

"Aunt Esther awaits, Caroline," said Bingley, his voice carrying a hint of warning. "It would be nothing to write an express to her and send you to the north. Why, she would not mind if I put you on a coach heading north without informing her."

Miss Bingley glared at her brother, a mutinous glint in her eye, but his return glare was without waver, without mercy. In the end, she looked away and stared in moody silence out the window for the rest of the journey. To the gentlemen, the silence was a blessed relief.

CHAPTER XXV

The day after their return to Hertfordshire, the gentlemen visited Longbourn. Accompanying them were Mr. and Mrs. Hurst, but also Miss Bingley, though it was obvious the last of the company was not at all pleased to be there. They calculated manner of their greeting to deliver a message, the contents of which were left to the imagination of no one present.

"Mr. Bennet, Mrs. Bennet," said Mr. Bingley leading the way. "How good it is to see you again after our short absence."

"Mr. Bingley," greeted Mrs. Bennet. "It is good to have you returned. There was some talk of your business consuming more of your time than you thought."

No one missed the reference in her words, but Miss Bingley did not even have the grace to appear embarrassed. "There was never any chance of that, Mrs. Bennet," said Mr. Bingley, refraining from glancing at his sister. "I charged Louisa with passing my regrets along and informing you of my plans. The matter for which I was summoned was not difficult, but it was urgent."

"Your sister informed us," said Mrs. Bennet, nodding with a smile to Mrs. Hurst. "I hope your journey was pleasant."

It was a tactful way of changing the subject, though Elizabeth could not imagine traveling with Miss Bingley was in any way pleasant. Mr. Bingley, showing the gentleman he was, alluded to good roads and pleasant weather, and the conversation moved to other subjects. Miss Bingley, it seemed, was not inclined to continue with her previous behavior, though Elizabeth was uncertain of the reason. The lady's continued scrutiny of the Bennets and the palpable sense of distaste which hovered over her like a cloud was not dispelled. If she was quiet, that was enough for Elizabeth.

Though Elizabeth might have expected to be in Mr. Darcy's company as soon as the gentleman arrived, he approached her, whispered to her of the need to speak to her father, and then made his way thence. Elizabeth waited practicing patience, knowing they were speaking of the gentleman's confrontation with his aunt, certain Mr. Darcy would speak of it to her when he joined her. The slight sense of relief her father displayed was enough to inform her of the result of Mr. Darcy's endeavors.

"I hope you will allow me to thank you for your assistance, Mr. Darcy," said Elizabeth when a few moments later he made the brief communication to her. Mr. Bennet was, at the same time, informing her mother, who was regarding Mr. Darcy with obvious gratitude. "It is my understanding your aunt can be a difficult woman. I hope she accepted your advice in the manner you intended it."

Mr. Darcy's slight grimace informed Elizabeth of the lie of her words, a sight which gave her no little amusement. "She was not so sanguine. Lady Catherine has the singular ability to believe herself correct in any circumstance, which makes convincing her otherwise a perilous proposition."

The irony in his voice was such as to provoke outright laughter in Elizabeth. "Then it is well you escaped unscathed."

"Again, not unscathed. But unharmed at least." Mr. Darcy paused and regarded her with his usual serious demeanor for a moment, and then he continued: "A larger part of the argument was my insistence of not following my aunt's dictates, especially pertaining to those regarding her daughter."

"Oh," said Elizabeth, uncertain what to make of his comment. "I was not aware you intended to raise that subject."

"Do you think I could brave my aunt in her den and not be drawn into such a discussion?" asked Mr. Darcy, mirth twinkling in his eyes. "I assure you, Miss Elizabeth, I was not required to raise the subject, for my aunt was more than willing to do it herself."

"And what was the result?"

"Lady Catherine is, as you might expect given everything you have heard of her, not pleased. It has led to a break between us, though I doubt her objections are at an end. My uncle has assured me he will stop any attempts she might contemplate to interfere. With that, I must be content."

Conscious as she was that the argument had come about because of his recent attentions to her, Elizabeth did not know how she should respond. Mr. Darcy seemed to understand this, for he changed the subject. They spent a pleasant time in each other's company, speaking of many things, and if Elizabeth noted Miss Bingley's cold glare, which was on them more than on the rest of the company put together, at least the woman kept her opinions to herself. There was little more for which Elizabeth could ask.

Miss Bingley's behavior would persist beyond that first day. The Bennets returned the visit the next day, and while Miss Bingley was present, she spoke little and sat with her discontented glare fixed on them all. Elizabeth decided not to concern herself with the reasons for the woman's sudden tact. Not only did she not care, but it was enough she was silent more often than not.

Three days after the gentlemen's return to Netherfield was the day the Bennets had been invited for dinner. That dinner party was notable for a few reasons, not the least of which was a change in the management of Netherfield. But that was not to be made known to them until they were called into dinner.

Once again, Kitty and Lydia had begged, and been allowed, to attend the dinner, and while they were disappointed the colonel was not present to entertain them, they were still pleased to feel like part of the company, like the adults they were becoming. The Bingley party welcomed the family with all the warmth of new acquaintances becoming close friends, and they sat together while waiting for the call to dinner. It was then, to no one's surprise, that Kitty and Lydia began to giggle louder than perhaps they ought.

"It is to be expected, I suppose," drawled Miss Bingley in a loud voice. "Young girls brought out into society before they are ready cannot help but misbehave."

Elizabeth, whose attention had been consumed by Mr. Darcy, turned to see what the fuss was about, but she could see nothing out of the ordinary. The girls had stopped to stare at Miss Bingley for her impudence, but as their voices had not intruded on Elizabeth's senses, she had no notion their behavior had been truly reprehensible.

"Perhaps you are correct, Miss Bingley," said Mr. Bennet, his look quelling any further noise the sisters might have made. "However, I have always understood that young girls should be given a taste of society before they are out. It not only teaches them what is expected when they debut, but it gives them something to anticipate." Mr. Bennet turned a fond eye on his elder progeny. "It seems to have worked with my older daughters."

Miss Bingley sniffed, her manner dripping with disdainful conceit. "Then it is incumbent upon their minder to ensure they do not disrupt the rest of the company."

Mrs. Garret, sitting near to the youngest Bennets, did not bother to make a response to the supercilious woman, though she glanced fleetingly in her direction. Elizabeth was certain Mrs. Garret considered Miss Bingley herself in need of some manners, a sentiment with which Elizabeth agreed without reserve.

"It is," interjected Mrs. Bennet, her hard gaze fixed upon Miss Bingley. "In this instance, however, I cannot say my girls have misbehaved to any great degree."

It was fortunate Miss Bingley did not seem eager to continue to speak, for more than one member of the Bennet family was becoming annoyed with her criticisms. And more than one member of Miss Bingley's own family, if Elizabeth's observation was correct. Her silence and the call to dinner which occurred soon after was a relief to them all.

When they sat down to dinner, the change in the household was made known to them, and Elizabeth understood it was likely that which in part fueled Miss Bingley's disgruntled manner. Rather than Miss Bingley, it was Mrs. Hurst whom Mr. Bennet escorted to dinner. She was seated at the foot of the table, with Mr. Bennet by her side, denoting her current position as mistress of the estate. Miss Bingley appeared quite annoyed with her position in the middle of the table, one determined because she was the lowest of them all, being neither married nor the daughter of a gentleman. It was fortunate that those seated on either side of her had other partners with whom to converse, for Miss Bingley gave all the indication of a desire to snap at anyone who spoke to her.

Mrs. Hurst was a competent hostess, for the dinner had been planned with flare and included dishes which would appeal to them all. There was a ragout for Mr. Hurst's more eclectic tastes, as well as the plainer dishes that had always appealed to Mr. Bennet. Where she might have procured this intelligence Elizabeth did not know, for she had not been present when Mr. Darcy, Mr. Bingley, and Miss Bingley had dined at Longbourn. If Miss Bingley had been left to plan the menu, Elizabeth thought it equally likely she would have wished to overwhelm them with an elaborate dinner as wish to feed them nothing but stale bread and water.

"It seems to me you appreciate the repast," said Mr. Darcy to Elizabeth. The gentleman had made certain to offer his arm to Elizabeth when they were called to dinner.

"Who does not enjoy good food?" asked Elizabeth. "Any good hostess must take the different tastes of the diners into consideration — it seems to me Mrs. Hurst has done well, everyone seems satisfied."

"Indeed, they are," replied Mr. Darcy. "Is there anything present which is an especial favorite of yours?"

"Not in particular, Mr. Darcy. I am, my mother informs me, easy to please at the dinner table, for I have a wide variety of tastes and few foods I detest."

"That is fortunate," replied Mr. Darcy. "When she was a child, my father always had difficulty inducing Georgiana to eat, for she was very fussy."

Elizabeth grinned. "Is she still fussy? If so, perhaps you could send her to Longbourn for a time. We would cure her of such habits."

A disgusted snort reached Elizabeth's ears, and she turned slightly to see Miss Bingley regarding them with contempt. Not caring for the woman's opinion, Elizabeth ignored her, turning back to Darcy.

"That is a good suggestion, Miss Elizabeth," said Mr. Darcy, ignoring Miss Bingley in his turn. "Though she is not so difficult to please as she was when she was a child, her tastes are still rather narrow."

"Most of my family eat with little coaxing, Mr. Darcy. Mary has more she dislikes than the rest of us, but my mother is not often required to avoid serving something because we will not eat it."

"I have often observed," said Mrs. Bennet, "that it is incumbent upon a parent to introduce their children to a wide variety of foods to avoid such persnickety behavior. From the time they were young, all my girls were given what the family ate and required to finish it. Sometimes they ate those foods which were not appealing to them, but it taught them to have good appetites and to try new foods which they might otherwise reject."

"That is wisdom, indeed, Mrs. Bennet," said Mr. Darcy. "It is a path my father took with me. Over time it helped with Georgiana's palate, though I suspect hers is naturally more finicky than that of your daughters."

Mr. Darcy's words to support Mrs. Bennet's words seemed to remove whatever Miss Bingley was about to say, likely in condemnation of the Bennets, for she had opened her mouth to speak and subsequently closed it. The manner in which she looked at Mr. Darcy suggested confusion. Miss Bingley did not know Mr. Darcy so well as she thought she did.

After dinner, when the party retired back to the sitting-room, Elizabeth's conversation continued unabated with Mr. Darcy. As Jane was occupied by Mr. Bingley's ardent ministrations, that left the rest of the company to make do with one another, though Elizabeth noted that Miss Bingley stayed nearby to where Elizabeth spoke with Mr. Darcy. For the most part, she remained quiet, but there were a few times she interjected into their conversation with an observation, sometimes pointed, sometimes innocuous. As this went on, Elizabeth noted her actions seemed more directed toward understanding Mr. Darcy, than disparaging Elizabeth. She still could not resist denigrating a rival from time to time.

"I did not realize your cousins were so young," said Mr. Darcy in response to a comment Elizabeth made about her relations. "In my extended family, Georgiana is the youngest. As I am twelve years her senior, Georgiana comprises most of my present experience with children."

"My uncle is younger than his two sisters," said Elizabeth by way of explanation. "As building his business occupied his younger years, he married a little later than might usual."

"A man of industry," said Mr. Darcy with evident approval. "Since you speak of them often, I assume you get on with your uncle's family."

"We get on with them very well. Uncle and Aunt Gardiner are excellent people and had much influence on Jane and me before their own children arrived to preoccupy them. Though Uncle is in trade, if you met him, you would not know it unless you were informed of it, for his manners are that of a gentleman."

"It is my opinion that people should not strive to appear anything other than what they are," interjected Miss Bingley.

"That is an opinion with which I can heartily agree, Miss Bingley," said Elizabeth easily. "My uncle never attempts to hide his profession."

Then Elizabeth turned away from Miss Bingley, though not before noting the woman was gazing at Mr. Darcy with curiosity, rather than offended by Elizabeth's rebuttal.

"As for Aunt Gardiner, she is the daughter of a parson, who was himself the son of a gentleman. Thus, she is well aware of how to behave properly herself. They are the most wonderful relations, and despite whatever anyone says about their position in society, one could never be ashamed of them."

"It is my hope I shall make their acquaintance someday," said Mr. Darcy.

"If you remain for Christmas, you shall," said Elizabeth, "for they visit us at Longbourn every year."

From there, the conversation meandered around other such topics, relations, children, proper behavior, and to other similar matters. Eventually, they began to speak of childrearing, Mr. Darcy contrasting what he experienced with his father and some of the practices he tried to implement with his younger sister when he became responsible for her, Elizabeth responding with what she herself had known as a child.

"My sister, as I have said before, is at heart a shy creature, though it is true she has gained more confidence these past months. There has been little need for discipline as she has always been very obliging."

"Of course, she has," inserted Miss Bingley. "Miss Darcy is quite the most excellent young lady I have ever met."

"Thank you, Miss Bingley," said Mr. Darcy.

It was of interest for Elizabeth to note that however Miss Bingley had used Miss Darcy as a means to get close to the brother, her regard for the girl seemed genuine. As was their custom by this time, Mr. Darcy made a gracious response to Miss Bingley and they returned to their conversation.

"Perhaps your sister is a quiet girl, but my youngest sisters are not," said Elizabeth. She directed a fond glance at Kitty and Lydia, who were seated beside Mrs. Garret, whispering to each other, though punctuated occasionally with a giggle. "Lydia, in particular, has always been high-spirited, and while Kitty shares many of the same characteristics, she is not so fearless as Lydia. Instead, she follows where Lydia leads."

"That is curious, Miss Elizabeth. It is the elder sibling who leads most often."

Elizabeth could only shrug. "Usually you would be correct. In this instance, however, Lydia is most decidedly the leader." Elizabeth paused and sighed. "When Kitty is of age to come out formally, it will be a trial, I am sure, for Lydia will still be two years from coming out and will feel her exclusion keenly."

"Do you not hold to the notion of younger sisters not coming out until the elder sisters are married?" asked Miss Bingley. Again Elizabeth was interested to note the woman seemed genuinely curious, rather than trying to shade her character in Mr. Darcy's eyes.

"If the Bennets were prominent in London society, I might agree with you," said Elizabeth. "In the country, however, it is customary to allow that rule to lapse. It would not do to provoke hard feelings in younger siblings when the elder are not inclined or unable to marry. Do you not agree?"

The question was as much for Miss Bingley as it was for Mr. Darcy. The former, however, seemed curious to hear the latter's opinion on the subject, for she did nothing more than look to him. Mr. Darcy was quick to give his response.

"I do. In the country, there is little harm in girls coming out while their sisters are unmarried. In London, however, it would not be contemplated." Mr. Darcy paused and smiled. "It seems to me unlikely your sisters will be required to concern themselves on that regard. It is little likely you or Miss Bennet will remain unmarried long enough to cause problems, and with only Miss Mary unmarried for the present, there should be little impediment."

Elizabeth felt her cheeks heating at his obvious inference, and Miss Bingley's expression darkened. Unwilling to pursue that line of conversation, Elizabeth directed it back toward her earlier comments.

"Lydia, I suppose, will do tolerably well, though she will feel ill-used. Mrs. Garret is capable of controlling her outbursts, and by the time Lydia comes out, she will be the focus of attention, which is all she will ever want."

"Discipline is, of course, paramount," replied Mr. Darcy. "I would not consider my father a disciplinarian, but he did not tolerate foolishness either."

"Were you often the target for his reprimands?" teased Elizabeth. "A determined boy such as yourself must have been difficult to control. Did you and Colonel Fitzwilliam get up to much mischief as children?"

Mr. Darcy was quick to laugh at Elizabeth's characterization. "Having met us both, do you believe that *I* was the instigator of our exploits?"

"Your cousin *does* strike me as a . . ."

"Troublemaker?" asked Mr. Darcy when Elizabeth paused to search for a word.

"An active man who was as active as a boy," rejoined Elizabeth.

"Aye, he was at that," said Mr. Darcy. "Though I will not attempt to assert I did not create my fair share of mischief, I was more often pulled into his schemes. Being two years older than me, it was natural I should follow him more than the reverse.

"As I was saying earlier, my sister has not followed my wilder ways, and as such, I have not been required to discipline her."

"Do you mean punish her?" asked Miss Bingley, intruding on the conversation again.

"Discipline can be had without punishment, Miss Bingley, though sometimes punishment must be meted out when rules are broken."

"And what is your opinion concerning what form that punishment must take?"

Mr. Darcy regarded Miss Bingley for a moment, attempting to understand her, and for the lady's part, she seemed to realize her question might be considered accusatory. Or perhaps merely challenging—Elizabeth was uncertain.

"I only ask because my father believed punishment must be a reminder of the offense," said Miss Bingley, as diffident in manner as Elizabeth had ever seen. "Charles often received such discipline, and while Louisa and I did not so much, sometimes our father used harsh methods with us too."

"It is difficult to say," said Mr. Darcy, "as I am not a father—I have only acted as one to a much younger sister, one who has needed little correction. When I have children of my own, I may understand differently, but at present, I think boys and girls require different measures to ensure good behavior. It is said that to 'spare the rod, you spoil the child,' and I believe that is true. However, there are many ways to rear children to be good and upright in their decisions, rather than to resort to such devices as a belt, particularly for girls. I would have to say I think it is much more effective to be an active teacher, instilling good values, and supporting that instruction with appropriate penalties when necessary. Consistency, above all, is paramount."

"I agree, Mr. Darcy," said Elizabeth, delighted their opinions should align so closely in such a matter. Miss Bingley made some noise of agreement, but for the rest of the time the Bennets were present at Netherfield, the lady was quiet, deep in thought. Since she had not given her opinion, it was difficult to say, but Elizabeth thought she was considering her father's harsher standard of child rearing and the differences between herself and Mr. Darcy for perhaps the first time.

The evening progressed as most such were wont to do. After tea in the sitting-room, those ladies who played performed for the rest of the company. Mrs. Hurst and Miss Bingley, and thereafter Elizabeth and Mary followed suit, then Mary played while Elizabeth and Jane sang, to the appreciation of all the company. Even Mr. Bennet, who was not a connoisseur of the musical arts, was effusive in his praise for all the ladies.

When it came time to depart, Mr. Darcy took care to ensure he escorted Elizabeth from the room, and while they were walking, he addressed her:

"Do you still often walk in the mornings, or has the threat of Wickham made you more cautious?"

"Oh, I am more cautious, certainly," replied Elizabeth. The sudden memory of the morning of Mr. Darcy's departure and her meeting with Mr. Campbell entered Elizabeth's mind, but she pushed it aside. "I still walk, though I do not range far from Longbourn of late."

"Do you plan to walk tomorrow? Might we meet on the path I first met you where Wickham was accosting your sisters?"

"That would be acceptable, Mr. Darcy," said Elizabeth warmly. "It is near to Longbourn and public enough we would not be questioned should we be discovered."

"It would not cause me a moment's concern should someone see us, though I would avoid misunderstanding." He leaned in close and said in a low tone: "I would also speak with you in a setting more private than this."

"Then I shall strive to walk there by eight in the morning."

"Excellent," said Mr. Darcy. "I shall anticipate it."

As the carriage was departing from Netherfield, Elizabeth looked back at the gentleman, standing with his friend and the Hursts, watching the carriage as it rumbled away. Her heart full, Elizabeth realized she could not wait to be in his presence again in the morning.

CHAPTER XXVI

*T*he excitement coursing through Elizabeth was such that it surprised her to obtain any sleep at all after returning to Longbourn. The first part of the night was long, to be certain, for she lay in bed alternately thinking about what the morrow might bring while contemplating the various perfections of Mr. Fitzwilliam Darcy. Thereafter, when she had succumbed to sleep, her nighttime ruminations were replaced by dreams filled with scenes of what might be, mixed with glimpses of the man's face. In the morning, when she woke, Elizabeth felt as if she had slept a week, rather than only a few hours.

While a woman in similar circumstances might feel it necessary to take great care with her appearance, the appreciative glances she often saw directed at her by the gentleman informed her he would find her beautiful if she dressed in a burlap sack. A simple knot sufficed for her hair, as did a dress, well worn, but much loved because of the comfort it provided. Then, mindful of the late season chill, Elizabeth descended below stairs to seek her pelisse, her fur-lined gloves, and a thick bonnet, and she was ready to depart. Before she could exit the house, Elizabeth discovered her escape was not to be unnoticed.

"I see you are to go out walking this morning," came the voice of

Mr. Bennet as she was preparing to go. The figure of her father emerged from the hall leading to his study, a wide smile of affection gracing his countenance. "Dare I accuse you of ignoring the restrictions put in place for your safety, or will someone be nearby for your protection? I dare not suppose you will be meeting someone on such an early morning walk."

Honesty had always been a pillar of the relationship between father and daughter, and while Elizabeth had not thought to inform her father of the morning assignation, she could not tell him a falsehood.

"Mr. Darcy is to meet me near Longbourn."

"Is he?" asked Mr. Bennet, his eyebrow raised. "I might never have guessed, had I not seen you both speaking so earnestly last night."

Elizabeth gazed at him with curiosity. "You knew I was to meet him?"

"I suspected," replied Mr. Bennet. "It was not something anyone with any discernment might not see if they only looked." Mr. Bennet paused, considering. "He is to meet you close to Longbourn?"

"Yes, Papa. Near the place where Mr. Wickham accosted my sisters and me and we first met Mr. Darcy."

"That is a curious place for a proposal?"

Elizabeth's cheeks burned at his observation and Mr. Bennet laughed. "I do not know that he is planning to propose!"

"If he is not," said her father with evident affection, "he is not the decisive man I know him to be, and blind as well. But I know he is neither of these."

"Should I accept him if he does?" asked Elizabeth, feeling suddenly shy and unsure. "It has not been long since I made his acquaintance."

"That is a question I cannot answer for you, Lizzy." Mr. Bennet approached and put his hands on her shoulders. "The only person who can answer that question is you. Though it is true you have not known him long, it is also true that some need not know their spouses long before they are sure of their feelings. Whether you or Mr. Darcy are two of those people, I cannot say.

"What I would advise is that you listen to your heart and judge his proposal—should he choose to make it today—based on what you feel when he does. Is he a good man, one who will devote his life to making you happy, or is he a charlatan, intent upon misleading a beautiful young woman to accept him for some other reason?"

"Mr. Darcy is no charlatan, Papa," said Elizabeth. "He is the most genuine man I have ever known. And the best."

"Then the only question is your feelings for him. I trust you are capable of discerning the contents of your own heart."

"I believe I am," whispered Elizabeth.

"In that case, you have your answer, and I shall lose a daughter to the north." Mr. Bennet paused and regarded her with evident mirth. "Then again, if what I have heard of his library is the truth, I shall gain much in the bargain too!"

"Oh, Papa!" scolded Elizabeth. Mr. Bennet remained unrepentant, grinning at her, unabashed glee flowing from his eyes. Then he turned serious once again.

"Since this Mr. Wickham is still unaccounted for, I have half a mind to accompany you, if only until you meet with your beau."

"I am certain I shall be fine. Mr. Wickham has not been seen since his departure from the neighborhood."

Mr. Bennet nodded slowly. "That is true, though I do not trust he will stay away. Since you are not to walk far, I believe all should be well, and I must look at the ledgers this morning."

"Then I shall leave you to it, Papa. There will be no trouble."

"Very well, get along with you. I shall be waiting for your young man's visit when you return."

Elizabeth said nothing in response, instead choosing to stand on her toes and kiss her father's cheek. Then she slipped through the door, knowing he would watch her as she departed. The future awaited, however, and Elizabeth was eager to meet it, to discover what it held for her.

The path down Longbourn's drive took Elizabeth only a moment to traverse, and soon she had gained the road beyond which would lead through the few homes clustered around the church in Longbourn village. Before she gained the town, however, she struck off on the smaller path, winding through the woods, bisected neatly by a small bubbling brook, to the north and her meeting with Mr. Darcy. While she walked, the tower of their small church rose above the foliage, but while she could see it for some moments, even it fell beneath the rising trees.

Alone, Elizabeth pondered the upcoming meeting with Mr. Darcy, eager to learn if he intended to propose, or if there was something else in his request. Would he offer nothing more than a courtship? A part of Elizabeth was disappointed at the thought. But the prospect of a courtship also held some charm—Elizabeth was not vain but receiving a handsome man's ardent attentions before the entire neighborhood was appealing.

Or it would be until Mrs. Bennet decided she should be paraded in front of the people of the neighborhood from sunup until sundown. Elizabeth knew her mother still possessed an excitable nature despite all her improvements, and a courtship would release it. If only Mr. Bingley had already proposed to Jane! Then her focus would be on the elder daughter, who had always been a favorite.

"Well, well, well. What do we have here?"

The sound of a man's voice broke into Elizabeth's reverie, and she came to an abrupt halt, noting the sudden appearance of the man she least wished to see. Mr. Wickham—for he it was—standing, insouciance in his bearing, leaning against a tree by the side of the path. He wore rough leathers, weather-beaten and bleached by the sun, and a hat pulled down to cover his face. Elizabeth did not need to see him to know it was he, for it was written in his posture, in the curly brown hair which formed a ring below his hat, and most of all, in the insolent mockery evident in his voice.

Then he pushed the brim up, revealing his face. The glower he fixed upon her did not disturb Elizabeth so much as the wild and sickly light which shone in his eyes. His smirk Elizabeth had seen before and had stood up to on more than one occasion. The disquiet of his presence, however, sent a frisson of fear running up her spine, for she well knew this man detested her and was dangerous besides.

"It is fortunate I have met you, my dear Lizzy," said he, still not moving. "It has been many weeks since we have last been in each other's company and I have longed to renew our acquaintance."

"An eternity would not be enough to remove the stain of your presence," said Elizabeth, determined not to give into fear. "With a man such as you, the indies would not be enough distance to remove your stench from the neighborhood."

Mr. Wickham threw his head back and laughed. "Oh, you always were a saucy one! It is a significant part of your charm. Given the circumstances, however, it may be best if you refrained from angering me. I am not inclined toward geniality as it is."

While Mr. Wickham chuckled and shook his head, Elizabeth took stock of her situation. Outright flight she ruled out except at the last resort—Mr. Wickham was much larger, possessed longer legs, and while Elizabeth was not unable to run, she doubted it would be long before he caught her. The situation, here on a secluded path, however, was not tenable. Then again, Mr. Darcy had promised to meet her, and Elizabeth did not doubt he would keep that promise. He would be along any time now, the fact that Elizabeth had left a few minutes before their agreed upon time notwithstanding.

"You see, my dear Miss Elizabeth," said Mr. Wickham, unaware of her thoughts, "it has been much on my mind of late that you have caused me much misfortune, and I am not a man who forgets those who have wronged me."

"Wronged you?" asked Elizabeth, infusing every ounce of scorn she could into her voice. "How could I have wronged you?"

"By interfering with my designs," replied Mr. Wickham. He remained unmoving, every word, every gesture, his very being suggesting confidence. "Had you allowed matters to rest, none of this would have happened." Mr. Wickham shot her an expressive leering grin. "In time, you might even have come to enjoy the . . . benefits of having me as a brother."

"Thank you, Mr. Wickham," said Elizabeth, standing bravely before her tormentor. "You have confirmed my long-held opinion of your worthlessness. My disgust for you is beyond anything I have ever felt for any man."

"Then I have succeeded in my purpose," said he, unmoved by her contempt. "Be that as it may, I am also not a man who allows others their offenses without reprisal."

"So you have come to attack an undefended woman? Typical of your brand of cowardice."

In a motion so sudden it caught Elizabeth by surprise, the man pushed himself away from the tree and stalked toward her, his expression determined. "Vengeance, Miss Elizabeth, is something you should never provoke. The time to pay for your misdeeds is at hand."

All thoughts of defiance fled and Elizabeth turned to run from this deranged man. She ran, as fast as she ever had, imagining his hand clamping about her wrist at any moment. She ran uncaring, unseeing, wild to escape, her heart thudding in her chest. On she ran, desperate to escape.

Then she impacted with something hard and came to a sudden stop. The fetid odor of his breath caused her to gasp and retch. His grip tightened about her wrists. Elizabeth fought and kicked, claws extended desperate to escape. A keening wail sounded in her ears, frightening her even further.

"Miss Elizabeth!"

The sound of her name on his lips broke through Elizabeth's terror, and the scream faded away. In a moment of clarity, Elizabeth realized it had issued from her own throat. Then she looked up into the demon's face. Only it was not a demon. It was not Mr. Wickham at all. It was Mr. Darcy.

A sense of relief so powerful it overwhelmed her surged through Elizabeth, leaving her boneless. She sagged, and Mr. Darcy's arms tightened around her, otherwise she was certain she would have fallen to the ground. Heart thumping, sending a ringing through her ears, Elizabeth rested her head on his broad chest, feeling lethargic and spent. It was beyond pleasant to be held in such a manner, she decided, and while his light stroking of her back was not in any way proper, Elizabeth did not wish him to stop.

"What is it, Miss Elizabeth?" A chuckle sounded in her ear. "It seemed to me the hounds of hell were hard on your heels."

The reminder of her ordeal flooded into Elizabeth's remembrance, and she gasped, pushing away from him. Mindless of his surprise, Elizabeth blurted: "Mr. Wickham!"

The gentleman's countenance turned from shock to fury in an instant, and he turned, peering down the path while drawing her closer to his side. "You saw Wickham?"

"There!" said Elizabeth, pointing at the path behind her. "I saw him and argued with him, then he began to chase me. Did you not see him?"

A frown settled over Mr. Darcy's countenance, and he shook his head. "I had just dismounted as I thought I was close to where we agreed to meet when you dashed around the corner there and ran headlong into me." Mr. Darcy smiled, though it was a feeble effort. "You are able to attain great speed, Miss Elizabeth, for you almost bowled me over."

"I thought him about to capture me," whispered Elizabeth.

"It seems you thought he *did* capture you," replied Mr. Darcy. "I believe I shall have bruises from our encounter, though I was fortunate to escape your claws."

"Now," said Mr. Darcy, his manner more businesslike, "please remain here while I attempt to see if he is still about."

Though Elizabeth little wished to remove herself from the protective circle of his arms, she nodded, allowing him to step away. Mr. Darcy strode down the path toward the little bend he had indicated earlier, continuing beyond a short distance, though remaining within her sight. After a moment of peering down the path, he turned and made his way back to her.

"It appears he has fled, unsurprising, I suppose." Mr. Darcy snorted with derision. "It was always his way to tend to cowardice. There is little chance he would brave a confrontation with me, though how he knew I would be here I have little understanding."

"I called him a coward myself," said Elizabeth.

Mr. Darcy regarded her, his fondness showing through his concern. "It would be best to return you to your father. Though I do not wish to lose any time in chasing him down, I would not leave you and risk his coming on you again."

Elizabeth had little argument to voice, and she accepted his arm, allowing him to lead her back to Longbourn. As they hurried along, Elizabeth related to him the gist of her conversation with Mr. Wickham, noting his growing anger as she did. When she had related all, Mr. Darcy shook his head and gazed at the church, which had risen above the trees again, though unseeing in anger.

"When we were boys, I could never have imagined the depths to which he could fall. I am glad my father cannot see it, for he would be heartbroken."

There was nothing to say to Mr. Darcy's words, and Elizabeth did not attempt it. She instead drew closer to him, clutching his arm more tightly in a gesture of support and affection. Mr. Darcy noted it, for he clasped his free hand over hers, his thumb drawing circles over the flesh of the back of her hands.

"This day has not proceeded as I might have expected, Miss Elizabeth."

The reminder of her speculations from earlier crossed Elizabeth's mind, and she turned a questioning look on him. Mr. Darcy was caught up in his own ruminations and did not reply, leaving Elizabeth to reply.

"Oh? Did you have some particular purpose in mind? Perhaps you wished to inform me of your efforts to attract Miss Bingley's attention. Or did you wish my advice on how best to go about it?"

Elizabeth's tease had the desired effect, for he turned a raised eyebrow on her, prompting Elizabeth's laughter. "I assure you, Miss Elizabeth, I have little desire to speak of Miss Bingley when I am in your presence, for there are much more pleasant subjects to discuss."

"I am happy to hear it, Mr. Darcy. But the reason you wished to see me today is still a mystery."

"In truth," said Mr. Darcy, sounding very much like he was confessing, "I am unable to determine what I meant to say. Or perhaps it is more correct to say I do not know to what extent I would speak this morning."

"Extent?" asked Elizabeth. "There are varying degrees of speech?"

Mr. Darcy turned an amused look on Elizabeth. "There are when you are trying to decide whether an acquaintance has been long enough in duration that a proposal will not be considered precipitous."

The words prompted Elizabeth's heart to fill near to bursting, and she stopped and turned to face him. "It seems like we have known each other longer, does it not?"

"A lifetime," was all he said.

"Then we shall have another lifetime to come to know each other better, Mr. Darcy. I believe you may proceed in whatever way you choose."

"I believe, my dear Miss Elizabeth, you do not understand to what you have just agreed."

With care, watching her to see if she would draw away, Mr. Darcy leaned forward and brushed his lips against hers. Elizabeth sighed and melted into the kiss, once again feeling like putty in his hands, and while she was not experienced in the art, it felt like she knew exactly what to do, where to move, to raise her hand to cup his cheek as he gathered her close, his arm around her back. It lasted only a moment, but the promise, the sheer bliss it provoked in her, was as if they had stood on that path kissing for an hour.

"It seems to me, my dearest, loveliest Elizabeth," murmured he as he drew away, "I had best return you to your father. You are already far too tempting as it is."

"Then I must retaliate, Fitzy," said Elizabeth with a gay laugh, "for you have used my Christian name without my permission."

"William, if you will," said he. "Fitzy was what my cousin used to call me when he was teasing."

"Then he should take care," said Elizabeth, once again accepting his arm, "for that moniker would apply to *him* as it does to *you*."

The sound of Mr. Darcy's laughter prompted Elizabeth's own. "And it did, more than once. Though I am two years younger, I gave as good as I received."

By this time, Longbourn came into view. The pair hurried down the walk, Mr. Darcy eager to deliver her into the care of her father. They had not reached the door when it opened, and Mr. Bennet stepped out, grinning in anticipation of their news. It was not long, however, before his face fell at the sight of their grim countenances.

"What is it?" asked he before they could speak.

"Wickham," was William's short reply. "He accosted your daughter before I found her."

Stricken, Mr. Bennet inspected Elizabeth, looking for signs of damage, a curious desperation about him, so unlike her unflappable father. "I should never have allowed you to go alone! Did he hurt you in any way?"

"No, Papa. I escaped him and found Mr. Darcy soon after."

William turned an expressive look on Elizabeth for her avoidance of the use of his name, but Elizabeth shook her head. Now was not the time to speak of such matters with her father.

"I assume you mean to search for him?" asked Mr. Bennet having assured himself of Elizabeth's safety.

"As soon as I return to Netherfield, I will assemble the estate's footmen and stable hands and scour the area. If I can prevent his escape again, I shall do it."

Mr. Bennet nodded, his calm demeanor replacing his concern, and augmented by determination. "I shall gather what I can of Longbourn's manservants and begin to search here." His eyes flicked to Elizabeth and he added: "But I will leave one footman, for it would not do to leave the estate unprotected should Wickham evade us and come here."

"That is prudent," replied William. "Now, if you will excuse me, I shall be on my way."

The gentlemen shook hands and William then bowed over Elizabeth's hand before turning and climbing into the saddle. Within moments the dust of his passing was swirling through the air, and the sounds of his horse's hooves pounding into the turf receded into the distance.

"Come, Lizzy," said Mr. Bennet, "let us get you into the house. Your mother and sisters have not yet arisen, but I am sure they will soon. I will have left by the time they are about, so I will leave it to you to inform them that no one is to leave the house until I inform everyone it is safe to do so."

"Yes, Papa," said Elizabeth.

"Now, please tell me what happened while I am preparing to leave."

Mr. Bennet gave a few low instructions Mr. Hill, the butler, and then Elizabeth told her father the tale of her fright that morning, only leaving out the more intimate parts of her time with William. As she told him what happened, Elizabeth noted the darkening of Mr. Bennet's countenance, the way he muttered imprecations when she informed him of her sudden flight. It was not a long recitation, for he was eager to depart, and once she had finished, he turned and pulled her into an embrace, which surprised Elizabeth, since he was not a tactile man.

"My dearest daughter! What a fright you have had. I heartily apologize I did not insist on accompanying you or insisting you did not walk out—I know you value your time with your gentleman, but it is not worth the risk to your safety!"

"Do not blame yourself, Papa," said Elizabeth from the safety of his arms. "I did not expect to see Mr. Wickham this morning either."

"No, but we have had ample warning of his perfidy to know you should not be walking out. I know you have valued your freedom in the past, but these walks must stop until the threat of Mr. Wickham has passed."

"I cannot agree more," said Elizabeth.

A thought tickled the back of her mind and she paused, her lips pulling down into a frown. Mr. Bennet noted it, but he seemed to recognize her introspection, for he did not interrupt. Then Elizabeth remembered, and she gazed at her father in consternation.

"Mr. Wickham may have been stalking me for some time!"

"What do you mean?"

"The day Mr. Darcy left for Kent, I walked out near the Campbell farm and had the distinct sense I was being followed. As I walked, a flock of birds took to the air from the middle of the woods, and I thought I heard the snapping of a branch behind me. But then Mr. Campbell hailed me and I did not think on it further."

"Then perhaps Mr. Wickham has been more focused on my family than I thought." Mr. Bennet nodded to himself. "That makes it more imperative than ever you all follow my instructions to the letter."

"Do not worry, Papa," said Elizabeth. "I have no intention of disobeying."

"Good girl. Inform your mother and sisters when they awake, Lizzy. I shall be back when I can, I hope with good news."

Then Mr. Bennet departed through the open door to the horse which was waiting for him. Two stable hands and a footman were already mounted and waiting, and after imparting a few terse instructions, the party rode through the gate. As they left, Elizabeth noted her father's rifle was strapped to his saddle, and the other men were similarly armed.

CHAPTER XXVII

"*D*arcy!" exclaimed Bingley as Darcy entered Netherfield, handing his gloves and great coat to the butler with a softly spoken instruction to keep them at hand. "Whatever is the matter?"

The sight of Miss Bingley descending the stairs after her brother, looking at them with keen interest, stayed Darcy's response. Instead, he beckoned his friend down the hall which led toward the study, and after glancing behind to ensure they were not being followed, undertook to explain the morning's events to his friend.

"Wickham is in the area."

Bingley gasped. "Wickham? Did you apprehend him?"

"I wish I had, but I did not see him. While on her morning walk, Miss Elizabeth encountered and was forced to flee from him—I met her soon after."

It seemed Bingley had no indication of Darcy's purpose for being out that morning nor any reason to suppose he had meant to meet with Miss Elizabeth. Though they had not been engaging in anything improper, Darcy preferred to keep his friend from any notion of the truth. Bingley was not noted for being the soul of discretion, and Darcy did not wish to give Miss Bingley any reason to speak of Miss

Elizabeth.

"Are we to search for him?" asked Bingley after a moment.

"I suspect he has already fled far from here," said Darcy. "Wickham has ever been a coward. But we must make the attempt. If you have not yet broken your fast, please do so while I send an express to Fitzwilliam."

"Join me when you have finished," said Bingley. "Hurst and Louisa have already descended—I am certain Hurst will offer his assistance. Either way, I believe you could some tea would do you good."

"Though I am uncertain there is time, I will join you."

The two men parted then, Darcy heading for the library. The letter was quickly written and sanded, which Darcy then gave to the butler with the instructions to ensure its immediate disposition. Then Darcy instructed him to gather as many stable hands and footmen with mounts as could be spared and meet out near the front door. When this was complete, Darcy made his way to the breakfast room, heedless of the riding leathers he still wore.

Four sets of eyes looked up at him as he entered, and while he noticed the concern on Mrs. Hurst's face and the determination on the part of the gentlemen, Miss Bingley's appraisal was not welcome at all. It was the younger woman who spoke first.

"Mr. Wickham is again in Hertfordshire?"

"It seemed best to warn my sisters," said Bingley by way of apology. "Though I would not expect him to come to Netherfield, I cannot put anything past him at this point."

"It is only prudent," said Darcy with a curt nod. "It may be best to warn the other gentlemen of the neighborhood as well."

Bingley nodded. "I shall ask the butler to see to it."

"It is strange the gentleman continues to come here, Mr. Darcy," said Miss Bingley, apparently unwilling to be ignored. "One might wonder if there is anything that draws him back. And I understand Miss Eliza was the one to see him?" The woman sniffed in disdain. "That is curious, for she was the last one to see him in Hertfordshire before he fled, I believe."

Darcy turned the full force of his displeasure on Miss Bingley, taking a measure of dark glee at her sudden pallor. "In the company of her sisters, Miss Bingley. Surely you are not suggesting she was engaged in some assignation when he forced her to flee from him."

Especially since the assignation was with me.

"Of course not," replied Miss Bingley, eager to deflect his displeasure. "But one cannot help but wonder what he means by continuing to return."

"I cannot speak to his thoughts, for they have forever been a mystery to me. It seems, however, that he has developed a taste for vengeance, for the words he spoke to Miss Elizabeth suggested anger that his schemes were not fruitful. Beyond that, I cannot say, for as I said, his thoughts are unfathomable to me.

"Bingley, Hurst, are you prepared to depart?" asked Darcy, unwilling to trade further words with this woman.

"Yes, let us leave," said Hurst, rising from his chair with a glance at his brother.

The three men took their leave and stepped quickly out of doors where the party of stable hands and footmen were already waiting. After a few instructions, where Darcy informed them of the identity of their quarry and the location where he was seen, they set out.

Thus began a frustrating morning of fruitless searching for a man who, Darcy was certain, was no longer in the neighborhood. They found Mr. Bennet and the Longbourn men quickly, a few words from the other gentleman revealing they had not as yet had any luck in sighting Wickham either. They fanned out from there, searching the nearby area, scouring the woods and gullies of Mr. Bennet's land. But Wickham was nowhere to be found.

"What do you suggest now, Mr. Darcy?" asked Mr. Bennet when the morning had surrendered to afternoon. "Should we go further afield than we have? There are only so many places on the estate that a man can hide."

"I cannot say, Mr. Bennet," said Darcy. "It was my firm opinion that Wickham would avoid the neighborhood after he discovered my presence. Enduring discomfort has never been Wickham's forte, and as such, I might have thought he would move on to the next likely target of his schemes."

"It appears he has changed much in the years since your estrangement," replied Mr. Bennet. "Can he have been receiving assistance?"

"My cousin believes he has a confederate who has been providing him aid but has not been able to discover who it is. But that was in London, not Hertfordshire."

"Could he have been holed up in some copse of woods nearby?" asked Hurst.

"It is possible," was Darcy's reluctant reply. "Again, I should not have thought him willing to endure the simple conditions of a campsite."

"The question is where," said Mr. Bennet. "There are any number of small copses or larger groves in the area. It will take some time to search them all. At present, I do not believe it is worth our time to continue this search."

Little though he appreciated it, Darcy could not disagree. "At this new sighting of him, my cousin will almost certainly join me here. It is possible he might think of something I have not."

Mr. Bennet gave a tight nod in response. "Then I suppose there is little to be done except to ensure we are protected against the possibility of his return. To that end, I shall keep my girls at home—it may be too dangerous for them to even walk into Meryton."

"I shall ensure my sisters also stay close to the house," said Bingley.

"It may be best to avoid riding alone as well," said Mr. Bennet peering at Darcy in particular. "This Mr. Wickham's behavior is becoming ever more unpredictable and dangerous. If he finds you alone and is armed, there is no telling what he might do."

Again, Darcy did not like the insinuation, but he knew Mr. Bennet was correct. "That would be for the best."

The gentlemen all agreed and the search was called off. Hurst, it appeared, was eager to return to Netherfield—a morning in the saddle did not agree with him, though he had been more than willing to assist. For Darcy's part, he was more interested in seeing Miss Elizabeth once more that day and assuring himself of her wellbeing.

"Well, this is more excitement than we have seen in our neighborhood for many a year," said Mr. Bennet as they turned to ride back to Longbourn. "Your coming to Netherfield was enough to excite the wagging tongues of every gossip within ten miles without all this intrigue!"

"I think I speak for my friend, Mr. Bennet," replied Bingley, who had been as eager to see his lady as Darcy had been to see *his*, "I would have been happy without it."

"This is so unlike Wickham," said Darcy. Though he had spoken out loud, his words were more introspective. "He has always been a coward, one to run at the first sign of trouble. Though I could see him conceiving a plan to compromise my sister, the threat of his current actions is unlike anything I have ever witnessed from him."

"People change," was Mr. Bennet's reply. "The years after the sundering of your acquaintance have not yielded the riches he was hoping to amass, and that has likely altered him, given him a sense of desperation. With desperation comes a man's willingness to accept risks he might not otherwise."

Darcy grunted. "That is possible. But I have always observed that those who are cowards stay cowards. And yet Wickham has somehow become more daring."

"I cannot help you, Mr. Darcy," said Mr. Bennet. The elder gentleman reached across the distance between their mounts and rested a hand on Darcy's shoulder. "I believe there is little we can do but focus on what is before us. Perhaps once he is apprehended, his motivations will become clear."

Uncertain though he was that Wickham would ever be made to speak with any truth, Darcy decided Mr. Bennet had the right of it and allowed the subject to drop. It might have been a pleasant day had the situation been different. The late November sun was shining down on them, now past its apex, the warmth it provided meager, though the lack of wind allowed the day to remain pleasant. So concerned was Darcy for Wickham's actions, the entire return distance to Longbourn he imagined his childhood friend hiding behind a tree with a rifle, to attempt a more direct approach to their longstanding enmity. Nothing happened, however, and soon they had reached the drive to Longbourn.

And there they discovered a commotion about the manor's entrance. As the sound reached their ears, Mr. Bennet spurred his horse forward, his edginess about the morning's events the equal of Darcy's own. They covered the distance down the drive with alacrity, and they dismounted in front of the door to a strange sight. Rather than Wickham, as Darcy had feared, the tall figure of a parson could be seen trying to force his way past Longbourn's butler and remaining footman, who were standing barring his way.

"I am sorry, Mr. Collins, but the master has left strict instructions to admit no one to the house."

"The master!" sneered Mr. Collins. "When I have had my cousin put aside, *I* shall be the master, and *you* shall be let go without reference. Let me enter!"

"What is the meaning of this?" thundered Mr. Bennet.

The gentleman stepped forward, his baleful glare fixed on the parson, who started in surprise at the sudden voice of his cousin. While the situation might have been amusing in other circumstances, at present Darcy had little desire to continue to exchange words with Mr. Collins. Mr. Bennet, however, put himself nose to nose with his cousin

"What are you doing, Collins? Why have you returned?"

"I have come to claim what is mine!" exclaimed the parson, his shrill voice climbing the heights of the register. "You shall not cheat me. I shall have your eldest daughter as my wife, and your family may stay at the estate, but I *will* have her."

"Are you out of your senses?" demanded Bingley. The normally genial man surged forward and joined Mr. Bennet in confronting the hapless parson. Collins did not seem to know where to look. "What kind of a man attempts to barge into another's home, demanding the hand of a woman? What kind of parson are you?"

Mr. Collins sniffed with disdain. "I am the man who was cheated out of his inheritance by my cousin's unjust and, may I say, dishonest scheme with his solicitor. But I shall not be defrauded! I know my rights!"

"It is apparent you know nothing," said Mr. Bennet, his voice sounding like rocks rolling down a hill. "I have already informed you that you may seek redress with the courts if you feel I have misused you. The only result you will accomplish is to make a fool out of yourself — or more of a fool, as you already the most ridiculous man I have ever met."

Mr. Collins drew himself up to his full height. "The only fool, it appears, is you. Did you think I would not retaliate when you have committed such a grievous sin of avarice I can scarcely comprehend it? You hide behind this action you have taken, and do not even deign to respond to my patroness's letter. Instead, you send Mr. Darcy to persuade my aunt away from her just course of action."

"Mr. Bennet did not *send* me to Kent, Mr. Collins."

The parson whirled around and blanched at the sight of Darcy, who he had not realized was present. There was little Darcy wished to see other than the back of this man, so he could enter and ensure himself of Miss Elizabeth's wellbeing, but as the estate belonged to Mr. Bennet, the pleasure of evicting Collins must rest with him. That did not mean Darcy could not inform the man what he thought of him.

"I went willingly, for I could not allow my aunt to be deceived into a proceeding which would not end well. And I would not see my friends, the Bennets, endure a pointless and frivolous lawsuit when it was in my power to ensure Lady Catherine never supported you."

Eyes narrowed, Mr. Collins said: "I believe I begin to see the reason for your interference. Lady Catherine spoke of your interest in one of Longbourn's daughters. You covet the estate for yourself, though I cannot imagine why a man of your wealth would attempt to defraud me of my inheritance."

"Let us be clear on one matter," said Darcy, amused the man had misconstrued the situation, "do not accuse me of attempted fraud, sir, or it will go ill for you. Furthermore, I am not paying any sort of attention to Miss Bennet. That privilege has been bestowed on my friend."

Mr. Collins glanced back at a decidedly unfriendly Bingley, who said: "Your friend who has never been closer to planting a facer on another man than I am now."

"So, you see, Mr. Collins," said Mr. Bennet, "your accusations are meaningless, and your cause is hopeless. Personally, if I never see you again, it will be too soon. Now, I require you to depart and never darken my doorstep again."

Not allowing the parson to say anything more, Mr. Bennet motioned the servants standing nearby to take control of his cousin. "See him to Longbourn's borders and ensure he does not return. Collins, if you trespass on my land again, I shall call the constable."

The parson did not cease his complaining, but the men about him were implacable, and they walked off, John, Longbourn's largest footman, and David, one of the stable hands, escorting him.

"Do you think he is gone for good this time, Mr. Bennet?" asked Bingley.

"I know not," replied Mr. Bennet. "But I shall follow through on my threat if he returns. At one time I believed having him as a correspondent would provide amusement, but I have since concluded that a little of Mr. Collins goes a long way."

"Now," said Mr. Bennet, turning back to them, "if you will step this way, I believe your purpose for accompanying me was to bask in the company of my eldest daughters."

The ladies were gathered together in the main sitting-room, engaged in various activities according to their temperaments. Even the youngest sisters were present, though Darcy thought they might usually be engaged in their lessons at such an hour. Darcy had no interest in them, nor in any of the other ladies. His eyes immediately found the person of Miss Elizabeth, who brightened at the sight of him, and he approached her, without regard for anything else.

"Are you well, Miss Elizabeth?"

"As well as I was when you left me here this morning, Mr. Darcy," said she. "Can I assume you were unable to locate Mr. Wickham?"

"I suspect he has once again retreated, though I am not so certain he shall not return. This time, Miss Elizabeth, I strongly urge you do not put yourself in a situation where you may come across him alone."

"You need have no worry of that, Mr. Darcy," said Miss Elizabeth, grinning at him with amusement. "Unless something is amiss with my memory, however, I seem to remember my sojourn this morning was at another's request."

"The request shall not be made again," replied Darcy. "In the future, I shall to visit you here or receive you at Netherfield — or at least I shall until Wickham has been captured."

"Mrs. Bennet, girls," said Mr. Bennet, drawing Darcy's attention, as well as that of the rest of the room. Something in his mirthful glance at Darcy suggested he had heard his exchange with Miss Elizabeth, but he instead addressed his family. "If you do not already know, Mr. Wickham accosted Lizzy again this morning while she was out walking."

There was no surprise among his family, indicating Elizabeth had already vouchsafed the matter to them.

"Though we searched for him, he remains undiscovered. As such, until he is apprehended, I insist upon you all refraining from putting yourselves in harm's way. Until I inform you otherwise, walks on the estate, walking to Meryton, or even to Lucas Lodge, is forbidden."

Darcy noted that Miss Lydia was about to protest, but Mr. Bennet expected it and stopped her before she could speak. "This is for your own protection, Lydia. I do not mean to deny you Maria Lucas or your other friends, but I will keep you safe to the best of my abilities. Please do not force me to lock you in your room until you can behave."

"I shall keep Kitty and Lydia with me," said Mrs. Garret.

"Good," replied Mr. Bennet. "Even walking on the back lawn may only be undertaken with severe restrictions. Call John to accompany you if you decide to go at all. When traveling by carriage, the footmen are to escort you bearing arms. I do not know what this Wickham will attempt, but I mean to make it as difficult for him to succeed as I can."

"Do you think it will be long before he is caught?" asked Miss Elizabeth.

"It is difficult to say," said Darcy. "I have informed my cousin, and I expect him to come when he is able. Finding no trace of Wickham leaves us with few clues as to his whereabouts, and his skill at remaining hidden in London renders it difficult to know when we will apprehend him. It is only a matter of time, but I cannot say how long that time will be."

Darcy paused and turned to Mr. Bennet. "If you are willing to see to their lodging, there are several footmen I can call down from Pemberley, Mr. Bennet. The additional men would not go amiss especially as you would then have the numbers to mount a night watch as well."

"I would much appreciate it, Mr. Darcy," said Mr. Bennet with a nod.

"I shall send an express before returning to Netherfield if you will provide me with paper and a pen."

The second express of the day was soon written and secured in Darcy's pocket, where he intended to seek out a rider when they went to Meryton. After a few more moments of conversation, Darcy knew it was time he and Bingley departed. Miss Bennet and Miss Elizabeth accompanied them to the door, Mr. Bennet walking behind them. As they walked, Miss Elizabeth paused and turned to her father.

"Papa, this visit Mr. Collins paid to us is on my mind. Do you think there might be some connection between him and Mr. Wickham?"

"I should not think so, Lizzy," said Mr. Bennet. "They are two very different men and have had little occasion to meet."

"Their presence in Meryton *did* overlap, if you recall," insisted Miss Elizabeth.

"But their goals are the same—they both want an estate. I do not think they could form alliances under such circumstances."

"In this instance, I must agree with your father, Miss Elizabeth," said Darcy. "It is not beyond Wickham to deceive Mr. Collins into assisting him. Having said as much, I do not think they could be confederates. Wickham would have little patience for Mr. Collins's foolishness, and Mr. Collins has been in Kent these past months. Though I do not know where Wickham has been hiding, I believe we would have had some word if he had gone to Kent."

Though Miss Elizabeth seemed unconvinced, she allowed the matter to drop. With her father in attendance, Darcy was allowed little more than a kiss to her hand in parting. The circumstances were trying, but Darcy knew they would prevail. They needed to locate Wickham before he could cause any further harm.

CHAPTER XXVIII

$\mathcal{D}$arcy arose the next morning, intending to spend the day at Longbourn. Unfortunately, it seemed fate decided there were other ways of spending his day, to his chagrin. While the morning had been pleasant, other than the constant worry over the situation, and due to the absence of a certain resident of Netherfield, he knew it would be much more pleasant at Longbourn. Before he and Bingley could saddle their horses and depart, however, a visitor joined them earlier than they might have expected.

"Ho, Darcy!" greeted his cousin as he entered into the breakfast room, dusty from his long ride.

"Colonel Fitzwilliam!" greeted Bingley with surprise. "To have come at this hour you must have set out early this morning."

"Aye, well before six," agreed Fitzwilliam. "This business of Wickham appearing in Hertfordshire again is so unlike him, I thought I would come and do a bit of poking around of my own. But I would appreciate a cup of tea before we set about it."

"Of course," said Bingley, gesturing to one of the nearby footmen. "If you need to break your fast, please help yourself."

Fitzwilliam grinned and filled a plate to overflowing. "I troubled Darcy's cook for a roll before I departed, but the ride was long and cold, and I am eager to be warmed by your excellent fare."

"Do you think you can find what we could not?" asked Darcy. "I expected you to join us, but I hope you have not left Georgiana unprotected."

"Thompson is there," said Fitzwilliam around mouthfuls of breakfast. "Even I would be reluctant to attack him with the whole regiment at my back. I believe our Georgiana is ready to join you here if you were to extend an invitation."

"It would be my pleasure!" said Bingley. "We are more than happy to welcome her here."

"Then when I return to London, I shall gather her up and escort her back here. Now, please inform me of what happened and what you have done to locate our friend Wickham."

Darcy took the lead in relating the events of the previous day, with Bingley adding a few observations of his own. While Fitzwilliam ate, he listened intently, interjecting a few questions, and when the account was complete, he fell silent, considering what he had learned as he finished his breakfast.

"There is something . . . something I dislike about this." Fitzwilliam paused and shook his head, pushing his chair back from the table. "I cannot put my finger on it, but something about Wickham's behavior bothers me."

"The whole situation bothers me," replied Darcy. "Wickham has never been the most courageous of men, and he was always eager to move on to the next target when his last did not yield the riches he desires."

"Perhaps," replied Fitzwilliam. "It is more than that, though I will acknowledge your point. Let us ride out, shall we? If you will show me the place he accosted Miss Bennet, perhaps we can start from there."

Thus agreed, the three men soon departed from Netherfield, their mounts directed toward Longbourn village and the estate beyond. They set a quick pace, the ground flowing by, little conversation passing between them until they were cantering through the village. The manor house rose in the distance as did the track Miss Elizabeth had chosen for their meeting, but Darcy noted Bingley looking longingly at Longbourn and took pity on his friend.

"You may proceed to Longbourn if you wish, Bingley."

Fitzwilliam laughed and shooed Bingley away with his hand. "By all means, to Longbourn with you, and your fair maiden. There is little enough chance we will find anything of value—Wickham has likely left the area, so I doubt we will require numbers to keep him at bay."

With a grin, Bingley spurred his horse on, his voice floating back to them, saying: "I shall inform the Bennets of Fitzwilliam's arrival."

"Excellent man, that Bingley," said Fitzwilliam. "Under normal circumstances, I would be inclined to make sport with him over his mooning after Longbourn's eldest daughter. But since *you* are currently mooning after the second, I doubt my jests would be well received."

"Let us get on with this," growled Darcy. "I prefer Miss Elizabeth's company to yours."

Fitzwilliam shook his head and chuckled, following Darcy down the path. As their horses plodded on, Fitzwilliam turned to Darcy and eyed him with interest.

"It is strange, Cousin," said he. "I might have thought your overt interest in Miss Elizabeth might bring Miss Bingley's jealousy to the fore, but she was not in attendance this morning."

"Just because you have not seen it does not mean it is not present," replied Darcy. "The woman has grown more hateful the longer we have been here. But I have hope she now understands the extent of my distaste for her."

"Oh?" asked Fitzwilliam. "Do you refer to something in particular?"

"Last night we exchanged words that should have left her in no doubt."

If Darcy was honest with himself, he was not proud of the way he had behaved. A sense of unease, the tense atmosphere rendering him out of sorts and snappish punctuated the rest of the day after departing Longbourn. That Bingley was in the same straits was no comfort to Darcy, who had always striven to maintain a gentlemanly manner, regardless of the situation.

"Do you wish we had stayed at Longbourn?" asked Bingley late in the afternoon when they were waiting for dinner.

Darcy grunted in the affirmative, knowing Bingley would understand him.

"I know Mr. Bennet is adequately protecting them," continued Bingley, "but I cannot help but thinking I would prefer to see to it myself."

"The feeling is mutual, Bingley," said Darcy. "And though Wickham's recent target was Miss Elizabeth, it may as have been Miss Bennet to meet him on a secluded path. They are all in danger, and yet

I still do not know why."

"If they would not practice such unladylike habits as traipsing all over the countryside, they would not be in danger."

Both men turned at the sound of Miss Bingley's voice, and Darcy knew his scowl matched Bingley's. Mrs. Hurst, eager to be the peacemaker, interjected before anyone could throw further fuel on the flames.

"Walking near one's home cannot be deemed unladylike." Mrs. Hurst turned to Bingley. "Perhaps you should spend the day there tomorrow, Charles. We are well here with Hurst and the footmen to protect us."

The snort from Miss Bingley informed them all what she thought on the matter, but no one paid her any heed.

"Then we shall do that," said Bingley with a nod

Darcy had no objection at all, his concise response informing her of that and his appreciation for Mrs. Hurst's efforts. Though he had never cared much for the woman, she was providing a valuable check on her sister.

"I am certain your presence there will be agreeable to your ladies," continued Mrs. Hurst.

"Of course, it will!" snapped Miss Bingley, proving she still had much to say. "Why should they not? It is clear they have sunk their talons into you both, as you are so eager to put yourselves in their power again. I never thought I would see the day you both are so eager to consort with those so wholly unsuitable as the Bennets."

"For my part, Miss Bingley," said Darcy, his voice cold, yet tightly controlled, "I could never consider them to be unsuitable. They are kind, gracious, welcoming, and descend from a long line of gentlemen. I find your comments insulting and would appreciate it if you would refrain from making them in my presence!"

"Yes, be silent, Caroline," said Bingley. "No one here wants your opinion. It is better to be thought a fool than to open your mouth and remove all doubt."

For a time, Darcy thought his cousin would fall from his mount, he was laughing so hard. "Bingley actually said that to his sister?"

"And would have said more if she had not fallen silent," replied Darcy. "I apologized to him later for speaking so to her, but Bingley would have nothing of it, insisting she brought it on herself."

"Genial *and* intelligent," said Fitzwilliam. When Darcy looked at him, Fitzwilliam waved him off. "Perhaps you might have spoken with less anger or more tact, but I dare say she has been provoking you since you made her acquaintance. Miss Bingley could use a hint of humility, Darcy, for she is envious of others, grasping, and selfish. She deserved more than the rebuke she received."

"There is no question she did," agreed Darcy, deciding there was little reason to further castigate himself. "After dinner, Miss Bingley only stayed in the sitting-room for a half hour before excusing herself to retire. Of late she has been waking early to attend me, no doubt hoping to persuade me from my path. This morning, however, she did not appear. I find I can endure her incivility without any reason to repine."

"Of course, you can," agreed Fitzwilliam.

"This is where I met Miss Elizabeth," said Darcy, looking about. "Or near enough. I believe that bend in the path is where Miss Elizabeth was fleeing Wickham."

Fitzwilliam nodded and spurred his horse into a canter, rounding the bend. After a short time of this, he stopped and looked about.

"There is no path leading away, though I suppose Wickham might have gone through the woods. When you first met Miss Elizabeth, you did not search the area?"

"It was of more importance to return her to Longbourn and ensure her safety."

"It seems to me this woman is addling your wits, for this is the second time you were close to Wickham and allowed him to escape." Fitzwilliam grinned, showing his words were a jest. "But I understand the allure of a woman so exquisite as Miss Elizabeth. Where did you search when you returned?"

"All throughout these woods, as far as the church and Longbourn village, and further to the north."

Fitzwilliam considered. "If I recall my geography of the area, Netherfield is to the east, Longbourn a little to the south and west, and further south is a smaller estate. Is that not correct?"

"Lucas Lodge," replied Darcy. "It is not large—I suspect it is only about two thirds the size of Longbourn."

Turning, Fitzwilliam gazed toward the north. "What is in that direction?"

"I believe most of Longbourn's land is to the north and I have heard them speak of some tenants, though I do not know how many there are. Beyond Longbourn is another estate, though I do not know its name. Miss Elizabeth has also spoken of Oakham Mount, which is the prominence you see in the distance. I believe before the troubles with

Wickham began, she used to walk there frequently."

"Then with more estates to the south and an unclaimed hill to the north, I suspect if Wickham was in the area for any length of time, he must have been hiding somewhere up there. Let us have a look, shall we?"

Darcy motioned his cousin forward, and they began to canter toward the north. As they rode, Darcy noted his cousin gazing out over the land, watching with great care, though he knew not what Fitzwilliam was looking for. There was no reason to suppose they would come across Wickham as they rode.

"Lady Catherine paid a visit to my father," said Fitzwilliam after some minutes of this.

"Did she?" asked Darcy. "And what resulted from that?"

"Bedlam," was Fitzwilliam amused reply. "She complained of your recalcitrance, my support, Anne's indifference, Miss Elizabeth's perfidy — though not by name — and in general the entire world for not falling in with her schemes. My father sent her away with a bee in her ear, warning of breaks in the family should she attempt to interfere. The way he put it, I doubt she will attempt anything."

"The break has already occurred," said Darcy. "I have no intention of visiting Rosings again, and I will not welcome her into my homes. If she assures me she will not berate my future wife, I may be inclined to mend the distance between us, but only if I have her solemn promise."

"Do you think she would honor the promise?"

Darcy shrugged. "If she does not, then she will break the possibility of all congress between us forever."

"Happy thought, indeed," said Fitzwilliam.

The appearance of a man dressed in the rough coat and trousers of a tenant interrupted their conversation. Though he eyed them with suspicion, he greeted them, tipping his straw hat in response to Fitzwilliam's hail.

"My good man," said Fitzwilliam, "I am Colonel Fitzwilliam, and this is my cousin Mr. Darcy, and we were hoping you could give us some information."

"I am Campbell," replied the man. He looked at them with a little more respect. "I have heard of you, Mr. Darcy. Seems like you have become friendly with the master, though I cannot say how the likes of me can help you."

"There has been a man bedeviling the Bennets of late by the name of Wickham," said Fitzwilliam. "He was a member of the militia until he deserted and has recently returned to the area. Have you seen anyone suspicious loitering about?"

The farmer scratched his head in thought. "There is no one loitering about that I have seen, though I have heard tell of this Wickham." Mr. Campbell spat in his disgust. "Accosting the Bennet girls like that—the man should be hanged!"

"I could not agree with you more," said Fitzwilliam.

"Now, I have seen no one," continued Mr. Campbell, "but I have seen smoke to the north, a small campfire or some such. There is an old hunting lodge on the northwest slope of Oakham Mount. I assumed it was Mr. Pearce, as the lodge is on his land, but it could be the man you have been looking for."

Darcy glanced at Fitzwilliam, who nodded and thanked Mr. Campbell. "That is as good a lead as any we have had."

The man tipped his hat again, wished them luck, and went on his way after pointing the direction to the lodge of which he had spoken. Fitzwilliam took the lead, setting his mount to a quick canter, down the path the farmer indicated. After a few moments of travel, they struck another path which led around the side of the promontory—which was more of a rounded hill than a mountain. It was not many moments later when Fitzwilliam's sharp eyes caught sight of a narrow track leading up into the woods, which soon opened up into a clearing where a small building sat.

"Careful, Darcy," said Fitzwilliam, dismounting and peering at the ramshackle hut. "We do not know he is not there."

Though Darcy followed his warning, it soon became clear the shack was abandoned. It was a rough building, constructed from the wood likely cut from the forest surrounding them, smoky windows set into various locations about the exterior. The door they found, when they pushed it open, was in good condition, proving the building had been used in the recent past. When they entered, they discovered it to be only two rooms, with a bed in one, a pair of chairs, both of which appeared ready to collapse if used, and a hearth to warm the interior. The charred remains of a fire still rested in the hearth provided one more piece of evidence of the hut's recent use, though by now it was cold. Darcy could also see signs of someone having hunted, as there were a few bones strewn about the hearth, uncaring as to their resting place.

"There is no saying Wickham was using this place," said Fitzwilliam. "Someone has, but it may be nothing more than a woodcutter or the local gentleman."

Darcy was about to agree when the twinkle of reflected light caught his eye. Leaning over, Darcy plucked the object from the floor by the wall where it rested and turned it over in his hands.

"A cufflink?" asked Fitzwilliam, looking over Darcy's shoulder.

"A cufflink which belonged to my father," said Darcy, anger coursing through him. "If you look, you can see the curious design here, the stones making the shape of a stylized D."

"For Darcy," said Fitzwilliam.

Darcy nodded. "After my father's death, I could never find these, though they were my father's favorite set, given to him by my mother as a Christmas gift when I was young. I cannot say how Wickham got his hands on them, but I always suspected he might have had something to do with their disappearance."

"Then it seems we have our proof," said Fitzwilliam. "That cufflink could not have made its way here on its own. Wickham *has* been here."

"But why would he have even brought it here?" demanded Darcy. "If his financial straits are what I believe them to be, I would have thought he would sell them long ago. Even stolen they would have fetched a pretty penny."

"I cannot say," replied Fitzwilliam. "But it appears we have located his hideaway. I believe we should have a word with the local gentleman and have him set watch on this place for the possibility of Wickham's return."

"Is it worth it?" asked Darcy. "Do you think he will use this place again?"

"I am certain of nothing when it comes to Wickham anymore, for he has defied our understanding of him over and over. I think we would be wise to alert him of what we have found, for it is one more avenue to finally getting my hands on his hide."

"Very well," said Darcy. "Let us go."

The arrival of Mr. Bingley without William in attendance set Elizabeth's nerves on edge, though the gentleman did what he could to ease her concerns. "Colonel Fitzwilliam is with him, so I doubt he will come to any harm. I expect we shall see them here at some time or another, likely before the morning is gone."

Though she appreciated his reassurance, Elizabeth still worried, and as he took his seat beside Jane, she felt a pang of jealousy. It was unreasonable, Elizabeth knew, but at that moment she wished for nothing more than to have William's comforting presence at her side, assuring her there was nothing to fear. While she waited, Charlotte came to visit, full of tales of her courtship with Mr. Pearce and eager to hear of Elizabeth's stories in return. Though Elizabeth attempted to give her friend as much of her attention as she could, she found herself distracted and unable to focus. It was fortunate Charlotte was such a good friend, for she endured Elizabeth's distraction without comment until it was time for her to depart.

When the sight of William and his cousin riding up the drive appeared through the window—Elizabeth had set herself close for just that purpose—she rose and went out to greet him, not caring for her less than proper actions. She arrived at the door as the gentlemen were dismounting, the stable boy on hand to take their mounts. It was only a lifetime of proper behavior that reminder her to curtsey at all, and Mr. Darcy's look at her, drinking in the sight of her, made Elizabeth feel weak about the knees.

"Miss Elizabeth." The sound of her name on his tongue was like the gentlest caress. "I see you have anticipated our arrival."

"Indeed, she has," said Colonel Fitzwilliam, amusement coloring his features. "Is your father in his study?"

"Yes, he is," came the voice of Mrs. Hill. "I shall show you to him."

With a slap of Mr. Darcy's back, Colonel Fitzwilliam departed, leaving them alone together. For a moment, Elizabeth could not think of what to say, her heart so full she wished to say everything and nothing all at once. Mr. Darcy's hand rose to touch her cheek, then lowered to grasp her hand.

"All day yesterday I wished I had stayed at Longbourn," said he, his voice rough with emotion.

"You would have been welcome," replied Elizabeth. "I longed for your presence."

The barest ghost of a smile reached Mr. Darcy's lips—she thought he might have kissed her again had they not been standing on Longbourn's front step. Instead, he bowed and kissed her hand, a lingering warmth which left the appendage tingling from the exquisite sensations it engendered.

"Soon, Miss Elizabeth. Soon we will not part again."

"Do you promise?" asked Elizabeth, a hint of her playfulness coming out.

"Of course," replied he. "But at present, I think we should deal with the practicalities. Shall you join me in your father's room?"

With a shy smile, Elizabeth led him into the house, never relinquishing her hold on his hand. It seemed to her like Mr. Darcy had no more wish to end the physical contact between them than she. The door to her father's study was open, and they entered, noting both Mr. Bingley and Colonel Fitzwilliam were already present.

"Mr. Darcy," greeted Mr. Bennet, shooting an amused glance at their still joined hands. "Your cousin has informed me of your adventures this morning. It is my understanding you have discovered Mr. Wickham's lair."

"His lair in Hertfordshire," said Mr. Darcy while Elizabeth looked on with interest. "Before we returned we stopped at Mr. Pearce's estate and informed him of our suspicions. He was not happy that someone was trespassing on his land and likely poaching too."

"No, I imagine he would not be. Pearce is more than a little indolent, but I expect he will take the matter seriously."

"He promised to lock the place up tight, though I think it may be best to allow Wickham to return and then surround him."

"What I do not understand," said Mr. Bennet, "is why he seems to have targeted Lizzy. Should he not have attempted to compromise my Jane to force her to marry him?"

No one missed the anger Mr. Bingley displayed, though he made no comment.

"By now," said Colonel Fitzwilliam, "he must realize he will gain nothing by marrying your daughter. If you will pardon my saying, I suspect you have little ready assets he can extort?"

"My daughters' dowries," said her father. "But even that is not a fortune. The bulk of my capital is tied up in the estate and several investments managed by my brother in London."

"Then it is not what Wickham requires," replied Colonel Fitzwilliam. "Now we know where he is, he would not risk attempting to become a gentleman, as he must know we would not allow him to gain a foothold here. No, Wickham needs money, and he needs it without delay. I suspect he means to flee the country when he has it."

"Then why Lizzy?" asked Mr. Bennet.

"It may be for nothing more than revenge," said Mr. Darcy. "But he may have heard of my interest in Miss Elizabeth. He knows me well enough to understand that should he take her, I would pay much in ransom to have her returned."

Mr. Bennet looked at Mr. Darcy, an amused sort of gaze. Though Mr. Darcy had not made his intentions known by word, they were plain to see—but this was the clearest sign he had given any of them, other than to Elizabeth herself. The other two gentlemen were grinning openly.

"There have, I assume, been no developments on that regard?"

"There has been no time," said Mr. Darcy.

"Very well. I do not know that we can unravel this mystery. But I will keep my girls close to home, so he cannot prey on them. When we find him, I intend to see he is no longer a threat to any of us."

"I believe, Mr. Bennet," said Mr. Darcy, "we are all determined on that score."

The conversation continued for some moments after, but nothing more came of it, and no one had any answers. For her part, Elizabeth concentrated more on Mr. Darcy than the troubles with Mr. Wickham. Though the gentleman was a threat, she was not of a mind to allow anyone to interfere with her happiness.

CHAPTER XXIX

※ ⟨⟩ ※

After spending the entire day at Longbourn, Darcy, Fitzwilliam, and Bingley returned to Netherfield, though with more reluctance than Darcy had ever felt in his life. It was not only the fascination for Miss Elizabeth that drew him—it felt like he was the only one qualified to see to her safety. It was silly, he knew, for Mr. Bennet had the matter well in hand, his staff on alert for anything out of the ordinary. Even so, the manservants he employed were few, and Darcy would feel much better when the contingent of Pemberley footmen arrived to assist.

"Buck up, Darcy," said Fitzwilliam as they rode down the driveway toward Netherfield. "It is only for the night. We shall return to Longbourn tomorrow where you may bask again in the presence of your young lady."

"It is *not* long," said Bingley. "But it will feel like an eternity."

"I am surrounded by mawkish gentlemen unable to be out of the company of their ladies for more than a few hours!" Fitzwilliam put his hand to his head in a show of mock despair. "Whatever shall I do? I shall go to Bedlam with such despair surrounding me."

"Keep digging your grave," said Bingley, directing a dark look at Fitzwilliam. "When a young woman captures *you*, Darcy and I shall return your teasing tenfold."

"Darcy does not know how to tease," said Fitzwilliam with a sly look at Darcy.

"If you had not noticed," said Darcy, "I shall have an excellent teacher. I agree with Bingley—your tongue is far too glib and apt to get you in trouble."

"So you have told me before," said Fitzwilliam with a wave of his hand.

They continued this banter the remainder of the short distance to the door, and after a time, Darcy felt his spirits rising ever so slightly. The butler met them with a group of stable hands who took their horses in hand, and they made their way to their rooms to change for dinner. The evening in company with Bingley's family was unremarkable, and even Miss Bingley, who could be counted on to make caustic statements at every opportunity remained silent. Perhaps the set down both Darcy and Bingley had given the woman had made an impact, as unlikely as the notion sounded.

When they finished dinner, the company spent a short time together in the music room, but even Mrs. Hurst and Miss Bingley's playing was not enough to remove their thoughts from the situation. After a short time of this, Hurst suggested they adjourn to the study.

"None of you seem eager to be here, and I would like some of Bingley's excellent brandy. Speaking of the matter may bring clarity, or at least some measure of peace of mind."

The gentlemen all agreed to his suggestion and excused themselves, Mrs. Hurst wishing them luck in unraveling the mystery, while Miss Bingley watched without comment. Soon the four ensconced themselves in the study, lounging about on the various chairs in the room. Hurst poured himself a brandy as he had suggested, but when asked, Darcy decided against it. For whatever reason, he was feeling lethargic, and he knew the drink would dull his senses further. Fitzwilliam followed his example, though Bingley accepted a glass.

"What makes little sense to me," said Fitzwilliam, "is Wickham's focus on Miss Elizabeth. In the past, he has never held a grudge against those he could not charm. He tended more toward forgetting them and moving on to his next target."

"That and the possibility of his capture seems greater here," added Darcy. "The last several months have proven the efficacy of his ability to hide in London."

"I should have thought you searching for him would induce him to take ship," said Hurst around sips of his drink.

"Perhaps," said Darcy, "but to do so requires capital, and I am certain Wickham has had little of that for some time now. And he has convinced himself he will make his fortune in England."

"It seems rather short-sighted," said Hurst.

Fitzwilliam snorted and said: "Short-sightedness is a defining characteristic of our Georgie. Else he might have made something of his life."

"It seems to me," interjected Bingley, "that Wickham has always considered you a means by which he may procure the fortune he craves."

Though Darcy opened his mouth to protest, noting Wickham had always schemed to marry into wealth, among other plots, Fitzwilliam preempted him by saying: "I think Bingley may have a point. Yes, he has often set his sights on other targets, it always seems to come back to you. His attempt at Georgiana in Ramsgate points to that, as does his demand of money in lieu of the living, his renewed petition after, not to mention his actions in Cambridge and Lambton."

"This man made an attempt on your sister?" asked Hurst, eying Darcy with interest. "I have not heard this tale." When Darcy hesitated, Hurst said: "Whether to inform me of the incident is, of course, your decision. If you choose to, you may be assured of my secrecy."

"Last summer, when Georgiana was in Ramsgate with her companion," said Darcy, deciding in an instant that Hurst was trustworthy, "Wickham attempted to enter the house at night."

Hurst's eyes widened in shock. "I can see why you would not wish it to become common knowledge. Do you know if he intended kidnapping or compromise?"

"At this time, I do not know," replied Darcy. "Compromise seems more likely, as it would have been difficult for him to spirit her from the house without raising the alarm. If he had reached her room, he could have demanded to marry her."

Fitzwilliam snorted with contempt. "Another sign of Wickham's thoughtless insistence on his own infallibility. If he thought for an instant we would allow it, he would soon have discovered how wrong he was."

"How was he thwarted?" asked Hurst.

"A footman in my employ, Thompson, was on duty that night and came upon him as he was making his way to Georgiana's room."

"I have met that footman of yours," said Hurst with a laugh. "This Wickham must have only just escaped with his life."

"If it had been me, he would not have escaped with that much," muttered Fitzwilliam.

"This sheds new light on the situation," said Hurst, his tone thoughtful, as he swirled the amber liquor about in his glass. "I do not blame you for not informing me of the matter of your sister before, but when I learn of that, along with these other matters, including the money he received from your family, I believe Bingley may be correct. Wickham *does* seem to have a compulsion to extort as much money from your family as he can. The Ramsgate incident may be nothing more than an ill-conceived attempt to extort more."

"It is possible," said Fitzwilliam, rising from his chair to pace the room. "We could never locate him after Ramsgate, and our questions have remained unanswered. Though marriage to Georgiana would have secured ready funds and served as personal vengeance against you, Darcy, I cannot imagine Wickham with a wife."

"It is an avenue to a life of ease he has attempted many times in the past," disagreed Darcy. "For that matter, if he had succeeded with Georgiana, he could have left her in my care. He knows I would never allow her to suffer when it was in my power to assist."

"That is true," said Bingley. "But it seems to me we have established his obsession with you, Darcy."

"We have always known of his obsession," said Fitzwilliam. "I am uncertain, however, that we have ever thought in terms such as this."

"Then what now?" asked Hurst.

Bingley nodded. "Knowing he wishes to gain as much of Pemberley's wealth as he can does little to inform us of what he means to do to gain possession of it."

"Well," said Darcy, "as I suggested before, it seems he has realized my interest in Miss Elizabeth, and he knows me well enough to understand that I would pay a great sum in ransom for her return."

"The question is, how he learned of it," said Hurst. "My understanding is that he departed Hertfordshire in great haste when he learned of your presence. Since you were, as yet, unknown to Miss Elizabeth, he would not have been able to see it for himself."

"Could one of his former friends in the regiment be in contact with him?" asked Bingley.

"Unless they are excellent actors, I doubt it," said Fitzwilliam. "I suspect he was in Hertfordshire for some time living in that shack we found. If he had a spyglass, he could have been watching from Oakham Mount, or even risked coming into the town or the paths of the estates. It would not take much to learn of your interest, and even if he did not, he might have thought to take her and hold her for ransom anyway. Though demanding a large sum would have been his preference, he might have accepted whatever Mr. Bennet could muster."

"And he knows would step in," added Bingley, looking at Darcy. "Even if you were not enamored of Miss Elizabeth, you would not wish the family to suffer."

Darcy gave a distracted nod. Though his father had always taught him to care for the family's legacy, it was not inconceivable he might have acted in just such a manner if he had been at all friendly with the Bennets. Darcy did not think this was any great good in his character — it was the gentlemanly thing to do.

"With Bingley here," said Hurst, "not to mention me, he might have counted on all of us doing our part. In fact, one look at my brother and Miss Bennet reveals his regard for her — Wickham could have used that to his advantage too."

Hurst turned a lazy grin on Bingley. "Sorry to describe you in such a way, old man, but you are transparent when you have a young lady to admire."

"No offense taken," said Bingley. "I am happy should all the world know of my affection for Miss Bennet. I intend to make her my wife before long, so there shall be no doubt of it regardless."

"That still brings us no closer to an answer concerning Wickham," said Fitzwilliam. He resumed his pacing, which had halted while they were talking.

It was a puzzler to be certain, and Darcy did not know what to make of it. Before these last several weeks, he would have sworn he could predict what Wickham would do given any situation. The man had ever been predictable if one knew of his greed, his resentment toward Darcy, and his limited imagination. Recent events, however, had turned everything he knew on its head, and Darcy felt himself adrift without a rudder. What action Wickham would take next was a complete mystery.

"Here is a question," said Hurst. "Do we know for certain the Bennet girls are Wickham's true target?"

Fitzwilliam frowned and halted, peering at Hurst. "He accosted Miss Elizabeth on the path only yesterday, did he not?"

"He did," answered Darcy. "But I thought it was odd from the beginning. Escorting Miss Elizabeth to her home was more important than chasing after Wickham, but I looked a little and could see no sign of him."

"Was she not fleeing from him?" asked Fitzwilliam. The genial and frivolous gentleman Fitzwilliam sometimes displayed to the world had been replaced by the professional colonel, the soldier who allowed nothing to stand in the way of his purpose.

"She was," replied Darcy. "When they met on the path, I believe she was still some distance away from him, and after they exchanged words, he approached her, causing her to flee."

"Do you know how far she ran to escape him?"

Darcy thought for a moment and said: "I am not sure, but not far. Perhaps less than an eighth of a mile."

"Then why was he not hard on her heels?" asked Fitzwilliam. "Could he have known you were there?"

"If he did, I do not know how," said Darcy. "We had agreed to meet on the path the evening before when the Bennets were dining with us at Netherfield." Darcy paused and fixed his cousin with a curious look. "What are you thinking, Fitzwilliam?"

"At the moment, I do not know," replied his cousin. "It occurs to me that he came across Miss Elizabeth on a secluded path, threatened and frightened her, causing her to run from him, and yet he made little attempt to take her."

"Why would he do such a thing?" asked Bingley.

"He would if he wished to establish the fact of his presence in Hertfordshire," said Hurst.

As one, the three remaining gentlemen looked at Hurst, for he had spoken in a tight and concerned voice, which was so unlike the careless man with whom they were all familiar.

"What do you mean?" asked Darcy.

"Wickham knows you have been looking for him," said Hurst, ticking off each point on his fingers as he proceeded. "Though a disreputable man, he is not a stupid one. While he has remained hidden in London for some time, it seems to me you will find him, sooner or later. Thus, he must throw you off the trail. Showing his face here and threatening a young woman with whom he has known to have had disagreements in the past seems an easy way to do so. By establishing his presence in Hertfordshire, he draws your attention here. By the time you arrived at the shack, he had already been gone for some time—is that not so?"

"That is my suspicion. But why?"

"To turn your attention away, to distract you," said Bingley, catching on to what his brother was saying. "If you had come close to discovering his lair, a distraction would turn your attention away, giving him much needed relief."

"It is more than that," insisted Hurst, his countenance now stony. "In fact, he has attempted it before. Wickham appeared to Miss Elizabeth and frightened her away, you searched for him in Hertfordshire when he has already returned to London, calling Fitzwilliam here to assist in the search, meaning Fitzwilliam is not in London any longer."

"And with Fitzwilliam in Hertfordshire, he might think he has a chance at the real prize," said Darcy, understanding what they were saying.

Hurst gave a curt nod and said: "Georgiana. She must be his target."

Miss Caroline Bingley suppressed the gasp which almost escaped her lips and decided it was time to withdraw, to consider all she had heard. Her sister had been so easily diverted with the suggestion they seek their rooms early that evening, for Caroline, annoyed with how their time in Hertfordshire had gone, had determined to learn something of what the gentlemen were speaking. It appeared she had uncovered more than she had bargained for.

The moment Louisa's door closed behind her, Caroline made her way back down the stairs and to the door of her brother's study, and when frustrated by her inability to hear through the door, had risked opening it just a crack. When the door was open, the first thing she heard was the matter of Miss Darcy's near disaster in Ramsgate which had shocked Caroline, for she well knew how such a story could harm the reputation of a young woman, even if she was not at fault. The rest had proceeded from there, leaving Caroline as shocked as she had ever felt in her life.

It was fortunate no servant had come on her as she had listened behind that door, for it would have been difficult to explain her presence. As she hurried back up the stairs, convinced Mr. Darcy and Fitzwilliam would soon emerge from that room like bloodhounds following a scent, Caroline considered what she had learned.

The possibility she could use the information and attempt to turn it to her own ends flitted about the back of Caroline's mind. The knowledge that Miss Darcy had been the target of an unscrupulous man would not ruin her in society, but it would make for salacious gossip which would affect her coming out. Mr. Darcy would wish to avoid such an outcome—could she use that as leverage to force him to offer for her, rather than the detested Eliza Bennet?

If she had come across such information only a week before, Caroline might have jumped at the chance. But the knowledge of Mr. Darcy's disdain for her—and disdain it was, given some of the things he had said to her of late—caused her to pause. Since their father's death, Caroline had always exerted great influence over her brother, and she had grown accustomed to subtly directing him. Mr. Darcy, however, was a horse of another color—she would not succeed in guiding him in any meaningful way.

His anger should she succeed, she discounted without a second thought—he was such a gentleman she knew he would not mistreat her, regardless of whatever resentment he harbored. In fact, that might almost be better that way, for as soon as he got an heir or two from her, they could live separate lives, he with his beloved estate, she in London where she most wished to be.

There were several problems, however. Mr. Darcy's stature was such that he might weather whatever gossip there was, for there was every possibility he would refuse her attempts to force his hand. That was if he did not call her bluff, inform her brother of the matter, and between the two of them send to Scarborough on the next mail coach, never to be heard from again. The thought of being banished to that dingy place caused Caroline to grimace, as she opened the door to her suite and stepped inside. Her maid she had dismissed, so disrobed and prepared to retire.

The greater consideration was that it was Georgiana Darcy she would harm should she follow through with her notion. Georgiana was, as Caroline had always noted, a pleasant young girl, though perhaps tending toward shyness which made her insipid. However, she was a good girl, and regardless of Caroline's tendency to speak of her with praise, she found that she did possess an affection for the girl. Could Caroline threaten to harm such an unassuming creature, even for the possibility of realizing her most cherished dreams?

As her head hit the pillow, Caroline could not help but glower at the offending article beneath her head. If it had been Eliza Bennet, Caroline could well imagine doing whatever necessary without heed to her wellbeing, for the woman was that contemptible. Georgiana Darcy, however, was a different matter, and Caroline could not find it in her heart to act to harm her. It was surprising to Caroline, but closer examination informed her she might not have acted, even had she been assured of the success of her plans.

"This business of yielding to one's conscience is most inconvenient!"

The words spoken in the darkness caused mirth to well up within Caroline's breast, and she could not stifle the giggle which escaped. Caroline well knew that envy, spite, covetousness, and greed were not admirable qualities, though the desire to ascend the heights of society had been nigh overpowering and had overwhelmed her better nature more often than not. Some boxes, however, as Pandora had discovered, were best left unopened.

For the first time in many months, as Caroline drifted off to sleep, she felt light, almost free as a bird that winged through the skies. A great weight had been lifted from her shoulders.

"You think Georgiana is Wickham's target."

Though Darcy spoke words with what he thought was admirable calm, inside he was a churning mass of emotions and worry. If he was to guess, he thought Fitzwilliam was in the same position, likely seasoned with a liberal helping of self-reproach.

"Can we take that chance?" asked his cousin.

"Of course, you cannot," said Bingley. He moved to his desk and opened a drawer, producing paper and a pen. "Perhaps it would be best to dispatch a letter to your uncle so he may take Georgiana under his protection. I can have one of my footmen ride to London at once."

"Or we can go," said Fitzwilliam, turning to Darcy.

"That would be for the best," said Darcy. "A footman would make good time, but unless he is familiar with London, he would need to search for my uncle's house, and then my uncle would have to make his way to mine. We would arrive more quickly."

"I agree," said Fitzwilliam.

Bingley grinned and put the supplies back in his desk. "I expected you might say that. If you will excuse me, gentlemen, I believe I shall stay here and take word to the Bennets."

"There is no need for you to go, Bingley," said Darcy. "I would appreciate your continued vigilance while we are away. If I have your permission, I shall return here with Georgiana regardless of what we discover in London."

"In the morning, I shall have Louisa prepare a room," replied Bingley. "Miss Darcy is welcome at any time."

"Before we depart," said Fitzwilliam, staying Darcy's desire to leave at once, "I wish to know your opinion of Mr. Collins. You mentioned that Miss Elizabeth had some suspicion concerning his involvement—do you think he is unconnected with Wickham?"

"I cannot see how he is," said Darcy. "Their goals are by no means compatible, and while Mr. Collins feels he is being ill-used in the matter of Longbourn, I doubt he would descend to such methods Wickham employs without thinking."

"You do not know that man," said Bingley.

"No," acknowledged Darcy.

"I do not believe we can trust Aunt Catherine's judge of character," said Fitzwilliam. "I would not suspect most men of the cloth to become involved with such intrigues, but in this matter, I do not wish to take anything for granted. When we arrive in London, could we not dispatch someone to Kent to see if Mr. Collins has returned to his parish? If he is there, that would negate any notion of their being in league."

"A footman should suffice," said Darcy. "He would not need to go to Rosings—visiting the tavern in the village and observing the parsonage to determine if Mr. Collins is present should be enough."

"Then let us see to it," said Fitzwilliam.

The appropriate preparations complete and farewells were given, and after Darcy and his cousin had changed to their riding leathers, they departed. It was a cold, miserable journey, for though the weather had not turned too wintry, they easily felt the lateness of the season through their great coats and jackets, and the mist of their breath rose in the air, falling behind as they pressed on.

Throughout the journey, they said little, an occasional comment on the subject of Wickham, Georgiana, Collins, or even the Bennets, or an infrequent comment on their progress. When the lights of London rose in the distance, Darcy, who had started to feel like they had been on the road for weeks, released a sigh of relief. The city never truly slept, but it was still and calm, greeting their coming with indifference, the denizens awake at this time of night going about their tasks in a swift and efficient manner.

Soon, the trotting of their horses brought them to Mayfair, and they entered the street on which Darcy's house lay, noting the utter silence of the neighborhood. Beyond the end of the street, the dark expanse of Hyde Park rose, and the bark of a dog rent the air. Darcy House was situated on a corner, a small garden his mother had adored on one side next to a bisecting street, the whole surrounded by a high fence. All was still as they approached the front door.

CHAPTER XXX

$\mathcal{T}$he bulk of Darcy house rose before him, a monument to wealth unimaginable, to freedom and security, a life of luxury, the power to have anything. It was nothing to Pemberley, that great estate in the north with its ten thousand a year, its wide and spacious halls, reeking of affluence and power. But the London house held a special allure, for it was in the center of society, decadent and hedonistic as it was.

The house had no particular attraction for Wickham, though he knew its master possessed more wealth than he could imagine. It was a residence, no more, regardless of its finely appointed rooms and rich décor. There were many others like it, for the street and most of those beyond groaned under the weight of all that wealth. No, the house was not important to Wickham — it was the owner of the house, the history between them and the just desserts Wickham meant to mete to the sanctimonious bastard which dominated his thoughts. Darcy would not miss the money Wickham meant to have for he had more of it than he could ever use. But to Wickham, it meant everything.

Perhaps some vengeance was in order. Wickham grinned at the possibility, rubbing his hands together as much with glee as in a way to keep them warm in the cold of the late night. Ruining his sister would be exquisite though not the level of revenge Wickham wished to take on his old friend. Miss Elizabeth might be another avenue, he supposed. However, Wickham knew he could not allow such matters to distract him, for it was the prize of his freedom which was important. Such thoughts could wait until later.

A glance at his watch revealed it was almost the agreed upon time; only a few more moments and he would have what he deserved. Last time that accursed Thompson had intervened through means Wickham did not care to know. This time, however, it was certain to go as planned, for Thompson, along with most of the rest of the house, would be sound asleep. Wickham would abscond with the girl would before they knew, and with Fitzwilliam gone to Hertfordshire chasing the phantoms he had left behind, there was no one to stop him.

When the time arrived, Wickham made his way from his place of concealment down the side street toward the back of the house. There, not far from the stables, set in the side wall stood a small servant's entrance. It was always barred, for the butler was a conscientious sort who had been in his position for many years, knew every inch of the house and checked everything it seemed like twenty times over. But this evening, Wickham had an edge, a failsafe which would allow him entrance.

Sending a quick look down both directions, Wickham noted there was no one in evidence. All was still. Knowing the time had come, he stepped up to the door and knocked, three times in rapid succession, followed by three slow taps, and then one more after a short pause. A trick of the night, a hint of the danger of what he was doing, caused the raps to echo in his ears as if it had been the ringing of the Westminster bells. For a long, agonizing moment he waited, and then he heard the latches grating against the door.

A grin settled over Wickham's countenance, one that might have been described as feral, had anyone been present to witness it. A moment later the last latch clicked out of place and the door swung open revealing the face of his confederate.

"Sarah," said he, his voice silky soft, caressing her name. "How beautiful you appear tonight. How beautiful it will be when we possess Darcy's lovely money. Is everything ready?"

Had Wickham not known he held this woman in the palm of his hand, he might have been concerned at the severe look with which she regarded him. As it was, he knew she was a serious sort, though when given the right encouragement could be a tigress. They complemented each other in many ways, his flair with her dependability, his schemes and her planning, his charisma and manners and her ability to mingle in polite society. It was unfortunate Mrs. Sarah Younge had no notion that Wickham did not mean to share the money he extorted from Darcy with her. It was unfortunate, but Wickham knew money flowed through his fingers quicker than water, and a woman of her expensive tastes would soon deplete the fortune he knew he could deplete himself, and far more rapidly than he would wish. Wickham's confidence was that he knew he could increase his wealth this time, but he did not need some female hanging onto him, no matter how pleasant her company.

A pinch of the same substance he had given her for the servants of this house, and he would be rid of her, and what she did he did not particularly care. Then freedom would be his, freedom from Darcy and his scruples, freedom from this woman's neediness, freedom from restraint. It was all he had ever wanted.

"Wickham," said Mrs. Younge, still regarding him in her inscrutable way. "I had wondered if you would come."

"I am exactly on time," said Wickham. "Surely you did not expect me earlier."

"No, I did not. Given what happened last time, however, I wondered if you would reconsider."

"Not when the prize is within my grasp. Are the servants asleep?"

"The entire house is asleep," said Mrs. Younge.

"Excellent. Then let us be about our business."

"A moment, George," said Sarah, blocking his way into the house. "Before we proceed, I wish to know the truth of one matter."

Wickham regarded her, exasperation worming its way into his thoughts. "Can it not wait until we have secured Georgiana? Time is wasting, and Darcy may be along at any moment." Wickham snorted with disdain. "Though I hesitate to give him any credit, he *is* clever and may see the truth behind my ruse. If he does, he will fly here like an avenging angel."

Mrs. Younge peered at him, the slight lift of the corner of her mouth somehow offending Wickham. A moment later it disappeared, and she regarded him as seriously as ever. Wickham made a note to himself to ask her about it later.

"It will only take a moment."

"What is it?"

"Just this," said Mrs. Younge. "I wish to know how long it will be before you intend to betray me."

A fleeting hint of surprise flicked its way across the edges of

Wickham's consciousness. He should have expected her to guess his intentions, for Mrs. Younge was not deficient herself. Wickham knew she was lying in wait to betray him as much as he was to rid himself of her — the trick was to act before she did. There was no honor among thieves, after all.

"I am shocked you believe me capable of such treachery," said Wickham, pulling out his surprise and offense and hanging it about himself like a cloak. "Have I not demonstrated over and over my love for you?"

"Save your words, Wickham," said she, glaring at him. "You profess love with an assurance born of much practice, and I am not deceived. You claim to love me, but I am capable of observing that you will only ever love one person — yourself."

"Had I the leisure to consider your words, I might take offense. As it is, the night is waning, and I have little desire to speak of such matters in a cold doorway. You are familiar with my character, and I well know yours — do not play the martyr, for it becomes you ill.

"Now, shall we proceed?"

"I was a fool for ever trusting you. I doubt it would be two days after we secured the funds before you would leave me destitute."

"Then we can split it in half as soon as we receive it," growled Wickham. "What has become of you? Have you become timid in your old age?"

"Timid, no," said Younge. "But perhaps I have grown a little wiser — wise enough to see through you, for certain."

"There is no need to argue," said Wickham, trying a different tack. "We can arrange matters between us in a satisfactory manner. But we need to act now, while we still have the opportunity."

Mrs. Younge regarded him for several moments before the fateful words spilled from her mouth. "I did not use your powder, Wickham. I poured it in a chamber pot."

Shocked, Wickham could only stare at the woman. "You did what?" the feral growl did not even sound like his voice.

"I rid myself of it," said Younge. "I want no further part of your schemes. You should leave at once."

The door swung closed, but Wickham stuck his foot in the jam, pushing it back inward and forcing her back into the entrance. He realized as he stepped close that she betrayed no fear, did not retreat as he might have thought, though she was a diminutive woman, and he a tall man. The look she directed at him was without fear, even if she was regarding him as one might a wild animal. At present,

Wickham was feeling rather wild, indeed.

"What has become of you?" hissed Wickham.

"I have considered the matter and concluded there is little chance of success in this plot and every chance of disaster."

"Have you lost your mind? If you had put the powder in the food as I directed you, there would be no one to stop us! How is that every chance of disaster?"

"You *do* know Mr. Darcy and Colonel Fitzwilliam, do you not?"

Sarah smiled at him, a cruel gesture showing her triumph, for fear of the colonel's retaliation had always been the one part of the plan over which Wickham had agonized. Several scenarios had come to him, each one examined and rejected until he had come on the perfect ruse to ensure he received his money and fled from the reach of Darcy and Fitzwilliam's vengeance before they realized he had departed.

"I can see you do, though your overconfidence is once again your weakness," continued Sarah. "It is best you leave, Wickham. After much thought, I have determined it is not *you* that I should fear—it is Mr. Darcy and Colonel Fitzwilliam. At present, they have little reason to suspect me, and I intend to keep it that way."

"Should I illuminate them to your own actions?" Wickham sneered. "What do you think Colonel Fitzwilliam would say if he learned you applied for the position at my urging? Do you think you would escape his wrath?"

"You may be correct," said Mrs. Younge. "But it will be infinitely worse if I actually *do* something to endanger their charge. Thus far I have done nothing."

"I will have what I want, Younge," said Wickham, stepping close and looming over her. This time she retreated, keeping him at arm's length.

"Not now, you will not," said she. "As they have not taken the drug, the staff will awaken easily, and Mr. Thompson is, even now, prowling the halls of the house. I shall scream if you do not leave at once."

"You will bring suspicion down on your own head," said Wickham, feeling control of the situation slipping away from him.

"Better that than to inform them of my involvement by drugging the house and disappearing with you." Mrs. Younge glared at him, still poised to flee. "Leave now, or I shall scream. Then we shall see if Thompson can free us all from your schemes forever."

For a moment, Wickham peered at her, trying to determine if she would do as she said. The consequences for her could be severe, though perhaps not as severe as those he might face. Though Darcy and his uncle did not exercise the power they held, it was possible they could have him hanged if they captured him this night, especially if they learned what he planned. Mrs. Younge was only likely to be transported, a grim fate to be sure, but one which would at least preserve her life. Wickham judged the distance between them, assessing whether he could reach her and silence her before she cried out. The odds were not good, given the noise a scuffle would raise.

It was the hardness of her eyes which told Wickham she would do as she had said, would raise an alarm before he could reach her. She was no shrinking violet, a woman as hard as life had made Wickham. She would do what she promised.

"I *shall* have what is mine," hissed Wickham. "You may be certain of that. And when I have it, a certain letter will make its way into Darcy's hands, informing him what a wonderful underling you have been."

Then Wickham turned on his heel and departed through the door, turning as he reached the street and stalking off to his horse. Perhaps she had thwarted him with respect to Georgiana Darcy. But there were other ways to achieve his aims.

The house was quiet with nothing seeming amiss as they approached. A glance down either street when they came to the corner told Darcy nothing for no one was in evidence—he began to wonder if they had raced off to London chasing after specters. The sound of his cousin's voice brought Darcy's thoughts back to the house before them.

"Let us enter quickly. There may be nothing amiss, but if Wickham has already made his move, it may have remained undiscovered."

Darcy nodded, clucking his horse forward at a faster pace, its gait taking him to the front door, Fitzwilliam close behind. When they reached the drive, Darcy swung down from his mount, still watchful in the gloom of the late night. But nothing met his questing gaze.

A sharp rap on the door brought the footman on duty nearby to open it just a crack. The set of eyes peering at him was at first puzzled, then shocked, and the door swung wide, revealing the man in Darcy livery.

"Mr. Darcy!" exclaimed he, though he possessed the presence of mind to stay quiet and avoid waking the entire house. "We did not expect you, sir!"

"I am not surprised, Wilson," said Darcy, greeting the junior footman. "Is all quiet in the house?"

"It is, sir," said Wilson, his brow furrowed in confusion. "Thompson stopped by only fifteen minutes ago and then sought his bed. It is as quiet as the grave, sir."

Darcy nodded, thinking it certain they had arrived before Wickham made his move if their conjectures were even correct. "Then stay at your post. Fitzwilliam and I will see ourselves to our rooms and retire for the night. When you see Gates in the morning, inform him of our presence."

"Of course, Mr. Darcy. Good night."

Leaving the man behind, Darcy's long strides took him to the stairway leading to the second floor, and he bounded up, taking the steps two and three at a time, Fitzwilliam on his heels. The second floor was as dim as the lower one had been, the only light that filtering in through the long window at the end of the hall. The family wing lay to the left, and Darcy turned toward his sister's room, only to halt in surprise at the sight of a shadowy figure approaching from the opposite direction.

"Mr. Darcy?"

It was Mrs. Younge. The shock of seeing her halted Darcy's progress for the moment, and she stepped into a patch of light. The woman was not her perfectly coiffed self, for she had woven her hair into a braid for sleep and the dress she wore hung a little askew as if she had donned it hurriedly.

"Mrs. Younge? Why are you about at this time of the night?"

Mrs. Younge's smile and her appraisal of him suggested she had thought of asking him the same thing. She did not voice that thought, however, instead saying:

"I arose a short time ago to walk the house and ensure everything is in order." The woman paused and gave him a wry smile. "It has become a habit since the events at Ramsgate—it seems I am unable to sleep unless I assure myself that everything is well."

"Is Georgiana in her room?"

"I checked on her not ten minutes ago," replied Mrs. Younge. "After dinner, Miss Darcy indicated she was fatigued and wished to retire early. She has been sound asleep ever since."

"Nothing is out of order?" asked Fitzwilliam, suspicion coloring his voice. "You have not seen Wickham since Ramsgate?"

"Though I responded to the commotion between Mr. Wickham and Mr. Thompson," said Mrs. Younge, "I could not obtain a good look at Mr. Wickham, and as such, I would not know him if I saw him."

Darcy could see the suspicion in his cousin's set jaw, though his countenance was obscured in the night's gloom. In Darcy's mind, all appeared to be well, and he was grateful that Mrs. Younge had taken it on herself to ensure the safety of his sister. Unable to rest, however, until he checked on her, Darcy excused himself, leaving Mrs. Younge to Fitzwilliam.

Careful he did not make a sound, Darcy stepped into the sitting-room attached to Georgiana's rooms and then hurried to the door to her bedchamber. Upon easing it open, Darcy stepped into the room, noting the light through the window from a nearby lantern. The soft sound of his sister's breathing reached his ears, and Darcy followed the sound, stepping close and looking down into her face. Georgiana was deep in repose, her mouth slightly open, her breathing deep and even. Nothing had disturbed her sleep, not even a hint of whatever dreams she was seeing.

Relief swept through Darcy, weakening his knees and allowing his shoulders to slump. Tense and concerned the entirety of the ride, Darcy's shoulders now felt stiff and the cramps in his legs pained him enough to cause a groan. A sense of exhaustion swept through him, rendering him drained and eager to seek his bed.

With a final look at his sister, Darcy turned and departed, careful to close the door without disturbing her. Fitzwilliam had retrieved a candle from a nearby table, which ow illuminated the hall outside the room, giving him a better sense of Mrs. Younge's dishabille and Fitzwilliam's stance, which was still wary, but now more relaxed as Darcy's had become.

"I trust Miss Darcy is still well?" asked Mrs. Younge.

"She is, I thank you, Mrs. Younge. Your care of your charge has been exemplary, as usual."

Mrs. Younge inclined her head. "It is no trouble, Mr. Darcy. I have grown fond of Miss Darcy since I came to your employment—if a short nighttime stroll will ensure her safety, I am more than happy to do it."

Darcy nodded, already considering what must now be done. Given the uncertainty of the situation and the unpredictability Wickham had shown of late, there was no choice.

"Tomorrow, I shall return to Hertfordshire, and this time, I mean to take Miss Darcy with me, Mrs. Younge. I understand the difficulty this will cause, given the lateness of the hour, but I wish to leave by no later than nine. Can you ensure everything is prepared?"

"I will see to it." The woman paused, as if considering her next words, and when she spoke, it was with a wealth of deference. "Excuse me, Mr. Darcy, but may I ask if there is anything amiss?"

"Mr. Wickham was seen in Hertfordshire yesterday," said Darcy, deciding there was no reason to keep Mrs. Younge ignorant of the matter. "While we have discovered the lair he was using while he was in the district, there is some question as to his plans and some suggestion he might attempt to get to Georgiana again. I feel much better now I am on hand to protect her, and I mean to keep her with me for the foreseeable future."

Mrs. Younge nodded. "One would think he would desist since he was so spectacularly unsuccessful the first time he made the attempt."

"That would be a reasonable assumption," replied Fitzwilliam, "if we were not speaking of George Wickham. His arrogance and misplaced confidence in his own abilities are such that he would think he could enter at a time of his choosing and spirit her out from under our noses."

The look Mrs. Younge gave Fitzwilliam was devoid of emotion. "A dangerous man, then."

"Only if you turn your back to him, Mrs. Younge."

There was some undercurrent of the conversation that Darcy could not quite capture, though he wondered at it. But the night was late, and he longed for his bed. Perhaps he could induce Fitzwilliam to be explicit later.

"You had best retire, Mrs. Younge," said Darcy.

"That would be best, Mr. Darcy. I wish you a good night."

The companion curtseyed and turned to make her way back to her room, her footsteps soon ceasing altogether as the door closed behind her. When she was gone, Darcy turned an arched brow on his cousin, noting Fitzwilliam's pensive gaze down the hall.

"What is it, Cousin?" asked Darcy.

Fitzwilliam started as if he had forgotten Darcy's presence. "It is nothing, Darcy," said Fitzwilliam, regaining his wits in an instant. "I believe your suggestion that we retire is for the best. I am eager to turn in after our long ride."

Though Fitzwilliam attempted to move away toward his usual room, Darcy reached out a hand to grasp his arm. "What were you saying to Mrs. Younge?"

"Nothing in particular," said Fitzwilliam with an insouciant shrug. "I questioned her to see if she had any more information, any odd happenings of late. However, it seems London has been dull, for there has been nothing but lessons and visits with my mother."

For a moment Darcy was uncertain if his cousin was telling the truth or prevaricating. Then a wave of exhaustion once again swept over him and turned his thoughts to his bedchamber. Should Fitzwilliam deem there was something of importance he needed to know, Darcy was certain he would do so at the earliest opportunity. As such, he wished his cousin a good night and made his way to his room.

CHAPTER XXXI

*M*r. Bingley's visit the following morning carried an eerie similarity to a visit to Netherfield only a few days before. Both imparted news of the sudden departure of a member of their party, and while Mr. Bingley did not mean to sow confusion and doubt as his sister had, it was still a matter of some concern. Elizabeth had not considered the possibility of Mr. Wickham making another attempt on Miss Darcy, and the thought sent a chilling sensation through her

"Do not concern yourself, Miss Elizabeth," said Bingley when he saw her worry. "There is no doubt in my mind that Darcy and his cousin will head off whatever Wickham plans. We expect them to return this afternoon with Miss Darcy in tow, for Darcy will not wish to allow her out of his sight until Wickham is no longer a threat."

"What a wicked man this Mr. Wickham is!" exclaimed Mrs. Bennet. Had Elizabeth not possessed the memories of her mother's former behavior, she might have termed her mother's tone a wail. "It is difficult to fathom how such a man can exist! And Mr. Darcy, who was raised in the same house, is everything gentlemanly and obliging. How can a man as evil as Mr. Wickham be worked upon?"

"I do not believe there is anything left to work upon," replied Mr.

Bingley, his manner colder than Elizabeth could ever remember from the genial gentleman. "When we capture him, the best he can hope for is prison or Botany Bay. In my opinion, the gallows might be best for him."

"Well, I wish Mr. Darcy well," said Mrs. Bennet. "When he returns to Hertfordshire, you must inform him that he is welcome to bring his sister to meet us whenever convenient. It would please my girls to make her acquaintance."

"Believe me, Mrs. Bennet," said Mr. Bingley, though he directed a sly glance at Elizabeth, "I suspect no such admonition is needed."

Mrs. Bennet did not miss his glance, nor did Elizabeth, though she thought she weathered it well without a hint of embarrassment. Given the reports of the young woman, Elizabeth was very much anticipating making her acquaintance.

"The crux of this matter," said Mr. Bennet, "is that Wickham is a danger — we are all now well aware of the threat he poses. Thus, we must not allow him the opportunity to make his move, if that is what he plans. We must continue to ensure there is no walking the paths of the estate, no walks to Meryton, or even to Lucas Lodge until he is brought to justice."

"For my part," said Elizabeth, knowing her father's words were directed toward her, "I am eager to avoid being Mr. Wickham's target again. You need not fear I will disobey."

"Thank you, Lizzy," said Mr. Bennet. "I appreciate your willingness to restrain yourself, and those hairs on my head which will not turn prematurely grey thank you also."

The company laughed, and the subject of Mr. Wickham for other matters. By other matters what happened was that Mr. Bingley focused all his attention on Jane as was his custom, and only a few comments from anyone else were enough to capture his attention. Elizabeth watched this all with interest and appreciation, for Jane, she knew, would attain her happiness with a man she esteemed. Elizabeth was not the only one to recognize this.

"Jane has had a time of it, has she not?"

Elizabeth turned to Mary, who had spoken, and grinned. "I suppose she has. After the insincere flattery and utter wickedness of Mr. Wickham and the silliness of Mr. Collins, I would not have expected her to find another man with so little trouble. Then again, she *is* Jane and has been the focus of attention since she was fifteen. I suppose sooner or later *one* of them must prove himself acceptable."

The two girls laughed together. "The odds must eventually be in her favor!" said Mary. "Heaven knows she has had the other kind in abundance, even before Mr. Wickham came to bedevil us. Do you not recall that young man who wrote poetry to her while she stayed with Aunt and Uncle Gardiner?"

"Ghastly verse it was, too!" exclaimed Elizabeth. "But it was no worse than some of the antics men of the neighborhood used to capture her attention."

"Perhaps there is a disadvantage to having a respectable dowry," said Mary, seeming introspective.

"Oh, aye, there most certainly is," said Elizabeth. "A dowry gives a woman a measure of freedom to be sure, but there are always those who value the money more than the woman. A union with such a man cannot be agreeable."

"I dare say that those in society who are more concerned with pecuniary advantages far outnumber those who do not."

"I cannot say you are incorrect. Fortunately, though you and I will have a little money, we shall not be wealthy enough to attract the Mr. Wickhams of the world."

Mary grinned with delight. "There are many in society who would consider us witless to suggest that the lack of thirty thousand pounds is anything other than a punishment."

"Thou shalt not covet," quoted Elizabeth. "I find myself content with my lot."

"That is no surprise, considering Mr. Darcy will return and propose within a few days. I have heard it said that he is a very wealthy man."

"So I understand. But I honor the man, not the position."

"He is a good man, Lizzy. I only hope I am as fortunate to gain the love of a good man, no matter what his place in society."

With those final words, Mary excused herself, and soon the sound of the pianoforte rose throughout the house, the music practiced by a skillful hand. As the morning progressed, Elizabeth watched Mr. Bingley with Jane, reveled in every word and gesture which passed between them, and contented herself with the knowledge of Jane's good fortune. The first steps of the family's future were being taken in the company of this good man, and Elizabeth anticipated many more to come.

When the gentleman departed, citing the expected return of Mr. Darcy to Hertfordshire, Mrs. Bennet excused herself to go to her room for a rest. As their father had taken himself to his library, Elizabeth and Jane were left alone in the sitting-room. It was their wont, in times such as these, to discuss the morning's events. On this occasion, their conversation turned more to their expectations and hopes for the future.

"Mr. Bingley is attentive to you, Jane," observed Elizabeth, intending no hint of a tease.

"As Mr. Darcy is to you," replied Jane.

"Perhaps he is. So, tell me—do you think he will propose soon?"

Jane blushed and looked down at her hands. "Would I surprise you if said I hope he will?"

"That would not surprise me in the slightest," said Elizabeth. "But do you think his addresses are imminent?"

"I cannot say," said Jane. "He has left me in no doubt of his affection, but I cannot say when he will feel our connection is strong enough to propose." Jane paused and turned a questing eye on Elizabeth. "What of you, Lizzy? When shall Mr. Darcy propose to you?"

"It is my opinion he might already have done so had this situation with Mr. Wickham not arisen again."

Jane gasped. "Mr. Darcy tried to propose?"

"No, he has not been interrupted. The morning I met Mr. Wickham, Mr. Darcy had arranged to meet me, and while he did not say outright, he inferred enough to suggest that he intended to."

"Then it seems like you are further along than Mr. Bingley and I."

"That is not surprising," said Elizabeth. "If you recall, when Mr. Bingley came, you were still recovering from your experiences with Mr. Wickham and Mr. Collins."

A slow nod was Jane's response. "That is true. At first, though I knew I liked him, I did not know if it was wise to give him my heart."

It was Elizabeth's turn to laugh. "And yet, he has been here only a month and already you expect his addresses. I always thought several months were necessary to know a man well enough to accept him, and yet here we are, in love and wishing to marry the men who have captured our attention. What a strange time this has been!"

"But I would not change it for the world, Lizzy—even those experiences with Mr. Wickham and Mr. Collins. For had I not had them, I might not have known a good man from the bad—I may not have been as open in my regard as I have been."

Elizabeth smiled, rose, and kissed her sister on the forehead. "That is the optimistic Jane with whom I am intimately familiar. Being able to see the good in all situations is an estimable skill, Jane. I have every confidence in your eventual happiness with your Mr. Bingley."

"As I am in you with your Mr. Darcy."

"Then we shall be content."

With one last smile, Elizabeth excused herself to return to her room. There, she indulged in a brief rest, replete with memories of Mr. Darcy, allowing her imagination to run wild thinking of what the future might hold for them.

It was early afternoon before Darcy and his party arrived back at Netherfield, and given the travel he had undertaken recently, Darcy was eager to stay for a time with his friend, paying attention to his beloved. Mrs. Younge was a godsend, for she had managed the disposition of Georgiana's trunks with such a level of efficiency that they had been ready to depart a half hour before the designated time. Furthermore, she had not seemed at all fatigued by her early and busy morning, for she was awake and alert the entirety of their journey, though Georgiana indulged in a nap.

Conversation, however, was sparse among the travelers. Fitzwilliam sat gazing out the window at the passing scenery, and while Darcy might not have credited the possibility, it seemed his cousin was out of sorts. What might have caused him to descend to this state, Darcy could not say, and his conversations that morning with his cousin had revealed nothing, though Darcy knew Fitzwilliam had met with those he had set to searching for Wickham, leaving them with instructions.

"What is it, Fitzwilliam?" Darcy had asked when his cousin had returned less than a half hour after leaving the house. "Is there some word of Wickham?"

The sour look Fitzwilliam turned on him gave the lie to that supposition. "No, he remains as slippery as ever. While I suspect he is in town now, once he learns of our departure, I expect he will follow us to Hertfordshire."

"I suspect you are correct," said Darcy with a tight nod. "Then what instructions did you give? Do you hope to leave men in wait and capture him when he follows us?"

"That is a good notion," replied Fitzwilliam. "I have arranged it, but I suspect Wickham will be too canny to be taken in by such stratagems. When will your contingent from Pemberley arrive in Hertfordshire?"

"If they depart soon after my express reaches them, perhaps tomorrow or the next day."

Fitzwilliam nodded, though appearing distracted. "We may have need of them, so I hope they will make good time. You mean to station them at Longbourn?"

"There are servants enough at Netherfield to ensure Georgiana and the Bingley sisters' safety without augmenting the staff, and that does not even count Thompson, who will travel with us. At Longbourn, there are only two footmen, two stable hands, and the butler. An infusion of extra manservants will boost security and make me feel much better. I have already dispatched a man to Kent, as per our conversation from last night."

A grunt was Fitzwilliam's response. When he did not speak again, Darcy fixed him with a level look, wondering at how far he might push his cousin. Gregarious and open he may be, but when he decided to close himself off, he became difficult to read.

"Do you expect something, Fitzwilliam? It seems to me you have been out of sorts since our arrival last night."

"There is nothing the matter with me," replied Fitzwilliam. "I am only considering the tangled web we are attempting to unravel. Should Wickham strike—and I am convinced he will—we must consider every angle to frustrate his designs."

Something informed Darcy that Fitzwilliam was not telling him everything, but as he had no proof and their departure was looming, he allowed it to rest for the moment. Several times during their journey, Darcy thought to speak to Fitzwilliam again, but something stayed him. Trust was something he possessed to excess for Fitzwilliam, so he allowed his cousin to keep his thoughts to himself.

As the manor arose in the distance, Georgiana, seated as she was with Mrs. Younge on the rear-facing bench, turned to catch a glimpse of it. "Oh, Netherfield is quite a pretty estate, William!"

"I believe you will find the house to be rather unlovely on the outside," said Darcy. "But it is situated in a pleasing location with groves about and a pretty garden to the rear, though it is not what it would be in the summer."

"How far distant is the estate of your lady?"

A laugh by his side alerted Darcy to Fitzwilliam's return to his jovial self—or at least an echo of it. Intent upon ignoring his cousin, though he was feeling rather amused himself at Georgiana's eagerness, he did nothing more than respond.

"About three miles. To go to Longbourn, we must take the road back to Meryton, and from thence we go to the west."

"Shall we visit them today?"

This time both cousins laughed, though Georgiana folded her arms and huffed., Mrs. Younge took up the conversation.

"Perhaps it would be best to continue on to Netherfield first and meet our hosts, Georgiana. Longbourn is not going anywhere—you shall visit tomorrow unless I miss my guess."

With a thankful nod, Darcy addressed his sister: "I believe it would be best to go tomorrow. For this evening, let us give our attention to Bingley and his family as our hosts."

The oblique inference of the Bingley sisters was not at all welcome if Georgiana's suppressed grimace was any indication. She made no comment, however, choosing to look out the window at the passing trees. Darcy thought she might be pleasantly surprised by the sisters—or at least one of them.

The two sisters were standing on the steps waiting for their arrival as the carriage pulled to a stop, though there was no sign of the gentlemen. When the step was in place, Darcy alighted from the carriage, followed by Fitzwilliam, and then turned to assist the ladies out. As they were descending, a horse and rider raced up to the steps, and Bingley vaulted from the saddle, joining them with cries of laughter and welcome.

"You made excellent time, Darcy. I had thought I would return in plenty of time to welcome you."

"At present," said Darcy, "London is not to my liking."

"When is London ever to your liking?" asked Fitzwilliam.

"I must agree with William," said Georgiana, shooting her cousin a mock glare. "London holds no attraction for me, not with so many interesting goings-on in Hertfordshire."

Bingley welcomed Georgiana with a bow to her curtsey, and Darcy noted a wistful expression with which Miss Bingley regarded them. Long had he known of her design to match Georgiana to her brother, and while he could not quite interpret her current mood, it seemed she now understood the death of that scheme. It was just as well—Darcy had considered Bingley a good match for Georgiana, but as she was some years from even coming out, no attachment could be formed until then. Now that Bingley admired Miss Bennet so assiduously, there was little chance of Miss Bingley's designs coming to pass.

Within moments, the two ladies had gathered Georgiana between them and were showing her into the house, Mrs. Younge following behind. As was their wont, they were eager to see her and complimentary of everything from her dress to her hair, but in Mrs. Hurst, Darcy sensed a new and more genuine attitude. Even Miss Bingley, who was not as voluble as her sister, seemed to display pleasant interest, rather than the avarice Darcy had so often detected in the past.

The guests were taken to their rooms where they refreshed themselves, and soon the company gathered together in the sitting-room. Seeing Georgiana ensconced with the sisters, Mrs. Younge in close attendance, Darcy turned his attention to the gentlemen.

"If you please," said he, "I have not informed Georgiana yet of our suspicions with respect to Wickham."

"Is that wise?" asked Hurst with a frown. "You cannot coddle her forever, Darcy."

"As it happens, I quite agree with you," replied Darcy. "It is my intention to inform her of the matter this evening, but I did not wish to distress her while we were traveling."

"That is likely for the best," said Bingley. He eyed the cousins, saying: "Can I assume you found nothing when you arrived at your house last night?"

"Everything was silent, nothing was out of place, except for Georgiana's companion wandering the halls in the dead of night."

Fitzwilliam's steady look at Mrs. Younge confused Bingley. "Why would she do that?"

"She informed us she has done it since Ramsgate," said Darcy. "I understand her concern. It is a relief she takes such care for my sister's wellbeing."

"Just because you found nothing," said Hurst, "it does not mean our conjectures are incorrect. Wickham will almost certainly follow you here, and with his growing desperation, will be ever more dangerous."

Darcy nodded. "Your staff must be alert for anything out of the ordinary. Also, Thompson has accompanied us, and he will bear the responsibility for Georgiana's safety. If you can integrate him into your staff, it would make his task much easier."

"Of course," was Bingley's reply. He paused for a moment, and then said: "Do you think Georgiana will remain his target? I mean, he *has* accosted Miss Elizabeth, and he had Miss Bennet's inheritance firmly in his sights . . . ."

"I should think any of the ladies would be of equal use for Wickham's purposes," said Fitzwilliam. "Darcy would move heaven and earth to protect Georgiana and Miss Elizabeth, and any one of her sisters could provide an avenue of attack."

Bingley grimaced. "Should he target Miss Bennet, he might affect all three of us, given my interest, her connection to Darcy through Miss Elizabeth, and Hurst's connection to me."

"That is true," said Fitzwilliam. "But it would not be as satisfying for Wickham, as Georgiana or Miss Elizabeth would provide him a means to sate his desire for vengeance."

"It matters little either way," said Hurst. "Though he might prefer Miss Elizabeth or Miss Darcy, I am certain he will take whomever crosses his path."

"I agree," said Darcy. "When the contingent of footmen I requested from Pemberley arrives, I shall dispatch them to Longbourn. The more protectors the Bennets have at their disposal, the better."

The gentleman agreed and turned their attention to the ladies. It seemed that old habits die hard, for Miss Bingley, as had been her wont in the past, was doing her best to flatter Georgiana as she ever had.

"We are so pleased to have you here, my dear Miss Darcy. Have you had much opportunity to practice while you were in London? Your playing is exquisite—we have been eager to hear you play again."

"Thank you, Miss Bingley," said Georgiana, giving no hint of embarrassment or discomfort. "As you know, the pianoforte is my favorite way to pass the time, and I play often."

"One might almost say constantly," interjected Mrs. Younge, directing a fond smile at her charge. "There are times when it is difficult to interest her in anything else."

"Which must be why you play so well," said Miss Bingley. The woman paused and eyed Georgiana, saying: "It is good you show such interest in it, and a reason you have become so accomplished. But remember, my dear, that true accomplishment is obtained when you are skilled in many disciplines. Do not allow your other studies to lapse, for whatever knowledge you amass will assist when you come out."

"Yes, Miss Bingley," said Georgiana.

"Now, shall we retire there? Louisa and I would love to play together with you."

Georgiana agreed, and the ladies clustered around the pianoforte, the sounds of their efforts soon filling the room. Darcy watched Miss Bingley with Georgiana, noting how she was still profuse in her praise, but he thought there was a more genuine quality inherent in it than he had seen in the past. Soon he noticed Bingley watching his sister, and when Darcy raised an eyebrow at his friend, Bingley shrugged.

"There seems to be a softer side of Caroline of late. I cannot determine from whence it sprang, but though she was eager to welcome your sister again, there seemed to be something different from what I have seen in the past."

Though careful to avoid offending his friend, Darcy could only say: "It seems like she has faced the reality of the situation."

"Perhaps," replied Bingley. He grinned darkly and said: "Or perhaps she has developed some other stratagem."

"That is as likely as anything else," said Hurst.

"Come now, that is a rather ungentlemanly way to talk of a lady," said Fitzwilliam. "I have never thought your sister deficient, Bingley. She is determined and rather eager to see things the way she wishes to see them."

Bingley smiled and shook his head, declining to continue the conversation. For the rest of the afternoon and evening, they stayed in company together, and gradually Darcy's concerns for Miss Bingley's behavior faded. The woman was attentive to Georgiana and eager to praise her, but she crossed no lines as she had so often done in the past.

Later that evening as the company was nearing the time to retire, Mrs. Younge indicated her desire to speak to him. At first, he was a little concerned, for her manner was grave, but then when she spoke, he could not contain his surprise.

"I wanted to inform you, Mr. Darcy, that I must leave your service."

"You do?" asked Darcy. "I had hoped you would stay on, for my sister has blossomed under your guidance."

"You have my thanks," said Mrs. Younge. "It has been a pleasure to know your sister, for she is an excellent young lady and will do you proud. But there are matters which have arisen which will make it impossible for me to continue in this role. I am willing to wait until you have found a replacement. However, I will ask you to expedite your search, for I will need to leave within a month or two at most."

"Of course," said Darcy. "I shall initiate a search at once. Is it possible you might suggest any candidates?"

Mrs. Younge showed him a slight smile, the most he had ever seen from her. "I know of no one searching for a position now, Mr. Darcy. You have my apologies. As for Miss Darcy, I shall inform her of my decision myself."

"Thank you," said Darcy, allowing the woman to depart.

It was a bother to think of replacing his sister's companion at such a time as this. Then again, it was possible he would not have to. Miss Elizabeth Bennet, as his wife, would fill the role of Georgiana's confidante admirably.

CHAPTER XXXII

᠅🌊᠅

E lizabeth was excited, for two days after William's sudden journey to London, the gentleman was to bring his sister to Longbourn to introduce her to the family. Not insensible to the honor of Mr. Darcy's wish to introduce his dearest sister to Elizabeth, she waited until they could be reasonably expected with a sense of anticipation. That the Darcy carriage was sighted far sooner than Elizabeth might have expected was a source of gratification, though it also filled her with nervous anticipation.

"Remember, Kitty, Lydia," the sound of her father's voice reached to where Elizabeth was looking out the window, "the young lady visiting us today is about your age but of an entirely different level of society. I am allowing you to stay as I know you wish to make her acquaintance. Do not behave in a fashion which would provoke me to regret my decision."

As Elizabeth turned, she watched the two girls give their father solemn assurance they would behave—from Lydia it was as solemn as the girl could manage. Nearby, Mrs. Garret sat, as watchful as always, though she also seemed rather sanguine.

When the guests arrived, Elizabeth first impression was surprise that Miss Bingley had accompanied them. Elizabeth might have thought Miss Bingley would avoid them as had often been her wont, especially since the man interested in Elizabeth was introducing his sister to her. Soon, however, the sight of the girl who must be Miss Darcy came into her sight, and Elizabeth had no more notice to spare for Miss Bingley.

At the tender age of sixteen, Miss Darcy was already a little taller than Elizabeth's diminutive height. The girl was willowy, her head crowned with blonde curls, tied back in an elegant knot, her dress a soft pastel, though made with fine materials as befitted her station. William's tales of his sister had led Elizabeth to believe she was excessively shy, but at that moment, other than a little reticence, understandable given she was among those who were unknown to her, Miss Darcy was looking at them all with more curiosity than shyness.

"Mrs. Bennet," said Mr. Darcy, addressing the Bennet matron as was proper, though it was clear in his manner he wished to approach Elizabeth directly. "Please allow me to introduce my sister to your acquaintance."

A proper introduction ensued, in which Mr. Darcy named each member of the Bennet family in order. Mrs. Bennet approached Miss Darcy and caught her hands, giving them a light squeeze.

"We are pleased to meet you, Miss Darcy," said she, "and hope you will feel comfortable among us. But I also know you are not eager to meet *me*. Please, do not feel bound by society's strictures. Sit with my daughters, for they are wild to make your acquaintance."

Though Miss Darcy started a little in surprise at Mrs. Bennet's informal manner, she thanked her and approached Elizabeth and Jane, guided by her brother. Into the gap she had vacated, Mrs. Hurst and Miss Bingley stepped forward and began to speak to her mother. Elizabeth had no opportunity to hear their conversation, for Miss Darcy was soon before her.

"Miss Elizabeth," said Miss Darcy, the awaited shyness entering her manner, "I am thrilled to make your acquaintance, for my brother has told me much of you."

"It seems we are in a similar position, for he has been a positive fount of information concerning *you*."

"Then I must assume you have quite an unrealistic expectation of my virtues, Miss Elizabeth," said Miss Darcy with a mischievous glance at her brother. "William is far kinder to me than I deserve."

"That is not possible," said Elizabeth, charmed already. "For it is clear his words were understated."

"Lizzy!" said Jane *sotto voce*. "There is no need to flatter the man's sister, for I believe you have already captured him!"

Those nearby laughed at Jane's jest, Elizabeth as hard as anyone else. After she had allowed her mirth free rein, Elizabeth drew herself up and fixed her sister with a mock frown.

"You will teach Miss Darcy to believe I am mercenary, Jane! And what has become of my demure sister who never puts herself forward?"

"Perhaps you have rubbed off on me a little," said Jane sweetly.

"If there are two now," interjected Colonel Fitzwilliam, "that is terrible news for us all. One is enough!"

"Enough, Anthony!" admonished Miss Darcy. "Come, Miss Elizabeth, let us sit for a time, for it appears we are surrounded by jesters, intent on making a joke."

In fact, they all sat together in a large group, for Mr. Bingley had joined them to be near to Jane, and Mary was sitting about the edge of the group. Elizabeth soon discovered that Miss Darcy was a delightful girl, intelligent and though quiet, one who could speak at length if she was comfortable and the topic interested her. Elizabeth made it her mission to ensure both of those conditions were met, and soon they were all calling each other by their first names.

After a time of this, Elizabeth noted her youngest sisters watching with ill-concealed impatience, their restraint because of nothing more than the proximity of their companion. Though she wished to speak more with Georgiana and come to know her better, she knew she would have years to come to know Mr. Darcy's sister. As such, she suggested they sit together, which earned her grateful smiles from her youngest sisters. Georgiana went willingly, though it was clear she was more hesitant than she had been to meet Elizabeth; within moments, however, the girls' cheerful openness had drawn her out and they were speaking like old friends.

"Thank you, Miss Elizabeth," said William, "for making my sister feel welcome."

"It is no trouble at all," replied Elizabeth. "She is everything you told me she was and more." Elizabeth paused and directed a searching look at him. "Can I assume you have not told her the truth of her presence and the threat of Mr. Wickham?"

"You would have been correct had you asked me when we arrived yesterday," said William. "I did not wish to frighten her before or during our journey. But it was not prudent to leave her in ignorance once we arrived, so I informed her last night."

Elizabeth nodded. "I concur. Though she knows of his true character, it would not do to leave her unaware of his possible appearance, especially should he show himself when she is alone."

"That will not happen, I assure you," replied William. "Thompson will attend her at all times when she is not in the house, and we have warned the servants of the possibility of his appearance."

Smiling, Elizabeth touched his cheek and said: "Your determination to protect her is admirable. However, it is possible Mr. Wickham will succeed, despite all your precautions."

"At present, we have had no indication it is she Wickham has targeted," said William with a pointed look. "The only person he has accosted is you."

"Which is why I shall take care. What I will not do is fool myself into thinking he cannot wreak havoc, regardless."

"I know. Though I have not respected Wickham in many years and have considered him among the worst of men the entirety of my adult life, I can acknowledge he can be resourceful when he takes the trouble to be so."

"Come, Mr. Darcy, let us speak of other matters, for the subject of Mr. Wickham is most disagreeable."

They began to canvass other matters, Mr. Darcy's journey from London, their arrival the previous day, along with Elizabeth's doings since he had gone away. There was little enough to tell, though by this time such confidence existed between them as to render the most mundane of subjects interesting and enjoyable. Then they turned to other matters and debated various topics of literature, music, and current events, and once again Elizabeth found herself enthralled by the gentleman.

When they had been speaking for some time, Elizabeth became aware of a conversation occurring near to where she and William were sitting and noted it had become a larger discussion of the company.

"I had thought to hold a ball during my stay in Hertfordshire," Mr. Bingley was saying to Jane, though Elizabeth noted that there were many interested ears listening. "You have all welcomed my family with such enthusiasm—it would be a means of giving my thanks to you all."

"Oh, yes, do hold a ball!" said Lydia, her enthusiasm unsurprising. "I am sure we would all be grateful for such an amusement, for it has been so dull here of late."

"It would be agreeable to the ladies, to be certain," said Mr. Bennet, directing a fond, though stern look at his youngest. "However, I will remind you, Lydia, you are not yet out, and as such, would be unable to attend."

"But, Papa," said Lydia, her voice little more than a whine, "surely a ball such as this, given by a good man of the neighborhood cannot be inappropriate for us to attend. In fact, it would be good practice for when we come out." Lydia looked to the other girls for support. "I am sure Kitty and Georgiana would be eager to attend too."

While Kitty's agreement was a foregone conclusion, Georgiana appeared startled when Lydia included her in her scheming. Elizabeth noted the surreptitious glance she directed at her brother, who grinned at her in response, but the girl said nothing to support her new friend.

"In this instance," said Mrs. Garret, "I believe I might agree with Miss Lydia. Under certain conditions. You are *not* out yet, Lydia, and certain proprieties must be observed."

The beaming smile which Lydia had shown was dimmed when conditions were mentioned, but she seemed to think they were better than denial. Thus, she nodded to Mrs. Garret, as if giving her permission to make her case.

"Dancing only with those of our party and bed after dinner?" suggested Mr. Bennet.

"Yes, sir," said Mrs. Garret. "It will give them experience in a situation which will not be difficult or intimidating, and it may, in fact, be safer than leaving them at home."

"But then we shall only have a few dances," said Lydia.

"It is better than none at all, is it not?" asked Mr. Bennet.

Though Lydia pouted, she glanced about the room, noting the gentlemen consisted of her father, Mr. Darcy and Mr. Bingley, Mr. Hurst and Colonel Fitzwilliam, and seemed to understand this was the best offer she was likely to receive.

Mr. Hurst, who seemed to understand her glance, laughed and told her: "If it is for such a cause, I suppose I can be persuaded to dance, though I am not fond of the activity."

"But what of the officers?" asked Kitty. "Surely we shall be allowed to dance with them?"

"Are the officers part of our party?" asked Mr. Bennet, his tone mild but pointed.

Lydia, who had nodded to agree with her sister was brought up short, and a glance at her father seemed to suggest resignation. For his part, Mr. Bennet turned a questioning look on William, who was the only other one in the room with an underage ward. William, in turn, looked at Colonel Fitzwilliam, with whom Elizabeth understood he shared guardianship of Georgiana, and the colonel shrugged his indifference.

"If you have no objection, I shall agree," said Mr. Darcy, turning back to Mr. Bennet.

"Then I believe you may plan your ball for whenever you please, Mr. Bingley. The entire Bennet clan will be in attendance, though I shall beg to allow my youngest daughters to stay the night since they will not attend to the end."

The girls squealed their delight, and even Georgiana appeared excited at the notion of participating in the amusement. For several moments there was no talk of anything else, and even Miss Bingley was speaking on the subject with composure, though perhaps not enthusiasm, with her sister. Since it was the two ladies who would be tasked with planning the event, Elizabeth could well understand her hesitance. What she could not quite make out was Miss Bingley's general behavior that morning.

"Am I seeing things or is Miss Bingley much changed?" asked Elizabeth quietly of Mr. Darcy.

The gentleman shook his head. "If you are seeing things, then I am as well, Miss Elizabeth. Since our return, it has seemed to me that Miss Bingley has been more genuine and less insistent, either with myself or her compliments to Georgiana. It seems perhaps something has happened to mellow her disposition."

"Will wonders never cease?" said Elizabeth. "I had not thought it possible."

"Nor had I, Miss Elizabeth. Nor had I."

The next several days saw much congress between the two estates, with nary a day passing without one company visiting the other. As it was a time when there was a lull in the local society, they were not in wide company with other families, though the normal visits proceeded apace. As one who was not fond of company and on the watch for Wickham's next move, Darcy found himself unmoved by that lack. It was enough for him to be in Miss Elizabeth's presence as much as possible.

Wickham's continued absence was a source of concern. As Fitzwilliam had said, it would be better to have the confrontation at once rather than wait for it, as Wickham controlled the timing, leaving them all tense and irritable.

"He has not returned to the lodge?" asked Darcy of his cousin the next day.

"Mr. Pearce has kept a close watch," said his cousin. "I rode to his estate this morning to ask him about it. It is possible Wickham has found some other hole in which to hide, or it might even be possible the coward has not left London."

"I wish he would show himself," said Darcy. "This waiting is wearing on us all."

"Which is why he is waiting," replied Fitzwilliam. "At the moment, our vigilance is at its apex. The longer he waits, the more complacent we become."

"It also raises the chances of his capture," Darcy pointed out.

"It does," agreed his cousin. "That is why it is a delicate balance— if he moves too soon, we will anticipate him and increase the chances of his failure, while if he waits too long, he might lose all chance of getting what he wants. If you ask me, nothing will happen this week. I would expect him to try something on Monday or Tuesday."

Darcy grunted and allowed the subject to drop. At least his men from Pemberley had arrived—a contingent of six footmen, all chosen for their burly frames, their pugilistic skill and familiarity with arms, and their loyalty to the Darcy family. Though he was not on hand to greet them when they arrived at the estate, Darcy met them during his morning visit and instructed them as to their tasks. The increase in security was a relief, for the estate was now under constant watch both day and night.

Eventually, as Fitzwilliam had predicted, the tension began to diminish, and after the Sabbath, Monday and Tuesday passed without incident. A report arrived from London of a possible sighting of Wickham, but the snake still eluded his pursuers.

"I think I shall not go to London this time," declared Fitzwilliam after he received an express notifying him of the incident. "The men in London may pursue—I was pulled away last time, and I still wonder if we arrived before he could act."

Darcy nodded, grateful his cousin's support would continue to be available. "It is possible he staged it to focus our attention on London and away from here."

"If he did, it was a dangerous way to do it," said Fitzwilliam. "They might have captured him and ended all his pretensions. The men looking for him are professionals."

At Netherfield, plans for the ball continued apace, Mrs. Hurst proceeding with growing interest and excitement. Miss Bingley, while not showing her sister's enthusiasm, still appeared to be a willing participant. And when the Bennet ladies were present, they offered their assistance whenever asked. Soon the plans began to take shape, and the invitations were dispatched to the families of the neighborhood.

The latter part of the week continued to pass away, and complacency began to settle in, as Fitzwilliam had predicted. For his part, Darcy began to wonder if Wickham had made his escape—he was a greedy man, one supremely confident in his abilities and convinced of the wrong done to him. But eventually a man must bow to the inevitable, and for Wickham, that conclusion must be the longer he persisted in remaining, the greater his chances of being captured.

Of further interest was the arrival of word that nothing had been found in Kent to bring anyone suspicion. After being removed from Longbourn, Mr. Collins had returned to Kent and stayed there, and there was no sign he knew anything of the intrigues in Hertfordshire. Satisfied, Darcy allowed any thought of the parson's complicity to rest.

On Friday, Darcy and the rest of the Netherfield company visited Longbourn as was their wont, and as the day was mild, they proposed to go to the back lawn to enjoy the sun and fresh air to be found there. Elizabeth, he knew, could be convinced without difficulty, and the rest of the party were also eager. Soon they were scattered about the lawn, laughing and talking, the youngest Bennets along with Georgiana clustered about a rough swing hung there, Fitzwilliam pushing them each in turn. Darcy stood with Elizabeth, walking about the grounds, stopping for a few moments every so often to speak to one of the group. After a short time, they found themselves on a distant corner, with the woods looming beyond.

"This is idyllic," said she, removing her bonnet and raising her face to the sun, welcoming its warmth on her skin. As she did so, Darcy watched, mesmerized, for her countenance seemed to glow with health and vitality.

"A veritable paradise," said Darcy, more for lack of anything intelligent to say.

Elizabeth opened her eyes and gave him an impish smile, ducking a little further away into the waiting branches. The house remained in sight, but most of those out on the lawn were now hidden from view. A memory of the previous months crossed Darcy's mind, and he glanced about the woods. There was nothing there—only the trees, bereft of their summer mantle, swaying in a gentle breeze.

"Are you now suggesting Longbourn is the equal of fabled Pemberley?" asked Elizabeth, pulling his attention back to her. "I have only heard you refer to your own home as a paradise."

"I think, Miss Elizabeth, the presence of paradise often coincides with one's company, and not a specific location."

Elizabeth regarded him, a half smile playing about her mouth. "Then, yes, I suppose we may call this little patch a paradise. The question is, what do you intend to do now you have found it?"

"What should I do?" replied Darcy lazily, enjoying these games with his love. "Do you have any suggestions?"

"Oh, I do not know," said she, sauntering away from him a short distance. "Perhaps we should return to the others, for this situation in which we find ourselves is improper."

"There is nothing improper about it. We are within shouting distance of the house, and anyone may discover us with a cursory search. Or do you not trust me?"

"I trust you as much as any man I have ever met," said she, her words full of feeling.

"Then I am grateful for your trust," said Darcy.

Stepping close, he looked down into her beloved face, drinking in the sight of her button nose, her glorious eyes, and from then to the plump, red lips which framed her mouth. And with great care, he lowered his mouth to hers, stroking her lips with his, a kiss deeper and more exciting than the last time he had attempted it. A soft sigh was the only sound she made as she melted into his arms, breaking the connection, but creating a new one when she laid her head on his chest. For a moment they stood thus, each cherishing the closeness of the other.

"You said there was nothing improper, William," said she, still standing in the circle of his arms. "That kiss was not proper, nor is our current attitude. What shall I do when you are continually pushing the boundaries of what is acceptable?"

"Marry me," replied Darcy.

Darcy felt the change in her stance and instinctively knew she now sported a wide smile. After a moment, she pushed away, looking up at him, her eyes framed with happy tears, a slight tremble about her lips. Darcy once again lowered his head to kiss the trembles away.

"Is that a proposal, sir?"

"It was an answer to a question," said Darcy. "I believe, my dearest, loveliest Elizabeth, you asked me what we could do to make this situation proper. If you will consent to marry me, it shall never be improper again."

"I agree. But a woman cannot answer unless given the opportunity to do so. Would you have me answer an answer?"

"Of course not," said Darcy. "It is in every way unthinkable.'

Grasping her hands, Darcy said: "Miss Elizabeth, it would be my great honor if you would consent to marry me. I have not flowery words or grandiose statements to offer you—what I have is my undying devotion, my heart, and my commitment to spend the rest of my life making you happy. Will you do me the honor?"

"I will," replied she. "Nothing would make me happier than to be your wife."

Darcy leaned down once more to seal their agreement with a third kiss, to which Elizabeth responded and with more of the passion Darcy knew existed deep within her. The moment was perfect.

Then it was not perfect. The sound of clapping interrupted that wonderful moment, and as one Elizabeth and Darcy looked up. It was Wickham. And he held a pistol pointed at them.

Chapter XXXIII

$\mathcal{E}$ lizabeth might have expected the sight of a weapon pointed in her direction, where a slight movement could end a life, would induce a sense of panic deep within her breast. When confronted by the reality of the situation, however, she felt nothing of the sort. Mr. Wickham was a dangerous man, for he had proven it time and again — but he was also a worthless man, and all she felt for him at that moment was contempt.

The first movement was William's as he put himself between them, an action Elizabeth knew a gentleman would take, but which still irritated her. Everything within her shouted at her to confront the man, to bludgeon him with the knowledge they would never be intimidated by anything he could muster. Knowing any sudden move may cause him to release the deadly ball of lead contained in his pistol, Elizabeth refrained from provoking him.

"I will own, I did not think you had it in you, Darcy," were the first mocking words out of the man's mouth. "A colder man I have never met — to be honest, I was uncertain you would know what to do with a woman, even if you caught her."

"Just because I do not consort with the sort of women *you* prefer, does not mean I do not enjoy their company."

Mr. Wickham laughed and shook his head. "The ladies always preferred me, Darcy. And for good reason."

"I cannot imagine *any* woman preferring you, Mr. Wickham," said Elizabeth, her voice dripping with scorn. "Any woman who puts her trust in you must inevitably expect betrayal."

"I care little for the trust of a woman, or anyone else," said Mr. Wickham, unaffected by her words. "I suppose I must give you your due, Darcy, though it pains me to do so."

Again Mr. Wickham laughed, and the weapon he held dipped ever so slightly toward the ground. "It seems you *do* possess exquisite taste. In some ways, Miss Elizabeth is finer even than her sister—had it been she who was the heir of her father's estate, I might have succeeded."

"You would be incorrect," snapped Elizabeth. "It was I who saw through you first. Jane has a good heart and has difficulty seeing the ill in others' motives—I counseled her against you from the beginning."

"It is of little matter," was Mr. Wickham's negligent reply. "Had I succeeded with your insipid sister, it would have tied me to this miserable hovel with an inadequate income. Instead, I have a much better plan, one which will ensure I have everything that is my due."

"Are you thinking this through properly, Wickham?" asked William.

The way he motioned with his hand suggested he wished Elizabeth to cease baiting their attacker. Though Elizabeth would have preferred to continue to inform Mr. Wickham just how little his bravado and threats affected her, she obeyed.

"On the contrary, my dear Darcy—I believe I have thought of everything."

"If you kill me, Fitzwilliam will pursue you to the ends of the earth. If you attempt the same with Miss Elizabeth, you can ensure *I* will stop at nothing to see you pay for your crime."

"That is the problem with you, Darcy," mocked Wickham. "All you could ever see was the narrow view before you. You worry yourself over whether I will murder you where you stand, yet you do not see how much more advantageous it is for me to leave you alive. Why should I kill the one who will provide me with the means of living my life the way I was meant to? Kill you, indeed!"

"Ah, so your desires run toward ransom." William made a guttural sound in his throat. "Typical. Not content to earn your bread as an honest man, you grasp for every penny you can extort, knowing it will all slip through your fingers in no more than a few weeks. I cannot imagine what it must be like to live like this, to be nothing less than a parasite on society, a desperate, avaricious, selfish caricature of a man."

"You may as well save your breath, Darcy," said Mr. Wickham. "Now, if you please, I believe the time has come to depart. If you will step this way, Miss Elizabeth, we shall leave this place at once."

Elizabeth did not move, instead fixing Mr. Wickham with a contemptuous stare. "And why would I do such a thing?"

"Because, Miss Elizabeth," said Mr. Wickham, his tone all that was pleasant, "you are my means of gaining what I want. You shall come with me to a location I have prepared for you, and when the time is right, Darcy may have you back—for a price. Then when I have what I deserve, I shall leave and you may reunite with your stodgy and uptight gentleman, to live as happy a life as you can muster. I, you may be sure, shall be very happy with the money Darcy will provide me. It was not even he who earned it, so I am certain he shall not miss it."

"And what is my assurance I shall be unharmed?"

Mr. Wickham bared his teeth in what might have been a smile. "You will have to trust me, Miss Elizabeth."

A derisive laugh was Elizabeth's response, followed by her scornfully said: "I would be better to put my hand in the mouth of an adder, for I would trust it more."

"Oh, I am far more dangerous than a simple adder, Miss Bennet. It seems to me, however, you have little choice."

"Come, Mr. Wickham," said Elizabeth, "you have already said you would not harm Mr. Darcy as you are hoping to extort money from him."

"Perhaps I did," said Mr. Wickham. The man moved in a circle, his pistol still held in a threatening attitude, staying out of range, but assuming a position where he could more easily fire on Elizabeth. "Or perhaps I shall kill *you*, my dear Miss Elizabeth, for there are other ways by which I may procure that which I desire from Darcy."

"If you fire on her, Wickham," said William, "I will kill you—of that, you may be certain."

"Oh, shut up, Darcy!" spat Wickham. "There is nothing you can do that I fear. Now, time is wasting, and I will not allow Fitzwilliam or anyone else at Longbourn to realize your disappearance before I can make my escape. Now, Miss Elizabeth, come with me or you will force me to do something I do not wish to do."

The menace of the weapon waving in front of her was not what made up Elizabeth's mind, for she maintained her calm and was not intimidated. It was the way William looked at Mr. Wickham, studied him as if to discover his secrets. It was apparent William did not like what he saw, for he shook his head, a slight motion, and turned to Elizabeth.

"This Wickham is not a man with whom I am familiar. It would be best not to give him a reason to use his weapon."

"Yes, I have changed much since you betrayed me, Darcy," said Mr. Wickham, the light of insanity shining from his eyes. "How clever of you to have noticed."

The weapon once again found Elizabeth. "Come here, Miss Elizabeth. I shall not tell you again."

"Oh, very well," said Elizabeth.

With a confident step, Elizabeth made her way around Mr. Darcy, smiling at him to assure him all would be well. As she went past, she winked at him, prompting a frown from her new fiancée. But Mr. Wickham did not notice, for his gaze was fixed upon William again, his countenance triumphant.

"See, Darcy? There is nothing you have I cannot take from you. Do not follow us, or it will go ill with Miss Elizabeth."

"You *will* return her to me unharmed, Wickham," snarled William, "or the threats I made concerning Fitzwilliam will be doubly true in my case."

"Arrogant to the last, Darcy," said Mr. Wickham.

As Elizabeth crossed the short space to him, she noted that Mr. Wickham's attention was firmly on William. As she reached him, Mr. Wickham held out a hand to grasp her wrist, fumbling as he did so.

"You expect the world to fall at your feet. Perhaps she is comely enough for me to dally with her. But you need not fear, for in the end, I wish for freedom more than anything else. I will return her to you when I have procured that freedom."

As Mr. Wickham groped for her wrist, Elizabeth pulled away slightly, which distracted him, prompting him to look down and grasp it more forcefully. Seeing her chance, Elizabeth pivoted and brought her knee up between Mr. Wickham's legs, impacting with satisfying force. The man gasped and turned his pain-filled eyes to her, his expression surprised then murderous. But before he could gather himself and take any action, William had crossed the space between them in two quick strides, hammering down on Mr. Wickham's hand, sending the weapon flying away, and then bringing his fist in contact with the libertine's face.

Finding her hand free, Elizabeth stepped away from the struggling men, though by now the struggle was over. Mr. Wickham dropped to the ground moaning, flexing his jaw and holding his hands to his groin, while William stood over him, making a fist and shaking his hand, looking down on his adversary with contempt. At a distance, Elizabeth saw the weapon Mr. Wickham had held lying the ground. Quickly retrieving it, she hefted it before giving it to William, knowing he would be better positioned to use it. William smiled at her before it turned to a frown.

"That was very dangerous, Elizabeth. You could have been irreparably harmed."

"If you will excuse my saying so, William," replied Elizabeth, "I believe I would have been in significantly more danger if I had gone along with him."

It seemed William had nothing to say to that. Instead, he grasped her hand, gently pulled her forward and enveloped her in a one-arm embrace.

"Please, Elizabeth," said he, his voice low and brimming with emotion, "never scare me again like that. I could not stand it if something were to happen to you."

"Do you think I am any different?"

Elizabeth looked in his eyes, seeing the love and concern deep within them. Not caring there was still had an audience in the scoundrel still prone on the ground, Elizabeth reached up on her toes and initiated their kiss for the first time.

"Let us agree we can neither live without the other," murmured she against his lips.

"Very well," said William, his voice hoarse with emotion. "At present, however, I suspect we should focus on the task at hand."

That "task," as William referred to him, had managed to gain a knee, though he braced his opposite hand against the ground, holding himself erect. The glare with which he regarded them was filled with hate and rage and every other ill emotion she could name. The darkness in those eyes suggested he would see them dead if he had the chance.

"Go and call for Fitzwilliam," said William. "I shall stay here and watch Wickham."

"And if he attempts to escape?" asked Elizabeth. "Are you prepared to prevent him from once again eluding your grasp?"

The tone of her voice startled William, and he turned to regard her, though still keeping Mr. Wickham within his vision. "I will do whatever it takes, Elizabeth," said William. "It seems you have become hardened by your experiences with this man."

"How could I be otherwise?" asked Elizabeth. "Perhaps Jane is forgiving enough to allow his offenses against us to rest, but I do not have her goodness. This man has threatened us, has made our lives a prison these past weeks. I have no pity for him and wish for nothing more than for him to meet his fate at the end of a rope."

"And you shall have it, my dear," said William. "Fitzwilliam will agree with you. Fetch him now, please."

Nodding, Elizabeth stepped away and made her way through the branches back to the house, hurrying as she went along. Now that Mr. Wickham was within their grasp, she was not about to allow him to flee once again.

"Now that is an impressive woman."

As the sound of Elizabeth's retreat faded away, coupled with the sound of her voice calling for help, Darcy turned the fullness of his attention back on Wickham, noting his introspective mien. It was clear Wickham's injuries still pained him, as they should, with the beating they had given him. His eyes, however, were trained on the place Elizabeth had been before she had departed, and there was a hint of a smile playing about his mouth.

"I am sure you well know my history with members of the fairer sex, Darcy," continued Wickham. "If I was to give up my bachelor status for any woman, I declare it would be Miss Elizabeth Bennet." Wickham paused and chuckled. "I never expected her to do anything other than come along with me like a good little docile English gentlewoman. It seems I misjudged her."

"That much is clear," said Darcy, unable to keep a hint of irony from his voice.

Wickham continued to chuckle, though it had taken on a hysterical quality. He shook his head, tears running down his face, though Darcy could not determine whether it was due to laughter or pain. Or both. The sight brought to mind a madman Darcy had once seen raving in the center of Lambton's busiest street, and he wondered if Wickham was losing all ability to reason.

"What a woman she is!" wheezed he amid his laughter. "Had she been inclined to a less upright character, I might have found myself a partner. With her at my side, there is no way I would ever have been defeated in anything I did!"

"Then it is fortunate for me she is inclined toward virtue," said Darcy.

At once Wickham stood, all trace of pain or mirth now gone, replaced by deadly seriousness. He stood, tightening his fists rhythmically, his jaw clenched, the hate emanating from his face like the light of the sun. And his eyes — they were dead, dark pools where any semblance of light or humanity had fled, leaving nothing behind but a strange and disturbing resolve. If Wickham had been dangerous before he was ten times as dangerous now.

"Virtuous or not, Miss Elizabeth is insignificant now," said Wickham, his voice matching the picture he presented. "It is now you and I, Darcy — exactly as it always should have been."

"Perhaps it is you and I now, but soon Fitzwilliam will come. Your campaign of terror is over."

Wickham snorted with disdain. "Yes, yes, I am certain Fitzwilliam will soon come to your rescue. But I do not mean to allow him to come between us, Darcy. This is between us, the favorite of your father, and his only son."

It was Darcy's turn to respond with contempt. "Do you truly believe my father favored you? That he preferred you to his own son?"

"Did he believe your tales of my excesses? I *know* he favored me, Darcy. I was his protégé, his favorite son. You were only the heir."

"That proves you did not know him, Wickham. I was never insecure in my father's love for me. And if you did not know, I never bore tales of your exploits to him."

The statement pricked Wickham's interest. "You did not?"

"No," replied Darcy. "Though I despised you, I saw how my father esteemed you, how you could lift his spirits in a way I never could. I am not so blind as to fool myself concerning your admirable traits, Wickham — you have always been more affable than I, and you had a way of helping my father forget his troubles."

Darcy's gaze bored into his one-time friend, and he saw, for perhaps the first time in many years, a flicker of humanity behind the all-consuming lust for wealth and a life of ease and dissipation. "After my mother died, my father was a shell of a man. There was little I could do to ease his suffering. Even Georgiana, who was the light of his life in his later years, could do little to bring him cheer. I remained silent because I would not remove that one person from his life who could bring him even a little joy. Had I informed him, he would have banished you from Pemberley and cut you off to shift for yourself — do not lie to yourself, Wickham. You know I am speaking the truth."

"You lie."

"I only speak as I know," replied Darcy. "You can deny it if you like, but both you and I know the reality of my relationship with my father. Yes, he esteemed you. I was his son. I know the extent of my father's love for me."

Darcy could see in the way the tension ran out of Wickham that he saw the truth. It demolished Wickham's carefully constructed web lies he had used to convince himself of his own worth. Had Darcy not had years of disgust for this man's behavior, coupled with his intent to take Darcy's beloved away from him, he might have felt a hint of pity for him. As it was, Darcy could muster nothing but resolve and disgust. Wickham had dug his own grave.

"Then I commend you, Darcy," said Wickham. He was now loose and uncaring in his stance, which was even more threatening than what it had been before. "It seems you have had your revenge on me, and whether you believe it or no, it is more efficacious than anything I might have mustered."

"Vengeance was never *my* province, Wickham," said Darcy. "I always left that to you."

Wickham smiled, baring his teeth. Behind Darcy in the distance, shouts rose, informing them both that Elizabeth had found Fitzwilliam and was leading the men to their current location. Darcy gave Wickham a thin smile.

"Justice, however, is something I desire. I do not need to see you punished because of hatred, or anything else. But justice will be served."

"Perhaps it will, Darcy," replied Wickham. "But not in the manner you think. Do you believe I would allow you to turn me over to the constable?"

"I think you have no choice."

"There is always a choice, Darcy." Wickham smirked. "In fact, I would be willing to wager that the memory of your precious father is enough to stay your finger on that trigger. I doubt you could kill me, especially when you could not even bring yourself to denounce me to your father."

"You would lose that bet, Wickham," said Darcy shortly. "I erred in refusing to speak to my father about you. Though you may not acknowledge it, I know he would be appalled to learn what you have become."

"It would be best if you allow me to leave," said Wickham. "I am not stupid. I know what awaits me if I should be brought to trial."

"You should have thought of that before."

"Perhaps I should have."

Quick as a cat, Wickham darted forward, his hands outstretched to take the pistol from Darcy's hands. At that moment, Darcy knew that his former friend was beyond caring what happened to him.

CHAPTER XXXIV

*G*unfire rang out over the area, the sound of a single, sharp blast, which echoed between the house and the woods. It was like a peal of thunder, reverberating through Elizabeth's heart, filling her with dread. Heart pounding painfully in her chest, fearful of what she might find, Elizabeth hastened forward, Colonel Fitzwilliam, Mr. Bingley, and several footmen hard on her heels. Then, when she rounded the break in the trees, the sight of William down on one knee caused her heart to skip a beat.

The truth of the matter soon made itself known to Elizabeth, for she strode forward, seeing William holding Mr. Wickham by his arms, the other man's eyes open wide with surprise. As Elizabeth watched, she could see the mist descending over them, like the onset of night. And to her surprise, she heard Mr. Wickham utter the last words he ever would.

"It seems you were more resolved than I thought."

Then his eyes closed, and his head slumped forward, his weight pulling him to the ground below, and to Elizabeth's eyes, the sight of a rapidly spreading patch of crimson in the middle of his chest came into view. Slowly, almost carefully, William lowered him the rest of the way, his own hands and coat stained with Mr. Wickham's lifeblood. On his face, he bore an expression of intense sorrow as if this man had not been the source of much misery throughout the entirety of his life.

"Darcy," said Colonel Fitzwilliam, first motioning for Elizabeth to hold back. "Come away, Darcy—it seems Wickham has made his final miscalculation."

"It was no miscalculation this time," came the dull sound of William's voice. "He knew he was bound for the scaffold."

"He would have been a simpleton if he did not," replied Colonel Fitzwilliam. "Wickham was not a good man, but he was not devoid of intelligence."

William shook his head. "No, he was not. Knowing he would face trial and execution if he should be captured, he had no choice."

"There is always a choice, Darcy. The choices Wickham made in his life led him to this."

"I suppose they did," said William. "It is a tragedy—a life wasted when it might have been so much more." William looked up, gazed in his cousin's face. "Am I not allowed to grieve for that which might have been?"

"If you must grieve," said Colonel Fitzwilliam, "let it be for that. Wickham deserves nothing else."

Nodding his head, William turned back to his contemplation of the body—it was odd, Elizabeth decided, but Mr. Wickham did not look like his violent death had occurred only a few moments before. He looked almost at peace. Colonel Fitzwilliam motioned to the footmen nearby, and one returned to the house, presumably to fetch Mr. Bennet or perhaps acquire some instrument with which remove the body. Elizabeth noted this with detachment. The sight of William well, though sore of heart and mind, dispelled the fear, replacing it with compassion.

Carefully, Elizabeth sank down to her knees close to William, and he glanced at her, his expression turning from heartache to love in an instant. Elizabeth did not know whether she reminded him of life and love in a time of sorrow, but she used whatever he felt to her advantage, reaching out and grasping his hand to provide support. It did not surprise her that William attempted to pull away.

"There is blood on my hands, Elizabeth."

"Yes, there is," said Elizabeth. "It will wash off, I am sure."

William turned to her, wonder in his eyes. "You are a singular woman, Miss Elizabeth Bennet. I cannot imagine another woman who would not run and scream at the sight of so much blood."

"Trust me, William," said Elizabeth, fixing him with a wry smile, "A large part of me wishes to do just that. There are more important matters to consider at present, and I refuse to allow my instincts to get the better of me now when you need me.

"I must insist, however, on your remembering one very important consideration." When William arched an eyebrow, Elizabeth continued: "Remember there is blood on your hands in a physical sense. But there is none staining your soul. Mr. Wickham did what he did. *He* forced you to defend yourself."

"Listen to Miss Elizabeth," urged Colonel Fitzwilliam, throwing a grateful look in her direction. "There was nothing else you could have done, for if you think Wickham would not have exchanged your life for his, you are fooling yourself."

"Was there nothing else I could do?" asked William, his tone distant. "Perhaps you are correct. I cannot say for certain what I would have done if he had instead attempted to run."

"If you will listen to my opinion," said Colonel Fitzwilliam, "It is better he made the choices he did, though I am not happy you were forced to take his life. With his passing, an unhappy element of your family's past has now concluded."

William bowed his head and might have stayed there had his cousin allowed him. But Colonel Fitzwilliam would not, putting his hand under William's arm and urging him to his feet.

"Come, Cousin, let us get you back to the house. We shall send for Snell and a change of clothes. Once you are cleaned up again, you will feel much better."

Though his cousin had promised healing, Darcy continued through that afternoon, feeling as if a thick fog enveloped his head, which allowed for no thought and little light through its swirling mass. Snell arrived soon after, clucking about his master's state, informing him the clothes ruined by Wickham's blood would be burned as soon as could be arranged. Then he went away, returning to Netherfield when Darcy informed him his services would not be required for the rest of the day. Soon the magistrate had arrived along with the constable—and Colonel Forster—and Darcy was forced to focus as much as he was able.

"Bad business, this is," said Sir William, the town's magistrate, with a disbelieving shake of his head. "I knew of the difficulty you had with the lieutenant, but I never thought he was capable of such actions as this."

"Given the testimonies of these gentlemen," said the constable, a man named Smith, "it appears to be a simple case of self-defense. There is no need for any further inquest."

There had been little doubt in Darcy's mind of any other result once the constable was informed of the events of the day. It still felt like an ignominious end to one who had been, after all, known to Darcy throughout his life.

"The question is, what would you like done with the body?" continued Smith, interrupting Darcy's thoughts.

"The army has no claim," said Colonel Forster. "The man so dishonored the uniform that we have little interest in his final disposition."

"Bury him in a pauper's grave," said Fitzwilliam. "He deserves nothing better."

That roused Darcy's interest, and he turned to Fitzwilliam, saying: "I believe my father would wish his remains to be interred next to his father's. We should transfer him to Pemberley for a proper burial there."

"If you will excuse my saying," interjected Mr. Bennet, "your father was not aware of what his godson had become. Had he known, he would have cut Mr. Wickham off — is that not true?"

"It is," said Fitzwilliam. "Do not deny it, Darcy, for we both know it is true. Your father was an upright, God-fearing man, one who raised you to be the man you are today."

"Given that fact," continued Mr. Bennet, "could he see Mr. Wickham today, it would disgust him, for not only did Mr. Wickham waste his life, he threatened his patron's children. Do you think your father would wish to honor such a man?"

"Let it be a pauper's grave, Darcy," said Fitzwilliam. "He deserves nothing more."

"I am not thinking of him," said Darcy, in the grips of introspection. "His father is foremost in my thoughts. Wickham was his son, the only heir to his father's name."

"Perhaps he was at that. But I doubt *his* father would be any happier with his son than *your* father."

In the end, Darcy was persuaded to concur with their assessment, though inside a nagging feeling of betrayal for two men who had been so influential in his life remained. With a few final words, Mr. Smith went away, taking custody of the body and seeing to its disposition. Sir William stayed only a few moments longer, most of that time spent in earnest conversation with Mr. Bennet. When he was satisfied, he made a few comments to Darcy and excused himself to return to his home.

There was little inclination for any of the visitors to return to Netherfield that day, and those left at the estate—namely the Hursts and Miss Bingley—soon came to Longbourn, having heard of what had happened. Though their arrival could be termed an imposition, given the lateness of the hour, the mistress of the house accepted their presence with little comment, inviting them all to stay to dinner. Darcy was grateful for her forbearance, for he did not wish to be parted from Elizabeth at that moment; she was his rock, his lighthouse on a sea filled with reef and rocks to tear a ship asunder. Without her comforting presence, Darcy was uncertain what he might have done.

Throughout the rest of the day, Darcy sat and brooded with Miss Elizabeth always nearby, accepting the words of reassurance everyone in the company seemed to think necessary to say to him. Even the most unlikely of the company felt compelled to say a few words, including some he might never have expected possessed the capacity.

"What a vile man that Mr. Wickham was!" said Miss Lydia at one point. "I cannot understand how you withstood him for so many years, Mr. Darcy, for I suspected from the first moment I met him that Mr. Wickham was trouble!"

"Did you?" asked Elizabeth, fixing her sister with a pointed look.

Miss Lydia blushed, but she held her head high and replied: "Well, it was clear soon after, was it not?"

"It was," replied Elizabeth. "Given our vulnerability when he first showed his face, I suppose we all must be grateful he did not harm us before Mr. Darcy informed us exactly what he was."

"It is fortunate you were spared," Darcy mustered his wits enough to say. "Even I, it appears, was not aware of the full measure of Wickham's depravity."

For once, Miss Lydia made no attempt to speak further; she nodded and turned away, returning to where her sister and Georgiana were situated on a sofa, speaking in quiet voices with each other. Noting Elizabeth's look, Darcy rolled his eyes. But Miss Lydia was not the only surprising well-wisher—even Miss Bingley approached them to say a few words of comfort.

"I am grateful you emerged from your trials without injury, Mr. Darcy," said the woman, the hesitance in her manners nothing Darcy might have expected to see. "And you, of course, Miss Eliza."

"Thank you," said Darcy. "Though I am heavy of heart at present, I suspect I will be well before long."

Miss Bingley paused for an imperceptible moment and then essayed to say: "I dare say it must be difficult to accept this outcome for one your father favored. It may help you to remember that to those who love you, it is much better for Mr. Wickham to perish than to leave your sister without a brother, my brother without a friend, and so on. It seems even Miss Eliza has a claim on you. If I were to give you any advice, it would be to live for all these people, Mr. Darcy, for you would be missed much more than Mr. Wickham will had the situation been reversed."

Then the woman curtseyed and returned to rejoin her sister, who, they noted, captured Miss Bingley's hand and squeezed it as if congratulating her for doing well. Miss Bingley sat in her chair as proper as ever, but with more ease than Darcy could ever remember seeing. The lady at his side was similarly bemused.

"Was that Miss Bingley, or has an imposter taken her place?"

"Though I cannot say how this change has come about, it seems genuine."

"Then I wish her the best," said Elizabeth. "If she goes about it in a proper manner, I am sure she has much to offer a man."

With that sentiment, Darcy could only agree. Many were the times he wished to be free of her ubiquitous attentions, but he had never wished her ill. Perhaps she would find what she was looking for.

Wickham dead! Though Mrs. Younge could not quite decipher what she felt on the matter, considering her ultimate decision to refrain from supporting his attempt to take Georgiana Darcy, inside she was a mass of contradictory emotions. While she had known for a while that Wickham was becoming more unpredictable, more violent, Mrs. Younge had never thought he would come to this end.

Their acquaintance, begun more than five years earlier because of a coincidental meeting, had been satisfying in some respects, and downright maddening in others. Wickham had been a mercurial man, one always searching, never finding, constantly on the run from one scrape or another. And underneath, the anger against the Darcy family had simmered and burned, never extinguished, always enough fuel to keep it ablaze.

Mrs. Younge had fancied herself in love with him at one time not long after they had met. Wickham had been, after all, *very* charming, and Mrs. Younge had not been immune to it. That she was five years his senior did not matter in the slightest — what had mattered is her growing understanding of the man he was. Heartache was the inevitable outcome for any woman foolish enough to harbor feelings for him, and woe betide the woman who fell victim to his slick tongue and effortless charm.

That she had long been aware of those simple facts did not lessen the shock she felt at his death. When she had refused him entrance into Darcy House in London, she knew she had only delayed him, switched his target, though a small part of her hoped he would divest himself of the business and leave to make his fortune elsewhere. If he moved on his own, however, it would protect her, allow her to maintain her innocence. Her resignation from the position she now held would forever remove her from any suspicion in the matter. Mrs. Younge had no illusions what Mr. Darcy's reaction might be if he ever discovered how she had applied for her position. He was an unforgiving man, one who could be vindictive when it came to protecting those he loved. Mrs. Younge was certain she had made a fortunate escape.

Or so she thought. Events would prove Mr. Darcy's close cousin was far more perceptive than she might have hoped, as she was to discover before the day was through. With her charge situated with the younger Bennets, Mrs. Younge had most of the time to herself, a matter which would often be a frustration for a companion. Companions were neither family nor friends, and when Georgiana was busy with other girls her own age amid a large company, Mrs. Younge tended to find herself alone amid the commotion. Even Mrs. Garret, the Bennet sisters' companion, kept her distance, more inclined to watch her charges than exchange pleasantries.

"Mrs. Younge," intoned the voice of the colonel, a surprise, as she had been caught up in her thoughts. Her confusion only lasted a moment before she controlled her racing heart and responded with a cool greeting.

"There is one thing I wish to know," said Colonel Fitzwilliam, his grave manner setting her heart to racing. "When you applied to become Georgiana's companion, did you do it at Wickham's urging, or did you have some devilry of your own in mind?"

For a moment, Mrs. Younge only stared at him, wondering if she should attempt to deny it. It seemed he could see her hesitation, for his steady gaze never faltered, though he spoke to forestall her rebuff.

"Before you attempt to contradict, I should inform you that I had you investigated." The colonel fixed her with a thin smile. "Imagine my surprise to learn that those you cited as references had never heard of you. Then, when I searched further, I learned of your house in London—which you have sadly neglected of late—not to mention your history with Wickham, the bulk of which I am certain I still do not know.

"I had long suspected there was someone assisting Wickham," continued Colonel Fitzwilliam, his tone conversational. "It never occurred to me to suspect you, though now that I look back on it, I cannot understand why it was not obvious. Therefore, I ask you once again: did you attempt to get the position yourself, or did Wickham direct you."

"If you believe Wickham had any power to direct me," said Mrs. Younge, knowing the time for falsehood was passed, "then you did not search out my history as much as you think. I had grown tired of living in the slums of London and thought to better my position. Not all of my references were false, and my late husband *was* a member of the clergy, which means I understand gentle manners. I left the house in the care of an agent, who continued to let rooms out for me."

Colonel Fitzwilliam snorted. "And he has done well, indeed. If you do not wish to lose the property altogether, I suggest you pay some attention to it."

There was nothing else to say, so Mrs. Younge gave him a tight nod. The suggestion she might be free to turn her attention to the house was one she latched onto. Uncertain though she was what game he was playing, any hope at all was welcome.

"So you were not in league with Wickham?"

"I was," said Mrs. Younge, refraining from licking her lips in fear. Anyone around the room watching her would see signs of distress, and she did not wish to bring any more attention to herself. "But I soon thought better of it."

Colonel Fitzwilliam's gaze bored into her. "Then you did not, for example, allow Wickham into the house in Ramsgate."

"I did not," replied Mrs. Younge. "His plan was to meet Miss Darcy by chance, ingratiate himself into her heart, propose an elopement when the time was right. When she suspected his motives and foiled his designs—it surprised him to learn Mr. Darcy had spoken to her of him—he conceived a plan to compromise her and force her hand. I had nothing to do with his second attempt."

Colonel Fitzwilliam seemed to consider this. "In some ways, your original plan was more insidious. Had Georgiana fallen for his charm, she would have been heartbroken by the knowledge he did not care for her."

Mrs. Young nodded slowly. "But in the end, it kept her safe."

"Then you did not know of his actions since then?"

"Some of them, I did," replied Mrs. Younge. "When he joined the militia, I knew of it, but I knew nothing of his attempts with the young lady here. I thought I was rid of him once he joined, but when he discovered Mr. Darcy's presence, he fled to town and inserted himself again into my notice. His anger was terrible, provoking him to threats against your cousin—I have never been so frightened by a man's behavior. He proposed to again spirit Miss Darcy away from London, and for this, he requested my help."

"Did he attempt to distract me away from London?"

"He did. He told me after you went away and then returned, that the next time you went in Hertfordshire, he would come and make his move, and that I was to allow him to enter the house. He provided me with a powder to put into the evening meal which would cause the entire house to sleep until morning."

"Then he moved too slowly," said Colonel Fitzwilliam, remaining thoughtful. "I might have thought he would not be so tardy, but it seems we arrived before he could." Colonel Fitzwilliam paused and then fixed her with a stern glare. "Unless that was the reason why you were gliding through the halls the night we returned to retrieve Georgiana."

"As you have guessed, he arrived before you did. But I disposed of the powder and would not let him in."

"Oh? And why is that?"

"Because, Colonel Fitzwilliam," said Mrs. Young, seriously, "not only did I believe his plan was doomed to failure, but I had learned to be terrified of him, for his moods were growing ever more violent. I, myself, felt the sting of his hand, though he begged my pardon after, claiming his hatred of your cousin had caused his loss of control."

Colonel Fitzwilliam fixed her with a searching look. "I do not recall any evidence of an injury."

"Do you think he would be so lost as strike me where a bruise might show?" When the colonel's countenance darkened, Mrs. Younge replied with a thin smile. "It was the only time he struck me, though I knew then he was capable of more. Wickham was calculated in his brutality—far more than even you or Mr. Darcy know. Had I done as he asked, it would only have been a matter of time before he betrayed me, leaving me destitute and at the mercy of the denizens of whatever hole in which he had hidden himself.

"But this is not all. Though you may not credit it, I have grown fond of Miss Darcy and did not wish to harm her. Had Wickham successfully spirited her away, I know not what manner of cruelty to which he might have subjected her. Miss Elizabeth was in even more danger, for Wickham hated her beyond reason."

Colonel Fitzwilliam regarded her, his thoughts a mystery. "That is nothing less than I expected. What of this business of you resigning your position?"

"Just as you said," replied she with a shrug. "My house has suffered since I have not been there to manage it myself. My late husband left it to me, and I would not lose it because of neglect. And it is the one possession in my life with which I may support myself."

"I suppose the thought of being discovered also played a role in your decision."

"You are not incorrect, though by now I considered that a distant possibility."

The next few moments were difficult for Mrs. Younge's nerves, for Colonel Fitzwilliam seemed to consider her and, for all she knew, judging her future, whether she was to be incarcerated for her crimes or sent to a penal colony. For those moments, Mrs. Younge cursed the circumstances which had led her to make Mr. Wickham's acquaintance, while lamenting she had not lived up to her husband's example of goodness.

"Very well," said Colonel Fitzwilliam. "Then if you carry through and resign your position and, furthermore, never attempt to pass yourself off as a gentlewoman's companion again, we will consider the matter closed."

A wave of relief passed through Mrs. Younge, as she fixed him with an incredulous gaze. "You mean to allow me to leave Mr. Darcy's employ and go my way?"

"Revealing the truth of the matter would only harm Darcy now, for he would blame himself for hiring you. It would also hurt Georgiana, for I know she is fond of you. Your association with the late and unlamented Wickham is a heavy mark against you, but your refusal to assist him when it mattered most is also a factor I must consider. I cannot condone what you have done, but I believe it would be best to allow you to step away as you already planned to do. If you had not already spoken of your intent to resign, I might have judged differently."

"That is what I shall do, Colonel," said Mrs. Younge. "You shall never have reason to concern yourself for me, for I shall not bother you again."

"See you do not. If I hear anything spoken of my cousin, I shall know where to look for the source. Remember, Mrs. Younge—I have a long arm and very little tolerance for those who willfully hurt my family."

Then with a final significant glare, the colonel turned and departed, leaving an elated, but determined woman behind. The feelings rushing through her were akin to that of the condemned being pardoned at the last moment. Mrs. Younge vowed she would foreswear all dealings with scoundrels of Wickham's ilk and never again have any dealings with members of the gentry. When displeased, they had much more power to harm than the lower classes.

After enduring William's poor spirits for the bulk of the afternoon, Elizabeth decided it was enough. "Mr. Darcy," said she, drawing his eyes to her, as if startled she had spoken. "I had hoped I would not have suffered the loss of your attention so quickly, but there it is. Since I have accepted your proposal, I cannot imagine how dull the days will be, for it seems I am far from first in your thoughts."

"Perhaps I have been brooding," said William. "I had thought we were now referring to each other by our Christian names."

Elizabeth arched an eyebrow. "We did, but is it not improper? You have not yet approached my father, though I have said yes."

"I believe, my dearest Elizabeth, I shall attend to that as soon as may be, though I hope you understand why I prefer not to do it today. Let us have some happy memories associated with our engagement."

"And the fact of becoming engaged is not a happy memory?"

"Please do not misunderstand my words," replied William, his voice uncharacteristically quiet. "This business of Wickham had marred what ought to be the happiest event of my life. The man witnessed what should have been a most private moment, and then there was everything that followed."

"Yes, he did," said Elizabeth. "But I think it has been a most auspicious day for two reasons." When Mr. Darcy looked at her askance, Elizabeth continued: "First, it has seen me engaged to the man I love, and nothing all the libertines in the world can do will ruin that for me. Second, it was *not* the man I love who died today, but one devoid of any good quality, a man who no one will mourn." Elizabeth gave him a wry smile. "Besides, we shall have a story tell our children that no other can matched."

Mr. Darcy chuckled and grasped her hand, squeezing it with affection. "In that, you are correct, Elizabeth. In time, perhaps the memory of this day will be softened such that I may remember it as you do."

"Perhaps you would like to tell me more of your past," suggested Elizabeth. "You have informed me yourself that not all of your memories of Mr. Wickham are unpleasant. If you spoke of such matters, it might help exorcise those demons."

With a smile, Mr. Darcy began to speak, though his manner was halting at first. As he grew more comfortable speaking, he abandoned restraint and continued ever more easily. They shared many confidences that afternoon, Elizabeth listening to whatever he had to say, while she, in turned, shared the deepest parts of her own soul, including some things she had never shared with another person. And through it, the healing began, starting them on the road to a better future. And Elizabeth found herself content. The future was bright. They only had to grasp it.

EPILOGUE

*I*n the years to come, the events of that day at Longbourn often returned to haunt William, plaguing him not only with remembrances of what might have been had Mr. Wickham become more like his father, but also that it was through his actions that a man had lost his life. Adept as she was at recognizing these moods and interpreting them, Elizabeth, with patience, love, and understanding, would guide him back to better thoughts, remind him of their life together and the difference between the two men.

"As much good as you do in life, my dear," said she during these times, "there is little question who between you and Mr. Wickham contributes more to society. Mourn what might have been, but do not blame yourself for what happened. Nothing good can come from reliving such scenes of the past."

When presented with her support and good sense, Mr. Darcy's response was always similar. He would catch her up in his arms, look lovingly into her eyes, and say: "There is one event in my past I can surely not repine, for I have gained the most perfect woman with whom to share my life. I would be lost without you, Mrs. Darcy."

Though painful memories would often intrude, the Darcy family lived a happy life. Retiring to Pemberley and staying there for most of the first year of their marriage helped put much of this past into perspective. When Georgiana attempted to remove herself from their presence, thinking the newlyweds would prefer to be alone together, Elizabeth showed her stubbornness by refusing to allow it.

"Pemberley is your home, my dear Georgiana. My marriage to your brother does not change that. There is nowhere we wish you to be other than at Pemberley with us for as long as you wish it."

Georgiana Darcy's residence at that great estate was to last a full five years after Elizabeth's marriage to William, for though she came out two years after, she did not meet a man who excited her imagination. For, as she said herself, having seen the felicity shared by her brother and new sister, she would accept nothing less. When she made the acquaintance of a baronet, Georgiana knew she had found her partner in life and accepted his overtures.

Elizabeth's favorite sister found herself engaged at the same time as Elizabeth, and so close were they—and their husbands to each other—that they shared a wedding ceremony. As Longbourn was to pass to Mr. Bingley's because of his marriage to Longbourn's heir, the gentleman purchased Netherfield Park to combine the estates into one. Mrs. Bennet, thus, would remain in the house at Longbourn for the rest of her days, as the venerable manor became the dower house for the larger estate. The entire estate, however, was to be called Longbourn, pleasing their father, and retaining the name by which it had been known for generations. What pleased him even more was to pass the primary care of the enlarged estate to his new son-in-law, retreat to his book room, and while away his days with his beloved books. That was when he was not traveling to Derbyshire when least expected to stay with his favorite daughter and plunder Mr. Darcy's library.

As for the younger Bennet sisters, their fates were happy ones, though not all the same. Mary, next eldest to Elizabeth, remained unmarried for several years until firmly on the shelf. Then by chance, she met a friend of William's, a widower, who fell in love with the quietest Bennet sister and asked for her hand. Mary, contrary to what she had told Elizabeth years earlier, had become resigned to her single status and was in a state of disbelief at capturing the gentleman's heart.

"I do not know what to do, Lizzy," confided Mary one bright spring afternoon. "He is a good man and I would not hurt him, but am I not past the age of marrying?"

"It seems Mr. Hardwick thinks you are not," said Elizabeth, feeling rather amused at Mary's distress.

"Mary," said she, catching her sister's hands in her own, "I would counsel you to consider what is in your heart. If you are content and do not feel what you ought for a potential husband, then do not accept him—we would be happy if you were to remain with us for the rest of your life. Do not, however, refuse him because of some misguided notion of not being marriageable, for nothing could be further from the truth. Follow your heart."

The advice did the trick, for Mary followed her heart and was married six months after. With the gentleman, she attained joy and children of her own, and she always remained close with Jane and Elizabeth.

By contrast, Kitty and Lydia were eager for society and happy to join the estate of marriage when their turns arrived. Kitty married a good young man of some property in Nottinghamshire, and while she remained ever after easily led, her husband was more than capable of leading her. Lydia was perhaps the largest surprise, for she made the acquaintance of a parson not long after her elder sister Kitty's marriage and was wed herself after a whirlwind courtship. Though the parish held by Lydia's husband was not one attached to the estate owned by Kitty's husband, the sisters were situated within five miles of each other, leading to their close associations for the rest of their lives.

From Mr. Collins, the family never heard another word, though that did not mean there was no news of the man. As expected, Elizabeth's marriage to Mr. Darcy offended Lady Catherine, but Anne de Bourgh became a surprising source of correspondence. The loss of his supporter and his final eviction from Longbourn served to resign him to his fate, and he never bedeviled the family again. Miss de Bourgh, who never married herself, reported that Mr. Collins found a woman of the area to marry and continued as the parson of Hunsford for the rest of his life. While no one could say, as he did not renew his contact with the family, it must be assumed Mr. Collins was at least content.

With Mr. and Mrs. Hurst, both Elizabeth and Jane remained friendly for the rest of their lives, though they were not, perhaps close confidantes. Mrs. Hurst *was* with child those months in Hertfordshire and gave birth to an heir the next spring, much to the joy of her husband. It also calmed his cantankerous father's resentment. Mr. Hurst was, invariably, as Elizabeth often commented, uninteresting and more than a little boorish, even if he provided adequately for his family. That her husband shared the same opinion meant they were not often in one another's company, though they would often see them at Longbourn, and occasionally they would extend an invitation to join the Bingleys in their annual visits to Pemberley.

The former Miss Caroline Bingley's eventual fate was a surprise to both Elizabeth and her husband, though it was William who was the more astonished. A year after their wedding, Colonel Fitzwilliam announced he had made Miss Bingley an offer and was accepted. Though William questioned his cousin's sanity, it seemed the couple was well-matched, both eager for society and ill-inclined to a retiring life in the country. Their primary home was in London, though they often visited Pemberley or his parents' estate, and with her dowry and his half pay after retiring from the army, along with some investments his father had made on his behalf, they did well together. This put Elizabeth in the former Miss Bingley's company more than she might have wished, though she bore it with grace and forbearance. Though Elizabeth could not say she was ever more than polite with Miss Bingley, the woman's husband was a good man she esteemed. And once the Fitzwilliams' two children arrived, the former Miss Bingley's demeanor further softened until she became almost agreeable.

As for Charlotte Lucas, Elizabeth's closest friend married Mr. Pearce and remained ever after near Longbourn. Elizabeth had occasion to see her dearest friend whenever she returned, and her husband was a good man, though not one Elizabeth found interesting. But her friend attained her happiness, and that was enough for Elizabeth.

As for the Darcys, Pemberley was their chief residence, though obligation drew then to London every year. In their marriage, there was often disagreement, though their mutual love was enough to overcome the occasional harsh word which must inevitably be exchanged between two such confident and independent people. Elizabeth found herself pleased with her situation, grateful her husband had possessed the discernment to see in Elizabeth a woman who would suit him so well, and for William's part, he appreciated the light his wife brought to his life. And though their beginnings had been mired in trying and uncertain times, the rest of their lives were spent happily.

The End

For Readers Who Liked
The Challenge of Entail

A Gift for Elizabeth
Sundered from her parents and sisters, a depressed Elizabeth Bennet lives with the Gardiners in London. When times seem most desperate, she makes a new acquaintance in Mr. Darcy, and the encounter changes her perspective entirely. With the spirit of Christmas burning within her, Elizabeth begins to recover from the hardships which have beset her life. Join Elizabeth in her journey to receive a special gift which will change everything.

Mr. Bennet Takes Charge
When Elizabeth Bennet's journey to the lakes is canceled, Mr. Bingley, along with his elusive friend Mr. Darcy, return to Netherfield, turning a quiet summer is topsy-turvy. Then Elizabeth learns her sister, Lydia, means to elope with a rake, and the very respectability of her family is at stake. Elizabeth takes heart, however, when her father rises to the occasion, in a way she would never have predicted. With Mr. Darcy's assistance, there may still be time to prevent calamity, and even find love, against all odds.

Murder at Netherfield
After the ball at Netherfield, a fault in their carriage results in the Bennet family being forced to stay at the Bingley estate, and when a blizzard blows in overnight, the Bennets find themselves stranded there. When a body is found, leading to a string of murders which threaten the lives of those present, Elizabeth and Darcy form an alliance to discover the identity of the murderer and save those they care about most. But the depraved actions of a killer, striking from the shadows, threatens their newly found admiration for each other.

The Impulse of the Moment
Mr. Darcy finds a young woman in Elizabeth Bennet who has matured from the girl he knew four years earlier. Elizabeth finds herself compelled by Mr. Darcy and attraction grows, a connection begins to be forged. But elements of Mr. Darcy's family, those who possess the power to exert great influence over his future, do not take kindly to his potential choice of a wife.

Whispers of the Heart
A different Bingley party arrives in Hertfordshire leading to a new suitor emerging for the worthiest of the Bennet sisters. As her sister has obtained her happiness, Elizabeth Bennet finds herself thrown into society far above any she might have otherwise expected, which leads her to a new understanding of the enigmatic Mr. Darcy.

For more details, visit

http://www.onegoodsonnet.com/genres/pride-and-prejudice-variations

About the Author

Jann Rowland is a Canadian, born and bred. Other than a two-year span in which he lived in Japan, he has been a resident of the Great White North his entire life, though he professes to still hate the winters.

Though Jann did not start writing until his mid-twenties, writing has grown from a hobby to an all-consuming passion. His interests as a child were almost exclusively centered on the exotic fantasy worlds of Tolkien and Eddings, among a host of others. As an adult, his interests have grown to include historical fiction and romance, with a particular focus on the works of Jane Austen.

When Jann is not writing, he enjoys rooting for his favorite sports teams. He is also a master musician (in his own mind) who enjoys playing piano and singing as well as moonlighting as the choir director in his church's congregation.

Jann lives in Alberta with his wife of more than twenty years, two grown sons, and one young daughter. He is convinced that whatever hair he has left will be entirely gone by the time his little girl hits her teenage years. Sadly, though he has told his daughter repeatedly that she is not allowed to grow up, she continues to ignore him.

Website: http://onegoodsonnet.com/
Facebook: https://facebook.com/OneGoodSonnetPublishing/
Twitter: @OneGoodSonnet
Mailing List: http://eepurl.com/bol2p9